OUTRAGEOUS SEAS

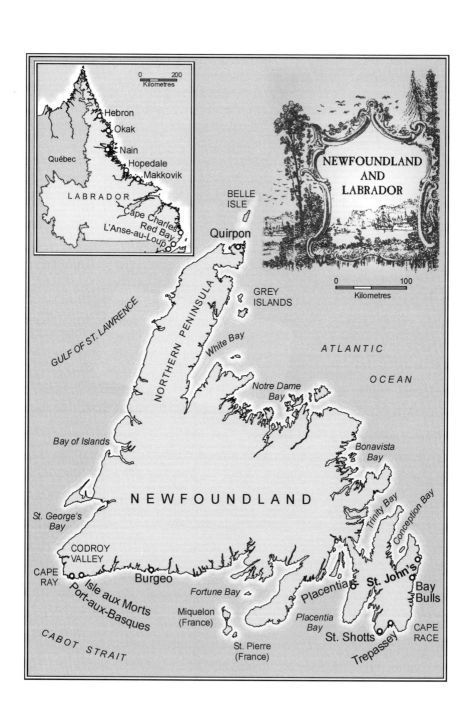

NEWFOUNDLAND
AND
LABRADOR

0   200
Kilometres

Hebron
Okak
Nain
Québec
Hopedale
Makkovik

LABRADOR

Cape Charles
Red Bay
L'Anse-au-Loup

BELLE
ISLE

Quirpon

GREY
ISLANDS

0   100
Kilometres

GULF OF ST. LAWRENCE

NORTHERN PENINSULA

White Bay

ATLANTIC

OCEAN

Notre Dame
Bay

Bay of Islands

Bonavista
Bay

NEWFOUNDLAND

Trinity Bay

Conception Bay

St. George's
Bay

CODROY
VALLEY

CAPE
RAY

Burgeo

Isle aux Morts

Port-aux-Basques

Fortune Bay

Miquelon
(France)

Placentia

St. John's

Bay
Bulls

Placentia
Bay

CAPE
RACE

St. Shotts

CABOT STRAIT

St. Pierre
(France)

Trepassey

OUTRAGEOUS
SEAS

Shipwreck and Survival

in the Waters Off Newfoundland,

1583-1893

Edited by

RAINER K. BAEHRE

PUBLISHED FOR CARLETON UNIVERSITY
BY MCGILL-QUEEN'S UNIVERSITY PRESS,
MONTREAL & KINGSTON, LONDON, ITHACA

Copyright © Carleton University Press, 1999

ISBN 0-88629-358-8 (cloth)
ISBN 0-88629-319-7 (paper)

Printed and bound in Canada

Canadian Cataloguing in Publication Data

Main entry under title:

   Outrageous seas : shipwreck and survival in the waters off
Newfoundland, 1583-1893

(The Carleton library ; #189)
Includes bibliographical references and index.
ISBN 0-88629-358-8 (bound).— ISBN 0-88629-319-7 (pbk.)

   1. Shipwrecks — Newfoundland — History. I. Baehre, Rainer,
1949-

FC2170.S5098 1999   971.8   C97-900246-X
G525.088 1999

Cover design: David Drummond
Cover photo: Schooner Aground. B12-93, Courtesy of the Provincial
Archives of Newfoundland and Labrador
Interior: BCumming Designs
Frontispiece: Cartography by David Raymond
Chapter heads: The Sinking of the *Nathalie*. From a lithograph by C.
Motte. Courtesy of the Department of Rare Books and Special collec-
tions, McGill University Libraries

Canadä

McGill-Queen's University Press acknowledges the financial support of
the Government of Canada through the Book Publishing Industry
Development program (BPIDP) for our publishing activities. We also
acknowledge the support of the Canada Council for the Arts for our
publishing program.

In memory of my late maternal grandfather, Walter Kramer, sailmaker,
my late uncle, Georg Kramer, lost at sea in the English Channel, 1944,
and my late cousin Werner Steinhauer, lost at sea in the Gulf of Mexico, 1952.
Also, for my uncle, Kapitän Gerhard Hinz (retired),
and Marie Croll's great-great-great-great-grandfather,
Matthew Gardiner,
an emigrant shipwrecked three times in 1817,
once off the coast of Newfoundland,
while en route from Sunderland, U.K., to Upper Canada.

CONTENTS

ILLUSTRATIONS

ACKNOWLEDGEMENTS

There are many people to thank for helping me complete this first of what I hope will be several projects relating to the early transatlantic experience. My sincere thanks to the staff of the National Archives of Canada, the Provincial Archives of Newfoundland, the Maritime History Archives and the Centre for Newfoundland Studies at Memorial University of Newfoundland, the Scottish Record Office, and the Public Record Office (Kew), London, England, as well as the Department of Rare Books and Special Collections in the McLennan Library at McGill University, and the Harriet Irving Library at the University of New Brunswick, especially Linda Baier. I also greatly appreciate the use of the microfiche material collected by the Canadian Institute of Historical Micro Reproductions [CIHM] under its director Pam Bjornsen.

Similar thanks are owed to Elizabeth Behrens and others at the library of Sir Wilfred Grenfell College, to the MUCEP and SWASP students over the years who carried out their duties admirably as research assistants, especially Doug Howell, Cheron Buckle, Carla Burden, and Justin Hulan, and to the indispensable assistance of Linda Taylor and Peggy Baxter, and Arlene Buckle, our divisional secretary at Sir Wilfred Grenfell College. I would also like to express my gratitude for research funding: a Vice-President's Grant from Memorial University of Newfoundland, several Principal's Grants from Sir Wilfred Grenfell College, especially one from the Anniversary Fund to help create the frontispiece for this book, and an indispensable grant from the Publications Subvention Board of Memorial University, without which this project might well have languished.

A special thanks to Dr. Naomi Griffiths and Dr. Robert Rutherford, and to my colleagues, maritime historians Prof. Lewis "Skip" Fischer and Dr. Olaf Janzen, for their encouragement and advice, especially the latter's unfailing humour (or is it flailing humour). Thanks also to former colleague Dr. Scott Jamieson, now of the Frecker Institute, for bringing the shipwreck of the *Belle-Julie* and the *Nathalie* to my attention and for his initial translations. Thanks to Jennie Strickland for patience beyond the call of duty, and to Jennie Wilson and Doug Campbell for editorial advice.

Most importantly, warm affection for Marie Croll, my spouse, for her attentive ear and unfailing support. Incidentally, Matthew Gardiner, the 1817 Newfoundland shipwreck survivor, to whom this volume is partly dedicated, became the great-great-great-great-great grandfather of our daughters Marta and Emma during the course of this project.

"For in that moment, the Frigat was devoured and swallowed up of the Sea."

— Edward Hayes, "Narrative of Sir Humphrey Gilbert's Last Expedition"

"From regions where Peruvian billows roar,
To the bleak coasts of savage Labrador."

— William Falconer, "The Shipwreck"

The breakers were right beneath her bows,
She drifted a dreary wreck
And a whooping billow swept the crew,
Like icicles from her deck;
She struck where the white and fleecy waves
Looked soft as carded wool;
But the cruel rocks they gored her side,
Like the horns of an angry bull.

— Longfellow, "The Wreck of the *Hesperus*"

On the first day of April
eighteen hundred and seventy two
The *City of Quebec* leaved London
with a choice of British crew,
'Twas seventeen men she had on board
when she leaved her native land,
But little did they ever think
they'd be drownded in Newfoundland.

— "The Loss of the *City of Quebec*" (a sea-ballad)

INTRODUCTION

RAINER BAEHRE

THE "LAND" IS COMMONLY THOUGHT to be a principal factor in shaping Canada's identity.[1] There is no denying that the confrontation of Euro-Canadian settlers with the backwoods strongly influenced this country's history and its culture. One sometimes needs to be reminded, however, that Canada is also "a nation with a significant maritime heritage."[2] Even in the late nineteenth century the sea could still be discerned as having a comparable role to that of the land in forging Canadian identity. As the organizers of a symposium held in 1987 at Mount Allison University, entitled *The Sea and Culture of Atlantic Canada: A Celebration of Art*, informed their audience, "The sea gives meaning to much that is of the Atlantic region; it should not — cannot — be ignored as we continue to search for our cultural identity."[3]

Indeed, prior to 1850 most of British North America was primarily a maritime world and only secondarily a landed one. The majority of settlers established themselves along the coasts, lakes, and rivers, and were linked by water to the Old World. The influence of the sea has been pervasive, and it has left a deep cultural imprint, particularly in Newfoundland and Labrador.[4] In some instances, the sea has influenced the use of language itself.[5] It is my contention that further insight into this past and present can be gleaned from shipwreck and related marine narratives or stories.[6]

THE STRUCTURAL DIMENSION

This collection is based on the premise that one can perhaps better understand the influence of the sea on the European migrants who visited or came to inhabit this country by looking at narratives of shipwrecks and other related accounts of marine disaster. Whether one views shipwreck narratives as stories-in-history or as history-in-stories, the common dimensions within which they exist require some background, comment, and clarification. To begin, the shipwrecks in history in this collection can only be properly understood within a wider structural context. They are the products of a combination of wide-ranging and largely uncontrollable factors: international events, global marine activity, changing economies, and technology. Moreover, in exploring their structural contours, one needs to recognize that shipwrecks are themselves a significant historical phenomenon.

In the early modern era, shipwrecks occurred most often as a consequence of very tentative economic and social linkages connecting the Old World and the New. Of course, there had been a few celebrated voyages of "discovery" following the Cabotos, notably by Cartier, who in the 1530s had reached central Canada. But in the formative period of European expansion into the New World, when, for example, Elizabeth I ascended the throne in 1558, there was only a fleeting European presence in present-day mainland Canada. In contrast to the North American mainland, such as in New France, Acadia, or Massachusetts, the level of activity in Newfoundland waters during this era was substantial, and it quickly attracted French, British, and other merchants.

Newfoundland waters, an extension of European waters, brought migrant fishers on a seasonal basis. During the height of the fishing season in the seventeenth century, these waters supported an estimated 100 Spanish fishing vessels, another 20 to 30 Spanish whale boats, 50 Portuguese sailing ships, 150 small French and Breton fishing boats, 50 English vessels, and thousands of seasonal fisherfolk.[7] This annual international presence, though fluctuating in its numbers, has been estimated to have often involved ten thousand and more migrants per fishing season. Even after the foreign presence in these waters diminished substantially in the early nineteenth century, Newfoundland fishing and sealing fleets equalled the traditional volume, numbering roughly 2,000 vessels and 20,000 fishermen.[8]

Exactly how many French, Spanish, Portuguese, Basque, and English vessels sailed here from the fifteenth to the end of the eighteenth century that sank, foundered, or were abandoned, will probably always remain something of a mystery. Some scholars have managed to compile useful though still limited estimates. For example, with the aid of notarial archives from Bayonne and Saint-Jean-de-Luz, historian Laurier Turgeon has counted 56 wrecks or abandoned vessels of Basque and French origin that sailed between mainland Europe and Newfoundland over a 70-year period from 1689 to 1759. Many sank near Cape Ray, St. Marie (Cape St. Mary's), and Plaisance (Placentia).[9] Other careful research by Jean-François Brière has shown that 1.9 to 2.5 percent of voyages in the eighteenth-century French cod fishery ended in shipwreck.[10] Consequently, given the volume and ongoing nature of the fishery, it comes as no surprise that overall estimates of shipwrecks for Newfoundland waters are in excess of 10,000 for the period from the sixteenth century through to the present. If the annual levels identified for the early fishery can be relied upon, there would only have needed to be as few as 40 to 50 wrecks annually over 200 years to reach this total. Apart from textual documentation, information concerning shipwrecks in the early period also includes physical evidence, such as sixteenth-century Basque and other European wrecks, including a whaling ship, a frigate, and smaller boats like a *pinaza* and a *chalupa*, which have been uncovered in the important excavations by professional and amateur marine archaeologists at a variety of sites: Red Bay, Trinity Bay, Bay Bulls, Isle aux Morts, Conche, and Brigus.[11] Based on all sources, the Northern Shipwreck Database lists more than 62,000 shipwrecks north of 40 degrees, of which many thousands relate directly and indirectly to Newfoundland waters.[12]

These enormous losses appear to be consistent with those for other parts of Atlantic Canada, as can be seen in several indices used to study ship losses in New Brunswick.[13] In a fine study of maritime labour, Eric Sager compiled figures based on ship cargo losses. His evidence suggests that, while the ratio of shipwreck to successful voyages was low, it was far from trivial. He found that, in the latter half of the nineteenth century for merchant ships registered at Saint John, New Brunswick, the percentage of tonnage lost at sea because of marine disasters ranged between 4.9 and 6.3 percent.[14] These figures agree with other estimates in this era for British wrecks in general and more particularly for wrecks associated with the timber trade between the mother country and

British North America, which was more dangerous, as indicated by its slightly higher loss figures.[15]

While the proportion of unfinished to finished voyages is thus low, it is not historically inconsequential. Yet only sometimes did shipwrecks affect specific historical events. Turgeon suggests, for example, that prolonged concern for the welfare of French ships and the difficulties posed by the winter ice pack were two significant reasons, among others, why, in 1713, France decided to move its centre of activity in the region from the harbour at Plaisance (Placentia) to the ice-free port of Louisbourg on Cape Breton.[16] Likewise, as a result of the d'Enville expedition of 1746, designed to recapture Acadia and Louisbourg, many vessels failed to return to France, and there was widespread sickness and devastating mortality among crews; this failed venture underscores the effect that storms at sea may have had upon history.[17] The losses from shipwreck among Acadians expelled from Ile-St.-Jean (Prince Edward Island) in 1758 is estimated at 679, with another 970 dying at sea from disease and illness, out of an original population of only 3,100.[18] Although the long-term impact on Upper Canada of the loss of the *Speedy* in 1804 can only be a matter of speculation, it did cause the deaths of a judge of the King of Court's Bench, a Solicitor General, an important merchant, and other individuals.[19]

On the other hand, examples of how history affected shipwrecks are frequent. To illustrate, during the era of "discovery," Newfoundland waters were initially shared by English and non-English vessels. In the late sixteenth century, when initial attempts to settle Newfoundland failed, the English imperial government decided to change its original intention to promote colonization. Disappointed by the private settlement schemes, English merchants placed their emphasis in the seventeenth and early eighteenth centuries instead on the exploitation of the island's most abundant natural resource, cod. In contrast to the tiny landed population which, in 1700, consisted of barely 1,200 settlers, the number of seafaring migrant workers in the eighteenth century rose as high as 30,000 persons annually. This migratory fishery off Newfoundland and Labrador continued to dominate the area after the Treaty of Utrecht of 1713, when the French were almost entirely displaced and the island became entirely British. Now France retained only St. Pierre and Miquelon and fishing rights along the west and northern coasts. Inevitably, in this early era, which drew thousands to a very sparsely inhabited region, some shipwrecked fishers and mariners never returned from fishing, and others only barely did so, in part because, once they found themselves wrecked there was little opportunity to encounter anyone on land who might rescue or aid them. In 1667, 180 mariners from three fishing vessels perished after hitting ice. More often, fishers were drowned when their small boats proved unable to withstand an unexpected gale.[20]

The eventual decline of the international migratory fishery, by the early nineteenth century, meant that there were fewer transatlantic fishing vessels, but this decline was matched by an increase in vessels involved in the resident Newfoundland fishery and the growth of the winter seal hunt. Also, following the end of the Napoleonic wars in 1815, timber exports to Great Britain increased dramatically, and the number of ships heading toward Canada climbed steadily, their holds filled with human ballast — the beginnings of the "great migration" to British North America. To protect emigrants, the British government passed the Passenger Act of 1803. Because it made it difficult for the poor to emigrate, this legislation was amended on numerous occasions and its strict provisions relaxed. Smaller vessels, including those of the Newfoundland fishery, were generally exempted from its protective clauses.[21] This circumvention of strict passenger safety contributed to the growing problem of shipwreck in the early nineteenth century, as timber market demands and problems in the mother country augmented the volume of traffic. Even after 1850, when more rigorous standards were put into effect on British vessels, Norwegian vessels played a significant role in transporting timber and emigrants between Canada and Europe, and they were often not subject to these laws.[22]

The problem of shipwreck became especially noticeable in the period from 1826 to 1840, because in these years more ships of suspect quality, especially in the timber trade, were used to transport peoples and goods, and this resulted in a relative rise in the number of shipwrecks. For these terrible years, the number of recorded shipwrecks in voyages to and from Canada, exclusive of those related to the seal fishery, totalled 589. Newfoundland wrecks, totalling 177, represented 20 percent of all wrecks involving British ships between 1826 and 1830, 33 percent between 1831 and 1835, and 25 percent between 1836 and 1840.[23] In 1834 a record 17 emigrant ships went down. It goes without saying that these numbers represent only a fraction, albeit a sizable one, of British shipwrecks throughout the world, which saw deaths reaching 2,000 persons annually, but they still raised strong concerns.

Death by drowning and other causes related to shipwreck were in fact an occupational hazard for merchant seamen. Sager has noted that drowning in a shipwreck accounted for 34.0 percent of all reported deaths among British seamen-in-service, the most common among numerous causes.[24] Fear of drowning at sea thus became a part of the seaman's and the travelling public's consciousness. Of course, to keep the incidence of shipwreck and drowning in perspective, it must be noted that not all shipwrecks ended in loss of life or in the total destruction of the vessels; that was the fate of a minority. Far more often than not, no loss of life was recorded, and many grounded ships were salvaged or returned to dry dock for refitting. Nevertheless, the volume and scale of marine catastrophes, especially between 1826 and 1850, attracted growing public attention marked by a series of inquiries by the British House of Commons into the construction of vessels, crew and passenger safety, a concern heightened by the preponderance of shipwrecks in the growing Canadian timber trade. The wages paid to seamen for these voyages are indicative of the level of danger associated with them. Mariners on northern transatlantic voyages received almost twice as much pay as did their counterparts heading into the Indian Ocean.[25]

In this era, certain parts of Newfoundland waters acquired distinctly negative reputations among seafarers, especially Cape Race, the south coast near the Isle aux Morts, Cape Ray, the Strait of Belle

St. John's Narrows, ca. 1842, a potentially treacherous entry into the safe confines of the harbour. A 45-59, Courtesy of the Provincial Archives of Newfoundland and Labrador

Isle, the St. John's area, particularly the Narrows and Cape Spear and, finally, along the Labrador coast. The documentary record has yet to be properly mined in order to provide an accurate geographical overview, but the degree to which a number of wrecks could be concentrated in a particular area is suggested by the record of the wrecking commissioner at Trepassey for the Cape Race vicinity in the late nineteenth century: he had filed 115 wreck reports in roughly a 20-year career.[26]

Apart from the growth and development of imperial expansion, the migratory fishery, and the timber trade, the history of shipwrecks in Newfoundland water was shaped throughout the centuries by real and potential military conflict, including the American War of Independence, and especially such conflicts between France and England as the Seven Year's War and the lengthy confrontation that emerged as a result of the French Revolution. The overall losses at sea from battle and shipwreck during these conflicts were considerable, though, admittedly, a far greater number of people died from disease. According to Dudley Pope, in the French Revolutionary and Napoleonic Wars (1793-1815) the Royal Navy "lost 1,875 killed in the six major and four minor battles fought by its fleets and four by its squadrons, compared with more than 72,000 who died from disease or accident on board and another 13,600 who died in ships lost by accident or weather."[27] In *Narratives of Shipwrecks of The Royal Navy*, William Gilly lists 515 naval shipwrecks for Great Britain between 1793 and 1849. The loss of life per wreck ranged from zero to 731, the latter figure resulting from the horrific wreck of the *St. George* off Jutland on December 24, 1811. Counting only those naval wrecks where exact figures are given, the Royal Navy lost more than 14,794 personnel in this 56-year period, or more than in actual conflict during the naval campaigns of the Seven Years War and the Napoleonic wars combined.

In Newfoundland waters, British military shipwrecks include the *Phyllis* (1798),[28] the *Fly* (1802), the *Aeneas* (1805), the *Avenger* (1812), the *Tweed* (1813), the *Warrens* (1813), the *Comus* (1816), the *Harpooner* (1816),[29] and the *Drake* (1822).[30] The worst toll among warships is that of the *Fly*, which lost all of its crew of 121 when it crashed on the coast.[31] In October 1805 the troop transport, the *Aeneas*, with 347 soldiers and their families aboard, hit a rock a mile off Newfoundland's coast and 300 miles from St. John's. Only 35 survived the sinking and the tragic aftermath.[32] The troop transport, the

"Loss of the *Aeneas* Transport." Woodcut. Only seven of 347 persons survived this terrible 1805 wreck on the Newfoundland Coast. From R. Thomas, *Interesting and Authentic Narratives of the Most Remarkable Shipwrecks ...*, London, 1835

Harpooner, was lost in November 1816 at Cape Pine near St. Shotts while on its way from Quebec (see Appendix C). It was carrying 385 men, women, and children, including veterans of the War of 1812. The dead numbered 208 persons.

Although the causes of shipwrecks, in whatever era, may have varied somewhat, most can be attributed simply to some combination of overwhelming and ultimately insurmountable natural conditions. Frequently, regardless of the vessel or its national origin, sheer bad weather, an unexpectedly large and devastating or "rogue" wave, boundless fog, or an encroaching ice pack were cited by observers as the dominant natural elements contributing to shipwreck.

Hurricanes and lesser storms now and again took an especially devastating toll. For example, in 1711, at least 2,000 persons were lost aboard numerous British ships at Egg Island, Labrador, as they were sailing toward Quebec.[33] According to Alan Ruffman, a hurricane struck the Avalon peninsula on 9-12 September 1775, quickly raising the sea by 30 feet, and resulting in the destruction of 700 boats and

11 ships, with the possible loss of 4,000 lives, and with another 100 and more vessels sunk in St. Pierre and Miquelon and 400 individuals lost there.[34] A Labrador gale in 1867, which was accompanied by a tidal wave, a *tsunami*, resulted in the loss of 100 people. In the "Great Labrador Storm" of 1885, winds reached 120 miles per hour and left hundreds of vessels sunk and thousands shipwrecked. Another similarly devastating storm pounded Labrador in 1894.[35]

Natural conditions leading to shipwreck were frequently matched or compounded by human choice and error. Sealers, in particular, consciously risked and sometimes courted disaster at sea. There were numerous occasions early on when the ice pack led to the destruction of large number of vessels, as detailed by Shannon Ryan in his acclaimed studies of the sealing trade, which was noted for its perils of "ice, blizzards, fire, explosion, [and] drowning."[36] The modern seal hunt had begun only in the 1790s, reaching its height a half-century later and then declining. Losses of at least 25 vessels were recorded in 1805 and 1811. The industry expanded in the 1820s after a hiatus during the War of 1812. In the late winter and spring of 1829, the seal fishery suffered the loss of 15 vessels. There was an estimated loss of 50 to 60 sealing vessels in 1852, with 1,000 sealers left shipwrecked. Despite an improvement in ship construction and the move toward steamers, heavy losses also befell the industry in 1864, when 1,500 sealers were shipwrecked, and there were other high losses in 1872 and 1898. The latter year proved a turning point: "For the first time, the people expressed their concern publicly over the risk to lives at the seal fishery. They were no longer satisfied with the view that disasters were 'Acts of God' for which no one was to blame."[37] Undoubtedly, the most famous sealing disaster in Newfoundland waters is the one of 1914, described best by Cassie Brown, when 132 persons were stranded on the ice-fields.[38]

It frequently happened that poorly constructed timber ships, such as the *Jesse*,[39] served as emigrant carriers which would be overinsured, overloaded with deck cargo, and then abandoned when they became waterlogged. Many of these vessels were recruited from leaky ships formerly in the Caribbean trade and now found unsuited to carrying dry goods. There were also occasions when captain or crew were blamed for having made a serious mistake or having demonstrated outright negligence; the collision between the large vessels *Vesta* and *Arctic*, whose captain was racing against time, is a case in point. Occasionally, ships were deliberately sunk or abandoned. In time of war, ships were scuttled as a way of keeping them from falling into enemy hands or being destroyed by foes; the *Sapphire* is an example. At other times, vessels disappeared mysteriously and owners collected handsome insurance claims. Still other factors that increased the risk of shipwreck include faulty ship construction, such that stability was affected, "pooping" (the sweep of an unexpectedly large wave over a vessel's stern), and the "canal effect," a disproportionate change in water pressure that pushes the ship toward the nearest bank.[40]

One must not forget the element of sheer bad luck. As one of our narratives informs us, sometimes, in fog, a larger vessel would collide with a small fishing dory, and the result would be an unreported or unidentifiable shipwreck. In one telling description of a "fine stout ship" accidentally hitting a fishing boat, it was noted that before any rescue could be attempted, the boat had already sunk with all on board, and with no one other than those who had caused the accident to know or record that it had happened or who had drowned. Interestingly, this event, while regarded by the author as tragic and regrettable, was not considered unusual for this region.[41]

In short, there was no simple formula to explain why a shipwreck happened or how it could have been prevented. Each case needed to be examined separately. In recognition of the complexity of the event, reforms to address the problem of shipwreck were multifaceted. In an important British House of Commons inquiry in 1836, a Select Committee itemized what it considered to be the avoidable causes: defective construction of ships; inadequacy of equipment; imperfect state of repair; improper or excessive loading; inappropriateness of form; incompetency of master and officers; drunkenness of officers and men; the nature and operation of Marine Insurance, which contributed to risk, neglect, and even deliberate destruction or abandonment of vessels; want of harbours of refuge; and imperfection of charts.[42] It was also in the 1830s that shipping reformers, including insurance companies, began to call for renewed and strict port regulation of the carrying trade, the proper training of crew, better ship construction, an end to deck-loading, and other measures to minimize the risks of shipwreck. Increasing efforts were also undertaken in Great Britain and British North America to improve safety conditions, including the building of more lighthouses, such as that at Cape Spear, which began operations in 1836.

Yet, in most instances, reforms and needed legislative modifications proceeded ploddingly, influenced as they were by ideological and political agendas.[43] Only after the long-awaited implementation of recommendations by several important government investigations into shipping safety — the building of lighthouses, the introduction of safety features such as buoys and flares, the development of resuscitation techniques, the predominant use of iron-hulled steam vessels, the compulsory presence of a ship's medical officer, and modifications to the Passenger Acts in the mid-1850s — did ocean travel become noticeably safer.[44]

Recognition of the problems and specific preventative measures did not eliminate shipwrecks or some of their traditional causes. At the turn of the twentieth century, one finds a prominent Newfoundland captain, when asked, continuing to cite human failings as the most common reasons for shipwreck: the overconfidence of shipmasters; ignorance of coastal and ocean currents, especially the force of tides; and the negligence of crews who used lead in their soundings to judge a ship's proximity to shore.[45]

THE CULTURAL DIMENSION

A second, equally important dimension within which the shipwreck narratives of Newfoundland and Labrador occurred and are given meaning is the cultural dimension. These narratives constitute an essential element in this colonial society's self-definition and self-image.[46]

It is important to recall that for more than a century after Cabot's "discovery," Newfoundland barely existed in the European consciousness, and that Labrador was even less well known. If known at all, Newfoundland was regarded simply as an extension of Europe. With the exception of a minor rash of publications on the island in the early seventeenth century, in fact little was written about Newfoundland and Labrador until the early nineteenth century.[47] This dearth of narrative extends, not surprisingly, to the shipwreck experience: despite the great number of shipwrecks in pre-twentieth century Newfoundland and Labradorian waters, accounts of them are rare. In a very real sense, the identity of this part of the French and British empires was forged on the margins.

Few survivors, apparently, chose to or were able to write about their shipwreck experiences. Perhaps this can be attributed in part to the high levels of illiteracy. There are also other possible explanations. In the testimony of shipowner James Ballingall before the Select Committee on Shipwrecks, concerning the causes of shipwrecks, he suggested that of all crews sailing an unsafe vessel "few or none" survive its demise, and that "scarce one in a thousand can explain the cause, or indeed has ever thought about it."[48] Yet, contrary to Ballingall's belief that most survivors rarely thought about the matter, virtually all of the extant narratives show clearly that survivors were preoccupied with their experiences, though they also expressed a reservation or reluctance about making their feelings public. The relative rarity of these accounts makes them particularly important to the historical record. They clearly influenced opinion, and as Zuckerman writes, "Awareness of the dangers of the sea voyage was widespread in England." While the voyage across the Atlantic became typified by its "ordinariness," it nevertheless represented for many travellers, as it did for the Puritans, "a literal rite of passage."[49]

In defining the historical and cultural contours of narratives of shipwrecks in Newfoundland waters, this distinct phase of the ocean crossing, our designation of "Newfoundland waters" needs first to be explained. Primarily, it is a term of convenience that reflects the natural

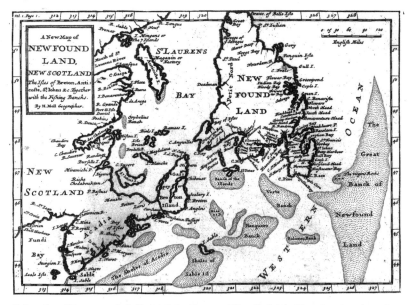

Map by Herman Moll, 1708. From *The British Empire in America*, Courtesy of Centre for Newfoundland Studies, Memorial University of Newfoundland

distinctiveness of a particular sector of the transatlantic journey; but these waters are somewhat indistinct. Of course, the designation relates to the present-day province of Newfoundland and Labrador, which is part of the political and geographical region of the Atlantic provinces, but this is not our meaning. It refers more specifically to the waters immediately along the province's island and Labrador coast lines, and to their extensions, which they share with Cape Breton, the Magdalen Islands, St. Pierre and Miquelon, and even New England. Included are the various fishing banks, the Cabot Strait, the Strait of Belle Isle, and much of the Gulf of St. Lawrence. Beyond these boundaries, one finds the shores of Sable Island, mainland Nova Scotia, Prince Edward Island, New Brunswick, Anticosti Island, and Quebec.

Newfoundland waters is also a designation fashioned in largely piecemeal fashion over a long period of time, the probable evolution of which included the early oral traditions of fishers, imprecise sixteenth-century cartographical fragments from the first Spanish, Portuguese and French navigational maps (which barely discerned the correct contours of "new founde lande"), early nineteenth-century British "sailing directories," Admiralty charts such as those prepared by James Cook, documenting hazards, as well as shipwreck and other narratives.[50]

This distinctive phase of the oceanic passage from Europe to mainland Canada was often difficult for mariners, less so during the period from May to September, but notably at other times of the year, because of the unpredictable nature of the spring ice pack, the frequent fogs that resulted from the meeting of the Labrador and Gulf currents, a rock-bound coast, the cold, unpredictable, and strong currents, the rapidly shifting winds, and the brutal storms.[51] Although Newfoundland and Labrador boasted many good harbours that could be used for protection against the elements, especially at St. John's, these waters and the island's coastline also held a special reputation for danger and marine accidents, many with tragic and fatal consequences.[52]

More importantly, these Newfoundland waters existed in the mind. For our purposes, the concept of region adopted here is primarily a cultural one, whose defining characteristics are of course its "natural" or physical settings but, more tellingly and in a dynamic way, a "region" is "the scene and effect of interaction in social relations," and structured by place and time.[53] It constitutes a somewhat "impure" cultural construction and a limited identity.[54] Two important modern literary works that have depicted the history of Newfoundland and Labrador in a cultural way through narratives are Patrick Flaherty and Peter Neary's *By Great Waters* and Patrick Flaherty's *The Rock Observed*.[55] In examining similar textual accounts,[56] I plan to turn these standard "landed" vantage points slightly askew.

The region of this collection is circumscribed by encounters on and of the waters. In other words, it is an indistinct place where inhabitants and visitors have lived and have passed through, and it is a place to which these residents and travellers, and those who have perceived their world only from the outside, have given a specific meaning. Within this definition, Newfoundland waters is a place where people have encountered shipwreck not only in their experience but also in their imaginations. It is the sea marked by the contours of Newfoundland waters and observed through the prism of shipwreck experience.[57]

Borrowing my approach from literary, anthropological, and cultural historical analysis, I propose that these narrative texts of Newfoundland shipwrecks illuminate a certain mental and historical perspective: "the way in which the text's subject of perception (its focalizer) mentally views the world, according to his/her psychological, cognitive, and ideological frame of mind."[58] In these texts, the "visual and mental perspectives coalesce in an almost exemplary fashion"; the geographical and the natural, the historical and the contemporary, the individual and the cultural, all merge to help us understand a unique regional experience. Such an approach helps to explain how a cultural identity emerges over time.

This collection is about storytelling in a particular setting and these stories are used to reconstruct a specific past. Individual shipwreck narratives, as stories, are artifacts of microhistory. More broadly, these shipwreck and other narratives of Newfoundland waters constitute a set of stories within a particular historical setting that are "stories-in-history" but also "history-in-stories."[59] This interrelationship is significant. "We inhabit storied space," Laura Cameron tells us,[60] and those who experienced these waters and wrote about them, or others who merely read about them, all inhabited this space, this region. These narratives, it is argued, therefore play an important role in shaping this regional consciousness, because, as Clifford Geertz has suggested: "The culture of a people is an ensemble of texts, themselves ensembles."[61] Whether one considers the places where these events occurred to constitute part of a regional landscape or waterscape, they reflect a region of the mind.

Despite the richness of their content, one needs to be cautioned that these narratives are by no means comprehensive nor all-encompassing in their representation of Newfoundland shipwrecks, nor can they be. The shipwreck accounts of this collection portend a multiplicity of meaning and subtexts. Individual shipwreck narratives also provide a perspective, an account of historical events, but each story provides only one of the many perspectives that are and were possible. Consequently, no narrative explains all that there is to know about the experience of being shipwrecked. No single narrative is representative of all others. And no single narrative or set of narratives adequately explains shipwreck culture and history in its entirety. Yet it is suggested here that the collective contents of these unique stories of local events metamorphosize into generic stories of shipwreck and cultural narratives of Newfoundland waters. Each account, though distinct from the others in its primary emphasis, incorporates themes common to all. Taken together they transcend the individual work.

In their entirety, they reflect much of the complexity of the phenomena of surviving and of succumbing to the sea. One can discern in their voices, therefore, a preoccupation with humanity's deeper issues of existence. In differing degrees, each narrative gravitates toward the sensational, toward adventure and suspense, toward religious and moral appeal, toward emotional catharsis, and toward the secular, the pragmatic, and the cultural. As such, they offer historical case studies of "humanity" and "inhumanity" within the context of crisis — the nature of courage, cowardice, and desperation, their interpreted meaning, and the complex emotions reflected in the thinking and actions of shipwreck victims and survivors,[62] and to some extent they provide insight into the reactions and practices of community and government towards shipwreck victims and survivors.

Yet, as narratives or stories or reports, they necessarily rest somewhere between the realm of "objective" historical documentation and that of the purely "subjective." In this form, as narratives, they reflect what the historian Lynn Hunt has argued are three levels of human experience: the most intimate level, the middle or cultural level, and the level of public power.[63] Even if they were to be considered for the moment to be absolutely "true" historical accounts, they are not merely detached "factual" accounts. They combine the subjective with the objective. In placing each narrative in its individual historical context, one must connect the private with the public world. Only so can one understand all three levels of this mental landscape, and the "langscape" of the sea.[64]

In assessing their historical and cultural value, one must ask the question, how influential have these stories been? No one living in Newfoundland and Labrador, and noting the popularity of shipwreck narratives, would deny that they have exerted a considerable cultural impact on this part of the country, thereby helping to define in the here and now this region of the mind. But was this always the case? Just as they are today, premodern stories of shipwreck were disseminated far and wide, though perhaps to a more limited audience. The ones in this collection, to judge from their places of publication, found readers in London, Manchester, Paris, Exeter, Glasgow, New York, Boston, Dublin, Bath, Cincinatti, St. John's, and doubtedly many other places. Moreover, the contents of individual narratives became part of the history of the Jesuits, the Moravians, and the Royal Navy, and were often incorporated into Newfoundland and Labrador's songs, hymns, and other folklore traditions. In addition, the diverse origins of ship-wrecked passengers and crew would have resulted in a broad dissemination in their respective communities of information concerning Newfoundland waters, because these stories found a place in newspapers, official reports, sermons, art, literature and poetry, and everyday letters and conversation.

In deciding which narratives to include, I have chosen different voices that suggest the variety, complexity, and range of shipwreck experience. In virtually every instance, the narrator is clearly identified. The subjects include a shipmaster, a Jesuit, a Labrador trader, a Moravian, a merchant mariner belonging to His Majesty's Service, a transported soldier, a migratory Scottish fisherman, two migratory French fishermen, several indentured seaman, wreckers, various emigrants, the wife of a Governor General, an obscure wife, daughter, and sister of fishers who failed to return, and a famous Newfoundland captain. In a few instances, the main subjects did not write down their stories but told them to another, an editor or benefactor, who wrote them on their behalf, or who wrote reports, or who recounted or trans-lated stories of which they had no first-hand knowledge but that were based on primary sources.

In a literary study of shipwreck narratives, Keith Huntress has suggested that in the past the primary reason for turning shipwreck narratives into print was the element of adventure and suspense, their titillating content. Secondarily, he contends, their publication served a didactic purpose in offering the reading public some religious, moral, pragmatic, or civic lessons.[65] Recent studies of the nature of the narrative have prompted further analysis along these lines. Part of the intrinsic cultural interest and historical value of this narrative analysis is certainly to be derived from our attempt to understand the psychological motivation behind the survivors' relating, writing, or publishing them. Herein one finds a complex illustration of the interconnectedness among the intimate, the cultural, and the public.

From the point of view of cultural anthropology, these narratives represent a form of social drama with a clearly intended social impact. Victor Turner has proposed that this drama, or crisis, about which nothing is predetermined or inevitable, is a matrix through which individuals and societies define or redefine their beliefs.[66] Thus, writing and reading narratives is a way to make cultural sense of indeterminate and abnormal events. Such cultural expressions, then, not only reaffirm existing norms and beliefs; they help to create new ones. If this is a compelling argument, and I believe it is, then shipwreck narratives from Newfoundland waters not only reflect that region's past culture, they indicate the way it has probably been shaped and remade. More than forgotten remnants of our past, they are embedded, by means of the written word and through the story, in our cultural psyche.

The symbolic significance of the sea and of shipwreck experiences in Western civilization has had a longstanding and universal influence on several other cultural forms.[67] It exists as part of a long European and North American religious, literary, and artistic tradition dominated by but not exclusive to text. Shipwreck voices have been expressed in public since at least the middle of the sixteenth century and are part of a continuum consisting of accounts of single voyages, anthologies of ship disasters, chapbooks, and other forms of non-fictional texts involving exploration.[68] Nineteenth-century fiction writers and poets, such as William Wordsworth, Lord Byron, Percy Bysshe Shelley, Henry Wadsworth Longfellow, Herman Melville, Edgar Allan Poe, and Joseph Conrad, have used the theme of shipwreck in their works. While Longfellow's contribution to Canadian cultural history, in the form of the poem *Evangeline*, has long been recognized, he also wrote *Sir Humphrey Gilbert*, commemorating this explorer's voyages to Newfoundland and his death at sea.[69] The nineteenth century's artists and some of their most famous paintings, including Théodore Géricault's *Raft of the 'Medusa,'* J.M.W. Turner's *The Wreck Buoy,* and Winslow Homer's *The Wrecked Schooner*, used man's clash with the sea to help define the content of their canvases.[70]

Like shipwreck accounts, these textual and painted images invariably reflect the contest between humanity, God, and Nature. In the case of Newfoundland waters, which share in this wider cultural tradition, this contest has often been represented in the visual imagery evoked by individual wrecks, in various media: votive paintings, wood cuts, oils, and prints.[71] There are numerous engravings of shipwrecks and sea-related themes, including Newfoundland ones, in popular publications such as the *Canadian Illustrated News* and the *London Illustrated News*.[72] Text, however, dominates the presentation of shipwreck experience. Newfoundland shipwrecks have also spawned stories, sea-ballads, sermons, hymns, and poetry. Recently, the region has once more been put on the cultural map with the unprecedented success of the film *Titanic* and its accompanying commercialization. This renewed interest affirms the more longstanding one that, in the case of the *Titanic,* amounts to a near-obsession. There can be little disagreement that the public's cultural gaze, its collective memory, constitutes a major dimension of the shipwreck experience, even today.

In closing this part of the discussion, one must note that there is also another dimension, the most intimate element implicit in these narratives. George Landow contends that, existentially and culturally, the crisis of shipwreck and death at sea is a metaphor for the human voyage through life, and stands at its centre.[73] Hence its power and attraction.

A nineteenth-century commentary by Henry Howe on the universal image of "man overboard" constitutes an insightful confirmation of this observation. He writes, "Death is at all times solemn, but never so much so as at sea. A man dies on shore; his body remains with his friends, and, 'the mourners go about the streets'; but when a man falls overboard at sea and is lost, there is a suddenness in the event, and a difficulty in realizing it, which give it an air of awful mystery. A man dies on shore — you follow his body to the grave, and a stone marks the spot. You are often prepared for the event. There is always something which helps you to realize it when it happens, and to recall it when it has passed. A man is shot down by your side in battle, and the mangled body remains an *object*, and a *real evidence*; but at sea, the man is near you — at your side — you hear his voice, and in an instant he is gone, and nothing but a *vacancy* shows his loss."[74] The forgotten voices of these Newfoundland shipwreck narratives and their attempts to give meaning to their survival offer some support for Howe's comments and Landow's conclusion.

Because those who have disappeared at sea have also often disappeared from history, these narratives, though written about personal loss and suffering, and mostly forgotten, have additional significance. They restore those individual tragedies to history and help to fill that "vacancy" and its cultural meaning for humanity. Indeed, one is consistently struck by the prevalence and the common experience of death that most of the survivors in these narratives relate. The rawness and the vivid detail of many of these near-death episodes — their authentic feel — reflects both a personal and intimate terror and the detachment that is consistent with modern research.[75] They embody the perceptions of a premodern society, which integrated death as a private, social, and public fact, and where personal meaninglessness was countered by religion and community integration, which in turn was based on traditional beliefs and values.

In his monumental history of death, Philippe Ariès has discussed how historically, "the death of each person was a public event that moved, literally and figuratively, society as a whole. It was not only an individual who was disappearing, but society itself that had been wounded and that had to be healed."[76] Ariès contends that it has only been since the nineteenth century that our encounter with death has become denied, privatized, individualized, feared, medicalized, and removed in its pristine state from public view. Therefore, death did not merely represent the "unspeakable" or "inexpressible" in the centuries from which this collection's narratives are taken. It was "a dramatic moment in life, grave and formidable, but not so formidable that they [the survivors] were tempted to push it out of sight, run away from it, act as if it did not exist, or falsify its appearances."[77] This former world stands in sharp contrast to the present one, where rationality and modern institutions are engaged primarily in "risk management."[78]

The power of these stories as cultural forms is suggested by their many dimensions and the strength of their appeal. At the most superficial level they were individual and sentimental accounts that elicited their readers' prurient interest. However, they also belong to what Thomas Laqueur has called "humanitarian narratives."[79] According to Laqueur, it is in order to involve the reader, and thereby to draw upon his or her compassion that the authors provide the many details of their experiences. Upon more careful reading and analysis, one finds that the writer's objective is less to entertain the individual reader than to gain the attention of the community. The author portrays the suffering body and mind in order to forge a bond between the reader and the victim. Significantly, all Newfoundland shipwreck narratives embody these elements of Laqueur's analysis, which suggest their multidimensional importance.

This "humanitarian" dimension also has importance specifically for the individual survivor. Writing down a shipwreck experience was likely vital to his or her intimate self. A recent analysis of Herman Melville's *Moby Dick*, in which Janet Reno draws parallels between Ishmael's narrative in the novel and modern survival literature, in turn tells something more about the narratives presented in this collection.

In her interpretation of this quintessential nineteenth-century novel of the sea, a shipwreck story, Reno suggests that writing about a disaster, such as a shipwreck, can be understood as an act of self-healing. It is an attempt by the narrator to find meaning amid the chaos of disaster, but it is also a way of communicating that event to those who have never had such an experience. Yet it often proves personally and technically difficult to write. Besides forcing the author to remember an unhappy event, the act of writing also requires him or her to make sense of what happened, to find meaning in the event's apparent senselessness. Reno writes, "A survivor needs to go through feelings of sorrow, helplessness, rage, guilt, and loss to tell his story."[80] An overwhelming sense of loss encompasses not only the loss of fellow human beings but also the loss of innocence. A survivor often feels that no one can truly understand not only what happened, but also the overwhelming sense of chaos and the accompanying feelings of guilt, the need to come to terms with the loss, and the need to mourn the dead.[81] These feelings are consistently conveyed throughout the Newfoundland narratives. Many times the survivors and narrators delve in some detail into what it felt like to be alongside those who died. The nature of such deaths and their own reactions appear to fit Reno's paradigm.

Even when no life was lost, which was the case more often than not, such shipwreck experiences provoked uncomfortable personal sensations. A comment in the autobiography of Captain Bob Bartlett, who in mid-career commanded the *C.B. Roosevelt*, which brought Admiral Peary to the North Pole, and whose illustrious career inspired several sea ballads,[82] effectively raises this point. Here, Bartlett writes about the early stages of his official sailing career, when he signed on with the *Corisande* so as to begin qualifying for his second mate's papers, and his reaction to its wreck. Throughout his last voyage aboard this vessel, he and the other members of the crew had a number of premonitions of disaster. As he notes in a serious way, superstition influenced the sailor's perceptions. Bartlett survived without personal loss, but he nevertheless found the event depressing for some time afterward. He states, "To my surprise I found I couldn't talk much about it. Since then I have learned that the loss of a ship affects a seafaring man much like the loss of a dear relative; and it pains him greatly to discuss the circumstances of the sorrow."

Bartlett's comment, which describes a psychological reaction much like those of survivors of other forms of crisis, speaks volumes and offers insight into human responses to tragedy and loss, as well as into the mentality of the mariner. Perhaps, as Landow suggests, "The sudden crash of the totally unexpected sea upon the ship produces a moment of crisis, a flash-point, one of those brief instants in time when the primal isolation and helplessness of the human condition are revealed."[83]

The fate of shipwreck victims in nineteenth-century narratives was not always to be regarded as inevitable, pitiable, or necessarily tragic. This fact demonstrates to the reader that the circumstances of victimization by the sea were in many instances a product of individual elements that could be mitigated or remedied by human intervention. The presence of reflections such as these in a historical context, envisioning as they do the possibility of a way of being that is not subject to natural fate, appears to anticipate the coming of a secular risk society. In short, whatever the underlying motivation in the past for publishing a shipwreck narrative — to lament, bemoan, and forewarn — the intimate, the cultural, and the public were inevitably intertwined.

THE NARRATIVE DIMENSION

The foregoing overview of the historical, structural, and cultural dimensions of Newfoundland shipwrecks provides a backdrop to our understanding of the individual narratives that, by themselves, offer observations on the relationship between humanity and the sea as expressed through the linkages of the intimate, the cultural and the public. In light of the inherent difficulties of ordering these stories thematically, it was decided to present the ones included in the collection in a chronological order. They carry us from Newfoundland's mercantilist origins to the mid-Victorian industrial era; they begin in the time of Sir Humphrey Gilbert and the second claiming of Newfoundland in 1583 and end with the early sailing days of Captain Bob Bartlett, the growing dominance of steamships, and the decline of sail. They end before the wholescale professionalization of the marine workplace, before the statutory insistence on government enquiries, in other words, before the risk management of the sea. The late nineteenth century was also chosen as a natural divide between the premodern and the modern eras, because much more is known, or rather remembered, and much more has been written about the twentieth century's Newfoundland-related marine disasters, from the S.S. *Greenland* disaster of 1898, and the sinking of the *Titanic*, the *Ethie*, and the *Flux*, to that of the oil-rig *Ocean Ranger*.[84]

Whether one wishes to place these narratives in the context of story-in-history or history-in-stories, they all encompass at least the one main connecting theme of marine disaster, and frequently a variety of other overlapping historical and cultural subthemes: the perils of "discovery" and early exploration; the interpretation of shipwreck and survival as divine "providence"; the rescue of Europeans by native peoples and contemporary enemies; the danger of the ship as workplace; military, national, cultural, and personal values reflected in human responses to shipwreck; the social welfare of merchant mariners; secular interpretations of marine disaster; wrecking; the gendered space aboard ship; and other topics. In ranging as widely as they do in their subject matter, they add indirectly but substantially to our knowledge of Canadian cultural history and the history of Newfoundland waters.

The first narrative that arguably mentions shipwreck in these waters, *The Greenlanders' Saga*, was recorded more than a thousand years ago when the Norse group led by Thorvald, brother of Leif Ericson, wintered in Vinland (possibly L'Anse aux Meadows in Newfoundland) and sailed their *knorr* eastward and then north around the coast. When a gale struck, off an unidentifiable headland, they were driven ashore and their boat's keel was smashed. After making rudimentary repairs, they continued their voyage looking for supplies. According to this account, a violent encounter then ensued between these Europeans and North American native peoples (they never recorded any non-violent encounters), whom they identified only as *skraelings*. The Norse came upon three skin boats with three men hidden under each, and then others arrived, whom they attacked, killing eight. Soon finding themselves pitted against a hostile flotilla of "hundreds of skin boats," they quickly made their escape.[85]

Five hundred years later other well-known explorers likely faced similar instances of shipwreck and aboriginal hostility. The island's reputed early modern European discoverer of 1497, Giovanni Caboto, better known as John Cabot, was quite possibly a victim of shipwreck in this region, for on his second voyage, like many mariners and ships, he went "missing." This event, it has been argued, may have delayed English interest in the colonization of Newfoundland for several decades. Likewise, Corte Réal, who sailed along the west coast of the island, did not return home; otherwise the region might have had a stronger Portuguese presence, for Newfoundland was initially also claimed by the King of Portugal.[86] Finally, although Jacques Cartier described the region as inhospitable, after his voyages in the early seventeenth century, France's interest in expanding its role in these waters gradually grew.[87]

Despite these initial failures, records indicate that French and Basque fishing and some trading vessels soon plied the western and southern coasts of Newfoundland and initially outnumbered the English.[88] In southern Labrador, the Basques were engaging in major whaling operations at Red Bay; they too had problems with shipwrecks, which disrupted their supplies and exports of baleen oil.[89]

After Cabot, a second and more formal English colonization of Newfoundland began with the voyages of the admiral and explorer Sir Humphrey Gilbert. He was more than once a victim of shipwreck, to which his failures were directly ascribed. William Cambden wrote a century after Gilbert's demise that the latter had "suffered so much by Shipwrecks and want of necessary Provision"[90] that he had finally been forced to turn his back on his colonization plans for England, give up his search for a northwest passage, and return to Europe. As fate would have it, during his final return to England, Gilbert was drowned when his vessel, the 40-ton *Golden Hind*, was "devoured and swallowed up of the Sea."[91] Cambden aptly described Gilbert's ocean experiences as an ongoing confrontation with "outrageous seas," to which description this volume owes its title.

One of Gilbert's losses was the sinking of the *Delight* in 1583. During this expedition he had insisted that the shipmaster Richard Clarke and his crew follow a dangerous course despite Clarke's protests;

this decision resulted in the shipwreck. Much later, the poet Longfellow recreated this event in verse:

> He [Gilbert] sat upon the deck,
> The Book was in his hand;
> "Do not fear! Heaven is as near,"
> He said, "by water as by land!"[92]

In recognition of Gilbert's importance to the island's history, an account from Clarke's perspective of the *Delight* misfortune and the crew's rescue, ostensibly by international rivals, begins this anthology.

Not surprisingly, many shipwreck narratives, including that of the *Delight*, raised spiritual issues and concerns, and highlighted contemporary religious values. From the beginning, the expansion of European empires into the New World was associated with the spread of Christianity. Some of the most prominent examples of the workings of "divine providence" entered into the narratives of missionaries, such as the Jesuits in Newfoundland and along the St. Lawrence River. On a number of significant occasions, Jesuit activities were affected by shipwrecks.

Spiritual preoccupations and interpretations, and the joining of private with public concerns, are evident throughout an important 1629 account of the shipwreck of an unnamed vessel by the eminent Jesuit Fr. Charles Lalemant; it is included in our collection. The vessel, forced to turn away from Quebec, which had been recently captured by David Kirke, sailed back into the Gulf of St. Lawrence, was blown southward off course toward Cape Breton, and met its doom on the Canso Islands. Its victims included crew members and fellow clergy. With the aid of local Mi'Kmaqs, the survivors made their way toward safety and were fortuitously rescued in Newfoundland waters by an unidentified Basque ship. Lalemant, a figure of historical importance, gave meaning to what had happened by presenting it as divine intervention.

Such "miracles," though apparently not in this case, frequently inspired votive (*ex-voto*) paintings, such as one commemorating the survival of a French captain in his journey from Plaisance to Quebec, as a way of thanks to God.[93] The letters of the *Jesuit Relations* describe several other shipwrecks that adversely affected the Jesuit order's activities besides the one described by Fr. Lalement. They include Father

Crespel's noted shipwreck on Anticosti Island[94] and that of an unnamed vessel in Newfoundland waters in 1649. We are told, in a lengthy description of the latter incident, that the ship's mainmast broke and pierced its bottom, in open seas near the "great bank."[95] This vessel carried a cargo of furs for sale in France on behalf of the Jesuits and the Company of One Hundred Associates, and a serious financial blow to the order was sustained.

Besides the usual spiritual and psychological themes, this narrative of 1649 introduces the topic of cannibalism and the interventionist role of women aboard ship, and is yet a further illustration of how the intimate became linked to the cultural and the public world. The crew, after being adrift for many days, was forced, in desperation, to draw lots in order to decide which one of its members to eat. Lots were chosen, but the group was initially reluctant to resort to cannibalism. Necessity forced a second drawing of lots. At the last moment, just as they were about to kill a fellow crew member, they met an English vessel and made a "miraculous rescue."[96] Their trials, however, were not over. The English crew objected to taking those they had rescued aboard because they lacked sufficient supplies for all, but "some English women on board this Vessel threw themselves at their husbands' feet, and besought them to take pity on those poor shipwrecked men, offering even to fast a part of the time, for their sake." According to Lalemant, the entire group was so grateful at being rescued that, on returning to France, they fulfilled their vows at a shrine and in church instead of immediately returning home to family and friends.[97]

A number of shipwreck narratives, including several in this collection, demonstrate the relief and gratitude felt by Europeans facing impending doom upon being saved by the goodwill and humanity of local indigenous inhabitants of Newfoundland and Labrador. One cannot help but wonder how many shipwreck survivors owed their lives to the region's aboriginal populations, with Lalemant's Cape Breton experience being a case in point.

Moravian missionaries and associated traders of Labrador had similar experiences. Foreign trade with the Inuit had been conducted by Europeans for at least two centuries before the appearance of the Moravians, certainly since the Basque presence at Red Bay and the Strait of Belle Isle between 1537 and 1542, when "peace and harmony" reigned between aboriginals and whalers, a state that did not always prevail.[98] Since then in the region, there had been contact and trade with the French, including the two traders, Courtemanche and Fornel, who had run independent trading posts at Bradore Bay and Northwest River until 1763; they were barred from the coast after the British Conquest. One exception was Makko, a Roman Catholic and French Canadian, who operated a post at Kaipohok Bay from 1780 to 1800.

Moravians, who had been active in western Greenland since 1721, together with independent English traders and larger trading companies, filled the void left by the French. The British government, anxious to keep others out, came to an agreement with the Moravians in 1769, when it granted them 100,000 acres and a virtual monopoly of trade and missionary activity in an effort to establish peace and Christianity in the region.

Efforts to bring peace to the area had not been easily accomplished, for in earlier European accounts the Inuit had more often than not been regarded as aggressive and opportunistic. This perception was borne out when many members of the first Moravian venture in 1752, in conjunction with the firm Nisbet, Grace and Bell, a company of English Moravian businessmen seeking baleen (whale-bone), were killed by hostile Inuit. Only in the late eighteenth century did their efforts begin to leave a permanent mark. The Moravians managed to establish their first mission at Nain in 1770, then Okak in 1776, and Hopedale in 1782.

When relations improved, however, the Moravian attitude was condescending, and sometimes they accepted necessary assistance from native peoples only reticently. For example, when Haven and other Moravian missionaries, upon founding the mission station at Nain in 1771, required aid from the local native population, Haven described such hospitality as "no slight ordeal to Europeans."[99] In 1774 the sloop *Amity* was wrecked and two missionaries lost. The survivors, including the leader Haven, were saved by a local Inuit, who piloted them to safety in his kayak.[100] Needless to say, rescue was attributed first to God, but they also managed to acknowledge the role of their wordly rescuer. The period 1779 to 1804 witnessed "a religious awakening" in the area of Hopedale, Nain, and Okak, as mission supply ships began to come regularly. This helps to explain the friendly assistance provided by the Inuit to these traders at this time and helps us to understand the background to a dramatic story from 1782 included in this collection, of an event typically experienced throughout Newfoundland waters from late October to mid-May, the breaking up of the winter ice pack.

Much has been written about the arrival of the Moravians, and their relationship with the Inuit and Innu populations,[101] but their travels by sea and ice while carrying out their proselytizing and trading activities are less commonly known. A second story concerns these marine experiences. This narrative describes the origin and nature of the various ships in the sect's service between the early and late nineteenth century, and gives an account of some wrecks and some close calls. As Gosling writes, "The history of the Moravian ships and their captains is one of the most remarkable in the records of navigation."[102] Based on an extract from the order's *Periodical Accounts,* the narrative includes some detail on seafaring that is of interest to the maritime historian, including the origins of crew members and the types of vessels; also it includes a cultural component, an original hymn.

Another fortuitous intervention by native peoples of this region that resulted in the rescue of shipwreck victims is related by John Smith, first mate of the *Neptune.* This brig, while on its way from Bristol to Quebec, was smashed in 1829 near Belle Isle off the Northern Peninsula during a violent January snowstorm. Smith movingly describes the experience of loss and the power of religious faith. He and five other survivors managed to make it to shore. They had endured "great hardships" for two weeks "on a wild and uninhabited coast," when they were "fortunately discovered and conducted to an English settlement by a friendly Indian." In light of his rescue by this native hunter, Smith felt compelled to change his preconceptions of "the savage." Not only does this story affirm the author's belief in divine intervention, but also he came to believe that the nature of truly Christian behaviour, even among "heathens," was a common trait of humanity. Focus on the spiritual and the intimate was not however exclusive to the religiously devout; it was common to many survival accounts in this era.

There are to be found several accounts of the migratory fishery to Newfoundland and Labrador that likewise illustrate aspects of life and danger at sea, and particularly offer insight into the ship as a workplace prior to the nineteenth century. They include one by Flavel of Dartmouth on the shipwreck of the English merchant vessel, the *Thomas and Ann,* which was bringing brandy, wine, and salt to Newfoundland in 1679. The ship was crushed by ice, and after great effort its survivors landed at Cripple Cove, near "Treposse" (Trepassey), there to be saved by "providence."[103] Another story involves Allen Geare, one of a group of nine who survived the 1702 wreck in ice of the frigate *Langdon*, a full 70 leagues (210 miles) off the northeast coast of Newfoundland. Geare and his fellow crew thanked God and wondered why they were saved.[104]

A third such revealing story, one included in our collection, was written in 1704 by an obscure seaman in the fishing trade, Henry Treby of Lympson, a survivor of the salt-laden ship, *Anne*. Originally from Topsham, near Exeter, the ship had been bound for Newfoundland from Lisbon when it was driven onto a huge island of ice roughly 50 leagues (150 miles) from the coast. In this narrative dedicated to the Archbishop of Canterbury, Treby describes the crew's attempts to save the ship, their psychological turmoil as they realized their fate, the dark nature of their despair, their pleading for divine intervention, and their eventual rescue. Sadly, after their prolonged ordeal in frigid, foggy conditions, adrift and lost in open water, some of the survivors died at St. John's shortly after being rescued.

Religious metaphors and beliefs in Newfoundland shipwreck narratives, though never entirely abandoned, gradually did give way to other less divine preoccupations and explanations. This trend toward secular explanation is evident in nineteenth-century shipwreck stories used to address the behaviour of the British navy and merchant marine in an effort to promote nationalism, secular ideals, and English upper-class models of behaviour and decorum.[105] The meaning ascribed to naval shipwrecks especially suggests the underlying military ethos of the day. The metaphorical and didactic application of naval disasters in this fashion is quite understandable in light of the fact that the tragic fate of many ships in service to the British Crown was perhaps avoidable. In this era of global rivalry, naval superiority was of crucial importance, and shipwrecks constituted very real losses to national and imperial prowess. Consequently, an understanding of the circumstances of naval shipwreck and the development of ways to avoid these circumstances were key instruments in promoting national strengths, virtues, and values.

To the author William Gilly, who made a study of late eighteenth and early nineteenth century disasters, "good order, good discipline and good feeling," as well as exemplary courage, were paramount in a ship's survival. In contrast with the scandalous episode of the French *Medusa*, immortalized by Géricault, which exemplified a crew's cowardice, the example of the military frigate *Drake*, whose story this collection includes, portrays Captain Baker as a model hero, who insisted on staying with his ship to the last, risking his own life. In fact Baker insisted on fulfilling his role to such an extent that he ordered his entire crew to abandon ship before him; they all refused to leave without him — a clear indication of their own nobleness of spirit. Tragically, after this valiant stand-off, the captain and some of his crew left the ship, but failed to find their way to safety; they ended up on a rock surrounded by a rising tide, where they were inevitably enveloped. According to the evidence of survivors, the captain's behaviour had created deep affection and respect among the crew. Subsequently, they sent a letter to the Lords Commissioners of the Admiralty lamenting the loss of their "worthy" and "lion-hearted" commander and praising his "manliness and fortitude." They also asked that their letter become part of the permanent public record. The Lords Commissioners complied, and also authorized a monument to be erected in the chapel of the Royal Dockyard at Portsmouth in memory of Captain Baker, an authentic hero. The themes of civility, discipline, responsibility, self-sacrifice, and compassion underly Gilly's accounts. In one sense, these interpretations promoted the nationalistic aspirations, sentiments, and idealized values of the British navy and merchant marine. In another sense, they espoused universal values.

In a similar manner, the stories of the *Cumberland*, shipwrecked in 1824, and the *Lady Hobart* (included in this collection), heap praise upon the "highly creditable" conduct of British merchant seaman, though not always upon members of the public. The needy survivors of the packet ship *Cumberland*, upon reaching St. John's, were not aided by officials, and "would have died for want of food and necessaries, had it not been for the kind offices of a mulatto tailor, who supplied them with clothes, beds, and provisions, and did them other kind offices of humanity."[106] Obviously, shipwreck survivors did not always automatically meet with benevolence and humanity. Sometimes help came from unexpected quarters.

Captain William Fellowes, in the employ of the Postmaster General, compiled the story of the *Lady Hobart* and its ill-fated voyage of 1803.[107] A vessel in the service of the merchant marine, it was also a packet ship and performed the essential task of delivering imperial mail. In the midst of the Napoleonic wars, while en route from Halifax to England, it sailed past Sable Island to avoid its French foes, and then northward above the Great Bank (Grand Banks) of Newfoundland, where it managed to capture a French vessel. Upon continuing its journey, now with several prisoners, the ship struck a massive iceberg in heavy seas and foggy weather. Unable to keep the vessel from sinking, this disparate group of crew, passengers, and prisoners was left to survive in two small, open boats, a "cutter" and a "jolly boat." After much suffering, they managed to reach St. John's. It is notable that an American ship's captain and citizen of a rival nation offered to return the crew, some of whom were suffering from frostbite and loss of their toes, and in dire need of medical attention, to England. The captain's willingness to help, according to the narrator, illustrated "benevolence and humanity that will ever reflect the highest honour on his character."

Neil Dewar's narrative of the wreck of the *Rebecca*, a schooner engaged in the cod trade off the Labrador coast in 1816, is included in this volume. It is a similarly depressing account of freezing conditions, fatigue, and hunger that lasted 14 days before the survivors found refuge in a fisherman's hut. The hapless victim, suffering from frost-bite and gangrene, had to endure the excruciating amputation of his limbs by the fisherman, who used a large seal-knife. The initial ordeal of this Scottish-born seaman, now legless, lasted from the date of the wreck on November 17, 1816 to May of 1817, when the return of the fishing season made it possible for him to find more suitable shelter nearby. According to his narrative, he was eventually taken to the general hospital at Quebec for treatment and returned in August 1818 to his home in Greenock. There he underwent a third amputation at the Royal Infirmary in Glasgow. The letter accompanying his narrative, which went through three editions from 1816 to 1843, suggests that the publication of his account was a means of alleviating his state of destitution.[108] It is common knowledge that in port the sailors' daily trials were compounded by the crimps and criminals who preyed on them.[109] Less well known is what happened to seamen like Dewar and his contemporaries if they suffered shipwreck, accident, or sickness which made them unable to work, or simply destitute.[110] Who, for example, took care of them or their surviving families?

The crews of merchant ships manning Canadian timber vessels probably enjoyed the lowest status and the least protection from the consequences of shipwreck. They served on "coffin ships," or *droughers*, built to last no more than four or five years, whose cargo holds were so generally overladen that crews were exposed to constant and unnecessary risks.[111] Conditions aboard such ships were typified in such narratives as that retold below by Thomas Goodwin and Joseph Shearer. In part, their account was published to praise the British government's efforts to regulate the workplace of seamen and to demand improvements in ship construction, though as evidenced by this horrific case, the same government had until then done little to diminish "the general dangers and hazards of a foreign voyage." It was also published to provide some income for the victims, who under existing laws as shipwrecked mariners were not entitled even to their outstanding wages up to the time of shipwreck. Their only other option was to sue the owners if someone managed to salvage the vessel or its contents.

Sailing from Quebec City to Limerick in late November 1835, Goodwin and Shearer's vessel, the *Marshal M'Donald*, encountered hurricane-force winds while sailing in the Gulf of St. Lawrence. The ship was virtually destroyed during the storm, though left afloat. After 15 days adrift and much death and misery among its crew, the wreck was pushed by heavy seas onto the shore at St. Shotts and, after a 15-mile trek, the survivors found their way to Trepassey. For reasons about which one can only speculate, the local magistrate Syms refused to give them accommodation or medical attention, despite the pleas of local fishermen; it was "a disgrace to the poorest or meanest person in the village." The local inhabitants, however, unlike the magistrate, did provide food, blankets, and a makeshift shelter in which Goodwin and Shearer spent four months, suffering from gangrene and in unimaginable pain. Their eventual fate was not much better, in that they ended their days in confinement and utter destitution. Upon their return to England as "helpless cripples," they were attended to by the parish and Poor Law authorities at Portsmouth and then sent to a "workhouse," the fate of many impoverished Victorians.

Two related stories of the French fishing fleet from the 1820s in Newfoundland, translated for this collection, show a far more compassionate attitude by the French government when it came to compensating shipwrecked mariners. The first concerns the *Nathalie*, the second, the *Belle-Julie*. Both ships belonged to the French fishing fleet in Newfoundland along the so-called French shore, which extended on either side of the Northern Peninsula into White Bay.

Written by Gaud Houiste, the first mate of the French fishing vessel, the first story tells of the loss of the *Nathalie* in late May of 1826 in ice near the Grey Islands. Houiste described to Commandant Brou of *la Station de Terre-Neuve*, at St. Pierre and Miquelon, how he and six other survivors held on to wreck debris and clung to ice-floes for 19 days. Eventually, only four survived and made it to land, where one

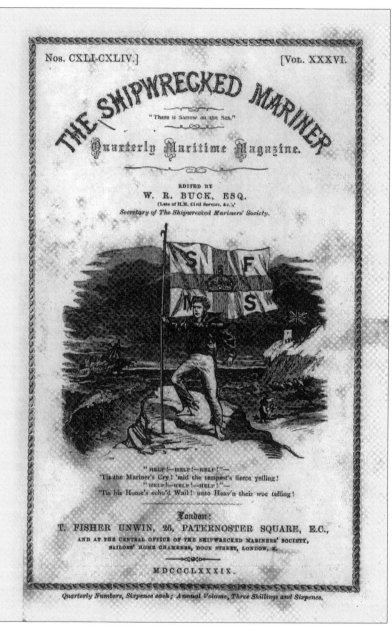

Cover of *The Shipwrecked Mariner*, a publication of the Shipwrecked Fishermen and Mariners' Royal Benevolent Society of London, 1889. Courtesy of the QEII Library, Rare Books Collection, Memorial University of Newfoundland

later died. They were rescued by an English schooner from St. John's and then from there transferred to a French ship bound for Granville. Writing on behalf of the last three survivors, including himself, Houiste attached medical certificates in his letter of request for assistance, or "bénévolence," from the Minister of the Marine, who was responsible for the relations between the French empire and its colonies, pointing out that two of the survivors were married, all remained in pain, and all were unable to work.

The second related incident occurred in the same sub-region late in June 1826, when a fishing flotilla of seventeen ships was coursing in this same general area toward Belle Isle and the Grey Islands when the *Belle-Julie* struck an ice pan that pierced its hull. One hundred and six of a crew of 143 drowned within 10 to 12 minutes of swimming in the icy seas. Two nearby ships, the *Élisa* and the *Comte d'Estourmel*, immediately sent out rescue boats and scoured the waters for additional survivors. This account includes an informative letter from one survivor, the ex-captain of the *Belle-Julie*, Clair Desiré Letourneur, suggesting the strategy a shipwrecked sailor and his rescuers might follow to improve the possibility of survival. On both these occasions, the government of France appears to have treated shipwrecked citizens much differently than its British counterpart. Not only was Houiste's plea given an attentive ear, but in 1826 the French king made the two remaining survivors, Houiste and Jourdan of the *Belle-Julie*, Knights of the *Légion d'Honneur*, and ordered that a sum of 6,000 francs be paid to each survivor's family.

Some shipwreck narratives were explicitly published "to rouse the dormant powers of sympathy — to display human nature struggling with adverse fortune ... to lessen the mass of ills within our reach."[112] Likewise, parliamentary reports occasionally addressed these questions.[113] On the basis of both types of information, laws were enacted to protect some of the wages of shipwrecked seamen.[114] Now tolls on the use of British lighthouses by ships provided sums for relief. The 1830s also saw the appearance of private charities and organizations in Great Britain devoted to the cause of seamen: the Society for the Relief of Widows and Orphans of Shipwrecked Mariners, the Naval and Military Orphan Society, the Seaman's Friend Society, and others, and somewhat later a journal, *The Shipwrecked Mariner*, which provided news on shipwrecks from throughout the British Empire.[115]

In the wake of public sympathy, compassion, outrage, and other motivations, philanthropic societies for seamen began to provide homes and medical aid for some. The British navy traditionally provided for its own rank and file on hospital ships and at the Greenwich Hospital. In Canada, Quebec City, Halifax, and Saint John boasted hospitals for seamen.[116] Merchants of St. John's, beginning in 1831, occasionally provided funds for sealers "lost or maimed" while working. Though there were rare calls for the establishment of a state-supported "asylum" for distressed seamen, this reliance on private charity remained in place until the twentieth century and applied to non-British sailors too.[117] By the late 1830s, registered British colonial seamen who were non-residents of Newfoundland but who were shipwrecked there found themselves billeted with local landlords until they could be transferred to facilities in the neighbouring colonies or in their resident colony. Some indication of the extent of the problem is found in an entry book of Disbursements to Distressed Seamen at St. John's. It reveals that between 1838 and 1844, a total of 360 shipwrecked seaman (see Appendix), all native to the neighbouring colonies, had their passage paid by the Lords Commissioners of the Admiralty.[118] However, the treatment and relief of shipwrecked British merchant seamen like Dewar, Goodwin, and Shearer remained largely unregulated. After Confederation and until the early twentieth century, the federal government of Canada took over the responsibility of providing for shipwrecked and ailing sailors, and it administered a dozen and more marine hospitals throughout the country.

That ships' passengers also contributed to the literature on shipwrecks is not unexpected. "Extreme hardships" generally characterized the carrying trade of the early nineteenth century.[119] The historian Oliver Macdonagh writes that before 1840 "shipwrecks and putting back in distress were almost everyday occurrences, with bad vessels, bad navigation and drunken ship's officers sharing the blame in more or less equal parts."[120] As Canadian and British merchants and shipowners increasingly imported manufactured and other unavailable goods into Canada and exported the New World's staples, fish, furs, timber, and wheat, this maritime route proved cheap and close, thus keeping steerage fares low. Sometimes cheated by unscrupulous ships' captains, passengers in steerage suffered dreadfully from hunger, thirst, and congestion during their six- to ten-week crossing.

Under such conditions, ships also became breeding grounds for epidemic diseases. The nadir of passenger traffic was probably

reached during the Irish famine migrations. In the late 1840s an estimated 17,000 people died aboard ship and thousands of others died
from contagious diseases initially spread on board ship and later at
the quarantine stations of Partridge Island at Saint John and Grosse
Ile above Quebec City.[121]

The grim realities of the timber vessel shipwreck experience are
confirmed in the narrative of the *Francis Spaight*, en route from Saint
John, New Brunswick (then St. John) to Limerick in 1836; it
constituted a well-known "unfinished voyage." As a victim of marine
disaster, it was one of many. In this year alone, an estimated one thousand men, women, and children died in marine disasters along the
coasts of North America, many in timber ships converted for passenger
travel. The victim of a fierce gale, the vessel had been abandoned by the
crew somewhere in the Banks. What happened next quickly acquired
wide notoriety, including retelling in official enquiries. In his narrative
describing the latter stages of the voyage, John Palmer tells how the
starving passengers left behind on board resorted to cannibalism, an
uncommon but not unique response.[122] In relating these events, also
included in our collection, the author explores how they affected his
own deteriorating mental state. Happily, he and other survivors were
eventually rescued by a brig heading out of Newfoundland. Shipwreck
accounts like Palmer's helped to shape public opinion and to highlight
the problems of the working mariner. By the end of the 1830s the
British government felt compelled to examine the causes and extent of
timber wrecks.[123]

Long before the *Titanic* gave Newfoundland waters their modern
reputation as dangerous, there were many major wrecks of passenger or
emigrant ships that heightened and reinforced existing fears about ocean
travel.[124] Apart from timber ships carrying passengers, emigrant vessels
from Great Britain, Germany, and Norway that were wrecked in
Newfoundland waters included the *Ark of Malacca* (1799), the *Despatch*
(1828), the *Florence* (1840), the *Monseo* (1857), and the *Hanoverian*
(1885). The worst disaster of the early nineteenth century was the wreck
of the *Lady Sherbrooke* (1831) at Cape Ray with the loss of 239 persons.
Rivalling these disasters was the sinking of the *Harvest Home* and the
Lady of the Lake, both of which succumbed to ice off Newfoundland in
1833, leading to the drowning of 170 passengers and crew.

This latter event appears to have inspired the following variation of
Psalm 107, King James version. The unnamed writer praised the

Late Dreadful High Wind!

They that in ships, with courage
- bold,
O'er swelling waves their trades
·pursue,
Do God's amazing works behold,
And in the deep his wonders view
Sometimes the ship's toss'd up to
· Heav'n,
On tops of mountain waves ap-
pear;
Then down the steep abyss are
driv'n,
. Whilst ev'ry soul dissolves with
/ fear.

They reel and stagger to and fro',
Like men with fumes of wine
oppress'd;
Nor do the skilful seamen know,
Which way to steer, what course
'—is best.

He does the raging storm appease,
And makes the billows calm and
' still;
With joy they see their fury cease,
And their intended course fulfil.

PSALM CVII.

Awful Disasters at Sea,

Wreck of the "Harvest Home," and Total Loss of the "Lady of the Lake," with 170 Passengers for Quebec.

THE Lima, Capt. Mardon, when about 400 miles from Newfoundland, being completely surrounded with ice, descried a boat at some distance. The captain instantly hove-to, and took the individuals in her on board. They, reported themselves to be the second mate and 12 of the crew of the Harvest Home, Captain Hall, of Newcastle, from London: they informed Capt. Mardon, the Harvest Home was struck by a piece of ice which stove in the bows, All hands were immediately put to tho-pumps, by which means they succeeded in keeping the vessel afloat for two days at the expiration of that time the second mate and 12 of the crew quitted her in the long boat; the captain and first mate having come to the determination of stopping on board. After they had been out one night, they returned to the vessel, and requested the captain and mate to leave her, but they refused, saying, that " they would stick to her while a timber remained afloat." The crew having again pushed off, they became bewildered among the masses of ice, by which they were surrounded and totally uncertain what course to steer. On the next day, they again fell in with their own vessel. This time they found the captain and mate had left her. Two of the crew now went on board and while busy in endeavouring to get more water and provisions, they were surprised by the sight of a boat containing about 30 individuals approaching in an' opposite direction; they immediately boarded the vessel, in the hope of succour. They proved to be the captain and crew, and part of the passengers (including two females) of the Lady of the Lake, of Aberdeen, bound from Belfast for Quebec, with upwards of two hundred passengers on board. Those who had boarded the wreck of the Harvest Home, when they saw the state she was in, with her hold full of water, made a simultaneous rush to return to the boat, which was at that moment pushed off, and several of them were precipitated into the water. One of them, however, was fortunate enough to make good his leap into the boat, which contained the crew of the Harvest Home, and he has now arrived in Liverpool, in the Lima. He states that the Lady of the Lake struck upon the ice, and immediately filled, when the Captain and crew took to the boat, leaving the sinking vessel crowded with the remainder of the despairing and shrieking passengers, to the number of 160 or 170. The crew of the Harvest Home state that after they left their vessel the last time they saw nothing more of the other boat. Several of the individuals who had fallen into the sea when the latter was pushed of, were drowning, but it was impossible for them to render them any assistance.

Late Dreadful High Wind.

On Tuesday last, there was a violent hurricane in the metropolis, that never, for its severity was ever felt in the month of June. Chimney-pots were blown off in all directions ; numbers of trees in the Parks and Gardens were torn up by their roots. At Half-way Reach between Greenwich and London, a boat containing a fisherman and boy, was blown over, and both drowned. The son of the Dean of Ripon, was, by a sudden gust of wind upset in a boat off Lambeth, and drowned. Vast numbers of ships were drove from their moorings in the river, and much injured. A girl gathering the fallen limbs of trees in Hyde Park, was killed by the falling of an elm tree ; in fact, it is impossible to calculate the extent of the havock and loss.

Smeeton, Printer, 74, Tooley Street, London.

courage of the crew and passengers of the *Lady of the Lake* as they faced a watery grave:[125]

> They that in ships, with courage bold,
>   O'er swelling waves their trades pursue,
> Do God's amazing works behold,
>   And in the deep his wonders view.
>
> Sometimes the ship's toss'd up to Heav'n,
>   On tops of mountain waves appear;
> Then down the steep abyss are driv'n,
>   Whilst ev'ry soul dissolves with fear.
>
> They reel and stagger to and fro,
>   Like men with fumes of wine oppressed;
> Nor do the skilful seamen know,
>   Which way to steer, what course is best.
>
> He does the raging storm appease,
>   And makes the billows calm and still;
> With joy they see their fury cease,
>   And their intended course fulfill.

Although government reforms of marine working and travelling conditions, together with the adoption by transatlantic ships of iron hulls and steampower, steadily and positively changed the nature of ocean travel, this gradual transformation did not immediately improve the security of passage. Consequently, for emigrants unaccustomed to the water, ship travel remained a fearful and extraordinary experience.[126] Some objected that shipowners and their captains continued to regard passengers, even those travelling first-class, as just another commodity. This became apparent during the mid-century sinking of the *Arctic*, a four-year-old wooden-hull sidewheel passenger steamship belonging to the New York and Liverpool United States Mail Steamship Company and the Collins Line, after colliding in 1854 with a French propeller, *Vesta*, on the Newfoundland Bank. This story, which became an international sensation, typified the growing commercialization of ocean travel and the perceived commodification of passengers.[127]

The *Arctic*, described as "one of the largest and noblest steamships in the world," had among its passengers on this voyage the wife, son, and daughter of the line's owner, Edward K. Collins, as well as his sister and her husband. In this instance, even the owner's family was not to be immune to death at sea. Estimates of the final death toll of the *Arctic* are conflicting, and range from 283 to 314; because the crew lists were incomplete, the exact number will never be known. It is a transitionary narrative that embodies the spiritual, but explains the causes of the wreck and the loss of life in strictly secular terms. The account presented here brings together the reaction of waiting families and friends in New York, survivor stories, official reaction and debate, and finally a shipwreck sermon.

Observers at first thought that the *Vesta* had suffered the most damage, but the French vessel survived intact, because the captain immediately jammed the holes in the hull with mattresses, and it slowly but steadily made its way to St. John's for repairs. In contrast, the hole in the *Arctic*'s hull soon proved fatal. The cause of the accident was officially stated to be "neglect of pilot rules." There was, however, also a shortage of lifeboats, and the ship's life-preservers proved futile in the cold waters. Notably, not a single female on board was saved. Some survivors maintained that the crew had deserted the passengers. The *Arctic* disaster was one of several that helped to provoke government to change marine safety regulations. The public impact of this disaster may only be comparable to the shock which followed the wreck of the *Anglo-Saxon*, of the Allan Line of Liverpool, at Cape Race in 1863. The tragedy resulted in 236 deaths, and was described extensively by Arthur Johnson.[128]

We have noted the intertwining of the intimate, the cultural, and the public in Newfoundland shipwreck narratives but there were other important themes too, including gender. Life at sea was predominantly, though not exclusively, a male preserve, and its records reflect that reality. Consequently, much more is known about the experiences of male than of female crew and passengers, although, clearly, women also worked and travelled aboard sailing ships.[129] Marine-related narratives that remark specifically on gendered space are few, but they do exist.[130] The actions of the mariners' wives who intervened successfully in 1649 to save the shipwrecked crew from the vessel carrying supplies for the Jesuits, and the debate over why so few female passengers of the *Arctic* were saved, offer some insights into this subject. There also exists one rare and significant example, *The Passage of the* Pique *Across the Atlantic*, a first-hand account written by an upper-class gentlewoman, Lady Aylmer, the wife of Canada's Governor General, about her ship and shipwreck experiences.

Her voyage of 1835 followed directly upon her husband's recall by the British government. In a short book published in 1837 and dedicated to Queen Victoria, then only recently ascended the throne, Lady Aylmer describes at some length the *Pique*'s departure from Quebec City, its shipwreck on the coast of Labrador, and its limping return home. She was hardly an ordinary ship's passenger, nor was her treatment during the trip typical. Even she found this trip trying and alarming although she was travelling under conditions which entailed both privilege and deference. In writing about her trip, she attempts to draw on some universal themes, including the role of men and women. Within this context, she not only analyses her own behaviour but informs the reader of what was expected of women in such circumstances.

In describing her experience on board the *Pique*, Aylmer comments repeatedly on the respective roles assigned to the sexes. She concludes that the women are "privileged to be cowards." In her words, they "should be grateful for that attention and care, which is usually bestowed on us [women], in order to spare our feelings on all occasions where danger is to be apprehended." Furthermore, moral courage was exemplified by men, whose duty it was to protect and preserve women from alarm and hazard.

This account is written at a crucial stage in the evolution of women's roles in English society, and can therefore be considered a significant and revealing narrative. Indirectly, through the shipwreck experience, this narrative, as evidenced in Aylmer's thinking, was used to legitimize the "domestic sphere" and changing upper middle-class values.

Another element of this narrative merits mention. An enduring ideal, even cliché, was that in the event of shipwreck women and children were the first ones to be saved, and the crew and captain the last. Lady Aylmer's account provides evidence for gallantry in the spirit of this ideal, on the the part of the *Pique*'s captain and crew. But, as with the case of the *Medusa*, such behaviour was neither automatic nor morally persuasive, and in some instances in the nineteenth century, passengers, including women and children, were abandoned by crew when a ship was in imminent danger. When this behaviour occurred it was of course publicly deplored, but that sentiment did not eliminate it. As noted, in the sinking of the *Anglo-Saxon*, few women and children were placed in the lifeboats. In fact, there was a disproportionate number of crew among the survivors, and the later evidence suggested that many crew members abandoned their charges to save themselves. Lady Aylmer's experience of crossing the Atlantic reflected her class and position as much as it did her sex. Paternalism and male gallantry toward women passengers was not historically a universal practice.

The *Pique* episode is also important in understanding shipwreck experience for another quite different reason. This ship was a well-built naval frigate, and there was no doubt that a merchant vessel would not have withstood a similar impact, as subsequent testimony to the Committee on Shipwrecks concluded.[131] The vessel had survived its ordeal, though only barely, because of its superior marine architecture and the crew's efforts; they had managed to guide it across the Atlantic from the Strait of Belle Isle to St. Helen's, on the Isle of Wight,[132] with a makeshift rudder that broke several times, faulty chronometers, and a leaking hole that had, without anyone's knowledge, been stuffed with a bag of biscuits, thereby reducing the flow. However, only its substantial construction had initially saved the vessel from sinking. A British merchant vessel of the same vintage would certainly not have been so lucky. Reformers used the occasion of discussing the *Pique*'s survival to lament the declining quality of British vessels.

Another aspect of shipwreck that captured the public imagination was the nefarious activity of "wrecking," or, in other words, the illegal pillaging of wrecks. This activity had long been part of the social and cultural landscape of the Old World.[133] Laws against wrecking extended back to the time of Edward I, and probably earlier. These laws were reinforced several times in the eighteenth century, and perpetrators of wrecking risked the gallows after 1753 if they were found to have taken goods directly from a ship or if they had put the lives of passengers or crew at risk. Evidently, the threat of capital punishment failed to eliminate the practice.[134] The problem, before the creation of a modern police force in the nineteenth century, was principally one of enforcement.

The following examples are perhaps typical. In 1747, observers of the famous wreck of the *Nympha Americana*, at Beachy Head in Sussex, England, saw "an assembly of human vultures" descend upon the victims, "destroying the morals and honesty of too many" before local people with "more humane intentions" and the local militia came to the aid of survivors. This event was recorded in a painting by Barrodell

Dory and Sailboat near Wreck. A1-40, Courtesy of the Provincial Archives of Newfoundland and Labrador

Lambert.[135] In another eighteenth-century example a British Captain, Robert Protton of the Orange Rangers, and a Lieutenant Hector, sailed from St. John's on the December 17, 1779. During its Atlantic crossing, the vessel encountered a gale that blew it to Bofin Island in Ireland; there, its wreck on January 29, 1780 resulted in the loss of one sergeant and 55 recruits. It was alleged that locals set the ship on fire. Moreover, the "unfeeling islanders" charged exorbitant fees for feeding the survivors. With the party facing starvation, the remaining officers paid for a ship out of personal funds so that they could leave. Without food, money, or orders, and with their men in rags, the hapless officers were forced to request help from Irish authorities before the matter ended.[136] In short, wrecking was already well known on the Irish, Scottish, and English coasts before similar events were reported in Newfoundland.

In the wake of early nineteenth-century legal and penal reform, wrecking-related offences were no longer listed as capital crimes. New measures came into effect with the Merchant Shipping Act of 1854, revised and consolidated legislation. Under this imperial legislation, British "ships"[137] and their crews throughout all British possessions, including Newfoundland, were subject to its clauses.[138] It sanctioned the government's right to use force to suppress wrecking, as well as to levy fines and prison sentences on offenders. Also under its terms, colonial authorities were permitted to pass legislation dealing with vessels registered in their respective jurisdictions. In 1866 the colony of Newfoundland passed legislation making provision for a Marine Court of Inquiry to conduct legal investigations into shipwrecks, losses, damages, and the competency of ships' officers,[139] only to repeal it the following year. Subsequently, the colonial governor retained the right to set up such a court when occasion required it.

There are many references to wrecking in Newfoundland waters, including those from the 1830s provided by Archdeacon Wix and recounted here. Whether wrecking was a cultural import or a product of the bleak social and economic conditions associated with isolated outports is subject to some speculation. This was especially so in Newfoundland, because settlement had long been discouraged, no grants of land were allowed before 1813, and no roads were built prior to 1840. Many of those who lived on the coast outside St. John's were isolated, poor, and self-reliant. The late Newfoundland magistrate and historian D.W. Prowse suggested that "the old toilers of the seas" believed the sea to be "their own special domain, and wrecks cast upon the shores as special interpositions of Providence in their favour."[140] In 1871, when Prowse was first appointed as an itinerant district judge and police magistrate, he investigated wrecking cases that "all happened in very out-of-the-way places." He was convinced that the proceeds of a shipwreck were regarded as providential and that to take possession of them was a sign of resourcefulness. Like Edward Wix nearly half a century earlier, he claimed that "everything specially good about the fishermen's houses" were probably from the proceeds of wrecks. In general, however, the extent of the practice is not known and the subject still requires further scholarly study.

There are nevertheless some examples of very aggressive wrecking in Newfoundland. In 1859, the *Indian*, a barque-rigged screw steamship, was wrecked off Cape Race, and although the mail and 130 of 157 crew and passengers were saved, there were many complaints that their possessions had been plundered by locals.[141] In another unspecified instance, Prowse was involved in trying "a very bad case of absolute piracy." Fishers attacked a schooner captain and crew, stripped the ship of its mast, and stole everything useful. Upon investigating the parties involved, the judge came upon a gasping, asthmatic elderly woman who ruminated, "Oh, why did they come so near the shore? Oh, why did they come so near the shore to timpt the poor peoples?"[142]

Stories about Newfoundland wrecking became well known outside the province and even fascinated the American literary audience early in this century. *Harper's Monthly Magazine* published an article on the "folk of Cape Race,"[143] which contended that in a 50-mile radius of the cape, there lived "diligent wreckers," "a hale, tough, genial crew, courageous to the point of an abandoned sort of recklessness, seasoned for the hazardous adventure of wrecking by seal hunting and the Banks fishery." Living in desolate surroundings dotted by small gardens and harsh coastland, they depended for their livelihoods on the fishery, supplemented by wrecking and salvaging. They were described as exceedingly resourceful, and willing to risk their lives to salvage any sort of useful cargo, especially when fishing was poor. The author also noted that salvaged goods were often sold from the community to companies in St. John's and Halifax that since 1850 had been active in the area.

According to the *Harper's* article, "It is not to be supposed that the folk wish evil to the vessels which go by their coast; but here, as elsewhere in bleak places, they joyfully 'take the goods the gods provide.'" "Supposedly, children were taught to pray, "God bless papa and mamma, and send another wreck." Along these same lines, the article cited court testimony. A witness, in reply to a lawyer's query, was reputed to have stated, "Well, as a rule, sir, we don't take no precautions to prevent wrecks." The article recognized that such anecdotes were passed along somewhat tongue-in-cheek, but noted that "Lives before salvage!" was "a proverb and a religion" here. To help balance the record, the magazine gave several examples of heroic attempts by community members to save passengers and crew from a watery grave.

The contradictory nature of wreckers and the discrepancies between myth and reality with regard to this social phenomenon are highlighted in Wix's diary and in the 1863 wreck of the *Anglo-Saxon*, which crashed onto the rocks at Clam Cove, Cape Race. Reporting in sensational style, the *Montreal Witness* claimed that 500 wreckers had come to the scene and carried away every useful item.[144] Even a local newspaper, in an article that was subsequently cited abroad, complained of the inhumanity of the Cape Race fisherfolk. Yet official evidence contradicted the press reports. Even if many people did come down to the shore at Cape Race to witness the wreck — and the exact number remains unknown — this group apparently also included officials and professional salvage workers. Moreover, the official record shows that, when the authorities arrived soon after the event, they found no desecration of the dead, but rather the decent burial by local people of over a hundred bodies interred in the frozen ground, with stones placed at their heads and feet. Under the law, wreckers were entitled to claim 5 percent of the value of a shipowner's property. On this day their concerns had been primarily with the *Anglo-Saxon*'s human cargo. Their courage in aiding the victims and their propriety toward the survivors and the dead were subsequently confirmed by dispassionate observers.

Several other stories by Prowse offer additional insight into the activity of wrecking. He describes how after the steamer *Gaspé* smashed to pieces at Miquelon and lost its cargo containing 2,000 five-pound notes, two fishermen discovered the notes and sold them to a junk dealer, who then sought and found help in forging the required signatures before attempting to cash them. The three culprits were quickly found out and received prison sentences ranging from 10 to 21 years. Apparently such criminal activities were not always limited to the fishers. Prowse stated that on one occasion he convicted two clergymen for the crime of wrecking.

In Labrador, "made to order" wrecking, or "scuttling" and "selling" a vessel in order to collect the insurance on the ship and its contents, was not unknown. Commenting on the occasional occurrence of insurance fraud, the Reverend P.W. Browne noted that the "opprobrium of this iniquitous business" invariably netted "unfortunate fishermen, if they *happened to be caught in the toils*."[145] Writing at the turn of this century, Browne believed that sanctions had made wrecking a "rare occurrence." Likewise, in 1904, Prowse suggested that such things had happened "years and years ago." In his view, they had disappeared because of better communications and transportation and the widespread "blessings of civilisation."[146] Also punishment was harsh. Wreckers in the colony risked "Barratry" court proceedings and a term in H.M. Penitentiary in St. John's. There they were subjected to a prison diet and penitentiary discipline.

The experience of shipwreck, though associated with tragedy, also gave rise to heroism. There are numerous instances in which Newfoundlanders were formally rewarded for their bravery in saving victims. Some of these heroes included wreckers. The most famous is perhaps George Harvey, described by Wix, who headed courageous efforts to save the passengers and crew of the emigrant ship *Despatch*, en route in 1828 from Londonderry to Quebec. When the ship crashed on Isle aux Morts at Wreck Rock, Harvey and his daughter used their dog "Hairy Man" to take a line out to the ship southwest of Burnt Island, and in so doing managed to save 163 passengers. For his efforts, Harvey received a Gold Medal from the Royal Humane Society of London and a reward of £100 from Lloyd's. Wix also praised another local man, Miessau [Mousseau?], for similar selfless acts.

There were many other examples of noble behaviour. In 1857, Captain Percey of the brig *Jessie* of St. John's received a medal and money for rescuing 63 crew and passengers from the American ship *Northumberland*. John Dower was given two medals in 1865 by Napoleon III for twice saving French fishers at Conche. For rescuing the crew of the Miramichi-based timber ship *Alfraetta* in 1866, Captain Mearns of St. John's was awarded binocular glasses. Captain William Jackman swam out to the schooner *Sea Slipper* during a hurricane off Labrador in 1867 to save 27 lives, and the Royal Humane Society of London gave him a diploma and a silver medal. Jackman was described as "modest as he is brave, and when spoken to on the subject will not allow that he did anything more than his duty."[147] On numerous other occasions, island residents received this Society's medals. Other donors of awards to Newfoundland captains and seamen included the British Board of Trade, several private companies, the Canadian, Portuguese, Spanish, and American governments, the Mercantile Marine Board of Greenock, and the Society of United Fishermen.[148]

Disaster at sea always involved more than a single person, whether it was the victim, the survivor, or the rescuer. Families, friends, and communities all shared in the event and its aftermath. Shannon Ryan has explored this dimension in his studies of community attitudes to marine disasters in the sealing industry. The impact was inevitably and consistently devastating. While the family and community response is rarely discussed in the narratives except in passing, these issues do frequently appear in Newfoundland sea ballads. One nineteenth-century ballad about the *Golden Hind*, which was wrecked near Cape Race, tells of the drowning of the captain, Jim Harding, and how he left behind "a loving wife /A-praying to God to take her too," as well as six small children, parents "nearly crushed," six sisters, and two brothers.[149] This traditional theme is also much in evidence elsewhere:

Waiting. The yearning of mariners' families for the safe return of loved ones remains a cultural constant. Engraver's plate, artist unknown, editor's collection

> "Oh mother dear," the children cried, "where is our father's boat?
> He said that he was coming home the last time he wrote."
> Grief-stricken was the mother's heart, the father and his crew,
> For they're cradled in their ocean beds beneath the ocean blue.[150]

A poignant glimpse into this private world is the very brief written memory of a 93-year old woman, Jessie Hale, of Placentia Bay. Her description, included in the following narratives, evokes themes found in the sea ballads, as she poignantly recalls her family's reaction on that day long ago when family and community members failed to return home from fishing.

A last word. The narratives from Newfoundland waters do not hold a monopoly on the many possible parts and variations of the phenomenon of shipwreck. There are shipwreck accounts throughout this country and abroad, and from all periods of the past. These particular narratives are however unique expressions of this specific region and its special identity. Some of these stories have been kept alive in our historical memory through text and song, and many were written by amateur historians who explicitly intended their stories to be popular histories. They were well received by the reading public. With some rare exceptions, however, these consisted almost exclusively of short summaries and contain little historical context. They dwell primarily on adventure, tragedy, and heroism.[151] They whet the appetite, invariably promote their subject matter with enthusiasm, and often prove useful to scholars — but only in a limited fashion.

Such popular studies are problematic for two important reasons. First, the original voices are often lost in these summaries. Secondly, in order to expand and advance our knowledge of the phenomenon of shipwreck in Newfoundland waters, a more systematic treatment of individual accounts of voyages and shipwrecks is necessary, and this can only been done by placing them more fully in the context of the region's social and cultural history. It is a way of integrating individual experience and memory with collective history.[152] This collection attempts to begin such a tack and to make these selected narratives more accessible. They are presented in their original published form with few modifications, together with short introductions to place them in a broader context. Many of these narratives have been housed in special collections of university libraries or archives, where they are seen only on those rare occasions when an enthusiast, a specialist, or a student retrieves them; some have rested in near-oblivion. It is time to revisit them.

NOTES

1. For a discussion of this heritage, see Gaile McGregor, *The Wacousta Syndrome: Explorations in the Canadian Langscape* (Toronto: University of Toronto Press, 1985).
2. Lewis R. Fischer and Gerald E. Panting, "Maritime History in Canada: The Social and Economic Dimensions," in John B. Hattendorf, ed., *Ubi Sumus? The State of Naval and Maritime History* (Newport, RI: Naval War College Press, 1994), 59.
3. "Foreword: A Multidisciplinary Perspective," in Larry McCann, Carrie MacMillan, eds., *The Sea and Culture of Atlantic Canada* (Sackville, NB: Mount Allison University, 1992), 9.

4. The popular works of Farley Mowat on Newfoundland and its ocean heritage are indicative of this imprint. See *The Farfarers* (Toronto: Key Porter, 1998), *The New Founde Land* (Toronto: McClelland and Stewart, 1989), and others.

5. T.K. Pratt, "Sea, Land and Language: Shaping the Linguistic Character of Atlantic Canada," in McCann and MacMillan, eds., *The Sea and Culture*, 127-41.

6. The importance of "stories" as underpinnings of cultural understanding has been recognized and explored recently in a number of disciplines. For a discussion, see Ken Plummer, *Telling Sexual Stories: Power, Change and Social Worlds* (London and New York: Routledge, 1995), 13-31.

7. Jean-Pierre Proulx, *Histoire et naufrage des navires le* Saphire, *la* Marguerite, *le* Murinet, *et l'*Auguste (Ottawa: Parks Canada, 1979), 5. A helpful study noted in this collection that illustrates and places in context the ships, from *knorrs* to clippers, is Roger Morris, *Atlantic Seafaring: Ten Centuries of Exploration and Trade in the North Atlantic* (Camden, ME: International Marine, 1992).

8. Keith Matthews, *Lectures on the History of Newfoundland, 1500-1840* (St. John's: Memorial University, Maritime History Group, 1973), 65-73; Gillian T. Cell, ed., *Newfoundland Discovered: English Attempts at Colonisation, 1610-1630* (London: Hakluyt Society, 1982).

9. Laurier Turgeon, "Naufrages des Terreneuviers Bayonnais et Luziens (1689-1759)," *Bulletin de la Société des Sciences, Lettres et Arts de Bayonne*, nouvelle série 134 (1978): 115-23. See also John Humphreys, *Plaisance*, Publications in History 3 (Ottawa: National Museum of Canada, 1970), 1-24.

10. Jean-François Brière, "The Safety of Navigation in the 18th Century French Cod Fisheries," *Acadiensis* 16, 2 (Fall 1987): 86.

11. James Tuck and Robert Grenier, *Red Bay, Labrador: World Whaling Capital, A.D. 1550-1600* (St. John's: Atlantic Archaeology, 1989); James Tuck, "1984 Excavations at Red Bay, Labrador," in Jane Sproull Thomson and Callum Thomson, eds., *Archaeology in Newfoundland and Labrador, 1984* (St. John's: Newfoundland Museum, 1985), 230-31; Willis Stevens, "Progress Report on the Marine Excavation at Red Bay, Labrador: A Summary of the 1983 Field Season," *Research Bulletin* (Parks Canada) 240 (March 1986): 1-15; James Ringer,

"A Summary of Marine Archaeological Research Conducted at Red Bay, Labrador," Research Bulletin (Parks Canada) 248 (March 1986): 1-19; Vernon C. Barber, "Newfoundland Marine Archaeology Society, Project Proposal," Unpublished paper, St. John's, 1975; Vernon C. Barber, "Shipwrecks of Newfoundland with Particular Comment on H.M.S. *Sapphire* (sunk in 1696)," Unpublished paper, Newfoundland Historical Society, April 23, 1975; Janette M. Barber and Vernon C. Barber, "The Trinity Site: A Shipwreck of a Mid-1700s Merchant Vessel," Unpublished paper, Newfoundland Historical Society, 1979; Sheli Smith, "The 1983 Isle Aux Morts Survey," Unpublished paper, Newfoundland Marine Archaeology Society, 1983; Janette M. Barber, "A Historic Shipwreck at Trinity, Trinity Bay," *Newfoundland Quarterly* 77, 2-3 (1981): 17-20; J.M. Barber, "The Newfoundland Marine Archaeology Society Survey Expedition in 1981," Unpublished report, St. John's, 1981.

12. David Barron, *Northern Maritime Shipwreck Database* (Bedford, NS: Northern Maritime Research, 1997). CD-ROM.

13. Brière, "The Safety of Navigation," 86.

14. Eric W. Sager, *Seafaring Labour: The Merchant Marine of Atlantic Canada, 1820-1914* (Montreal, Kingston and London: McGill-Queen's University Press, 1989), 206.

15. Report from *Select Committee On Shipwrecks of Timber Ships*, 18 June 1839, House of Commons, Great Britain (based on *Lloyd's Register Book of Shipping*). See Appendix in this collection.

16. Turgeon, "Naufrages des Terreneuviers," 120.

17. James Pritchard, *Anatomy of a Naval Disaster: The 1746 French Naval Expedition to North America* (Montreal and Kingston: McGill-Queen's University Press, 1995). The role of ships and smallpox is examined in Allan Everett Marble, *Surgeons, Smallpox, and the Poor: A History of Medicine and Social Conditions in Nova Scotia, 1749-1799* (Montreal and Kingston: McGill-Queen's University Press, 1993), esp. 13-72.

18. Earle Lockerby, "The Deportation of the Acadians from Ile St.-Jean, 1758," *Acadiensis* 27, 2 (Spring 1998): 81.

19. Brenda O'Brien, *Speedy Justice: The Tragic Last Voyage of His Majesty's Vessel* Speedy (Toronto, Buffalo and London: University of Toronto Press for the Osgoode Society, 1992), 111-24.

20. Matthews, *Lectures on the History of Newfoundland*, 82.

21. Oliver Macdonagh, *A Pattern of Government Growth, 1800-1860: The Passenger Acts and Their Enforcement* (London: MacGibbon and Kee, 1961); Kerby A. Miller, *Emigrants and Exiles: Ireland and the Irish Exodus to North America* (New York and Oxford: Oxford University Press, 1985), 193-96, 253-57; Maldwyn A. Jones, "Aspects of North Atlantic Migration: Steerage Conditions and American Law, 1819-1909," in Klaus Friendland, ed., *Maritime Aspects of Migration* (Cologne and Vienna: Bohlau, 1989), 321-32; Helen I. Cowan, *British Emigration to British North America: The First Hundred Years* (Toronto: University of Toronto Press, 1961), 144-72.

22. Helge W. Nordvik, "Norwegian Emigrants and Canadian Timber," 279-92, and Bard Kolltveit, "Scandinavian and Baltic Transatlantic Passenger Lines," 133-44, both in Friedland, ed., *Maritime Aspects of Migration*.

23. See Appendix, Table 2.

24. Sager, *Seafaring Labour*, 225.

25. See Evidence of Charles Walton, 2 May 1839, no. 562-69, *Select Committee on Shipwrecks of Timber Ships*, 37.

26. George Harding, "The Menace of Cape Race," *Harper's Monthly Magazine* 113 (April 1912): 674-84. This article was summarized in the *The Literary Digest*, 44 (January-June 1912): 960-63.

27. Dudley Pope, *Life in Nelson's Navy* (London: Unwin Irwin, 1987), 131; N.A.M. Rodger, *The Wooden Walls: An Anatomy of the Georgian Navy* (London: Collins, 1986).

28. Howard Douglas, "Account of the Wreck of H.M. Transport *Phyllis* 1795. Copy of Narrative of my father's shipwreck in 1795 — written by himself" [1880]. Douglas Papers. M.G. 24, A3, vol. 5, NAC [Copy held at Arts and Culture Library, St. John's].

29. See H., "Verses on the loss of the *Harpooner* Transport, respectfully inscribed to Miss Armstrong, the only person of that family saved from the unfortunate wreck," *Montreal Herald*, Jan. 7, 1817. Reprinted in *Mercantile Journal* [St. John's], May 30, 1817. See Appendix C.

30. Accounts of this event differ somewhat. Compare "Loss of the Transport *Harpooner*," in R. Thomas, *Interesting and Authentic*

Narratives of the Most Remarkable Shipwrecks (London, 1835; rpt. Freeport, NY: Books for Libraries Press, 1970), 341-45; *The Terrors of the sea: as portrayed in accounts of fire and wreck* (New York ca. 1890), CIHM 17909; Michael F. Harrington, "The Wreck of the 'Harpooner,'" *The Newfoundland Quarterly*, 45, 2 (September 1945): 26-28.

31. W.O.S. Gilly, *Narratives of Shipwrecks of The Royal Navy: Between 1793 and 1849*, 2nd rev. edn. (London: John W. Parker, 1861), 313.

32. "Loss of the *Aeneas* Transport," in Thomas, *Remarkable Shipwrecks*, 265-68.

33. Edward Rowe Snow, *Great Gales and Dire Disasters Off Our Shores* (New York: Dodd, Mead, 1952), 99-106.

34. Alan Ruffman, "The Multidisciplinary Rediscovery and Tracking of 'The Great Newfoundland and Saint-Pierre et Miquelon Hurricane of September 1775,'" *The Northern Mariner/Le Marin du nord* 6, 3 (July 1996): 12-17; Anne E. Stevens and Michael Staveley, "The Great Newfoundland Storm of 12 September 1775," *Bulletin of the Seismological Society of America* 71, 4 (August 1991): 1398-1402.

35. H.M.S. Cotter, "The Great Labrador Gale, 1885," *The Beaver* 263 (September 1932): 81-84; P.W. Browne, *Where the Fishers Go: The Story of Labrador* (Toronto: The Musson Book Company, 1909); "Sealers Wrecked Off Fogo," Unpublished notes by David Davis, Provincial Archives of Newfoundland and Labrador [PANF], 34-35.

36. Quoted in Shannon Ryan, "Newfoundland Sealing Disasters to 1914," *The Northern Mariner/Le Marin du nord* 4, 3 (July 1994): 15. The industry is thoroughly described in his *The Ice Hunters: A History of Newfoundland Sealing to 1914* (St. John's: Breakwater Books, 1994).

37. Ryan, *The Ice Hunters*, 307.

38. Cassie Brown, Harold Horwood, *Death on the Ice: The Great Newfoundland Sealing Disaster of 1914* (Toronto: Doubleday, 1972).

39. "Loss of the British Brig *Jesse*" [1835], in R. Thomas, *Remarkable Shipwrecks*, 358-59.

40. For a technical description of factors in shipwreck see K.C. Barnaby, *Some Ship Disasters and Their Causes* (London:

Hutchinson, 1968), 250-62.

41. John Palmer, *Awful shipwreck, an affecting narrative of the unparalleled sufferings of the crew of the ship* Francis Spaight, *which foundered on her passage from St. John's, N.B. to Limerick in November last. The survivors after remaining aboard the wreck 19 days, during which they were driven to the most awful extremities, were relieved by the Brig.* Angeronia, *Capt. Gillard, on her Passage from Newfoundland to Teignmouth* (Boston: G.C. Perry, 1837), CIHM 50787.

42. Great Britain, House of Commons, *Report From the Select Committee Appointed to Inquire Into the Causes of Shipwrecks* (1836). A proper charting of the Banks of Newfoundland by the British government did not exist in 1839, though French authorities had finally begun one. See Evidence of Alexander Bridport Becher, 30 April 1839, no. 349-352, *Select Committee on Shipwrecks of Timber Ships*, 25.

43. These matters are discussed at length in Kathleen A. Walpole, *Emigration to British North America under the Early Passengers Acts, 1803-1842*, Unpublished M.A. thesis, University of London, 1929, and Macdonagh, *A Pattern of Government Growth*.

44. Macdonagh, *A Pattern of Government Growth*, 335-36. See also David J. Molloy, *The First Landfall: Historic Lighthouses of Newfoundland and Labrador* (St. John's: Breakwater, 1994), 9-18.

45. Captain Thomas Fitzpatrick, Placentia, "Wrecks and Their Causes," Unpublished paper, H.F. Shortis Papers, Vol. 2.391 (74), [PANF].

46. For a discussion, see Introduction, Nicholas Camry and Anthony Pagden, eds., *Colonial Identity in the Atlantic World, 1500-1800* (Princeton, NJ: Princeton University Press, 1987), 5.

47. D.B. Quinn, "Newfoundland in the Consciousness of Europe in the Sixteenth and Early Seventeenth Centuries," in G.M. Story, ed., *Early European Settlement and Exploitation in Atlantic Canada* (St. John's: Memorial University of Newfoundland, 1982), 23.

48. Minutes of Evidence, 1 July 1836, in Great Britain, House of Commons, *The Select Committee on Shipwrecks*, 6.

49. Michael Zuckerman, "Identity in British America: Unease in Eden," in Camry and Pagden, eds., *Colonial Identity in the*

Atlantic World, 119.

50. For example, *The new sailing directory for the Island and banks of Newfoundland, the gulf and river of St. Lawrence* (London, 1827), CIHM 49076; *Sailing directions for the island of Newfoundland and coast of Labrador: including the straits of Belle Isle and banks* (London: 183?), CIHM 40624.

51. Michael Zuckerman, "Identity in British America," in Camry and Pagden, *Colonial Identity in the Atlantic World,* 119; see also Robert Cuff and Derek Wilton, eds., *Jukes' Excursions* (St. John's: Harry Cuff Publications, 1993), 110-11, the revised edition of Joseph Bette Jukes, *Excursions In and About Newfoundland During the Years 1839 and 1840.*

52. The Basques recognized the south coast of Newfoundland to be particularly dangerous, less so the Strait of Belle Isle. Selma Barkham, "A Note on the Strait of Belle Isle During the Period of Basque Contact with Indians and Inuit," *Études/Inuit/Studies* 4, 1-2 (1980): 52-53.

53. Definitions of "region" and a rethinking of Canada's regions are discussed in John Clarke and John Burrone, "Social Regions in Mid-Nineteenth Century Ontario," *Histoire sociale/Social History* 28, 55 (May 1995): 194-96; C. Gaffield, "The New Regional History: Rethinking the History of the Outaouais," *Revue d'études canadiennes* 26, 1 (1991): 64; W. Westfall, "On the Concept of Region in Canadian History and Literature," *Journal of Canadian Studies* 15, 2 (1980): 3-14.

54. For the problems associated with an "identarian 'purity'" in the Canadian context, see the discussion by Robert Schwartzwald, Introduction, *International Journal of Canadian Studies /Revue internationl d'études canadiennes* 10 (Fall 1994): 13. Special issue on "Identities and Marginalities."

55. Peter Neary and Patrick O'Flaherty, eds., *By Great Waters: A Newfoundland and Labrador Anthology* (Toronto: University of Toronto Press, 1974); Patrick O'Flaherty, *The Rock Observed: Studies in the Literature of Newfoundland* (Toronto, Buffalo and London: University of Toronto Press, 1979).

56. A study that leads the way in looking at the interrelationship between sea and culture as it pertains to Newfoundland is Peter Neary, "American Argonauts: Frederic Edwin Church and Louis Legrand Noble in Newfoundland and Labrador, 1859," in

McCann and MacMillan, *The Sea and Culture of Atlantic Canada*, 15-46.

57. There are, of course, precedents in the popular literature of Newfoundland and a prolific literature elsewhere of writings about the sea. For example, see M.F. Harrington, *Sea Stories from Newfoundland* (St. John's: Harry Cuff Publications, 1986); Tony Tanner, ed., *The Oxford Book of Sea Stories* (Oxford and New York: Oxford University Press, 1994).

58. Barbara Korte, "English-Canadian Perspectives of Landscape," *International Journal of Canadian Studies/Revue international d'études canadiennes* 6 (Fall/Automne 1992): 9.

59. Sarah Maza, "Stories in History: Cultural Narratives in Recent Works in European History," *American Historical Review* 101 (December 1996): 1494-95. See also William J. Cronon, "A Place for Stories, Nature, History and Narrative," *Journal of American History* 78 (March 1992): 1347-76.

60. Laura Cameron, "Old /New/Maps/Territories," *Histoire sociale/Social History* 28, 55 (May 1995): 241.

61. Clifford Geertz, *The Interpretation of Culture: Selected Essays* (New York: Basic Books, 1973), 452.

62. Compare American merchant marine survivor stories from World War II. See Arthur R. Moore, *"A Careless Word ... A Needless Sinking": A History of the Staggering Losses Suffered by the U.S. Merchant Marine, Both in Ships and Personnel During World War II* (King's Point, NY: American Merchant Marine Museum, 1983), 317-25.

63. Maza, "Stories in History," 1504.

64. An example of interpretative possibilities is Bernard Bailyn's reconstruction of the context and impact of the wreck of the emigrant ship *Bachelor* in his brilliant *Voyagers to the West: A Passage in the Peopling of America on the Eve of the Revolution* (New York: Vintage Books, 1988), 499-544. Also see Gilles Proulx, *Between France and New France: Life Aboard the Tall Sailing Ships* (Toronto and Charlottetown: Dundurn Press, 1984).

65. Keith Huntress, ed., *Narratives of Shipwrecks and Disasters, 1586-1860* (Ames, IA: Iowa State University Press, 1974), xiii-xviii.

66. See Maza, "Stories in History," 1498.

67. See W.H. Auden, *The Enchafèd Flood or The Romantic Iconography of the Sea* (New York: Vintage, 1967).

68. Huntress, *Narratives of Shipwrecks and Disasters*, ix.

69. *The Poems of Henry Wadsworth Longfellow* (New York: Thomas Y. Crowell, 1901), 126. See Appendix C.

70. Huntress, *Narratives of Shipwrecks and Disasters*, ix-xxxii; George P. Landow, *Images of Crisis: Literary Iconology, 1750 to the Present* (Boston, London and Henley: Routledge and Kegan Paul, 1982), 1-34.

71. See for example, "Ex-voto du capitaine Edouin" [1709], collection of Sainte-Anne-de-Beaupré. From Nicole Cloutier, *L'iconographie de sainte Anne au Québec*, Unpublished thesis, Université de Montréal, 1983, 622-38. I thank Christiane Matte, Adjointe, Musée de Sainte-Anne-de-Beaupré, for this reference.

72. For example, *Canadian Illustrated News*, Dec. 21, 1872; Feb. 8, 1873; April 5, 1873; April 12, 1873; April 19, 1873; Feb. 7, 1874; Mar. 7, 1874; April 12, 1873; *London Illustrated News*, May 9, 1855.

73. Landow, *Images of Crisis*, 128-30.

74. Henry Howe, *Life and Death on the Ocean: A Collection of Extraordinary Adventures, in the Form of Personal Narratives* (Cincinnati, OH: 1855), 589-90.

75. John R. Audette, "Historical Perspectives on Near-Death Episodes and Experiences," in Craig R. Lundahl, ed., *A Collection of Near-Death Research Readings* (Chicago: Nelson-Hall, 1982), 21-43.

76. Philippe Ariès, *The Hour of Our Death* (New York: Random House, 1982), 559.

77. Ariès, *The Hour of Our Death*, 405.

78. Recent sociological discussions of modernity and contemporary values include Anthony Giddens, *Modernity and Self-Identity: Self and Society in the Late Modern Age* (Cambridge: Polity Press, 1991), and Ulrich Beck, *Risk Society: Towards a New Modernity* (London: Sage, 1992), originally published as *Risikogesellschaft: Auf dem Weg in eine andere Moderne* (Frankfurt: Suhrkamp Verlag, 1986).

79. See Maza, "Stories in History," 1512.

80. Janet Reno, *Ishmael Alone Survived* (Lewisburg, PA: Bucknell University Press, 1990), 25.
81. Reno, *Ishmael Alone Survived*, 30.
82. "Captain Bob Bartlett" and "Ballad of Captain Bob Bartlett, Arctic Explorer," in Shannon Ryan and Larry Small, eds., *Haulin' Rope & Gaff: Songs and Poetry in the History of the Newfoundland Seal Fishery* (St. John's: Breakwater Books, 1978), 82-85.
83. Landow, *Images of Crisis*, 4.
84. Stories of these events are retold by Cassie Brown, *The Caribou Disaster and Other Short Stories* (St. John's: Fianker Press, 1996).
85. *The Greenlanders' Saga*, trans. George Johnston (Ottawa: Oberon Press, 1976).
86. For background on early exploration of Newfoundland waters, see James Williamson, ed., *The Voyages of the Cabots and the English Discovery of North America under Henry VII and Henry VIII* (London: The Argonaut Press, 1929); J.J. Sharp, *Discovery in the North Atlantic from the 6th to 17th Century* (Halifax: Nimbus Publishing, 1991); Robert H. Cuff, *New-Founde-Land at the Very Centre of the European Discovery and Exploration of North America* (St. John's: Harry Cuff, 1997); and D.B. Quinn, *Explorers and Colonies: America, 1500-1625* (London and Ronceverte: The Hambeldon Press, 1990).
87. Marcel Trudel, "Cartier, Jacques," *Dictionary of Canadian Biography*, Vol. 1 (Toronto: University of Toronto Press, 1967), 165-72; L.-A. Vigneras, "Core-Réal, Gaspar," ibid., 234-35; Vigneras, "Corte-Réal, Miguel," *ibid.*, 236.
88. Proulx, *Histoire et naufrage des navires*.
89. An overview of this heritage site is James Tuck and Robert Grenier, *Red Bay, Labrador*.
90. "Extract from Cambden's *Annals*," in David B. Quinn, ed., *The Voyages and Colonising Enterprises of Sir Humphrey Gilbert*, Vol. 2 (London: Hakluyt Society, 1940; reprinted 1967), 428.
91. "[October 1583?]. Edward Hayes' Narrative of Sir Humphrey Gilbert's Last Expedition," *The Voyages ... of Sir Humphrey Gilbert*, Vol. 2, 420.
92. Longfellow, "Sir Humphrey Gilbert," in *Poems*, 129. See Appendix C.
93. See John Russell Harper, *Painting in Canada: A History* (Toronto: University of Toronto Press, 1966), 17-20.

94. Emmanuel Crespel, *Voyages of Rev. Father Emmanuel Crespel in Canada and his shipwreck while returning to France* (Frankfort-on-the-Meyn: Louis Crespel, 1742), CIHM 35453.

95. Reuben Thwaites, ed., *Jesuit Relations*, vol. 34 (New York: Pageant Book Company, 1959), 229-35 [1649].

96. Thwaites, Preface, *Jesuit Relations*, vol. 1, 17.

97. Thwaites, *Jesuit Relations*, vol. 34, 233, 235 [1649].

98. Réginald Auger, *Labrador Inuit and Europeans in the Strait of Belle Isle: From the Written Sources to the Archaeological Evidence.* No. 55 (Québec: Université Laval, Centre d'études nordiques, 1991), 5-19; Selma deL. Barkham, "A Note on the Strait of Belle Isle during the Period of Basque Contact with Indians and Inuit," *Études/Inuit/Studies* 4, 2 (1980): 53.

99. John Carey, "The Rescue of a Race: A Brief Account of the Saving of the Eskimo," *Moravian Missions* 3 (1905): 58-60.

100. Carey, "The Rescue of a Race," 59-60.

101. Réginald Auger, *Labrador Inuit and Europeans in the Strait of Belle Isle*, 5-14; David William Zimmerly, *Cain's Land Revisited: Culture Change in Central Labrador, 1775-1972*, Social and Economic Studies No. 16 (St. John's: Institute of Social and Economic Research, Memorial University, 1975); James Hiller, *The Foundation and the Early Years of the Moravian Mission in Labrador, 1752-1805*, Unpublished M.A. thesis, Memorial University of Newfoundland, 1967; J.K. Hiller, "The Moravians in Labrador, 1771-1805," *The Polar Record* 15, 99 (1971): 39-54.

102. W.G. Gosling, *Labrador: Its Discovery, Exploration and Development* (London: Alston Rivers, 1910), 266.

103. "Shipwreck Off Newfoundland," in *Sea Sketches about Ships and Sailors* (London: Leisure Hour Office Religious Tract Society, 1853), 23-37.

104. Allen Geare, *Ebenezer; or, a Monument of Thankfulness* (London: A. Bettesworth, 1708).

105. Gilly, *Narratives of Shipwrecks of The Royal Navy.* See Preface, ix-xxxv, written by Gilly's father, William Stephen Gilly, vicar of Norham and canon of Durham, on the lessons inherent in these stories. A more recent work is W.P. Gossett, *The Lost Ships of the Royal Navy, 1793-1900* (London: Mansell, 1986).

106. "Loss of the *Cumberland* Packet," in *Shipwrecks and Disasters at Sea or Historical Narratives of the Most Noted Calamities, and*

Providential Deliverances from Fire and Famine on the Ocean
(Manchester: S. Johnson, 1837), 360-66.

107. William Dorset Fellowes, *A Narrative of the Loss of His Majesty's Packet, the* Lady Hobart, *on an island of ice in the Atlantic Ocean, 28th of June 1803* (London: J. Stockdale, 1803).

108. Evidence of recent interest in this narrative is found in John Fowles, *Neil Dewar of Greenock* (London: Cape, 1974).

109. Judith Fingard, *Jack in Port* (Toronto: University of Toronto Press, 1982), 82-139.

110. See Nick Nyland, *Skørbug, beskøjter og skibskirurger: Traek af søfartsmedicines historie* (Esbjerg: Fiskeri-og Søfartsmuseet, Saltvandsakvariet, 1994). This Danish book deals with the medical history of the sailing era. It includes an English summary.

111. These ships are described in detail in Roger Morris, *Atlantic Seafaring: Ten Centuries of Exploration and Trade in the North Atlantic* (Camden, ME: International Marine, 1992), 167-70.

112. *Shipwrecks and Disasters at Sea*, 2.

113. Great Britain, House of Commons, Select Committee Appointed To Inquire Into the Causes of Shipwrecks (1836); Select Committee on Shipwrecks of Timber Ships (1839); First Report from the Select Committee on Shipwrecks (1843); Second Report from the Select Committee on Shipwrecks (1843); Report from the Select Committee on Lighthouses (1845); Unseaworthy Ships: Preliminary Report from the Royal Commission, I (1873); Unseaworthy Ships: Minutes of Evidence before the Royal Commission with Digest of Evidence and Appendix, II (1873).

114. Under American nautical laws, shipwrecked mariners were entitled to receive their wages from any proceeds from salvage operations. See "Abstract of American Nautical Laws," in Henry Howe, *Life and Death on the Ocean*, 606-08. There were statutes relating to the recovery of wages for British seamen in Admiralty courts or in the Court of the Quarter Sessions, but also in consular or foreign courts. See Walter Murton, *Wreck Inquiries: The Law and Practice relating to Formal Investigations in the United Kingdom, British Possessions and before Naval Courts Into Shipping Casualties and the Incompetency and Misconduct of Ships' Officers* (London: Stevens and Sons, 1884), 171. The relative

success of shipwrecked sailors' civil cases in courts is noted in Fingard, *Jack in Port*, 179-80.

115. *Shipwrecked Mariner* was a publication of the Shipwrecked Fishermen and Mariners' Royal Benevolent Society of London, England, established in 1839.

116. Fingard, *Jack in Port*, 108-26.

117. Ryan, *The Ice Hunters*, 317-19.

118. GN2/19 No. 4. Disbursements to Distressed Seamen by the Accountant-General of the Navy in Account with the Lords Commissioners of the Admiralty, 1838-1844, PANF. This document includes an undated memo and an unsigned document, *Seamen lodged by Sundry persons. Account Book*. The Accountant-General of the Navy complained that the charges for passage were unnecessarily high because of the great risk associated with winter travel and the difficulty in procuring a vessel.

119. Macdonagh, *A Pattern of Government Growth*, 48.

120. Macdonagh, *A Pattern of Government Growth*, 44.

121. André Charbonneau and André Sevigny, *1847 Grosse Ile: A Record of Daily Events* (Ottawa: Canadian Heritage, 1997).

122. The most famous incident of cannibalism in Newfoundland followed the shipwreck of the *Queen of Swansea*, documented in the extant diary of one of the shipwreck victims, Felix Dowsley. See Edward P. Morris, "The Wreck of 'The *Queen*': A Christmas Memory of Forty Years Ago," *The Newfoundland Quarterly* 6, 3 (December 1906): 7-9; "The *Queen of Swansea* Tragedy," *Atlantic Guardian* 8 (March 1952): 52-54; Moses Harvey, "The Cast-Aways of Gull Island," *Maritime Monthly* 1 (April 1873): 435-46; Don Morris, "The Castaways of Gull Island," *The Atlantic Advocate* 67 (May 1976): 40-43; Mike McCarthy, "Letters from Gull Island, The *Queen of Swansea* Tragedy, December 12, 1867," in Galgay and McCarthy, *Shipwrecks of Newfoundland and Labrador*, 27-32.

123. Great Britain, House of Commons, The Select Committee Appointed to Inquire Into the Causes of Shipwrecks (1836). Also see Appendix A, Table 1, this volume.

124. For a description of emigrant ships, see Roger Morris, *Atlantic Seafaring* (Camden ME: International Marine, 1992), 160-63.

125. See broadside, *Particulars Of The Fatal Effects Of The Late Dreadful High Wind!*, Baldwin Room, Toronto Regional Library.

126. Today, we know much more than we did 20 years ago about the world of sailors and Canadian shipping history, but scholarly literature on the transatlantic passage has made little progress since the publication long ago of the standard but somewhat outdated work of Helen Cowan and Edwin Guillet and the more recent and specialized studies by Sager and Panting, by Matthews, and by Houston and Smyth. See Bibliography.

127. Alexander Crosby Brown, "Women and Children Last: The Tragic Loss of the Steamship *Arctic*," *American Neptune* 14, 4 (October 1954): 237-61.

128. A detailed account of this disaster is given by Arthur Johnson and Paul Johnson, *The Tragic Wreck of the* Anglo Saxon, April 27th., 1863 (St. John's: Harry Cuff, 1995).

129. Sager, *Seafaring Labour*, 234-38; Valerie Burton, "The Myth of Bachelor Jack: Masculinity, Patriarchy and Seafaring Labour," in Colin Howell and Richard J. Twomey, eds., *Jack Tar in History: Essays in the History of Maritime Life and Labour* (Fredericton: Acadiensis Press, 1991), 179-98.

130. Shipwreck narratives that focus on women include *Carrie Clancy, the heroine of the Atlantic* (Philadelphia: 1873), CIHM 55081; Saunders, *Narrative of the shipwreck and sufferings of Miss Ann Saunders* (Providence, RI: Z.S. Crossmon, 1827), CIHM 40276; Joan Druett, *"She was a Sister Sailor": The Whaling Journals of Mary Brewster, 1845-1851* (Mystic, CT: Mystic Seaport Museum, 1992).

131. Great Britain, House of Commons, Report From The Select Committee Appointed To Inquire Into The Causes of Shipwrecks, 15 August 1836, 39-41.

132. A modern shipwreck tale with historical ramifications is Ken Coates and Bill Morrison, *The Sinking of the* Princess Sophia: *Taking the North Down with Her* (Toronto: Oxford University Press, 1990).

133. John G. Rule, "Wrecking and Coastal Plunder," in Douglas Hay et al., eds., *Albion's Fatal Tree: Crime and Society in Eighteenth-Century England* (New York: Pantheon Books, 1975), 167-88.

134. A discussion of the early history of wrecking is found in Frederick Whymper, *The sea: its stirring story of adventure, peril and heroism* (London and New York: Cassel, Petter and Galpin, 1878), CIHM 17843.

135. Peter Marsden, *The Wreck of the Amsterdam* (New York: Stein and Day, 1975), 63-65.

136. Michael Redington, "An Island's Story," *Journal of the Galway Archaeological and Historical Society* 10 (1917-18): 156.

137. What constituted a ship was a matter of much legal discussion. Under the Merchant Shipping Act of 1854, it was defined as "every description of Vessel used in Navigation not propelled by Oars." Of course, not all ships were registered. Those in operation before this legislation came into effect, those less than 15 tons used in river or coastal navigation, or ships less than 30 tons used in fishing or trading in Newfoundland and the Maritime Provinces remained exempt. All Newfoundland ships were, however, considered British ships. See Murton, *Wreck Inquiries*, 72-79.

138. See Rev. Lewis Amedeus Anspach, *Summary of the Laws of Commerce and Navigation, Adapted to the present State, Government, and Trade of the Island of Newfoundland* (London: Heney and Haddon, 1809), recommended for publication by Vice-Admiral J. Holloway, Governor and Commander-in-Chief of Newfoundland and its dependencies.

139. "An Act to make Provision for the Constitution of a Marine Court of Inquiry in this colony," *Statutes of Newfoundland,* c. xiii. (1866). The Act was slightly amended in 1867. See *Statutes of Newfoundland,* c. viii. This legislation gave the court power to enact the provisions of the Merchant Shipping Act of 1854 and the amended Merchant Shipping Act of 1862. It was not, however, to affect the jurisdiction of the Vice-Admiralty Court of Newfoundland.

140. D.W. Prowse, "An Old Colonial Judge's Stories: Wrecks and Riots," *The Newfoundland Quarterly* 10 (July 1910): 17-19.

141. Kenneth Hudson and Ann Nicholls, *The Book of Shipwrecks* (London and Basingstoke: Macmillan, 1979), 85.

142. D.W. Prowse, "Old-time Newfoundland," *Cornhill Magazine* 89, 16 (April 1904): 542.

143. Harding, "The Menace of Cape Race," 674-84.

144. May 29, 1863. Cited in Johnson, *The Wreck of the* Anglo-Saxon, 64.

145. Browne, *Where Fishers Go*, 141-42.

146. D.W. Prowse, "Old-time Newfoundland," *Cornhill Magazine* 89, 16 (April 1904): 539-47.

147. "Heroism," *Youth's Companion* 48 (January 1868): 11.

148. James Murphy, *Newfoundland Heroes of the Sea* (St. John's: the author, 1923).

149. "The 'Golden Hind,'" in Kenneth Peacock, ed., *Songs of the Newfoundland Outports*, Vol. 3, Bulletin No. 197, Anthropological Series (Ottawa: National Museum of Canada, 1965), 922.

150. "The Loss of the 'Barbara Ann Romney,'" in Peacock, ed., *Songs of the Newfoundland Outports*, Vol. 3, 937-38.

151. The best recent popular histories are Captain Joseph Prim and Mike McCarthy, *The Angry Seas: Shipwrecks on the Coast of Labrador* (St. John's: Jesperson Publishing, 1999); Galgay and McCarthy, *Shipwrecks of Newfoundland and Labrador*, *Shipwrecks of Newfoundland and Labrador*, Vol. 2 (St. John's: Creative Publishers, 1990); and *Shipwrecks of Newfoundland and Labrador*, Vol. 3 (St. John's: Creative Publishers, 1995). Other articles and books are included in the Bibliography. There are several helpful general reference texts, including G.E. Bass, *Ships and Shipwrecks of the Americas* (London: Thames and Hudson, 1988); K.C. Barnaby, *Some Ship Disasters and Their Causes* (London: Hutchinson, 1968); Charles Hocking, *Dictionary of Disasters at Sea During the Age of Steam Including Sailing Ships and Ships of War Lost in Action, 1824-1962* (London: Lloyd's Register of Shipping, 1989); Charles A. Armour and Thomas Lackey, *Sailing Ships of the Maritimes: An Illustrated History of Shipping and Shipbuilding in the Maritime Provinces of Canada, 1750-1925* (Toronto: McGraw-Hill, 1975); Robert Gardiner, ed., *The Advent of Steam: The Merchant Steamship before 1900* (London: Conway Maritime Press, 1993).

152. See Susan A. Crane, "Writing the Individual Back into Collective Memory," *American Historical Review* 102 (December 1997): 1372-73.

I

THE CASTING AWAY OF THE *DELIGHT* (1583)[1]

RICHARD CLARKE

After the voyages of Giovanni and Sebastian Caboto to North America on behalf of the merchants of Bristol and the British crown, when they "discovered" New-founde-lande,[2] nearly seven decades passed before England again attempted colonization. The Oxford-educated Sir Humphrey Gilbert, with a background in academic geography, reclaimed the land in 1583, making it Britain's first colony outside of Ireland. His goal was to establish a series of settlements and to find a northwest passage to Asia. He may well have provided "a general ideological framework which linked America and the passage directly with Asia, the East Indies, the Moluccas, Japan, China and Cathay."[3] His hope was to establish "a great new state" in America, with himself as Lord Paramount.[4] He failed, whereas his younger half-brother Walter Raleigh fared better in Virginia.

The *Delight*, also known as the *George*, was sailed under Richard Clarke, master mariner, as part of Gilbert's expedition. At one point, Gilbert directed Clarke to sail in a direction that displeased Clarke. When the ship's master raised his objections, he was ordered on "her Majesties person" to obey. Despite his better judgment, Clarke submitted, for he would have committed a capital crime and risked Gilbert's wrath and, at minimum, the loss of his ears by refusing. Gilbert had a reputation for ruthlessness. When stationed in Ireland, he had impressed visiting dignitaries by making them walk to his tent, the path marked by rows of the heads of decapitated enemies. Likely acquainted with his superior's predilections, Clarke obediently sailed the ill-fated route.

Buffeted by bad weather, the *Delight* was pushed south roughly 60 nautical miles, to Sable Island, where the vessel was wrecked, and one hundred persons drowned. There were some survivors. Sixteen men, including Clarke, managed to secure a boat, with but one oar, and in "foule weather" they made their way for seven days, mostly without food and water and not knowing their ultimate destination. Eventually they made it to shore, "so weake that one could scarcely helpe another of us out of the boate." Finding themselves on a river somewhere along the west coast of Newfoundland, they rowed their way northwards for five days toward the Strait of Belle Isle (Grande Bay) before they were fortuitously picked up by a Basque vessel, "Spanyards," engaged in whaling or the Gulf of St. Lawrence fishery.[5] It is noteworthy and attests to his humanity that the Basque captain not only befriended them rather than killing them, but that upon their arrival in Biscay lied on their behalf, describing them as "poor fishermen" rather than the English enemy, thereby saving their lives. This shipwreck was one of many suffered by Gilbert's expeditions prior to his own drowning, and his costly failures contributed to the temporary abandonment of Newfoundland as an English colony.

DEPARTING OUT OF SAINT JOHNS HARBOROUGH in the Newfound land the 20. of August unto Cape Raz, from thence we directed our course unto the Ile of Sablon or the Isle of Sand, which the Generall Sir Humfrey Gilbert would willing have seene. But when we came within twentie leagues of the Isle of Sablon, we fell to controversie of our course. The Generall came up in his Frigot and demanded of mee Richard Clarke master of the Admirall what course was best to keepe: I said that Westsouthwest was best: because the wind was at South and night at hand and unknowen sands lay off a great way from the land. The Generall commanded me to go Westnorthwest. I told him againe that the Isle of Sablon was Westnorthwest and but 15. leagues off, and that he should be upon the Island before day, if hee went that course. The Generall sayd, my reckoning was untrue, and charged me in her Majesties name, and as I would shewe my selfe in her Countrey, to follow him that night. I fearing his threatnings, because he presented her Majesties person, did follow his commaundement,

and about seven of the clocke in the morning the ship stroke on
ground, where shee was cast away. Then the Generall went off to Sea,
the course that I would have had them gone before, and saw the ship
cast away men and all, and was not able to save a man, for there was
not water upon the sand for either of them much lesse for the
Admirall, that drew fourteene foote. Now as God would the day
before it was very calme, and a Souldier of the ship had killed some
foule with his piece, and some of the company desired me that they
might hoyse out the boat to recover the foule, which I granted them:
and when they came aboord they did not hoyse it againe that night.
And when the ship was cast away the boate was a sterne being in bur-
then one tunne and an halfe; there was left in the boate one oare and
nothing els. Some of the company could swimme, and recovered the
boate and did hale in out of the water as many men as they coulde:
among the rest they had a care to watch for the Captaine or the
Master: They happened on my selfe being the master, but could never
see the Captaine: Then they halled into the boate as many men as
they could in number 16. whose names hereafter I will rehearse. And
when the 16. were in the boate, some had small remembrance, and
some had none: for they did not make account to live, but to prolong
their lives as long as it pleased God, and looked every moment of an
houre when the Sea would eate them up, the boate being so little and
so many men in her, and so foule weather, that it was not possible for
a shippe to brooke halfe a coarse of sayle. Thus while wee remayned
two dayes and two nights, and that wee saw it pleased God our boate
lived in the Sea (although we had nothing to helpe us withall but one
oare, which we kept up the boate withall upon the Sea, and so went
even as the Sea would drive us) there was in our company one master
Hedly that put foorth this question to me the Master. I doe see that it
doth please God, that our boate lyveth in the Sea, and it may please
God that some of us may come to the land if our boate were not
overladen. Let us make sixteene lots, and those foure that have the
foure shortest lots, we will cast overboord preserving the Master
among us all. I replied unto him, saying, no, we will live and die
together. Master Hedly asked me if my remembrance were good:
I answered I gave God prayse it was good, and knewe how farre I was
off the land, and was in hope to come to the lande within two or
three dayes, and sayde they were but threescore leagues from the
lande, (when they were seventie) all to put them in comfort. Thus we

continued the third and fourth day without any sustenance, save onely the weedes that swamme in the Sea, and salt water to drinke. The fifth day Hedly dyed and another moreover: then we desired all to die: for in all these five dayes and five nights we saw the Sunne but once and the Starre but one night, it was so foule weather. Thus we did remaine the sixt day: then we were very weake and wished all to die saving onely my selfe which did comfort them and promised they should come soone to land, by the helpe of God: but the company were very importunate, and were in doubt they should never come to land, but that I promised them the seventh day they should come to shore, or els they should cast me over boord: which did happen true the seventh day, for at eleven of the clocke wee had sight of the land, and at 3. of the clocke at afternoone we came on land. All these seven dayes and seven nights, the wind kept continually South. If the wind had in the meane time shifted upon any other point, wee had never come to land: we were no sooner come to land, but the wind came cleane contrary at North within halfe an houre after our arrivall. But we were so weake that one could scarcely helpe another of us out of the boate, yet with much adoe being come all on shore we kneeled downe upon our knees and gave God praise that he had dealt so mercifully with us. Afterwards those which were strongest holpe their fellowes unto a fresh brooke, where we satisfied our selves with water and berries very well. There were of al sorts of berries plentie, & as goodly a Countrey as ever I saw: we found a very plaine Champion ground that a man might see very farre every way: by the Sea side was here and there a little wood with goodly trees as good as ever I saw any in Norway, able to mast any shippe, of pyne trees, spruse trees, firre, and very great birch trees. Where we came on land we made a little house with boughes, where we rested all that night. In the morning I devided the company three and three to goe every way to see what foode they could find to sustaine themselves, and appointed them to meete there all againe at noone with such foode as they could get. As we went aboord we found great store of peason as good as any wee have in England: a man would thinke they had bene sowed there. We rested there three dayes and three nights and lived very well with pease and berries, wee named the place Saint Laurence, because it was a very goodly river like the river of S. Laurence in Canada, and we found it very full of Salmons. When wee had well rested our selves wee rowed our boate along the shore, thinking to have gone to the

Grande Bay to have come home with some Spanyards which are yeerely there to kill the Whale: And when we were hungry or a thirst we put our boate on land and gathered pease and berries. Thus wee rowed our boate along the shore five dayes: about which time we came to a very goodly river that ranne farre up into the Countrey and saw very goodly growen trees of all sortes. There we happened upon a ship of Saint John de Luz, which ship brought us into Biskay to an Harborough called The Passage. The Master of the shippe was our great friend, or else we had bene put to death if he had not kept our counsayle. For when the visitors came aboord, as it is the order in Spaine, they demaunding what we were, he sayd we were poore fishermen that had cast away our ship in Newfound land, and so the visitors inquired no more of the matter at that time. As soone as night was come he put us on land and bad us shift for our selves. Then had wee but tenne or twelve miles into France, which we went that night, and then cared not for the Spanyard. And so shortly after we came into England toward the end of the year 1583.

NOTES

1. [1584]. "Richard Clarke's Account of the Casting Away of the *Delight,*" in David B. Quinn, ed., *The Voyages and Colonising Enterprises of Sir Humphrey Gilbert,* vol. 1 (London: Hakluyt Society, 1940), 423-26.
2. R.A. Skeleton, "Cabot (Caboto), John (Giovanni)," *Dictionary of Canadian Biography,* vol. 1 (Toronto: University of Toronto, 1966), 146-52, and "Cabot, Sebastian," *ibid.,* 152-58.
3. Luca Codignola, *The Coldest Harbour of the Land: Simon Stock and Lord Baltimore's Colony in Newfoundland, 1621-1649* (Kingston and Montreal: McGill-Queen's University Press, 1989), 36.
4. David B. Quinn, *Explorers and Colonies: America, 1500-1625* (London and Ronceverte: The Hambeldon Press, 1990), 215.
5. *Tabula Nautica,* a map published in 1611 or 1612 by Hessel Gerritz, the official cartographer of the Dutch East India Company, identifies northern Newfoundland as "Ilha de Bacalhao" (the Island of Cod), and a Portuguese (Basque) possession.

2

THE SHIPWRECK OF FATHER CHARLES LALEMANT,
PHILIBERT NOYROT, AND OTHERS,
OFF CAPE BRETON (1629)[1]

JOHN GILMARY SHEA

In his voyages between 1603 and 1634, nearly one hundred years after Jacques Cartier's voyages and twenty years after Gilbert's, Champlain "discovered" what came to be known as Acadia and New France, and he claimed these disputed lands for the King of France. The French government's intention in expanding its realms was in part to promote Christianity among native peoples as a way to secure possession and to promote the fur trade. The author of this narrative in the form of a letter is Paris-born Charles Lalemant (1587-1674), who became a Jesuit in 1607 and later a missionary of considerable distinction in what is now Quebec, at a time when European powers, notably France and England, were disputing jurisdiction over these new lands.[2]

The first attempt by the French to proselytize Aboriginal peoples had involved the austere Récollets, whose membership included both Hugenots and Catholics. By 1624 they had established six small missions on the mainland. Needing financial and other support, they sought help from the powerful and exclusively Catholic Society of Jesus, or Jesuits. In 1625 Father Charles Lalement, then the newly appointed Jesuit Superior of New France, successfully journeyed to the missions with supplies. He was accompanied by two other Jesuits and three Récollets. Two years afterward he returned to France for more supplies, but upon his return his ship was captured by the

Newfoundland-based, English-supported pirate Admiral David Kirke. The Jesuits were sent to England before finally returning home. On a second attempt to make meet their goal in the summer of 1629, Lalemant and the clergy who accompanied him only managed to reach the mouth of the St. Lawrence before learning that Quebec had been taken by Kirke on behalf of Sir William Alexander of Scotland, who in turn had acquired rights to these acquisitions from King James I.

Lalement describes to his Superior how the returning vessel was subsequently lost in the Gulf of St. Lawrence off Cape Breton. The ship had been blown southward while sailing through the Gulf of St. Lawrence and the Cabot Strait, where it was wrecked on the Canso Islands, roughly 45 nautical miles from Captain Charles Daniel's settlement at St. Anne's, north of the Great Bras d'Or Lake. The tragedy resulted in the drowning of 14 persons, including another leading Jesuit, Father Noyrot. With the assistance of sympathetic local Mi'kmaq, who alerted them to a hostile English presence in the area and who suggested their best escape route, the survivors fled to safety and were fortuitously rescued by an unidentified Basque ship, one in all likelihood engaged in the "wet fishery" and based for the fishing season off Newfoundland. Lalemant's account concludes with a second shipwreck on his return voyage, this time off the coast of Spain, resulting in the loss of the vessel and its entire annual catch. Meanwhile Kirke had sent the remaining handful of missionaries from Quebec back to France and briefly secured English control over the St. Lawrence.

French forces once again defeated the English in 1632. This allowed the Jesuits, under Lalemant's leadership, to re-establish their missions once and for all. When Lalemant arrived again in 1634, his noteworthy activities included attending Champlain on his deathbed. Upon his subsequent permanent return to France, he served as rector of the colleges of Rouen, La Fleche, and Paris, and eventually headed the Society of Jesus, as Superior of the Professed House, in Paris. His brother Gabriel was later killed in ritualistic and symbolic fashion at St. Marie-among-the-Hurons by Hurons angered at the diseases and cultural destruction brought by the Jesuits, and he became a martyr. In recommending Charles Lalement's appointment, the Company of New France praised him as "one of the first to expose himself to the usual perils for the conversion of the Savages, even to three shipwrecks which he suffered on those voyages."[3]

⚓

"THE LORD CHASTISING HAS CHASTISED ME; but he hath not delivered me over to death." (Psalms cxii. 18.) A chastisement the more severe, as the shipwreck has been attended by the death of the Rev. Father Philibert Noyrot, and of our brother, Louis Malot, two men who would, it seems to me, have been of great service to our seminary. Yet, as God has so disposed, we must seek consolation in his holy will, out of which there never was a solid or contented mind, and I am sure that experience has shown your reverence that the bitterness of our sorrows, steeped in the sweetness of God's good pleasure, when a soul binds itself indissolubly to that, loses all or most of its gall, or, if some sighs yet remain for past or present afflictions, it is only to aspire the more for heaven, and meritoriously perfect that conformity in which the soul has resolved to spend the rest of its days.

Of the four members of our Society in the ship, God, dividing equally, has taken two and left the two others. These two good religious, well disposed, and resigned to death, will serve as victims to appease God's wrath justly excited against us for our faults, and to render his goodness favourable henceforth to the success of our designs.

What destroyed our vessel was a violent southwester, which arose when we were off the coast; it was so impetuous that, with all the care and diligence of our captain and crew, with all the vows and prayers which we could offer to avert the blow, we could not avoid being driven on the rocks, on the 26th day after our departure, feast of St. Bartholomew, about 9 o'clock in the evening. Of twenty-four that were in the vessel, only ten escaped: the rest were engulphed in the waves. Father Noyrot's two nephews shared their uncle's fate. We interred the bodies of several, among others, of Father Noyrot and Brother Louis. Of seven others, we have had no tidings in spite of all our search.

To tell you how Father Vieuxport and I escaped, would be difficult, and I believe that God alone knows, who, according to the designs of his divine providence, has preserved us; for, for my own part, not deeming it possible, humanly speaking, to avoid dangers, I had resolved to stay in the cabin with Brother Louis, preparing ourselves to receive the death stroke, which could not be delayed over three *Misereres*, when I heard some one calling me on deck. Supposing that my assistance was needed, I ran up and found that it was Father Noyrot, who asked me to give him absolution. After

giving it, and singing the *Salve Regina* with him, I had to stay on
deck; for there was no way to get below; for the sea was so high and
the wind so furious, that, in less than a moment, the side on the rock
went to pieces. I was close by Father Noyrot when a wave broke so
impetuously against the side where we were standing, that it dashed it
to pieces, and separated me from Father Noyrot, from whose lips I
heard these last words: "*Into thy hands I commend my spirit.*" For my
own part, this same wave left them struggling amid four fragments of
the wreck, two of which struck me so violently on the chest, and the
other two on the back, that I expected to be killed before sinking
forever; but, just then, another wave disengaged me from the
fragments, sweeping off my cap and slippers, and scattered the rest
of the ship over the sea. I fortunately fell on a plank to which I clung:
it was connected with the rest of the side of the ship. There we were
then at the mercy of the waves, which did not spare us, rising
I cannot tell how many feet above our heads, and then breaking over
us. After floating thus a long while in the dark, for night had set in,
I perceived, on looking around me, that I was near the shore of what
seemed to be an island, which almost surrounded us, and was covered
with brambles. Looking a little more attentively, I made out six
persons not far from me, two of whom perceiving me, urged me to
do my best to join them; this was not easy, for I was greatly enfeebled
by the blows I had received from the fragments of the wreck.
I exerted myself, however, so much that, by the help of my plank, I at
last reached them, and by their aid got on the mainmast, which was
still fast to part of the ship. I was not here long; for, as we got nearer
the island, our sailors quickly got ashore, and, by their help, all the
rest of us were soon there. There we were, seven in all; I had no hat
or shoes; my cassock and clothes all torn, and my body so bruised
that I could scarcely stand up, and, in fact they had to support me to
enable me to reach the wood. I had two severe contusions on the legs,
especially the right one, which is still painful; my hands cloven open
and bruised; my hip torn, and my chest much injured. We now
retired to the wood wet as we came from the sea. Our first care was
to thank God for preserving us, and to pray for those who were lost.
That done, we lay down close by each other in order to try and get
warm, but the ground and the grass, still wet with heavy rain, was not
much fitted to dry us. Thus we spent the rest of the night, during
which Father Vieuxport, who, thank God, was unhurt, slept well.

The next morning, at daybreak, we began to examine the spot where we were, and found it to be an island from which we could pass to the main land. On the shore we found many things that the sea had thrown up; among which I picked up two shoes, a cap, cassock, and other necessary articles. Above all, Providence sent us, in our want, five kegs of wine, ten pieces of pork, oil, bread, cheese, and a gun, and powder, which enabled us to strike a fire. After we had thus gathered all we could, on St. Louis' day, all set to work to do their best to build a boat out of the fragments of the wreck, in which to coast along till we found a fishing-smack. We set to work with the wretched tools we found, and it was pretty well advanced on the fourth day, when we perceived a craft sailing towards the spot where we were. They took on board one of our sailors, who swam out near to where they were passing, and took him to their captain. That worthy man, hearing of our misfortunes, let down his boat, and came ashore to offer us a passage. We were thus saved; for the next day, we all slept on board. It was a Basque vessel, fishing about a league and a half from the rock where we struck, and, as their fishing season was far from being gone, we stayed with them the rest of August and all the month of September. On the first of October, an Indian came to tell the captain that, if he did not sail, he ran the risk of being taken by the English. This news made him give up his fishing, and prepare for the voyage home. The same Indian told us that Captain Daniel was building a house twenty-five leagues off, and had some Frenchmen there with one of our fathers. Father Vieuxport had already pressed me very hard to let him stay with this Indian, who was really one of the best that could be found. I now told him, Here, father, is a means of satisfying your reverence. Father Vimont will not be sorry to have a companion. This Indian offers to take you to Daniel's place; if you wish to stay there, you may; if you wish to spend a few months with the Indians and learn the language, you may do so, and both Father Vimont and yourself will be satisfied. The good father was quite delighted at the opportunity, and set off in the Indian's canoe. I let him have all we had saved, except the large painting which our Basque captain had taken, and which I would have made him give up, if another disaster had not befallen us. We left the coast on the sixth of October, and after more violent storms than I had yet ever seen, on the fortieth day of our voyage, as we were entering a port near San Sebastian in Spain, we were a second time wrecked. The vessel went into a thousand pieces, and all the fish was lost. All that I could do was to get into a boat in slippers and nightcap as I was, and, in that guise, go to our Father's at San Sebastian. I left there a week after, and, on the 20th of the present month, reached Bourdevac, near Bordeaux.

Such was the issue of our voyage, by which you may see how great we have to be thankful to God.

CHARLES LALEMANT, S.J.

Bordeaux, November 22, 1629

NOTES

1. John Gilmary Shea, *Perils of the Ocean and Wilderness: Narratives of Shipwreck and Indian Captivity, Gleaned from Early Missionary Annals* (Boston: Patrick Donahoe, 1856), 9-16. Originally published in *Voyages de Champlain* (Paris, 1632), CIHM 53412. A different translation is included in Reuben Thwaites, ed., *The Jesuit Relations and Allied Documents: Travels and Explorations of The Jesuit Missionaries in New France, 1610-1791*, vol. 3 (New York: Pageant Book, 1959), 235-45.

2. Leon Pouliot, "Charles Lalement," *Dictionary of Canadian Biography*, vol. 1 (Toronto: University of Toronto Press, 1966), 411-12.

3. "Letter addressed by Messieurs the Associates of the Company of New France to the Very Reverend Father General of the Society of Jesus at Rome," Paris, June 1651, in Thwaites, ed., *Jesuit Relations*, 36 (1650-51), 71.

3

SHIPWRECK AND DISTRESS SUFFER'D
NEAR THE COAST OF NEWFOUNDLAND:
THE *ANNE* (1704)[1]

HENRY TREBY

In 1700, the thousands of miles of coastline that define the island of Newfoundland were at best sparsely inhabited. The Anglican clergyman Thomas Bray described the island as consisting of 26 harbours under English control, 274 families, 1,120 permanent residents, 4,200 seasonal workers, and 3,150 ships' crew during the fishing season, with an additional 1,200 men arriving at the end of the season to transport the catch to the home market.[2] One might add to these groups a combined native population of Beothuk, Inuit, and Mi'Kmaq of less than 5,000. Overall, however, the small size of this population belied its importance to the mother country, for next to the woolen trades, the Newfoundland-based fish export trade was considered by some to be the most important and profitable sector of the British trading economy.[3]

The London and Bristol Company for the Plantation of Newfoundland had initially monopolized trade, and subsequent Royal Charters known as "Western Charters" gave rights of trade in Newfoundland to some West Country English ports. These controls were replaced in 1699 by the Newfoundland Act, which gave access to other centres, such as Exeter, which, with Topsham, was one of the minor ports that benefitted from the liberalization of trade, and in 1700 it returned 29 ships from Newfoundland.[4] The *Anne*, Thomas

Manson, master, was among those that did not make the final voyage home.

This narrative was written by Henry Treby, a survivor of the *Anne*. The ship had been engaged in bringing salt for the fishery, as was customary, from Lisbon, Portugal, to Newfoundland when, on April 21, 1704, it lost sight of the accompanying convoy of five other ships and found itself in islands of ice roughly 150 nautical miles off the coast. When the ship hit ice and became stuck on it, its tiller was broken, and when the crew managed to free the vessel it collided with ice a second time, its hold quickly filling with water. Treby's moving account describes in considerable detail the "terror" of this "direful calamity" and the crew's reaction to their impending fate.

In writing to the printer, Treby acknowledged that he liked to read about the "dangerous voyage," but he had found it extremely difficult to write his recollections and was often forced to break away from writing about these "matchless sufferings, terrors, and hazards," for he was "so terribly convulsed by this particular remembrance." It was "the stoutness and durableness of the animal part," according to him, that allowed six of his fellow fifteen crewmen to survive without resorting to cannibalism, although they were near starvation. Despite the "wonderful" nature of his narrative, Treby assured the printer, "it is all matter of fact."

Signing on for a voyage to Newfoundland was widely considered to be risky, and Treby's day-to-day observations of the ordeal remain a poignant reminder of this historical truth. His account also illustrates how shipwrecked mariners were received in St. John's, at a time when the English government had finally decided to build a battery to protect it as a permanent settlement. In the following year, the French recaptured St. John's, and their reception might not have been the same had they been shipwrecked then. On bringing their small boat into the Narrows, the survivors of the *Anne* were reunited with the four ships with which they had initially crossed the Atlantic. Together with two others, Treby had both legs amputated, despite medical intervention. Another crew member lost not only his legs but his genitalia.

Treby's description of their treatment and the reaction of others to their plight suggests that compassion and deep feeling were still to be found in an era of conflict and hardship. After a five-month convalescence, he managed to secure passage home, but his trials were not over. In this age of privateering and international rivalry, Treby was

subsequently captured by French pirates only 90 nautical miles from
Scilly but then, ironically, on the way to France this ship was retaken
by two Guernsey privateers. Treby finally managed to return home to
Exmouth, where his friends received him with "an equal measure of
grief and joy."

⚓

AMONG THE MANY WONDERS OF GOD in the great deep, may well be
recorded that experienced by the crew of a ship of Topsham, called
The *Anne*, Thomas Manson of Lympson Master; which, being
freighted with salt, and sailing from Lisbon, bound for
Newfoundland, on Friday April 21, 1704, being about 50 leagues off
that coast, in company with 5 other ships, the wind SE, the weather
so very foggy (*says the relater*) that we could scarce see a ship's length,
and every ship making the best of his way (having a fair wind) out of
that cold climate, we utterly lost all sight of 'em before night.

About 8 o'clock we thought proper to bring the ship to, under a
mainsail, and hauled up our foresail snug in the broyls, furling all the
rest of our sails. This we did for fear of the rocks, or rather islands, of
ice, which are so frequent in those parts about that season of the year.
We had the chance to escape all dangers of this kind hitherto, having
not seen any ice in the whole passage. But, as I said, the night being
prodigious dark, we acted prudently, tho' unsuccessfully, in being on
our guard. But, alas! About midnight, as we were thus lying to, tail of
a huge island of ice, that lay under water; and the air withal being so
full of black fog, we could not well discern when we first struck upon
it, (which we did with no small shock) whether we beat upon a fixed
rock, or upon floating ice; but supposing the latter, we, all of us,
looked out very sharp on all sides, if by any means we could discover
what danger we were in, and how to shun it. At length some of us
had spied some glimpse of an isle of ice directly upon our windward
quarter, which appeared to us of a prodigious height, and but a small
distance from us; but others could not perceive any such thing. We
however, at last, by much tugging, had again gotten our ship almost
before the wind; being to the leeward of the mountain of ice; the ship
beating pretty easy, what it did at first. We tried our pumps, and they
both sucked; and one of our men took an oar out of the boat, and,
sounding by the ship's side, found but 9 feet less than our ship did
draw. Some of our crew being on the forecastle, and one on the

bowsprit, fancied that the water just under the bowsprit appeared blacker than it did by the ship's side; if we could work her about her length forward, she would then be clear. This we soon accomplished, by letting fall our foresail, and setting both topsails; whereby every sea did help to launch us more and more into the deep; and at last we got clear of the ice; the rudder being the last thing that struck, by which was broke the tiller.

If we had been contented to have lain fast by 'til daylight, I believe we might have done well. But every man was in a distracted condition, and even at his wit's end, as only those who have ever encountered with such terrible dangers can justly conceive. The Master asked the man who looked after the glass, how the ship kept up when she first drove in upon the ice: who replied, SSW (South south west). Our master then was for making sail again, and ordered to keep NNE (having first put a capstan-bar into the rudder-head) under two topsails and a foresail. But we had not kept that course above four minutes, ever we again fell foul, of the same or another island of ice. At the first blow, the ship so rebounded, that we verily imagined all the masts would have fallen by the board. The vessel lay all on one side, the sea threatening to bury us every minute. We presently hauled up our foresail snug, and furled our topsails; then tried the pumps; but neither of 'em would suck. Two men were thereupon sent down to see what water was in the hold. The first who leaped down was up to the middle in water above the salt, and saw the empty casks floating thereon. They presently came up with the appearance of death and horror in their faces, and by their terrible outcries soon reduced us to their sad likeness. We all perceived the wound to be mortal and incurable, and our case altogether desperate and forlorn. What added to our terror and direful calamity was the hideous darkness we were encompassed with, and the boisterous raging of the sea, which continually made its passage over us. We looked one on the other with pale and ghastly countenances, appearing more like ghosts than living men. Dreadful hour! We lay awhile rumbling and sallying over from side to side, raking in every great wave which came, which sometimes filled our boat upon the deck; but the plug-holes being out, she soon was freed again. Our pumps rose an end both out of their places. We were justly apprehensive of the ship's falling in pieces every moment; but in the sad manner we lay beating on the fatal ice near the space of an hour, as near as I can guess; by no possible means being able to get out our boat, the only poor refuge we had left us; by reason of its being so exceeding dark, cold, and tempestuous, and the ship to be kept in no fixed steadiness.

I can't think it possible for any pen to express to the full our calamitous plight and circumstances at that time. After you have imagined everything that is terrible, and superlatively hideous, you will fall short in your conception of our dread and confusion. Here was seen one wringing his hands, smiting his breast, and in a hollow doleful tone begging mercy of God on his poor soul, which he supposed was upon the wing for eternity; there by him might be heard another with a voice altogether as deadly, crying out upon his wife and children; and the like. You may perhaps have noted the symptoms of agony which were visible in a wretched malefactor leading to execution; but considering he had long before had reason to expect the fatal hour, and time and help allowed him to prepare for his departure, what comparison can there be justly made between the horror of his case and that of ours, who were (as it may be said) thus hurried to our fates, altogether of a sudden and unprepared? All that can be urged any way to lighten the balance of our side, is the truth of the saying, *Whilst there is life there is hope!* Though our hope was but the smallest degree from utter despair. But to have a thorough sensible idea of *another's* distress and anguish, you must *yourself* have been under circumstances at least near akin to *his*. Yet God had mercy still in store for some of us, though we were all reserved for some of the greatest hardships that ever poor mortals endured.

Through providence, the sea at length, our deadly enemy, became our friend, in bearing the ship off from the ice; but as soon as she was clear, or in less than 4 minutes after, the sea ran in at the cabin windows. Having no runners, nor tackles up, whereby to hoist out our boat, we made haste, with the carpenter's axe, to cut her lashings (having first put in the plugs) and so launched her overboard by mere strength of arm into the sea, and several of us with incredible precipitation, head foremost, tumbled into her and presently took in the rest: All which was performed in less time than 3 minutes. We had but just opportunity to take with us the sea-compass, 2 skiff sails, a tarpawling weather-cloth, 3 oars, a small bag of bread all soused in sea-water, a cag of brandy containing about 6 or 8 pints, with 2 pieces of raw beef. Thus poorly furnished, we hasted to get as far off from the ship as

Coastal Wreck. Hearing breakers in fog or at night was often the first warning of disaster. From *The Shipwrecked Mariner*, vol. 36, Shipwrecked Fishermen and Mariners' Royal Benevolent Society of London, 1889

possible, for fear lest the indraught should have carried us down with her; And well for some of us we did so; for we were but just got out of reach of the danger ever we perceived her go down.

Our ship thus being sunk, and fifteen wretches of us thus confusedly, (but indeed happily, considering the more deplorable predicament we had just gotten out of) being huddled together in a frail boat, destitute of necessaries, of every kind, we could retain but very faint hopes of safety, without some speedy providence, or miraculous relief, in our favour. We were all of us so confounded and astonished by our sudden calamity, that we could neither of us reduce our prayers to any regular form; but I believe each of us most fervently lifted up our hearts to God: As who but the most unaccountably stupid and insensible could do otherwise? We had only fled from one danger into many others: For now we had the fear of perishing by cold and famine within, and the implacable element, whether liquid or congealed, dreadfully threatening us from without our poor sanctuary; the night, continued horribly dark, that we knew not which way to steer our course; for which reason, and for fear of again falling foul of ice, we thought it most advisable to lie by 'til daylight. Thus we endured greater hardships and fears than I can pretend to describe; many tedious hours, being only employed in bewailing our condition; which was reduced from a strong stanch ship to a weak leaky boat, and that deeply laden, her stern being no more than eight inches above water, and her head about eleven. At length the so much and long-wished for daylight began to appear, and our dead hopes a little to revive.

Saturday, April 22

As soon as it was light enough to distinguish one another's countenances, each beheld in his companion's face the image of desolation, despair, and death; not one of us but appeared as if smitten with thunder. I can't say we took courage, but considering that sighs and lamentations would not anywise better our circumstances, we assumed a resolution (if God permitted) to work out our deliverance. We all entered, upon consultation, into our master's opinion, that our most hopeful course lay towards Newfoundland, whither we had been bound before our ship foundered. We rejoiced not a little in our good chance to have taken the compass with us; but alas! what could we do without a mast and yard, though we had a sail? The wind continued still SE very fair, but pretty strong, almost half a storm; and if we had been furnished with those needful instruments, (viz. a mast and yard) we should not have doubted of making good way, without tugging at the oar. At length we contrived to make one of our three oars to serve for a mast, by working a hole in the blade of it with a sharp-pointed knife; and luckily finding the carpenter's axe on board, he split up some of the ceiling of the boat, where-with he made a kind of yard, at least a poor shift to square the sail; and moreover discovering about four fathom of deep-sea line, we made it serve for heilyards and stay to hoist the sail; and furthermore loosed the fenders of our boat to seize the pieces together for the yard. Thus, and with many other shifts, at length we sat our mast, and hoisted our sail. The wind still continuing south-east and blowing pretty quick, we made the best of our way for the land. We likewise took the before-mentioned tarpawling weather-cloth, which, being cut up, we nailed round the stern and quarters of our boat with some scopper-nails, which we happened also to find; having split up some more of the ceiling for stantions. So that, by this prudent means, we rose our boat eighteen inches more than before: which was a clever and happy defence against the dashings of the waves; or otherwise we should many times have taken in a hogshead or two of water at a time, if not filled and sunk our boat. I hope I shall ever preserve a thankful remembrance of God's providential provision of the aforesaid necessaries for our use: for indeed to me, without superstition, it seems more the care of the divine moderator and preserver of the universe, than the meer effect of what some may call chance, that such things as these were found in the boat.

Our hopes and wishes still were to discover one or other of the ships that had been in our company the preceding day, that they might take us up. And at last, about ten o'clock in the forenoon, we espied four sail, which we presently knew to be some of those, and did belong to Topsham, and also set sail with us from Lisbon. As our sorrow and consternation was extreme upon losing our own ship, so was our joy altogether as violent upon the sight of these. One of our men presently pulled off his white shirt, which was held up, and waved to and fro, on one of our oars, as a signal of distress; but in vain, we being so far from a period to our misery, that (at least with respect to our bodily sufferings) we had scarce as yet seen the beginning thereof. Methinks I still feel the cold damp which seized on my spirits at that fatal disappointment of our hopes: there was not a man whose countenance was not invaded with an additional paleness. The happy ships, before a brisk gale, made too great a way to give us any hope to come up with them; being at least two leagues to windward of us, and an island of ice above a mile long at the head of us; so that we were forced to go to the leeward of it, whilst they steered the contrary course. We however laboured hard, though but little encouraged so to do; but when we were gotten round the fatal ice, we had entirely lost sight of the ships.

The reader perhaps will scarce believe it, that I am yet so affected with the memory of our anguish on this second shipwreck, namely that of our chief hopes, that I have much ado to make my hand perform its office in penning this relation of it. Well! Tears and bewailing of our distress we found of no use to relieve us; wherefore having tired our eyes with keening towards the ships, or rather the way they took, all to no purpose, we finding the wind still fair, kept on as well as we could, in the same course; hoping we might, under God's protection, yet live to see the land. About two o'clock in the afternoon, we thought proper to examine a little into our store, all thoughts of sustenance and refreshment having hitherto been swallowed up in those of more immediate concern and moment, namely providing for our preservation and security. We took each of us a sup of brandy; but having no measure besides our mouths, some

I believe were not so moderate in their drinking as others. We also took each a morsel of the driest bread; but as for the beef, it being raw, and having no fire to dress it withal, none of us would touch it. The wind continued still south-east all the day and all the night, which, through the appearance of many stars, and fairer weather, was not quite so tedious and comfortless to us as the night before.

It has been a common saying, that *there is pleasure in recounting past dangers and calamities*: But however true this may be with respect to those whose *apprehensions* of it might be their only *real danger*, or who might have undergone some *light afflictions*, I for my part cannot entirely acquiesce in the verity and justness of the expression, who am so terribly convulsed by this particular remembrance and description of our matchless sufferings, terrors, and hazards, that I am often forced abruptly to break off in the midst of a sentence, and to write my short narrative at many different times. It would indeed be an act of basest ingratitude in me, not to reflect both with joy and thankfulness on God's wonderful mercy in my deliverance at last, and that I yet survive to declare the same: but the reader will perceive by the sequel such poignant sorrows necessarily attending our wretchedness and distress, as could not but take too fast a hold ever totally to be shaken off. But to proceed.

We weathered out, I say, another tedious night, which we spent indeed somewhat seriously, as the circumstance of providence we were under, I should think, would certainly oblige the most irreligious and abandoned wretches in like sort to do. When morning light began to dawn (being Sunday, April 23) we looked on the compass, and found the wind stood as it did the day before. We continued therefore our course in towards the land, 'til near ten o'clock of the same morning; at which time the wind veered to the northward, about north-east and blew very strong. We however, through much toil and struggling, kept the boat almost all the day before the sea, somewhat nighing the land. The sea ran very hollow, the foaming surges threatening to devour us every moment. Had it not been for our tarpawling weather-cloth, before-mentioned, we should have taken in many hogsheads of water more than we did, if not filled the boat; but that proved of mighty use to us.

A little before night the wind veered directly north blowing very roughly, into a little storm. We hauled down our sail, and with our oars kept up the head of our boat against the sea. We relieved each other by turns and thus all the Sunday night, two at a time, continually laboured at the oars.

The weather was not only tempestuous, but excessive cold. The ships that night upon the sea (as I afterwards understood) were obliged to reef their coasts. The sky indeed was clear, and the stars over our heads appeared like little moons: but, I say, the cold was extreme and insufferable, nor had we any defence against it, or relief under it; but lay open to all kinds of hardships that can be thought on. Our brandy was quite spent, so we had nothing to cheer our hearts; yea, though cold water, if but from a stinking ditch or horse-pond, we should have esteemed as a cordial, yet even that poor comfort was denied us. The small store of bread we had was also totally spoilt, being like sops with the salt water, it being impossible to preserve it from the spray of the sea, which could not be hindered from flying over us. The few thin clothes we had on us were all wet, nor had we any means to dry or shift 'em. The cold was so very pinching and intolerable, and our hands so benumbed therewith, that we could not clinch or wring them together to preserve their vital warmth; and 'twas with great difficulty we clinched 'em, or held the oars. Wherefore we that rowed were obliged to relieve our hands by turns, pulling with one, whilst we laid the other in our bosoms, and our fingers in our mouths, withal often beating 'em, to preserve a little heat. Never poor souls, I believe, were invaded, for so long a continuance, with such a complication of miseries. Our hearts, as it were, died with our hopes; and what could hopeless heartless wretches perform with their hands, that were also nearly dead? Yet under all this load of inconveniences, wants, pain, and despair itself, were we obliged incessantly to toil and labour, to preserve ourselves from immediate destruction.

We took in abundance of water continually; and the boat besides being leaky, some were imploy'd very busily, all night, in heaving out the water; so that the bucket was ever in action, both in foul weather and fair. Yet providence so ordered it, that though we took in a great deal of water, yet never a wave broke full home upon us; which if it had, we had doubtless been overwhelmed therewith, and perhaps sunk downright. We still wished for day, which might possibly bring forth something to our advantage. I say, might possibly do so; but cannot say we had any the smallest hope of it, the fell monster despair having fettered all our hearts. Skin for skin; and all that a man hath will he give for his life, hath been often approved a saying of truth, though uttered by the Father of Lies, but our case was so forlorn and comfortless, that had we had a title to the sway of the universe, we would have forgone our claims, for some present refreshment, and but barely probable means of safety. Thus harrassed and fatigued, we passed over one melancholy irksome night more.

Monday, April 24

At the first approach of daylight, we discovered on what coast we alas were driven; namely, the dreadful shores of DEATH; whose various armies surrounding us had already taken one of our miserable companions prisoner. We supposed he perished chiefly by the terrible extremity of cold. We looked on him as if on our own picture, and rather envied than pitied his condition, who by a pang or groan or two extraordinary had so happily escaped the superabundant woes and sufferings which stared the survivors in the face, if such as were half dead might be said to survive: for we that had any remains of life were so weak, so tired, and so benumbed with cold, that we could neither stand on our legs, nor arise from the places where we sat; and our clothes being stiff and frozen to our bodies, we appeared more like carved images than living men. However, uniting the little strength we had, we hove, or rather tumbled, the dead corpse overboard, to lighten the boat, and make more room for the living.

About nine o'clock this morning, the storm began to abate, and by noon we had a perfect calm; the sun shone forth, and not the least swelling to be seen on the sea. We had now a little respite from our toil; and again cast our eyes on all sides, praying God of his mercy to bring a ship to our relief and preservation: but, in vain. Between the hours of one and two, the wind began to spring up out of the SE quarter. We sat our mast (or oar), and hoisted our sail, and so stood away for land. The wind continued to freshen more and more; but as that increased, so a fog grew upon us thicker and thicker; insomuch that at last we could not discern ten boats length from us.

The wind still continued brisk and fair all this day, that we made considerable way: but the night coming on upon us was so exceedingly dark, by means of the prodigious mist, that none of us had ever known its like. The darkness was literally palpable; the black thick vapour which possessed all the air being really to be felt; and

was certainly an image of that horrible darkness which Moses by
God's command and power heretofore brought on Egypt for a plague.
This was no small addition to our distress; we being often obliged to
shut our eyes, to ease their smarting. Had we had the means to strike
and kindle a light, I can't suppose it would have been of any use and
service to us. Our compass therefore could be of no benefit; so that
we could not possibly tell which way we steered; but supposing, by
the run of the sea, that the wind stood fast as it did the day before,
namely southeast we kept on the boat before the sea. All this while
not a man of us, I believe, had stolen one wink of sleep. This was a
long, dismal, and comfortless night; but yet God enabled us to bear
up through it; and at length we saw the light breaking in upon us,
which was some small satisfaction to us, who as it may well enough
be expressed, came out of utter darkness.

Tuesday, April 25

I am by sad experience brought into an opinion, agreeable to a saying
which I have often heard repeated, that MAN of all *animal creatures* is
naturally the *strongest*: I mean with respect to what may (not to speak
profanely) be styled *self-existence*. No man can be thoroughly sensible
of the hardiness and vigour of his nature, before it has been put to the
utmost proof. We the fourteen poor remaining souls, in this bubble
of a boat, certainly were not composed of more durable flesh and
sinews, animated with spirits of force and temper superior to other
mortals. And yet if a person of the most robust and vigorous
constitution, or exalted courage, would but reflect on any past distress
he hath grappled with; as when he has a few hours been pinched with
hunger or parched with thirst, been benumbed with cold and wet,
and destitute of shelter, or been long debarred his natural rest; I say, if
he has ever been reduced to any thing like extremity, in either of these
gates, he would surely give it as his judgement, that he could not
possibly subsist or hold out long, under such miserable circumstances,
without some minute support. Now, then, let him a little consider
our woeful plight and calamity, and thereby know the innate
excellency of humanity, with reference to the stoutness and
durableness of the animal part. We had by this time, from Friday
to Tuesday morning, been exposed, in an open, frail, and leaky
cockboat, (as it were in the midst of the sea) to the most galling

weather, in a cold climate, being defenceless against wet (both from above and beneath) nearly so frozen as if we were petrified; withal pent up, and fixed in one place and posture (for the most part), so as we were debarred all means to prevent, by motion, a stagnation of blood in our lower parts; nor, for the major parts of the time, had we the least strengthening, refreshing, or cheering sustenance of either kind.

It has been looked on as an instance of the most extreme and poignant famine, when men have been so far reduced as to feed on household vermin, or to graze with forest beasts; and without dispute it must be granted to be a case very deplorable, when wretches are so sadly put to it to maintain life: but we, for our parts, who had not so much as wholesome air to subsist on, should gladly have banqueted on beetles, caterpillars, or the rankest roots, and even caroused on putrid stinking ditch-water, so as it had only been unsalted; but, alas! Wherever we could cast our eyes around us, we had no prospect of any relief for our parched throats, but the appearance of pale famine in all her ghastly forms. Add to this, that, under all these infinite wants and sufferings, we were obliged incessantly to toil and labour, without any refreshment or repose. Greater miseries therefore, I say, we endured than will easily be believed the human constitution is capable to sustain, for, in short, we had nothing little but sustenance, strength, and hope.

I have perused several narratives of other unhappy peoples being driven to sad calamities, wants, and dangers, both by sea and land; but among 'em all not one (in which the sufferers are said to survive their misfortunes, if of long duration) wherein there is not an account of some small succour or supply of nutriment, at least sufficient to support nature, bestowed by providence upon them. And where all kinds of ordinary nutriment have finally been wanting, they have often turned anthropophagi, and fed on one another. Whereas, blessed by God! we, though immersed in despair, still abhorred all thoughts of such a horrid practice, and submitted many of us to death, without ever muttering a word in favour of that (so much worse than wolfish) unnatural savage custom.

True indeed it is, water we might have enough; but then it must be what was salt, either that out of the sea, or what was strained through the vessels in our own bodies. At length we tried each of these, and, though both proved very odious and nauseous to our palates, we by far preferred the latter, but the misery was, this loathsome drink (even of which we were denied full draughts) did not assuage, but rather increased our thirst. Thus, (if in a relation of this sad nature I may be allowed such freedom) in the words of an excellent poet, may I partly describe our case:

> We laboured with eternal drought,
> And restless, thirsting, rav'd: Our parched throats
> Found no relief, nor heavy eyes repose.
> But found the settled thirst
> Still gnawing.

Well! To go on with my narrative (begging the reader's pardon for this digression); after having sustained another long tiresome night of gloominess and woe, we rejoiced, as much as dead hearts were capable, at the approach of morning light. As soon as we could discern anything distinctly, we looked on our compass; whereby we perceived that the wind (as we had imagined) stood all night on the same point it had done the day foregoing, and appeared likely so to continue. The thick foggy vapour, however, still possessed the air; though it was not quite so troublesome and frightful to us as during the night-season. And as before we had endeavoured all we could to shun the floating islands, so we now all of us looked out as sharp as possible to discover them; hoping for relief only from that which alone had proved our destruction. Miserable case! The use we designed to make of the ice was to suck; for never poor souls had a greater longing for something or other to moisten their dry and burning palates: this being the fourth day since we had drunk anything (besides our own urine, as above) save four drachms of brandy a man. And every person must be sensible, such kind of liquor (had we had a sufficient quantity) would not answer the end of common drinking: nor had we eaten above a biscuit each.

If any should object it to us as a piece of folly to expect such kind of ice, which at best was but the sea-water congealed, should afford a sweeter moisture than the fluid part: I answer, that a misty dew, often intermixed with snow and rain, frequently descending on the waves, already thus condensed, might reasonably be supposed to freeze into a consistence of itself, without incorporating with the salt ice on which it fell. But alas! This cold comfort was also now beyond our reach.

In this miserable condition we continued, making the best of our way, sparing no time, whilst a brisk gale thus favoured our course; conceiving a faint hope we should make the land before night. About five o'clock in the afternoon, the wind began to veer about to the south, and so round to the west; and thereupon ensued a calm, and the fog began to disperse.

Remaining thus long in a state of unparalleled distress and sorrow, all hope that we should be saved was long since taken away. But the black thick vapours, which had so long overspread the ocean, about five o'clock this evening, beginning to disperse, we looked out yarely, and to our exceeding joy discovered land between three and four leagues distant from us, as near as we could guess. The reader may better imagine than I describe what effect this long-desired vision wrought upon us. If he will but reflect upon the overflowings of pleasure which at any time have filled his breast, when awaking from a frightful dream of fancied danger, he may form a faint and imperfect notion of the superabundant tumultuous gladness which inveloped our hearts on this occasion. Certainly a reprieve brought to a condemned person, just on the point of expected execution, could not be more welcome than this happy view was to us. We thought ourselves, as it were, caught up into the third heavens. My own dead heart, I remember, sprung at the comfortable prospect; the only one of that kind we had been blessed with from the birth of our calamity, or at least from the moment of the ships' disappearance, on whose assistance (as before mentioned) we had chiefly relied for safety. 'Twould perhaps be incredible, if I related what strange alteration this pleasing, or rather most ravishing, sight wrought in our countenances, in which the marks of woe and despair had been so long deeply imprinted: nor will it easily be believed what a vast strange supply of vigour it administered to our limbs. A long-unfelt enlivening warmth suddenly diffused itself through all our veins.

The bare appearance of distant probable safety once more roused up our entombed hopes, cheered and animated our drooping spirits, and inspired us with a courage, which, a few minutes before, we thought ourselves utterly incapable of conceiving. The effect was soon visible by our uncommon activity and sprightliness in managing our make-shift tackle and oars. With hearts overwhelmed with joy, and mouths filled with tributary praises of our great deliverer, we eagerly bent our course towards the friendly coast, where our wishes had before been landed.

We were now arrived within three hours sail of the shore, and might have reached it by that time, had providence permitted. But alas! The reader will find himself disappointed, as we the most forlorn abandoned wretches so sadly were, in the expectation of so speedy a release from the unparalleled miseries which had chained us down. No, though we had the goal in our view, we were yet advanced but to the mid-way of our long and woeful race. We had scarce sailed five minutes, after we had made land, ever the wind, which (that little that was stirring) had favoured us before, suddenly sprung up, and chopping about blew directly in our teeth. Hard fate! Well; we put our utmost strength to it (which though seemingly superior to what we felt some hours before, you must needs think, could not be great) and taking in our sail, took our two oars in our hands to row; yet retaining some faint hope we might get into one place or other, though ever so desolate and barren. But what could such starved harrassed creatures do? We, however, joining prayers to our endeavours, used our best efforts, and struggled as hard as possible with the new adversity. Thus we laboured stoutly for the space of an hour; by which time the wind blew off shore so terribly strong, that we lost more ground between two strokes than we could gain in four.

I am reasonably persuaded, scarce a reader of the foregoing part of this tragic history would have imagined, that our prodigious distress would admit of an addition; in as much as we were already loaded with more grievous and ponderous troubles than mere humanity could be supposed to sustain the weight of, considering their long continuance. But, after all, we now laboured under a circumstance more painful and pricking to our minds and thoughts, than all the former ones together. It could not but seem to us, that God had immediately and visibly marked us out as examples of his power and wrath. Such a consideration must needs be most shocking to our consciences, which now begun too justly to reproach us, not only with our repeated affronts and provocations, but our willful forgetfulness of, and independence on, the great God of heaven and earth, whose voice alone both winds and seas obey.

Our condition must be owned to be a very melancholy one before; as how hope (the sheet-anchor of the soul) was lost. But to be deceived with a false or specious hope, could not but aggravate the direfulness of the case. I have heard it repeated, as expressed by an ingenious pen, *What is hell, but to know heaven, and know it beyond our reach?* And certainly, among all the punishments, feigned by the heathen poets, inflicted on the most egregious offenders in *Pluto's* confines, none, with respect to the mind's tortures, can be compared with those of *Tantalus*, who raging with extremity of thirst and famine, is cheated and bantered with a show of plenty, which he cannot possibly attain to the taste of.

The more to increase our sorrows, darkness drew on apace, filling us with most dismal apprehensions. The sea withal began to rage and swell most terribly, and with its hoarse voice threatened to swallow us every moment. The air moreover was insufferably cold; seeming much more sharp and piercing than all we had endured before. Our hearts again sunk like a stone in our bosoms, and the blood was all chilled in our veins; yet, however encompassed with such a variety of wretchedness, or rather a collection or huge mass of afflictions, with respect to mind as well as body, we were forced to lay our boat's head against the sea, incessantly tugging at the oars, as we had done the Sunday night before: not expecting that we should gain ground, but as much as possible to prevent our being again driven out to sea.

Thus we sat, under inexpressible pains of body, and horror of soul; all wet and frozen, shuddering with extremity of cold, *bewailing* our calamitous plight, *gnashing our teeth*; *weep* too indeed we should, but that all our moisture was quite exhausted. Never, I believe, could the wide ocean show such a company of forlorn wretches as it had this night upon its back. Notwithstanding we called often on the God of mercy to support our souls, and preserve us from wicked and fatal resolutions, yet I can truly say, that I believe hardly a man of us but secretly wished each wave that beat against us might become our tomb, and thereby end our lives and intolerable miseries together. We might, more reasonably perhaps than *Cain*, complain, that *our punishment was greater than we could bear*. This seemed to us the longest night we ever knew; and scarce either of us expected to see the morning light; supposing we were all driving into the vaster ocean of eternity. But I, particularly, have reason to adore and praise our almighty preserver, whose strength was sufficient for us, and who made a discovery of his power in our weakness. So that we all survived the tedious darkness, and saw the Wednesday morning breaking in upon us, to our surprise and astonishment, who never expected more to see a glimpse of this world's light.

Wednesday, April 26

The morning being come, the first thing we were concerned about was, in what situation we were. We therefore looked out yare for the land: But, having been driven out so far this night, could but just perceive any appearance of it. This morning died one more of our crew; whose happiness we envied. We tumbled him overboard, as we had done by the former, who, in like manner, had so fortunately escaped the miserable hardships reserved for the survivors.

About ten o'clock this forenoon the wind veered somewhat more westerly, about west-southwest and therefore we lay our boat's bead to the northward. But as the day advanced, the snow and rain together, or a kind of sleet, fell in great abundance upon us. This you might perhaps account most annoying and galling weather; and so indeed, in some respects, we found it; for all parts of our clothes were covered with icicles, and the cold was so extream, and our hands swoln to that degree, that 'twas with much difficulty we discharged 'em from whatever we held therein. But yet we exceedingly rejoiced at it, as a comfortable and benign providence, (being indeed the first true relief we had bestowed upon us) in that we had now some poor means to gratify our eager appetites, by greedily licking up the snow with our tongues, as it descended upon us. The sea-fowls, in numerous flocks, flew frequently about our boat, and often hovered over us. We hoped some of them would have pitched, that we might have caught or knocked them down, to have their warm blood to suck; for the snow was but cold comfort to any of us, and but of short gratification.

As for *eating*, we by this had laid all talk, thought, or desire of that aside. I don't remember to have heard any one complain of hunger after the third day; but each continually wishing for ice, snow, or puddle-water to drink, or but to wash the slime from his parched mouth. For our throats seem'd to be clung together, and every one complain'd grievously of the heart-burn. For my own part, I felt such a scorching pain in my stomach, as tho' a live coal of fire had been laid a-top of my heart.

About four a-clock in the afternoon, one more of our men bid us adieu; death doing him the kind office which she denied to the rest, who most importunately craved her assistance. As soon as his soul was discharged from her wretched prison, we put our united strength (which yet was scarce sufficient) to it, and by degrees tumbled him overboard; expecting soon to follow him, and each wishing his turn might be the next. I verily believe never mortals encountered with such difficulties, or underwent so great calamities before or since.

The land, as we first made it, appeared to me (into whose opinion our master and mate soon enter'd) to be that about the *Bay of Bulls*. The wind continuing still westerly, we at last were gotten within four or five miles of *Cape St. Francis*. But we were reduced to such a pitch of weakness, by so many complicated hardships, for so many days and nights together, without a moment's respite, that neither of us was now able to arise from the place where he sat; and our hands were so benumbed, that we could not hold an oar. To add more to our numberless misfortunes, the wind begun again to blow very strong; whereupon endeavouring to haul down our sail; (which, wanting the conveniency of a block, we had always been obliged some of us to heave after with our arms, by reason that the sea-line before-mentioned, which we made serve for the heilyards and stay, would not run free thro' the hole made in our mast or oar. I say, endeavouring to take in our sail) we brake our mast; being so very feeble, that we could not assist the sail, as we had been wont to do.

Seeing the night drawing on apace upon us, we made a hard shift to work an hole in the blade of another of our oars, with a sharp-pointed knife, as we had done before; and just as it was night sat it for a mast. The wind veering something to the northward, about NW we lay our boat's head to the southward. The snow showers continued all night, more terribly cold than they seemed in the day. The wind blowing strong, we with much difficulty hauled down our sail, and committed our selves entirely to God's providence, to be driven as the waves might chance to toss us.

Thus we sat shivering, and gnashing our teeth, expecting each wave would entomb us in its bowels; one tedious and sorrowful night more; concluding that the coming day must either give us some means of life, or end our protracted and long-spun miseries, by a double death, famine and drowning.

Thursday, April 27

The early morning (being the sixth from the birth of our misfortune) discovered to us another of our people dead. We at such a time should have thought it an unfriendly part to bewail his fate, who should joyfully have accompanied him, had it been the will of the sovereign arbiter of our destinies. We moreover, to our inexpressible grief of heart, found our sea-compass broken: the card, being all wet, would not traverse: And, to fill up the measure of the troubles which constantly pursued us, we had been the foregoing night driven almost out of sight of land; the air withal being so full of cloudy fog, but little wind stirring, and the sun scarce peeping out, that we were at a loss and much perplexed in our thoughts, which side of the land we lay. We remained some considerable time under a sad confusion and uncertainty on this account. We laboured hard to give our last-departed friend a water sepulture, and with great difficulty discharged the boat of its unnecessary and cumbrous load.

It indeed proved pretty fair weather (I mean, free from showers or storms) this morning; there being so little wind stirring, that not a wrinkle was discernable in the ocean's forehead. Could we have enjoyed one clear ray of the sun, we hoped to be able to make a shift to row speedily to land. Now we found the want of use of the absolutely necessary instrument in navigation, the compass. In this melancholy state we lay 'til about noon-tide, when, to our great comfort, the fog begun to disperse, and the sun a little to smile upon us; and moreover a small breeze of air sprung up out of the south east quarter. Sometimes we would row, with that very little strength we had; and at other whiles up with our sail: But when we did sail, we had but one spare

[pages 45-46 are missing]⁵

zed four of our miserable companions. That gentleman, being a jolly robust man, and of uncommon courage, struggled long with the grim tyrant; but the stoutest must yield the victory, at last, tho' they ever so long and manfully maintain the combat. Each of us would willingly have offered ourselves a ransom for him, if such condition might have been obtained; but as we were sensible the best and greatest in such a predicament must stand their own chance, the best proof we could give of our love and grateful respect for him, was to keep his earthly part, and carry it ashore, in order to its internment, if it pleased God either of us should arrive there ourselves. Our mate's son waited on him in his passage thro' the dark vale, whose remains we also resolved not to heave over-board, as we had done by the other four, as a prey for hungry fishes. Our Master well deserved our loves on many accounts; but especially in hazarding his own life for the sake of the general safety. For when our ship was even on the point of sinking, and he had seen all hands on board the boat before him, he ventured into the cabin, then half full of water, and brought thence the bag of bisket, before-mentioned, and threw it into the boat amongst us, before he would yield to our loud and repeated intreaties, of taking refuge therein with us. Such heroic generosity certainly merited better success, and its possessor a better fate had it consisted with the indisputable will of God!

As soon as we had light enough to take a clear distinct view of things, we looked around us for the land; which at length we espied right ahead of us; but a mist overspreading it, we could not certainly tell what land it was. We ran in about two cables length from it; Some said it was one place, and some another; but after a short dispute (for talk we could not maintain long) we supposed it to be that between *Cape Spear* and *Petty Harbour*. Between six and seven of the clock we came a-breast of *Cape Spear*. We found an huge sea going round the Cape, which had like to have swallowed us up; but by God's blessing we escaped or broke thro' the danger, and before a brisk wind stood away from *St. John's Harbour*.

Advancing at length over-against the new Battery at the harbour's mouth, the guard of soldiers then on the watch there hailed us, to know who we were, and whence we came. We made answer, as well as we could, "That we came from the sea: That that day se'ennight we had lost our ship on an island of ice, about 40 or 50 leagues off; and were come thither in our boat." We farther told 'em, "that we came into the boat fifteen souls; but had heaved four dead men over-board some days before; and had yet two more in the like state with us in the boat, *viz.* our master and a young lad." We then desired 'em, for God's sake, to give us a little beer or water to drink. The Serjeant then on duty appeared much affected at our melancholy relation, and took compassion on us, And bidding us bring our boat home to the stairs, he came with two armed soldiers down to us; and stepping into the boat, the wretched spectacles he met with caused a visible alteration in his face. For seeing some in such a manner actually dead, and so many others whom he knew not whether to reckon among the living or dead; scarce any of us able to wag hand or foot, or stir from the places where we lay or sat, the tears forced a passage thro' his eyes, & those of the two soldiers under his command, as doubtless they would from any thing humane, on the same occasion. We still prayed for some or other kind of liquor. Whereupon the Serjeant ordered one of the soldiers to fetch us some beer made of molosses. We thought he tarried a long while, tho' I doubt not he ran for it, and made all possible haste; but, at length we saw him come with three or four canns of beer, and a bottle of wine, which he divided amongst us equally with a little dish. We prayed him to give us some more; but were told, if we drank more, he was afraid it would kill us outright, and therefore he would not venture it.

Having thus a little refreshed ourselves, and gratified our thirsty appetites, we thought it advisable to make the best of our way up the harbour. But being so crippled with the cold, as scarce any of us capable of moving out of the places where we sat, or even to stir hand or foot, we implored leave of the Serjeant for the two soldiers to assist us in our passage; which he readily granted. As we advanced more up the harbour, we had sight of the ships which came out of *Lisbon* in company with us. This *Memorandum* of the Loss of our own, (being the womb from whence all our calamity took birth) forced a sigh from each of our breasts. We concluded to go on board our late Master's brother, Mr. *Henry Manson*. Coming by the ship's side, we found only the cook on board, who was a native of *Guernsey*, but spake the *English* tongue intelligibly enough. He having had knowledge of us, when we were in *Lisbon* together, at first knew not what to make of the surprising object; but having recollected the ideas he had preserved of us, he appeared like a person struck with thunder, his visage for paleness much resembling our own. Perceiving his astonishment, we in few words related our sad disaster, and begged him to give us a little beer, or some other liquor, to drink; for we were not satisfied with what had been bestowed upon us by the charitable soldiers. He instantly fetched us a good bottle of brandy, which passed but to four peoples' mouths, before the contents were exhausted. For my part, tho' my lower members were quite mortified I had yet so much vigour and courage remaining, as by meer strength of arm to draw my self up on board the ship by the entering rope.

We desired the *Guernsey Man* to take their boat and go ashore, to acquaint the harbour with our misfortune, which he immediately did. Coming ashore, the first person he met was Mr. *Philip Stafford*, of *Lympson*, a neighbour and very intimate acquaintance of our Master's, and several gentlemen in his company. Hearing the deplorable account of us, they presently took boat, and came on board. And, notwithstanding they had been in some measure prepared for the encounter, an extream astonishment seized each of 'em at the before-inconceivable misery in which they found us. Mr. *Stafford* seemed as if entranced in a mortal extasy, as soon as he beheld his dear friend, our poor master, void of sense and motion; and with much difficulty yielded to the belief of his being dead. He embraced him, wept over him; then jogged him, and rubbed his temples; kissed him, and begged him for God's sake to speak to him; vainly imagining to be able to bring him back to life by meer dint of cries and wailings. I assure the reader, every action of that gentleman was so very moving and pathetick, that however possess'd with a sense of our own misfortunes, we could not but sympathize and keep time with his (certainly unfeigned) sorrow and lamentations. Finding at length the vanity of his endeavours to recall the dear departed spirit of his friend, Mr. *Stafford* yielded to the reasons and intreaties of his company, and gave over his loud exclamations; the falling tears still witnessing the silent inward grief which hung about his heart. He demanded of us, as well as he could speak, when our Master died? We told him, about day-break that very morning. He shook his head; as much as to say, how he was grieved that he could not hold out a few hours longer, after having endured so many days and nights of misery, to enjoy his share of the relief he so well deserved, and had laboured with us for.

It was unanimously agreed upon by the gentlemen that we should be set ashore, the better to be taken care of. We were each of us helped out of the boat; and some of us carried upon hand-barrows up to *Gilbert Jane's* house; and others led between two men, who appeared to the spectators as if they walked on stilts. After we had been warmed by the fire, put on dry cloaths, (which masters of ships and other good people, in charity had bestowed upon us) and a little refreshing ourselves with a small modicum of victuals and drink, we were sent to different houses, and put to bed, to see after we had slept awhile, what the event would prove.

The harbour, according to each man's several station and ability, contributed generously towards our relief, each master of a ship giving a guinea, and every private person one shilling. There were three or four surgeons then in the place, who were sedulously employed about the care of us, to preserve life and limbs, by soaking our legs and hands in warm baths prepared for the purpose: But found several of us had our limbs so mortified, that no method would be effectual to save our lives without amputation. One poor wretch was invaded with a deadness up to his very waste, and his privy members so rotten, that they dropped short off from his body. I had first both my Feet, and soon after both my legs cut off. Another lost one of his; [And] a third (who is yet living) was found to have his feet as it were burnt as black as a coal. But by the blessing of God on the means applied to us, our lives were preserved, to praise his name among the sons of men. Some, not condescending to be dismembered, soon died; and others who underwent the operation speedily followed them. So that of fifteen persons who had taken shelter in the boat, six died on the sea, and other six submitted to fate soon after their being brought on shore. We the three survivors are yet under God's protection in the land of the living. Two of us dwell now at *Exmouth*, and the other is now actually engaged in the sea service on the same Coast, and I think at the same harbour; from whence he is speedily expected home. Our names are *John Salter* of *Cockwood*, *Edward Harris* of *Exmouth*, and (my own) *Henry Treby* of the same Place.

After we had been some time in the harbour, we had discourse with the masters of the four ships, which we had seen the day after we had lost our own; and they told us they were then about 45 leagues distant from the land. We told 'em what terrible nights of snow, and cold, and wind, we had following the Sunday, Tuesday, and Wednesday. They admired (very justly) how so small a boat as ours was could live in such storms and tempests as we met with. They moreover assured us, "That the Sunday night some of them were put under their two coasts, and some reefed their coasts; and that they arrived at *St. John's* Harbour's mouth the Tuesday four a-clock in the afternoon; when the wind blew out of the harbour so very strong, that they were obliged to warp in; and that as the water fell from their cables upon the deck, it instantly froze, that the ice at length was several inches thick."

I remained in the land near five months after my legs were cut off, before I could get passage home for *England*, and the mean while endured an incredible deal of pain and misery. And being at length got on board a ship bound for my own country, and arrived within 30 leagues of the Isle of *Scilly*, being then Sunday morning, *November* the 5th, a *French* privateer came up with us, took us, (the Wind then about WSW) and carried us away for *Morlaix* in *France*; and the Wednesday morning had gotten a pilot to carry us in over the bar. But Providence favoured us when we least expected it; there coming, in the nick, two privateers of *Guernsey* from that shore, and retook us, together with the enemy our keepers. We arrived at *Guernsey* the next morning; the inhabitants of which island were very kind and hospitable; among whom I remained other three weeks, and then happily got passage home for *Exmouth*, on board *Mr. Abraham Winter* of *Topsham*, where I soon arrived among my friends, who received me with tears, in the cause of which grief and joy had an equal share.

God's Name be prais'd! Amen.

NOTES

1. *A Narrative of the Shipwreck and Distress Suffer'd By Mr. Thomas Manson, of Lympson in Devon, and his Ship's Crew, near the Coast of Newfoundland, in the Year 1704* (London: Andrew Brice, 1724).
2. Thomas Bray, *A Memorial Representing the Present State of Religion on the Continent of North America* (London: William Downing, 1700); C. Grant Head, *Eighteenth Century Newfoundland* (Toronto: McClelland and Stewart, 1976).
3. For an overview see Gerald S. Graham, "Britain's Defence of Newfoundland," *Canadian Historical Review* 23, 3 (September 1942): 260-79; W. Gordon Handcock, "The West Country Migrations to Newfoundland," *Bulletin of Canadian Studies* 5, 1 (April 1981): 5-24.
4. W.B. Stephens, "The West-Country Ports and the Struggle for the Newfoundland Fisheries in the Seventeenth Century," in *Report and Transactions of the Devonshire Association for the Advancement of Science, Literature and Art* (1950), 95-97.
5. These pages are missing from the only copy of this narrative known to exist.

4

ACCOUNT OF A WONDERFUL ESCAPE
FROM THE EFFECTS OF A STORM IN A JOURNEY
OVER THE FROZEN SEA IN NORTH AMERICA (1782)[1]
WILLIAM TURNER [?]

The following narrative is not about shipwreck, but about a common marine phenomenon in this region that carries the potential for disaster: the break-up of coastal ice into a groundswell. In introducing the account, the unnamed editor of *Wonderful Escapes,* in which this account was published, marvelled at Labrador's climate, "so excessively cold during the winter, that wine becomes frozen into a solid mass, and the very breath falls on the blankets of a bed in the form of a hoar frost." He also commented on the Esquimaux [Inuit], and their mode of travel, the dogsled over the ice and snow. In the late winter, however, few dared to risk travelling by dog-team along the coast without great vigilance, as these European travellers found out.

An unidentified trader left Nain with a few helpers to visit Okak in distant northern Labrador. They travelled by dogsled over the frozen sea. A groundswell underneath the ice unexpectedly burst as the travellers rested, raising large fields of ice out of the water and smashing them against the shore. When the trader realized that a break-up was imminent, the group rushed to land, only to be turned back by the crashing sea ice. Their journey delayed by the rugged coast and lack of ice, they managed to endure until the ice returned, but only with the assistance of local Inuit who constructed a "snowhouse," or igloo, which they happily shared. This is not a story of the "noble savage," that idealized figure that emerged during the Enlightenment. Rather, it explores the subtheme of mutual dependency and co-operation and reveals a shared humanity, in the form of a healthy fear of the sea.

The editor identifies the narrator who experienced the ice break-up only as "an Englishman who had emigrated to America," and there is little more to aid in his identification except that he calls his friend Samuel. He was probably William Turner (1743-1804),[2] who made a trip to Labrador in 1782 with Samuel Liebisch (1739-1809). Liebisch, the future Moravian bishop, was then Superintendent at Nain, before leaving the next year for Germany to become a member of the United Elders Conference. Traders like Turner do not appear to have been Moravians; certainly this account makes no religious references. He was, however, part of the Ship's Company to the Society for the Furtherance of the Gospel (SFG), set up separately from the missionary branch of the Moravians; they eventually merged in 1796.

Turner and the Ship's Company were contemporaries of the most famous Labrador trader of the period, George Cartwright, whose published diaries drew attention to the area in his day.[3] Initially, one wonders if Cartwright, who was himself affected by marine mishaps, might not have written this account. Cartwright had returned to England in 1779 and had planned to return to this region shortly after, but in 1781 his ship, the *Countess of Effingham*, was "dashed to pieces" in Trinity Bay. His replacement schooner was also wrecked and then captured. Cartwright's problems were further compounded by financial difficulties and the death of his father. He therefore did not return to Labrador until 1783. So Turner, not Cartwright, was the likely author of this story.

What is also significant about this narrative, besides the terror of the sea, is the nature of the relations between Inuit and Europeans, and the way the life of the Inuit was characterized. By the late eighteenth century, when this narrative was written, the impact of European encounter on the native populations was considerable and had already taken effect over a long period of time.[4] Euro-Americans had become the traders and livyers, while the Hopedale Inuit acted as middlemen. The Okak trading store saw Inuit exchanging their baleen (whale-bone), blubber, and skins for iron tools, utensils, cloth, and rope. In part, the mission was established by the Moravians to dissuade native peoples from selling their wares to rival posts in southern Labrador. Because of the church's policy and its antipathy to secular trade, this may explain why the narrator makes no reference to the activities of several rival English trading companies from West Country England that had established posts along the south and central coast of Labrador, but south of the Moravian posts: Hunt and Henley Company, John Slade and Company, or King and Larmour and Company. Turner's depiction therefore wrongly reinforces the image of the isolation of the Inuit and their dependency on the Ship's Company for goods.

Finally, though this story would suggest that Labrador was forever cold and that the Inuit lived their lives in igloos, nothing could be further from the truth. Their lives were shaped by the seasons and by seasonal work. In the summers, when they hunted caribou, they moved inland and lived in tents.[5] From mid-October to mid-December Inuit bands inhabited semipermanent sod houses and engaged in whaling, then, until freeze-up, sealing from their kayaks. In winter, usually from mid-December to mid-April, they lived in these temporary snow houses, the igloos, and hunted seals detected through their breathing holes in the ice, as well as walrus, birds, and char. In the spring, usually April, when the ice quickly broke apart, they returned to their tents.

HAVING OCCASION TO VISIT OKKAK [Okak], about 150 English miles distant from Nain, my friend Samuel and I, with three other men, a woman and a child, left Nain on the 11th of March 1782, early in the morning, with very clear weather, the stars shining with uncommon lustre. Our company were in two sledges: An Esquimaux sledge is drawn by a species of dog not unlike a wolf in shape. Like them, they never bark, but howl disagreeably. They are kept by the Esquimaux in greater packs or teams, in proportion to the affluence of their master. They quietly submit to be harnessed for their work, and are treated with little mercy by the Esquimaux, who make them do hard duty for the small quantity of food they allow them. This consists chiefly of offal, old skins, entrails, such parts of whale-flesh as are unfit for other use, &c. &c. And if they are not provided with this kind of dog's meat, they suffer them to go and seek dead fish and muscles [sic] upon the beach.

When pinched with hunger, they will swallow almost any thing, and on a journey it is necessary to secure the harness within the snow-house over night, lest by devouring it, they should render it impossible to proceed in the morning. When the travellers arrive at their night quarters, and the dogs are unharnessed, they are left to

burrow in the snow, where they please, and in the morning are sure to
come at their driver's call, when they receive some food. Their
strength and speed, even with a hungry stomach, are astonishing. In
fastening them to the sledge, care is taken not to let them go abreast.
They are tied by separate thongs, of unequal lengths, to a horizontal
bar in the fore-part of the sledge; an old knowing-one leads the way,
running 10 or 20 paces a-head, directed by the driver's whip, which is
of great length, and can be well managed only by an Esquimaux. The
other dogs follow like a flock of sheep. If one of them receives a lash,
he generally bites his neighbour, and the bite goes round.

But to return to our expedition; we were all in good spirits, and
appearances being in our favour we hoped to reach Okkak in safety
in two or three days. The track over the frozen sea* was in the best
possible order, and we went with ease at the rate of six or seven miles
an hour. After we had passed the islands in the bay of Nain, we kept
at a considerable distance from the coast; both to gain the smoothest
part of the ice, and to weather the high promontory of Keglapeit
[Kiglapait]. About 8 o'clock we met a sledge with Esquimaux turning
in from the sea. After the usual salutation, the Esquimaux alighting,
held some conversation, as is their general practice, the result of
which was, that some hints were thrown out by the strange
Esquimaux, that it would be better to return. However, as we saw no
reason whatever for it, and only suspected that the Esquimaux wished
to enjoy the company of their friends a little longer, we proceeded.
After some time, the Esquimaux who drove the sledges, hinted that
there was a ground swell** under the ice. It was hardly perceptible,
except on lying down and applying the ear close to the ice, when a
hollow disagreeable grating and roaring noise was heard, as if
ascending from the abyss. The weather remained clear, except towards
the East, where a bank of light clouds appeared, interspersed with
some dark streaks. But the wind being strong from the North West,
nothing less than a sudden change of weather was expected. The Sun
had now reached its height, and there was as yet little or no alteration
in the appearance of the sky. But the motion of the sea, under the ice,

---

* The Sea in this country is frozen over in winter [original editor's
comment].

** A ground swell is a motion of the sea under the frozen part of it, which
can be easily heard by those who stand on the ice [original editor's
comment].

had grown more perceptible, so as rather to alarm us, and we began to think it prudent to keep close to the shore. The ice had cracks and large openings in many places, some of which formed chasms of one or two feet wide, but as they are not uncommon even in its best state, and the dogs easily lept over them, the sledge following without danger, they are terrible only to new comers.

As soon as the sun declined towards the West, the wind increased and rose to a storm: the bank of clouds from the East began to ascend, and the dark streaks to put themselves in motion against the wind. The snow was violently driven about by partial whirlwinds, both on the ice, and from off the peaks of the high mountains, and filled the air. At the same time, the ground swell had increased so much, that its effects upon the ice became very extraordinary and alarming. The sledges, instead of gliding along smoothly upon an even surface, sometimes ran with violence after the dogs, and shortly after seemed with difficulty to ascend the rising hill, for the elasticity of so vast a body of ice, of many leagues square, supported by a troubled sea, though in some places three or four yards in thickness, would in some degree occasion a waving motion, not unlike that of a sheet of paper accommodating itself to the surface of a rippling stream. Noises were now likewise distinctly heard in many directions, like the report of cannon, owing to the bursting of the ice at some distance.

The Esquimaux therefore drove with all haste towards the shore, intending to take up their night-quarters on the south side of the Nivak; but as it plainly appeared that the ice would break and disperse in the open sea, one of the Esquimaux advised to push forward to the north of the Nivak, from whence he hoped the ice to Okkak might still remain entire. To this proposal we all agreed, but when the sledges approached the coast, the prospect before us was truly terrific. The ice having broken loose from the rocks, was forced up and down dashing and breaking into a thousand pieces against the precipices, with a tremendous noise; which, added to the raging of the wind, and the snow drifting about in the air, deprived us almost of the power of seeing any thing distinctly.

To make the land at any risk, was now the only hope left; but it was with the utmost difficulty, the frighted [sic] dogs could be forced forward, the whole body of the ice sinking frequently below the surface of the rocks, then rising above it. As the only moment to land was that, when it gained the level of the coast, the attempt was extremely nice and hazardous; it however providentially succeeded; both sledges gained the shore, and were drawn up the beach with much difficulty.

We had hardly time to reflect with gratitude on our safety, when that part of the ice, from which we had just now made good our landing, burst asunder, and the water forcing itself from below, covered and precipitated it into the sea. In an instant, as if by a giant signal given, the whole mass of ice, extending for several miles from the coast, as far as the eye could reach, began to burst and be overwhelmed by the immense waves. The sight was tremendous and awfully grand; the large fields of ice raising themselves out of the water, striking against each other, and plunging into the deep, with a violence not to be described, and a noise like the discharge of innumerable batteries of heavy guns. The darkness of the night, the roaring of the sea, and the dashing of the waves and ice against the rocks, filled us with sensations of awe and horror, so as almost to deprive us of the power of utterance. We stood overwhelmed with astonishment at our miraculous escape, and even the heathen Esquimaux expressed gratitude for their deliverance.

The Esquimaux now began to build a snow-house, about thirty yards from the beach: but before they had finished their work, the waves reached the place where the sledges were secured, and they were with difficulty saved from being washed into the sea.

About nine o'clock, all of us crept into the snow-house, grateful for this place of refuge, for the wind was piercing cold, and so violent, that it required great strength to be able to stand against it.

Before we entered into this habitation, we could not help once more turning to the sea, which was now free from ice, and beheld with horror, mingled with gratitude for our safety, the enormous waves, driving furiously before the wind, like huge castles, and approaching the shore, where with dreadful noise, they dashed against the rocks, foaming and filling the air with the spray. We now took our supper, and lay down to rest about ten o'clock. We lay so close, that if any one stirred, his neighbours were roused by it. The Esquimaux were soon fast asleep, but my friend Samuel and I could not get any rest, partly on account of the dreadful roaring of the wind and sea, and partly owing to sore throats which gave us great pain.

Our watchfulness proved the deliverance of the whole party from sudden destruction. About two o'clock my friend perceived some salt water to drop from the roof of the snow-house upon his lips. Though rather alarmed on tasting the salt, which could not proceed from a common spray, he lay quiet, till the same dropping being more frequently repeated, just as he was about to give the alarm, on a sudden a tremendous surf broke close to the house, discharging a quantity of water into it; a second soon followed, and carried away the slab of snow placed as a door before the entrance. We immediately called aloud to the sleeping Esquimaux to rise and quit the place. They jumped up in an instant; one of them with a large knife cut a passage through the side of the house, and each seizing some part of the baggage, it was thrown out upon a higher part of the beach. We assisted the Esquimaux: the woman and child fled to a neighbouring eminence, where they were wrapt up by the Esquimaux in a large skin, and placed in shelter behind a rock, for it was impossible to stand against the wind, snow, and sleet. Scarcely had we retreated to this eminence, when an enormous wave carried away the whole house; but nothing of consequence was lost.

We now found ourselves a second time delivered from the most imminent danger of death; but the remaining part of the night, before the Esquimaux could seek and find a safer place for a snow-house, were hours of great trial to mind and body, and filled every one with painful reflections. Before the day dawned, the Esquimaux cut a hole into a large drift of snow to secure the woman and child.

As soon as it was light they built another snow-house, and miserable as such an habitation is at all times, were glad to creep into it. It was about eight feet square, and six or seven feet high. We now congratulated each other on our deliverance, but found ourselves in miserable plight. My friend and I had taken but a small stock of provisions with us, merely sufficient for the short journey to Okkak. The Esquimaux had nothing at all. We were obliged therefore to divide our small stock into daily portions, especially as there appeared no hopes of soon quitting this place and reaching any dwelling. Only two ways were left for this purpose; either to attempt the land passage across a wild and unfrequented mountain, or wait for a new ice track over the sea, which it would require much time to form; we therefore resolved to serve out no more than one biscuit and a half every day.

But as this would not by any means satisfy an Esquimaux stomach, we offered to give one of our dogs to be killed for them, on condition that in case distress obliged us to resort again to that expedient, the next dog killed should be one of the Esquimaux team. They replied that they should be glad of it, if they had a kettle to boil the flesh in, but as that was not the case, they must even suffer hunger, for they could not, even now, eat dog's flesh in its raw state. We now remained in the snow-house resigned to our situation, and even our rough heathen companions declared, that it was proper to be thankful that they were still alive, adding, that if they had remained a very little longer upon the ice, all their bones would have been broken to pieces in a short time.

Towards noon of the 13th the weather cleared up, and the sea was seen as far as the eye could reach quite free from ice. Some of the Esquimaux went up the hills and returned with the disagreeable news that not a morsel of ice was to be seen even from thence, in any direction, and that it had even been forced away from the coast at Nuasornak. They were, therefore, of opinion that we could do nothing but force our way across the mountain.

This day one of the Esquimaux complained much of hunger, probably to obtain from us a larger portion than the common allowance. We represented to him that we had no more ourselves, and reproved him for his impatience. Whenever the victuals were distributed, he always swallowed his portion very greedily, and put out his hand for what he saw we had left, but was easily kept by serious reproof from any further attempt. The Esquimaux ate this day an old sack made of fish skin, which proved indeed a dry and miserable dish. Whilst they were at this singular meal, they kept repeating in a low humming tone, "you were a sack a little time ago, and now you are food for us." Towards evening, some flakes of ice were discovered towards the west, and on the 14th in the morning, the sea was covered with them. But the weather was again very strong, and the Esquimaux could not quit the snow-house, which made them low spirited and melancholy. One of them suggested, that it would be well to attempt to make good weather; by which he meant, to practice his art as a Sorcerer, to make the weather good: but we opposed it; I told him his heathenish practices were of no use, but that the weather would become favourable as soon as it should please God.

This day the Esquimaux began to eat a filthy and worn out skin, which had served them for a mattress.

On the 15th, the weather continued extremely boisterous, and the Esquimaux appeared every now and then to sink under disappointment. But they possess one good quality, namely, a power of going to sleep when they please, and if need be, they will sleep for days and nights together.

In the evening, the sky became clear, and our hopes revived. Some of the Esquimaux went up the hills again, and brought word that the ice had acquired a considerable degree of solidity, and might soon be fit for use. The poor dogs had meanwhile fasted for nearly four days, but now in the prospect of a speedy release, we allowed to each a few morsels of food.

The temperature having been rather mild, it occasioned a new source of distress, for by the warm breath of the inhabitants, the roof of the snow-house got to be in a melting state, which occasioned a continual dropping, and by degrees made every thing soaking wet. We considered this the greatest hardship we had to endure, for we had not a dry thread about us, nor a dry place to lie down in.

Early on the 16th day the sky cleared, but the fine particles of snow were driven about like clouds. Two of the Esquimaux determined to pursue their journey to Okkak by the way of Nuasornak, and set out with the wind and the snow full in their faces. We could not resolve to accompany them, and yet our present distress dictated the necessity of venturing something to reach the habitations of men: we were afraid of passing over the newly frozen sea under the promontory, and could not immediately determine what to do. We went out again to examine the ice; and having strong hopes that it would hold, came at last to a resolution to return to Nain, and endeavour to retrace our perilous journey.

On the 17th the wind had considerably increased, with heavy showers of snow and sleet, but we set off at half past ten o'clock in the fore-noon, and about one o'clock we were out of danger and reached the bay. Here we found a good track upon smooth ice, and made a meal of the remnant of our provisions. Thus refreshed, we resolved to proceed without stopping, until we reached Nain, where we arrived at twelve o'clock at night.

Our friends at Nain rejoiced exceedingly to see us return, for they had been much terrified by several hints of the Esquimaux, who first met us going out to sea, and who in their own obscure way, had endeavoured to warn us of the danger of the ground swell. One of the Esquimaux who had made some article of dress for Samuel, addressed his wife in the following manner: "I should be glad of the payment for my work." "Wait a little, and when my husband returns he will settle with you, for I am unacquainted with the bargain made between you." "Samuel," replied the Esquimaux "will not return." "How not return! What makes you say so?" After some pause, the Esquimaux replied in a low tone, "Samuel and his companions are no more! All their bones are broken, and in the stomachs of the sharks." Terrified at this alarming account, my friend's wife called in the rest of her family, and the Esquimaux was examined as to his meaning; but his answers were little less obscure. He seemed so certain of our destruction, that he was with difficulty prevailed on to wait some time for our return. He could not believe that we could have escaped the effects of so furious a tempest, considering the course we had taken.

NOTES

1. "Account Of *A Wonderful Escape* From The Effects of A Storm In A Journey Over The Frozen Sea In North America," in *Wonderful Escapes!* (Dublin: Brett Smith, 1818), 148-62.
2. I would like to thank the Moravian expert, Dr. Hans Rollmann, Department of Religious Studies, Memorial University of Newfoundland and Labrador, for this information.
3. Charles W. Townsend, ed., *Captain Cartwright and His Labrador Journal* (Boston: Dana Estes, 1911), 292-94.
4. William W. Fitzhugh, ed., *Cultures in Contact: The Impact of European Contacts on Native American Cultural Institutions,* A.D. *1000-1800* (Washington and London: Smithsonian Institution Press, 1985), 19-43, 99-106; Susan A. Kaplan, "European Goods and Socio-Economic Change in Early Labrador Inuit Society," in *ibid.,* 45-69; François Trudel, "The Inuit of Southern Labrador and the Development of French Sedentary Fisheries (1700-1760)," in *Papers from the Fourth Annual Congress, 1977, Canadian Ethnology Society,* ed. Richard A. Preston (Ottawa: National Museums of Canada, 1978), 99-121.

5. J. Garth Taylor, "Moravian Mission Influence on Labrador Inuit Subsistence: 1776-1830," in D.A. Muise, ed., *Approaches to Native History in Canada* (Ottawa: National Museum of Man, 1977), 16-29. See also Charles A. Martijn, "The Inuit of Southern Quebec-Labrador: A Rejoinder to Garth Taylor," *Études/Inuit/Studies* 4 (1980): 194-98. It becomes evident from the discussion of the Inuit presence in southern Quebec and Labrador that migration to the island of Newfoundland had gone on for a long time.

5

VESSELS IN THE SERVICE OF THE MORAVIAN
MISSION ON THE COAST OF LABRADOR,
AND SOME SHIPWRECKS (1770-1877)[1]

AUTHOR UNKNOWN

The Moravians, also known as Unitas Fratrum and Herrnhuter, owe their religious origins to Jan Hus in the fifteenth century, making them reputedly the oldest Protestant sect. Forced out of Czechoslovakia by religious persecution, they moved to Berthelsdorf, Saxony, in 1722, under the patronage of Count Nickolas Ludwig von Zinzendorf. Believers in pietism, work, love, salvation, communal living, and a mystical relationship to God, this community sent forth missionaries to the New World, to such places as Greenland, Pennsylvania, Upper Canada, and Labrador, in order to convert heathens.[2] While much has been written about the Moravian arrival in Labrador,[3] their sea travels while carrying out their proselytizing activities are less commonly known. This extract on the Moravians' encounters with "outrageous seas" describes the origin and nature of the various ships in the sect's service during the later period, between 1816 and the late nineteenth century.

The dangers of the Newfoundland waters were evident from the early beginnings of the mission. Shipwreck, religious activity, and presupposed divine intervention marked the Moravian presence in Labrador. In 1774 the Moravian sloop *Amity* was wrecked and two missionaries lost. Native intervention played a role when a local Inuit piloted the survivors, including the mission leader Jens Haven, to safety in his kayak.[4] In 1851 and 1858, "Christian Eskimos" helped

Moravian and Hudson's Bay Company shipwreck survivors, "a striking testimony to the value of the instruction they had received, and the influence of the Gospel upon their hearts and lives." Based on the order's *Periodical Accounts*, this narrative includes descriptions of a few wrecks, some close calls, and other interesting detail for the maritime historian, including delivery of the mail by "post-kayak."

Such experiences culminated in the writing of a Moravian hymn, included here, on the centenary of the Society for the Furtherance of the Gospel (1841). Music was central to Moravian religious practices, to such an extent that various choirs virtually served as surrogate families among its membership. The hymn is also an artifact of the nineteenth-century religious, maritime, and cultural history of the province, and as one of the many sea and shipwreck ballads, a part of Newfoundland and Labrador's folklore and a distinct musical tradition produced by these waters.[5]

⚓

After spending the winter in England, Brother and Sister Kmoch returned to Labrador the following year, accompanied by the Brethern Korner and Beck. They were, however, destined to encounter perils on their passage out, exceeding in number and in magnitude even those which had rendered the voyage of 1816 so memorable. As a lively and correct account of the dangers, which are more or less attendant on Arctic navigation, even in latitudes much lower than those which have recently witnessed the achievements and endurances of our gallant countrymen, and as a record of the wonderful help and protection vouchsafed by the Lord to His feeble servants, the following extracts from the Journal of Brother Kmoch cannot fail to be acceptable to our readers. Graphic in themselves, and exhibiting considerable power of observation and description, they afford a pleasing insight into the character of the writer, who, as the patriarch of the Labrador Mission, at the age of more than fourscore years, entered the heavenly rest.

After describing the voyage of the Jemima *to the* Stromness, *whence she sailed on the 14th of June, and the favourable passage across the Atlantic, up to the close of the month, Brother Kmoch proceeds:*

BETWEEN THE 4TH AND 5TH OF JULY, we heard and saw many ice-birds. This bird is about the size of a starling, black, with white and yellow spots, and is met with about 200 English miles from the

Labrador coast. When the sailors hear it, they know that they are not far from ice. It flies about a ship chiefly in the night, and is known by its singular voice, which resembles a loud laugh.

7th. The morning was cold and rainy. In all directions, drift-ice was to be seen. In the afternoon it cleared up a little, and we entered an opening in the ice, looking like a bay. The continual rustling and roaring of the ice reminded us of the noise made by the carriages in the streets of London, when one is standing in the golden gallery of St. Paul's cathedral. The mountains and large flakes of ice take all manner of singular forms, some resembling castles, others churches, waggons, and even creatures of various descriptions. As we or they changed positions, the same objects acquired a quite different appearance; and what had before appeared like a church, looked like a huge floating monster. Sitting on deck, and contemplating these wonderful works of God, I almost lost myself in endeavouring to solve the question, "for what purpose these exhibitions are made, when so few can behold them, as they so soon vanish, by returning to their former fluid and undefined state." But surely everything is done with design, though short-sighted man cannot comprehend it. Having in vain exerted ourselves to penetrate through the ice, we returned at night into the open sea.

14th. Land was discovered ahead. It was the coast of Labrador, sixty or eighty miles south of Hopedale. We were close to the ice, and as a small opening presented itself, the captain ventured to push in, hoping, if he could penetrate, to find open water between the ice and the coast. For some time we got nearer to the land, but were obliged at night to fasten the ship with two grapnels to a large field. This was elevated between five and six feet above the water's edge, and between fifty and sixty feet in thickness below it. It might be 300 feet in diameter, flat at the top, and as smooth as a meadow covered with snow. The wind has but little power over such huge masses, and they move very slowly with the current. There are small streams and pools of fresh water found in all those large pieces. Our situation now defended us against the smaller flakes, which rushed by and were turned off by the large field, without reaching the ship. We were all well pleased with our place of refuge, and lay here three whole days, with the brightest weather, and as safe as in the most commodious haven; but I cannot say that I felt easy, though I hid my anxiety from the party. I feared that a gale of wind might overtake us in this

situation, and carry fields larger than that in which we lay, when the
most dreadful consequences might ensue; and the sequel proved that
I was not much mistaken.

On the 17th, the wind came round to the south, and we conceived
fresh hopes of the way being rendered open for us.

18th. The weather was clear, and the wind in our favour; we
therefore took up our grapnel, got clear of our floating haven, and
again endeavoured to penetrate through some small openings. Both
we and the ship's company were peculiarly impressed with gratitude
for the protection and rest we had enjoyed, and the warmth of a
summer's sun felt very comfortable among these masses of ice. The
clearness of the atmosphere today caused them to appear singularly
picturesque. It seemed as if we were surrounded by immense white
walls and towers. In the afternoon, we had penetrated to the open
water, between the ice and the land, but we durst not venture nearer,
as the sea is here full of sunken rocks, and the captain knew of no
harbour on this part of the coast. Having found another large piece
of ice convenient for the purpose, we fastened the ship to it. In the
evening, a fog overspread us from the north-east, and we were again
quite surrounded by ice, which, however, was soon after dispersed by
a strong north-west wind.

In the night, between the 19th and 20th, we were driven back
by a strong current to nearly the same situation we had left on the
17th, only somewhat nearer the coast. On the 20th, the morning was
fine, and we vainly endeavoured to get clear, but towards evening the
sky lowered and it grew very dark. The air also felt so oppressive that
we all went to bed, and every one of us was troubled with uneasy
dreams. At midnight we heard a great noise on deck. We hastened
thither to know the cause, and found the ship driving fast towards a
huge ice mountain, on which we expected every moment to suffer
shipwreck. The sailors exerted themselves to the utmost, but it was
by God's merciful providence alone that we were saved. The night
was exceedingly cold with rain, and the poor people suffered much.
We were now driven to and fro at the mercy of the ice, till one in the
morning, when we succeeded in fastening the ship again to a large
field. But all this was only the prelude to greater terrors. Deliverance
from danger is so gratifying, that it raises one's spirits above the
common level. We made a hearty breakfast, and retired again into our
cabins. At one o'clock the cook, in his usual boisterous way, aroused

us by announcing dinner, and putting a large piece of pork and a huge pudding upon the table, of which we partook with a good appetite, but in silence, every one seemingly buried in thought, or only half awake. Shortly after, the wind changed to the north-east and north, increasing gradually, till it turned into a furious storm. Top-masts were lowered, and everything done to ease the ship. We now saw an immense ice-mountain at a distance, towards which we were driving, without the power of turning aside. Between six and seven, we were again roused by a great outcry on deck. We ran up, and saw our ship, with the field to which we were fast, with great swiftness approaching towards the mountain; nor did there appear the smallest hope of escaping being crushed to atoms between it and the field. However, by veering out as much cable as we could, the ship got to such a distance, that the mountain passed through between us and the field. We all cried fervently to the Lord for speedy help in this most perilous situation, for if we had but touched the mountain, we must have been instantly destroyed. One of our cables was broken, and we lost a grapnel; the ship also sustained some damage. But we were now left to the mercy of the storm and current, both of which were violent; and exposed likewise to the large fields of ice, which floated all around us, being from ten to twenty feet in thickness. The following night was dreadfully dark, the heavens covered with the blackest clouds driven by a furious wind, the roaring and the howling of the ice as it moved along, the fields shoving and dashing against each other, were truly terrible. A fender was made of a large beam, suspended by ropes to the ship's sides, to secure her in some measure from the ice; but the ropes were soon cut by its sharp edges and we lost the fender. Repeated attempts were now made to make the ship again fast to some large field; and the second mate, a clever young man, full of spirit and willingness, swung himself several times off, and upon such fields as approached us, endeavouring to fix a grapnel to them, but in vain, and we even lost another grapnel on this occasion. The storm indeed dispersed the ice, and made openings in several places; but our situation was thereby rendered only still more alarming, for when the ship got into open water, her motion became more rapid by the power of the wind, and consequently the blows she received from the ice more violent. Whenever therefore we perceived a field of ice through the gloom, towards which we were hurried, nothing appeared more probable, than that the violence of the shock would determine our fate, and be attended with immediate destruction to the vessel. Such shocks were repeated every five or ten minutes, and sometimes oftener, and the longer she remained exposed to the wind, the more violently she ran against the sharp edges and spits of the ice, not having any power to avoid them. After every stroke, we tried the pumps, to find whether we had sprung a leak; but the Lord kept His hand over us, and preserved us in a manner almost miraculous. In this awful situation, we offered up fervent prayers to Him, who alone is able to save, and besought Him, that, if it were His divine will that we should end our lives among the ice, He would, for the sake of His precious merits, soon take us home to Himself, nor let us die a miserable death from cold and hunger, floating about in this boisterous ocean.

It is impossible to describe all the horrors of this eventful night, in which we expected every approaching ice-field to be fraught with death. We were full ten hours in this dreadful situation, till about six in the morning, when we were driven into open water, not far from the coast. We could hardly believe that we had got clear of the ice; all seemed as a dream. We now ventured to carry some sail, with a view to bear up against the wind. The ship had become leaky, and we were obliged to keep the pump a-going, with only about ten minutes rest at a time. Both the sailors and we were thereby so much exhausted, that whenever any one sat down, he immediately fell asleep.

During the afternoon, the wind abated and towards evening it fell calm. A thick mist ensued, which, however, soon dispersed, when we found ourselves near a high rock, towards which the current was fast carrying us. We were now in great danger of suffering shipwreck among the rocks, but by God's mercy, the good management of our captain succeeded in steering clear of them; and after sunset, the heavens were free from clouds. A magnificent northern light illumined in the horizon, and as we were again among floating pieces of ice, its brightness enabled us to avoid them. I retired to rest, but, after midnight, was roused by the cracking noise made by the ice against the sides of the vessel. In an instant, I was on deck, and found that we were forcing our way through a quantity of floating ice, out of which we soon got again into open water. The wind also turned in our favour, and carried us swiftly forward towards the Hopedale shore. Every one on board was again in full expectation of soon reaching the end of our voyage, and ready to forget all former troubles. But alas, arriving at the same spot from which we had been driven yesterday, we found our way anew blocked up with a vast quantity of ice. The wind also drove us irresistibly towards it. We were now in a great dilemma. If we went between the islands, where the sea is full of sunken rocks, we were in danger of striking upon one of them, and being instantly lost; again, if we ventured into the ice, it was doubtful whether the ship would bear many more such shocks as she had received. At length, the former measure was determined on, as, in case of any mishap, there might be some possibility of escaping to shore.

After encountering a succession of further perils and disappointments for three additional weeks, the Jemima *was brought safely into Hopedale harbour on the 9th of August.*

It being considered necessary, in prospect of the establishment of a fourth station, to provide a ship of larger dimensions for the use of the Mission, another Harmony, *the third of the name, was built at Yarmouth during the autumn and winter of 1831 and 1832, at an expense of about £3,500. Brother Taylor superintended the building, as in the case of her predecessor. She was a brig, or rather a snow, of about 230 tons burden, and proved herself well adapted to the performance of the service to which she was destined. Her first voyage, performed in the year 1832, a year remarkable as being the centenary of the Brethren's Missions, was marked by conflicts with the ice, more continuous and more alarming than had been experienced since the year 1817. The following extract of a letter from Captain Taylor to the Treasurer of the Society, describing the peculiar hazards encountered by the* Harmony *on her outward passage, will prove an interesting supplement to the particulars of Arctic adventure, already given:*

On the 6th of July (about five weeks after leaving the Thames) we first fell in with the ice, but, the weather being very hazy we stood off and on, till the 11th, when it cleared up a little, and the land appeared in sight. We now steered for the shore; but, the light failing us, we made the ship fast to a field of ice. We supposed that we were at this time not more than twenty-five or thirty miles distant from Hopedale. The next morning the fog returned, and was so thick, that we could not see any object two ships' length from us. Meanwhile the ice closed about us in such dense masses, that there was not water enough to dip a bucket into on either side of the ship. We remained in this state till the 13th, about noon; when the fog partially clearing away again, we beheld, to our no small alarm, an immense iceberg aground right in our way, our course being at this time in a direction to the SSE. It was not till about 3 p.m. that we could at all succeed in our attempts to move the vessel; and even then our utmost exertions, continued without interruption during the space of six hours, only brought her forward about three times her own length. Our object at this time was to get round the point of the ice-field to which we were moored, and thus place it between us and the iceberg, which was towering above us to the height of nearly twice the mainmast. Our position was indeed a fearful one; and I believe most on board were ready to give up all hope of saving either the ship or their own lives. The Lord, however, was better to us than our fears; He heard and answered the supplications we offered up to Him, and sent us deliverance in a way we least expected. May we never lose the remembrance of His great mercy! As soon as the field of ice to which we were attached came in contact with the berg, it veered round, and dragged us after it without the least injury, the distance between the ship and the latter being scarcely greater than a foot. Had we not succeeded in getting round the point in the way we did, we should probably have been crushed to pieces in an instant. We continued exposed to the same kind of perils till the 22nd instant, and, during the greater part of this time the frost was so intense, that our ropes were almost immovable. Even the small ropes were coated with ice to the thickness of four or five inches; so that we were obliged every morning to send up some of our people to the mast head, to strike off the ice with sticks, that the ropes might pass through the blocks. On the 23rd we succeeded, by dint of great exertion, and under press of sail, in getting clear of the ice and reaching the open water, and on the 21st, arrived at Hopedale in safety.

It may here be observed, that, up to this date, embracing a period of more than sixty years, the ship had always proceeded to Labrador by way of Stromness, though, in returning home, she had generally taken her passage through the Channel. The reasons for the northward course having been so long preferred, were various. In the first place, as the latitude of the Orkneys very nearly corresponds with that of northern Labrador, the portion of the Atlantic to be traversed was somewhat smaller by this than by the southern passage, especially in the alternate years, when Okak had to be first visited. Again, the danger from hostile cruizers [sic] was less imminent by taking this course, a convoy being ordinarily provided for the Hudson's Bay and Davis Straits ships. This was a consideration of some importance in time of war, and led to its being generally preferred, also on the passage home, up to the year 1815; and lastly, it has so happened, that nearly all the successive commanders of the vessel have been natives of the Orkney Islands, and the greater number of the crew likewise. It was natural, therefore, that they should prefer a course which brought them, at least twice a year, into personal contact with such of their relatives and friends, as were still residing in those islands, not to mention that the annual visit of the ship tended to excite and keep alive a very warm interest in the Labrador Mission, in the minds of not a few of the Christian people of Stromness and neighbouring islands, and to call forth their active and sympathising benevolence.

On the establishment of a fourth Missionary settlement on the coast of Labrador, an alteration took place in the Society's practice in this particular. It being found necessary to send the ship to Hopedale first, as the most southern, and consequently, under ordinary circumstances, the most accessible of the four stations, the Channel passage was for some time preferred in going out as well as in returning. The voyage of the *Harmony* in 1832, was the first in which this course was taken.

According to the testimony of the captain, the weather, that year, was more severe, and the hardships experienced by himself and his crew greater, than he had ever before known, in the twenty-eight voyages he had made in the service of the Society.

The year following, the ship was exposed to imminent danger, from a violent storm which she encountered while lying off Hebron. For some hours, the captain, who with two boys happened to be the only persons on board, the remaining hands being variously occupied on shore, expected almost every moment that the ship would part from her cable and be driven upon the rocks; but, by God's mercy, she rode out the gale, without sustaining any serious injury.

In 1836, the *Harmony* fell in with the ice, as early as the 24th of June, after a speedy and prosperous voyage to within 200 miles of the coast of Labrador. According to the statement of the captain, it was not merely the immense quantity of ice, that rendered the navigation difficult and dangerous, nor yet the number of icebergs that crowded the narrow channels, and of which he, on one occasion, counted no fewer than seventy; but more especially the character of the frozen masses, consisting chiefly of what seamen call bottom-ice, and the violent swells by which they were frequently agitated. The undulations hereby produced, exceeded, on one occasion, 100 feet in perpendicular height; a spectacle which, however sublime, could not be contemplated without the most lively sensations of alarm; for though the *Harmony* was at the time beyond the reach of the most violent agitation, the striking of the ice against the ship's side was sufficiently severe to cause the utmost apprehension for her safety. It was, in fact, only by the constant use of fenders of tow, or cable junk, let down beneath the surface of the water, and interposed between the vessel and the advancing masses, that the sailors were enabled, with the Divine help, to prevent her receiving serious, and perhaps, irreparable injury from their sharp and rugged edges. For eight days subsequent to this anxious period, the vessel remained completely entrenched in the ice, not a drop of water being visible on any side of her as far as the eye could reach. At length, however, the Lord sent deliverance from these accumulated perils and opened for her a safe, though toilsome passage, through the ice to the coast of Labrador. On entering Hopedale harbour, on the 4th of August, the captain learned, that it had become clear of ice only two days before; a circumstance, which led him to consider, as peculiarly providential, the many obstacles which had hitherto opposed his progress, having every reason to believe, that, had the ship been obliged to contend with similar ones, in the narrow and rocky channels between Hopedale and the islands, the destruction of the vessel would, humanly speaking, have been inevitable.

It was on returning from this voyage that Captain Taylor had the privilege of rescuing from a watery grave the nine survivors of the crew of the *Superior*, Captain Dunn, bound from Miramichi to Cardiff, which had been thrown on her beam ends, during a furious gale, on the 28th of September, and had become a total wreck. Eight of those poor mariners, including the captain, were brought in safety to England.

In 1837, the vessel encountered dangers of another kind. In the attempt, justified apparently by the state of the wind and weather, to enter the bay of Hopedale by a new channel, she struck three times on a sunken rock, which, however, she eventually cleared without sustaining any material damage. A similar accident befell her in 1840, on leaving the same harbour, though, in this instance, the channel was one with which the captain and mate thought themselves perfectly familiar. As she was going at the rate of six miles an hour, and the shocks were anything but slight, it was a matter of thankful surprise to all on board, that no leak appeared to have been sprung, nor any serious injury done to the hull of the vessel.

The year 1841, the centenary of the Society for the Furtherance of the Gospel, was marked by a state of the weather on the coast of Labrador, not very dissimilar to that which rendered the year 1853 so memorable. Being prevented by the storms which prevailed, from visiting Hopedale first, the captain steered for Okak, which he was enabled to reach on the 18th of August. Thence he proceeded successively to Hebron and Nain, where he delivered a portion of the stores destined for Hopedale, feeling very doubtful as to the practicability of reaching that settlement, owing to the lateness of the season and the continued prevalence of adverse winds. After a trying and difficult passage the *Harmony* reached Hopedale on the 20th of September, and, while lying in the harbour of that settlement, rode out a furious tempest, which at one time threatened to tear her from her moorings and drive her upon the rocks. Her return to Horsley-down was on the 23rd of October.

The year 1851 was again a year of icebergs and ice-fields, by which the progress of the ship was greatly impeded, both on her approach to the coast and on her passage from one station to the other. That Captain Sutherland was compelled by the quantity of ice which he encountered on leaving Hopedale for Nain, and, by the prevailing dense fogs, to put back to the former settlement, he had afterwards reason to consider a very providential circumstance, as it would have been scarcely possible for the ship to have weathered the storm which shortly after ensued, in a channel encumbered with ice and abounding with sunken rocks. Before, the *Harmony* was favoured to be the means of restoring to their families and friends the eight survivors of the crew of the barque *Graham*, Captain Froud, who, after enduring extreme hardships and sufferings, had found their way to Okak, from the entrance of Hudson's Straits, where the vessel had been wrecked, by coming into contact with a field of ice. The circumstances attending the rescue of the poor sufferers were such as to do great credit to the humane and generous feelings of the Christian Eskimos, who were the instruments of effecting it, and to afford a striking testimony to the value of the instruction they had received, and the influence of the Gospel upon their hearts and lives.

In August 1851, the *Harmony* was again preserved from the serious injury which might have been the result of her violent collision with a sunken rock, as she was entering the bay of Hopedale. In September of the following year, the Divine protection was not less manifestly vouchsafed on her approach to Hebron.

In 1853, the voyage of the *Harmony* was marked by a very serious and distressing failure. The vessel sailed on the 10th of June, and, on her voyage on the Channel and across the Atlantic, was much impeded by contrary winds, so that she did not enter the Hopedale Bay until the 25th of August. On the 3rd of the following month she left for the north; but, within twenty-four hours from quitting Hopedale, she was assailed by a violent storm from the N and NNW, and driven nearly 400 miles out to sea. An attempt to reach Okak was frustrated by a second violent storm, accompanied by a heavy fall of snow. At length, the ship having sustained serious injury from the violence of the weather, and several of the crew being disabled by sickness, the captain was reluctantly compelled to bear away for England, leaving the three northern stations unvisited. Happily, the European letters for all the stations had, as usual, been landed at Hopedale, whence those destined for the other stations were forwarded by post-kayaks, while of the most needful articles of consumption there was a sufficient stock on hand to avert absolute want in the mission-families at the northern stations.

The voyage of 1858, especially the homeward passage, was marked by circumstances of peculiarly trying character. The outward passage was rendered longer than usual by the large number of icebergs, and, subsequently on the coast, by calms and dense fogs. Yet the *Harmony* could sail from Hebron on her homeward voyage on the 25th of September. For five or six days, states the report issued at the time, the weather was favourable; but when off the south of Cape Farewell in Greenland, she encountered a heavy gale from the eastward, which continued several days; and from the first week in October there followed a succession of violent storms with short intervals of calm, quite sufficient to retard the progress of a vessel like the *Harmony*, firmly built, and well fitted to bear the shock of the waves and the crash of the ice, but bearing up indifferently against a head-wind. On the 18th of October, she was, nevertheless, almost within soundings, when another easterly gale sprung up, which drove her back, the sea breaking over the deck, and carrying away the stern boat. Between the 18th of October and the 22nd of November, the ship was driven into the Atlantic three successive times, her course varying from 46° to 52° N lat., and from 9° to 16° W long., often exposed to imminent peril from the fury of the waves. After making Dursey Island, north of Bantry Bay, on the last mentioned day, she came in sight of the Lizard on the 30th, and thence had a favourable run up Channel, passing Dungeness on the 2nd of December, and reaching Horsleydown on the morning of the 5th. Her homeward voyage of ten weeks, from port to port, is one of the longest recorded in the annals of the Society. To customary trials were added those arising from a partial failure of provisions, the supplies of more than one article of food running short during the last month or six weeks. The greater cause is there for thankfulness to the Lord, who visibly gave His blessing to the use of such as were left, suffering none of the passengers, whether adults or children, to want any real necessary of life, and preserving them in health, strength, and spirits, till the hour of their reaching the desired haven.

In the following year, the *Harmony* brought home the survivors of the crew of the *Kitty*, a vessel in the employ of the Hudson's Bay Company, which was wrecked in September of that year. Happily for them, these men, after enduring terrible sufferings, fell into the hands of *Christian* Eskimos, by whom their immediate wants were supplied, and they were conducted in safety to Okak.

As time advanced, it was found that the *Harmony*, after her long service, required very considerable repairs to enable her to endure the wear and tear of continued Arctic navigation. A somewhat larger vessel, having the advantage of modern improvements in construction, in many respects appearing desirable, it was resolved, after mature deliberation, to build one to meet the special requirements of the service. On the 24th of April, 1861, she was launched from the yard of the builders, Messrs. Fellows and Sons, at Yarmouth, in the presence of several members of the Committee and many Christian friends. W. Leach, Esq., the Vice-President of the London Association, gave to the ship the same time-honoured name, which had been borne by three of her predecessors. Shortly afterwards, a considerable number of Christian friends assembled on the deck, to dedicate the new vessel to the service of the Lord. Various ministers of religion took part in the devotional portion of the service, and the Secretary of the Society delivered an address containing an account of the ships employed by the Society since the commencement of the mission in Labrador, directing attention to the gracious protection afforded to them through so long a series of years, and commending the present vessel to the prayerful remembrance of the friends of the Christian Missions.

On her very first voyage, under the command of Captain Henry Linklater, the new vessel met with an accident which excited much alarm at the time, but was happily unattended with any serious results. Leaving the river, she struck with considerable force on a sand-bank; but, on the rising of the tide, was got off without injury.

The voyages since performed by the vessel, though marked by a continuance of the protection so long graciously vouchsafed, do not present any striking feature worthy of special mention.

For the sake of the numerous friends of the Labrador mission who have never seen the ship, a few descriptive particulars may be here given. The *Harmony* (the fourth of the Society's ships which have borne that name), is a barque of about 250 tons register. She has a slightly raised quarter-deck, by which additional height is gained for the cabins. The latter, though small, are neat and commodious, and the sleeping-places are comfortable. Though furnished with every additional protection required in case of contact with the ice, the outline of the ship is elegant, while the materials and style of the construction are good. The figure-head represents an angel with a trumpet, with the appropriate words of the Scripture on an ornamental scroll; Glory to God, Peace on Earth. On the stern are carved representations of various arctic animals, together with the Society's monogram, S.F.G. All these simple though characteristic decorations are in white and gold. For many years the Labrador ship had a berth in the river, but owing to some new harbour-regulations, she now lies at the West India Dock. Her usual crew consists of twelve hands, besides the captain.

In the year 1870 the development of the cod-fish trade in Labrador, which for the sake of the natives it was most desirable to encourage, as a substitute for the decreasing supply of seals and foxes, required far more space than could be supplied by the *Harmony*.

Hence the Society was obliged to purchase a second vessel, the *Cordelia*, a schooner of 160 tons register, which has made annual voyages to Labrador since the year of her purchase, always under the command of Captain J. Linklater, a near relative of the master of the *Harmony*. Her usual course is from London to Bristol to Cadiz, where she loads salt, thence to Newfoundland for mixed stores, and thence to Labrador; she is expected to reach the coast before the *Harmony*. Occasionally she has taken passengers out or home, but for this purpose the accommodation is very limited. From Labrador she returns laden with salt-fish, via Newfoundland, to some British port. The first return voyage across the Atlantic was marked by the only fatal accident which has ever occurred in the Society's vessels. During a violent storm a terrific wave broke over the ship, carrying away a portion of the bulwarks and the wheel, and killing two men on the spot. With this exception the *Cordelia* has been privileged to enjoy the same Divine protection in many perils as the *Harmony*; this the Society desires to acknowledge with deep gratitude to the Lord.

A small steam-launch has now (1877) been added to the Labrador vessels. She is 30 feet long by 7 1/2 feet beam, is furnished with engines of about 7-horse power, and is intended, during the summer, to convey letters and passengers, especially the superintendents along the coast, besides towing rafts of timber for firewood from distant bays, and occasionally the *Harmony* or *Cordelia*, when becalmed: in winter the engine can be utilized for sawing wood on shore. We trust that this little craft will prove of great convenience and advantage to our brethren on the Labrador coast in meeting the varied exigencies of the work entrusted to their care. A considerable portion of the cost of the steam-launch is provided by the liberality of the pupils in our Boarding Schools in England, who form together a Juvenile Missionary Association.

In reference to those on whom the important duties of commanders of these vessels have devolved, the following remarks are still appropriate: The Society cannot forbear a grateful acknowledgement of the goodness of God, in providing a succession of faithful, experienced, and able seamen to take the superior and subordinate charge of the vessels, in whose safety their missionary brethren and dear Christian friends, as well as themselves, are so deeply interested. In Captains Mugford, James Fraser, Thomas Fraser (no relation to his predecessor), William Taylor, James Sutherland,

and John White, a degree of confidence has been placed, which could only have been inspired by the belief that they considered themselves the servants of the cause rather than of the Society, that they acknowledged their entire and continued dependence on that Lord whom winds and waves obey, and that they were at all times, and especially in seasons of difficulty and peril, to seek His counsel, help, and blessing. To these remarks it may be added, that Captain White, whose acquaintance with all the landmarks on the Labrador coast was particularly valuable, retired from the service in 1862, in consequence of advancing age and the failure of his bodily powers. He, however, manifested his abiding interest in the cause he had so long served, by successfully navigating on her voyage to Labrador in 1866, the *Meta*, a small vessel which had been purchased for service on the coast. He was succeeded in command of the *Harmony* by Captain Henry Linklater, who fills his important post in such a manner as to enjoy in the highest degree the esteem and confidence of his employers. To him may without doubt be applied in its fullest sense the language used with reference to his predecessor sixteen years ago.

The worthy captain of the *Harmony* will, it is hoped, be more than ever prepared to admit, in practice as well as theory, that it is "under God" that "he is master for the present voyage," and that the friends of the Mission on the coast, and of the Society to whom he is more immediately responsible, will not fail to support him by their fervent prayers, and to unite in the utterance of the heartfelt wish, "And so God send the good ship to her destined port in safety."

Such aspirations will arise on behalf of the missionary vessel and those who navigate her, on the conclusion of a century of voyages. And surely, humble yet confident hopes for the future are abundantly justified by the experience of the past. Time indeed brings changes to all that is sublunary, and it cannot be expected that the mission in Labrador, and the arrangements found necessary for its welfare, and even its continued prosperous existence, will form an exception to the general rule. But there is One who changes not. He surely will not forsake the work of His own hands, but will, in His love and wisdom, perfect that which concerneth the dwellers in dreary Labrador. Nor need the hope be expressed with less confidence, that all who are concerned with the carrying on and the management of the Labrador mission, whether here or beyond the ocean, may continue to be favoured with the pardoning grace, the loving kindness, and the tender mercy, which have so abundantly been experienced through the century now drawing to its close.

The following stanzas, by the skilful hand of the greatest master of English sacred song whom this generation has known, the late Brother Jas. Montgomery, will, it is hoped, be considered to form no inappropriate sequel to the foregoing narrative. They form part of a beautiful hymn, composed in 1841, for the centenary of the Society for the Furtherance of the Gospel, of which the writer was an esteemed and faithful member:

> To-day one world-neglected race,
>   We fervently commend
> To Thee, and to thy word of grace;
>   Lord, visit and befriend
> A people scatter'd, peel'd, and rude,
>   By land and ocean-solitude
> Cut off from every kinder shore,
>   In *dreary* Labrador.
>
> Thither, while to and fro she steers,
>   Still guide our annual bark.
> By night and day, through hopes and fears,
>   While lonely as the Ark,
> Along her single track, she braves
> Gulphs, whirlpools, ice-fields, winds, and waves,
> To waft glad tidings to the shore
>   Of *longing* Labrador.
>
> How welcome to the watcher's eye,
>   From morn till even fix'd,
> The first faint speck that shows her nigh,
>   Where surge and sky are mix'd!
> Till, looming large, and larger yet,
> With bounding prow, and sails full set,
> She speeds to anchor on the shore
>   Of *joyful* Labrador.
>
> Then hearts with hearts, and souls with souls
>   In thrilling transport meet,

Though broad and dark the Atlantic rolls
>   Between their parted feet:
For letters thus, with boundless range,
Thoughts, feelings, prayers, can interchange,
And once a year join Britain's shore
>   To *kindred* Labrador.

Then, at the Vessel's glad return
>   The absent face: again:
At home, our hearts within us burn,
>   To trace the cunning pen,
Whose strokes, like rays from star to star,
Bring happy messages from far.
And once a year, to Britain's shore
>   Join *Christian* Labrador.

NOTES

1. Excerpt from *Brief Account of the Missionary Ships Employed in the Service of the Mission on the Coast of Labrador from the Year 1770 to 1877* (London, 1877). Based on *Periodical Accounts*, Vol. 6, 397; Vol. 21, 122-23, CIHM 02524.
2. Gillian Lindt Gollin, *Moravians in Two Worlds* (New York and London: Columbia University Press, 1967), 9-24. A very useful website by Dr. Hans Rollman, "Religion, Society, and Culture in Newfoundland and Labrador," that includes much information and a selection of documents on the Moravians, can be found at <www.mun.ca/rels/morav>.
3. W.H. Whitely, "The Establishment of the Moravian Mission in Labrador and British Policy," *Canadian Historical Review* 45, 1 (1964): 29-50; James Hiller, *The Foundation and the Early Years of the Moravian Mission in Labrador, 1752-1805*, Unpublished M.A. thesis, Memorial University of Newfoundland, 1967. See also, Hiller's "The Moravians in Labrador, 1771-1805," *The Polar Record* 15, 99 (1971): 839-54, and his "Jens Haven and the Moravian Mission in Labrador," Unpublished paper, Newfoundland Historical Society, 23 October 1968; Réginald Auger, *Labrador Inuit and Europeans in the Strait of Belle Isle: From the Written Sources to the Archaeological Evidence*. No. 55

(Québec: Université Laval, Centre d'études nordiques, 1991), 11-12.

4. John Carey, "The rescue of a race; a brief account of the salving of the Eskimo," *Moravian Missions* 3 (1905): 59-60.

5. Kenneth Peacock, Introduction, *Songs of the Newfoundland Outport*, vol. 1 (Ottawa: National Museum of Canada, 1965), xviii-xxv.

6

LOSS OF HIS MAJESTY'S PACKET,
THE *LADY HOBART* (1803)[1]

WILLIAM DORSET FELLOWES

There were a number of wrecks of naval packets, which performed the indispensable services of carrying the royal mail and troop transport in Newfoundland and Labrador waters during and immediately after the Napoleonic wars. Among the shipwreck stories that have been published either as narratives or poems are those of the *Cumberland* packet,[2] the transport *Warrens* (see Appendex C),[3] the transport *Harpooner*,[4] and the packet *Lady Hobart*.[5] Collectively, they are part of the early nineteenth-century maritime cultural heritage both in British North America and abroad. Apart from the drama and insight into human nature that the *Lady Hobart* narrative provides, it is also a testimony to the conduct of the captain and crew, and was recognized as such. Captain Fellowes, who wrote this narrative, was not only praised but rewarded with a promotion to Commander.

This narrative, like many others, encompasses both micro- and macro-history. Over the centuries, Newfoundland and Labrador had been drawn into international conflict, and the late eighteenth and early nineteenth centuries proved no exception. During the War of American Independence, for example, the Newfoundland fishery was designated "an excellent target" by the United States.[6] After a ten-year interlude of peace, the outbreak of conflict between Britain and France in 1793, at the height of the French Revolution, again resulted in "the beginning of a period of major disruptions in the Newfoundland fishery."[7] The wreck of the *Lady Hobart* in 1803 came at a time when war had just resumed between France and England after a brief lull. This helps to explain why the *Lady Hobart* attacked a French schooner and captured its crew.

The 11 survivors of the *Lady Hobart*, out of an original complement of 29 passengers and crew, were rescued on high seas by an American ship, the *Bristol Trader*, en route to Bristol, whose owner displayed "a benevolence and humanity that will ever reflect the highest honour on his character." This rescue was fortuitous. Despite competition in the fishery and renewed and growing tensions between the pro-French United States and Great Britain, culminating in the War of 1812-14, peace still existed in 1803 between the two countries and trade remained active. Incidentally, the presence of Americans in Newfoundland waters was considerable. For, while the British and French fishery in this region remained "sedentary," American fishers plied the coastlines, especially in Labrador and the Gulf of St. Lawrence, reaching a peak in 1804 of 1,360 vessels and 10,600 men.

Not only historical context and international developments played a role, however. Luck and happenstance also frequently combined to shape the fate of shipwrecks. The troop transport *Warrens*, for example, carrying part of the 70th Regiment from Quebec to Cork, was only stranded on the coast of Labrador, wedged onto rocks, but this was a "most providential thing," and inspired a regimental headmaster to write a poem. Had the vessel grounded only eight feet further toward the shore, its bottom would have been ruptured and everyone might well have drowned. The other vessels mentioned, including the *Lady Hobart*, were not nearly as fortunate.

ON THE 22ND DAY OF JUNE 1803, we sailed from Halifax for England, steering a course to the southward and eastward, to clear Sable Island. On the 24th, hauled to the northward, to pass over the northern part of the Great Bank of Newfoundland, with the intention to keep well to the northward, that we might thereby avoid the enemy's cruisers.

On the 26th, at seven a.m. being then on the Grand Bank, in lat. 44° 37', and long. 51° 20' west, Cape Race bearing NNW 1/2 W 123 miles distant, discovered a large schooner under French colours, standing towards us, with her deck full of men. From her manner of bearing down upon us, we concluded she had been apprized of the war, and that she took us for a merchant brig. Cleared ship for action. At eight being within range of our guns, fired a shot at her, when she struck her colours. Sent on board and took possession of the vessel; she proved to be *l'Aimable Julie*, of Port Liberté, of eighty tons burden, strong built, bound thither from the island of St. Pierre, laden with salt-fish, and commanded by Citizen Charles Roffe.

After taking out her captain and crew, I gave the prize in charge to Lieutenants John Little, and William Hughes, of his Majesty's navy (who were passengers in the *Lady Hobart*, and who most handsomely volunteered their services); and with them I sent two of our own seamen, and two prisoners, to assist in navigating the prize. At ten a.m. saw two schooners ahead; fired a gun, and brought them to: on finding them to be English, and bound to St. John's, I divided the French prisoners between them, excepting the captain, mate, and one boy, the captain's nephew, who requested very earnestly to remain on board the Packet.

Tuesday, June 28th. Blowing hard from the westward, with a heavy sea and hazy weather, with intervals of thick fog. About one in the morning, the ship then going by the log at the rate of seven miles an hour, struck against an island of ice, with such violence, that several of the crew were pitched out of their hammocks. Being roused out of my sleep by the suddenness of the shock, I instantly ran upon deck. The helm being put hard a-port, the ship struck again about the chest-tree, and then swung round on her heel, her stern-port being stove in, and her rudder carried away, before we could succeed in our attempts to haul her off. At this time the island of ice appeared to hang quite over the ship, forming a high peak, which must have been at least twice the height of our mast head; and we suppose the length of the island to have been from a quarter to half a mile.

The sea was now breaking upon the ice in a dreadful manner, the water rushing in so fast as to fill the hold in a few minutes. Hove the guns overboard, cut away the anchors from the bows, got two sails under the ship's bottom, kept both pumps going, and bailing with buckets at the main hatchway, in the hope of preventing her from sinking; but in less than a quarter of an hour she settled down to her fore-chains in the water.

Our situation was now become most perilous. Aware of the danger of a moment's delay in hoisting out the boats, I consulted Captain Thomas of the navy, and Mr. Bargus, my master, as to the

The Shipwreck of the Lady Hobart Packet.

A rare woodcut. Multi-storied iceburgs are brought south by the Labrador current when the ice-pack breaks up. From *Wonderful Escapes! containing the interesting narrative of the shipwreck of the* Antelope *packet* ... (Dublin: Brett Smith), 1818

propriety of making any further efforts to save the ship; and as I was anxious to preserve the sail, I requested their opinion as to the possibility of taking it into the boats in the event of our being able to heave them over the ship's side. These gentlemen agreed with me, that no time was to be lost in hoisting them out; and that, as the vessel was then settling fast, our first and only consideration was to endeavour to preserve the crew.

And here I must pay that tribute of praise which the steady discipline and good conduct of every one on board so justly merit. From the first moment of the ship's sinking, not a word was uttered expressive of a desire to leave the wreck: my orders were promptly obeyed; and though the danger of perishing was every instant increasing, each man waited for his turn to get into the boats with a coolness and composure that could not be surpassed.

Having fortunately succeeded in hoisting out the cutter and jolly-boat, the sea then running high, we placed the ladies in the former. One of them, Mrs. Cotenham, was so terrified, that she sprung from the gunwale, and pitched into the bottom of the boat with considerable violence. This accident, which might have been productive of fatal consequences to herself, as well as to us all, was unattended by any bad effects. The few provisions which had been saved from the men's berths were then put into the boats, which were quickly veered astern. By this time the main deck forward was underwater, and nothing but the quarter deck appeared: I then ordered my men into the boats, and having previously lashed iron pigs of ballast to the mail, it was thrown overboard.

I now perceived the ship was sinking fast; I called out to the men to haul up and receive me, intending to drop myself into the cutter from the end of the trysail boom, fearing she might be stove under the counter; and I desired Mr. Bargus, who continued with me on the wreck, to go over first. In this instance he replied, that he begged leave to disobey my orders; that he must see me safe over before he attempted to go himself. Such conduct, at such a moment, requires no comment; but I should be wanting to myself, and to the service, if I did not faithfully state to their Lordships every circumstance, however trifling: and it is highly satisfactory to me to have this opportunity of recording an incident so honourable to a meritorious office.

The sea was running so high at the time we hoisted out of the boats, that I scarcely flattered myself we should get them out in safety; and indeed, nothing but the steady and orderly conduct of the crew could have enabled us to effect so difficult and hazardous an undertaking: and it is a justice to them to observe, that not a man in the ship attempted to make use of the liquor, which every one had in his power. Whilst the cutter was getting out, I perceived one of the seamen (John Tipper) emptying a demijean, or bottle, containing five gallons, which, on inquiry, I found to be rum. He said that he was emptying it for the purpose of filling it, with water from the scuttle cask on the quarter deck, which had been generally filled over night, and which was then the only fresh water to be got and it became afterwards our principal supply. I relate this circumstance as being so highly creditable to the character of a British sailor.

We had scarce quitted the ship, when she suddenly gave a heavy lurch to port, and then went down head foremost. I had ordered the colours to be hoisted at the main-topgallant mast-head, with the union downwards, as a signal of distress, that if any vessel should happen to be near to us at the dawn of day, our calamitous situation might be perceived from her, and she might afford us relief.

At this awful crisis of the ship sinking, when it is natural to suppose that fear would be the predominant principle of the human mind, the coolness of that British seaman was very conspicuously manifested by his (John Andrews) exclaiming, "There, my brave fellows, there goes the pride of Old England!"

I cannot attempt to describe my own feelings, or the sensations of my people! Exposed as we were in two small open boats upon the great Atlantic Ocean, bereft of all assistance, but that which our own exertions, under Providence, could afford us, we narrowly escaped being swallowed up in the vortex. Men used to vicissitudes are not easily dejected; but there are trials which human nature alone cannot surmount. The consciousness of having done our duty, and a reliance upon a good Providence, enabled us to endure our calamity; and we animated each other with the hope of a better fate.

While we were employed in deliberating about our future arrangements, a curious circumstance occurred, which, as it was productive of considerable uneasiness to us all, deserves to be particularly mentioned here: at the moment when the ship was sinking, she was surrounded by what seamen term a school, or an incalculable number of whales, which can only be accounted for by their being known at this particular season, to take a direction for the coast of Newfoundland, in quest of a small fish, called Capeland [capelin], which they devour. We were extremely apprehensive, from their near approach to the boats, that they might strike and materially damage them; frequent instance having occurred in that fishery of boats being cut in twain by the violence of a single blow from a whale: we therefore shouted, and used every effort to drive them away, but without effect; they continued, as it then seemed, to pursue us, and remained about the boats for the space of half an hour, when, thank God! they disappeared without having done us any injury.

Having at length surmounted dangers and difficulties which baffle all description, we rigged the foremast, and prepared to shape our course in the best manner that circumstances would admit of, the wind blowing from the precise point on which it was necessary to sail, to reach the nearest land. An hour had scarcely elapsed from the time the ship struck, till she foundered. The distribution of the crew had already been made in the following order, which we afterwards preserved.

In the cutter, of the following dimensions, viz, twenty feet long, six feet four inches broad, and two feet six inches deep, were embarked three ladies and myself; Capt. Richard Thomas, of the navy; the French commander of the schooner; the master's mate, gunner, steward, carpenter, and eight seamen; in all eighteen people; which, together with the provisions, brought the boat's gunwale down to within six or seven inches above the water. From this confined space, some idea may be formed of our crowded state; but it is scarcely possible for the imagination to conceive the extent of our sufferings in consequence of it.

In the jolly-boat, fourteen feet from stem to stern, five feet three inches broad, and two feet deep, were embarked Mr. Samuel Bargus, master; Lieut. Col. George Cooke, of the Ist reg. of guards; the boatswain, sailmaker, and seven seamen; in all eleven persons.

The only provisions we were enabled to save consisted of between forty and fifty pounds of biscuit; one demijean, or vessel, containing five gallons of water; a small jug of the same, and part of a small barrel of spruce beer; one demijean of rum, a few bottles of port wine, with two compasses, a quadrant, a spy-glass, a small tin mug, and a wine-glass. The deck lantern, which had a few spare candles in it, had been likewise thrown into the boat, and the cook having had the precaution to secure his tinder-box, and some matches that were kept in a bladder, we were afterwards enabled to steer by night.

The wind was now blowing strong from the westward, with a heavy sea, and the day had just dawned. Estimating ourselves to be at the distance of 350 miles from St. John's Newfoundland, with a prospect of a continuance of westerly winds, it became at once necessary to use the strictest economy. I represented to my companions in distress, that our resolution, once made, ought on no account to be changed; and that we must begin by suffering privations, which I foresaw would be greater than I ventured to explain. To each person, therefore, were served out half a biscuit, and a glass of wine, which was the only allowance for the ensuing twenty-four hours, all agreeing to leave the water untouched as long as possible. During the time we were employed in getting out the boats, I had ordered the master to throw the main hatch tarpauling into the cutter; which being afterwards cut into lengths, enabled us to form a temporary bulwark against the waves. I had also reminded the carpenter to carry with him as many tools as he could: he had accordingly, among other things, put a few nails in his pockets, and we repaired the gunwale of the cutter, which had been stove in hoisting her out. Soon after daylight we made sail, with the jolly-boat in tow, and stood close-hauled to the northward and westward, in the hope of reaching the coast of Newfoundland, or of being picked up by some vessel. Passed two islands of ice, nearly as large as the first. We now said prayers, and returned thanks to God for our deliverance. At noon, observed in lat. 46° 33' north; St. John's bearing about W 3/4 N distant 350 miles.

Wednesday, June 29. This day was ushered in with light variable winds from the southward and eastward. We passed a long and sleepless night, and I found myself, at dawn of day, with twenty-eight persons looking up to me with anxiety for the direction of our course, as well as for the distribution of their scanty allowance. On examining our provisions, we found the bag of biscuit much damaged by salt water; it therefore became necessary to curtail the allowance, to which precaution all cheerfully assented.

It was at this moment that I became more alive to all the horrors of our situation. We all returned thanks for our past mercies, and offered up prayers for our safety.

A thick fog soon after came on; it continued all day with heavy rain, which as we had no means of collecting, afforded us no relief. Our crowded and exposed situation was now rendered more distressing, from being thoroughly wet, no one having been permitted to take more than a great coat or a blanket, with the clothes on his back.

Kept the oars in both boats going constantly; and steering at
WNW course. All hands anxiously looking out for a strange sail.
At noon served a quarter of a biscuit and a glass of rum to each
person. St. John's bore W by N 1/4 N distant 350 miles. No
observation. One of the ladies again read prayers to us, particularly
those for delivery after a storm, and those for safety at sea.

Thursday, June 30. At daybreak we were all forbenumbed with
wet and extreme cold, that half a glass of rum, and a mouthful of
biscuit, were served out to each person: the ladies, who had hitherto
refused to taste the spirits, were now prevailed upon to take the fated
allowance, which afforded them immediate relief, and enabled them
the better to resist the severity of the weather. The sea was mostly
calm, with thick fog and sleet; the air raw and cold: we had kept at
our oars all night, and we continued to row during the whole of this
day. The jolly-boat having unfortunately put off from the ship with
only three oars, and having but a small sail, converted into a foresail
from a topgallant steering sail, without needles or twine, we were
obliged to keep her constantly in tow. The cutter also having lost two
of her oars in hoisting out, was now so deep in the water, that with
the least sea she made little way, so that we were not enabled to profit
much by the light winds.

Some one from the jolly-boat called out that there was part of a
cold ham, which had not been discovered before: a small bit, about
the size of a nutmeg, was immediately served out to each person, and
the remainder was thrown overboard, as I was fearful of its increasing
our thirst, which we had not the means of assuaging.

At noon we judged ourselves to be on the north-eastern edge of
the Grand Bank, St. John's bearing W by N 1/4 N distant 246 miles.
No observation. Performed divine service.

Friday, July 1. During the greater part of the last twenty-four
hours it blew a hard gale of wind from the west-south-west, with a
heavy confused sea from the same quarter; thick fog and sleet throughout; the weather excessively cold, for the spray of the sea freezing as it
flew over the boats, rendered our situation truly deplorable. It was at
this time that we all felt a most painful depression of spirits: the want
of nourishment, and the continued cold and wet weather, had rendered
us almost incapable of exertion. The very confined space in the boat
would not allow of our stretching our limbs; and several of the men,
whose feet were considerably swelled, repeatedly called out for water.

On my reminding them of the resolution we had made, and of the absolute necessity of our persevering in it, they acknowledged the justice and propriety of my refusal to comply with their desire, and the water remained untouched.

At the commencement of the gale we stood to the northward and westward; but the cutter was so low in the water, and had shipped so much sea, that we were obliged to cast off the jolly-boat's tow-rope, and we very soon lost sight of her in the fog. This unlucky circumstance was productive of the utmost distress to us all. We had been roused to exertion from a double motive; and the uncertainty of our ever meeting again the companions of our misfortunes, produced in us the most lively affliction. To add to the misery of our situation, we lost with the boat a considerable part of our stores, but with them our quadrant and spy-glass. At about four a.m. the gale increasing, with a prodigious heavy sea, we brought the cutter to by heaving the boat's sail loose over the bow, and veering it out with a rope bent to each yardarm, which kept her head to the sea, so as to break its force before it reached us.

In the course of this day there were repeated exclamations of a strange sail, although I knew it was next to an impossibility to discern any thing, owing to the thickness of the fog; yet they were urged from the several seamen with such apparent certainty of their object, that I was induced to put the boat before the wind to convince them of their error; and as I then saw in a very strong point of view the consequences of such deviations, I took occasion to remonstrate with them upon the subject; I represented with all the force of which I was capable, that the depression arising from the disappointment infinitely overbalanced the momentary relief proceeding from such delusive expectation, and I exhorted them not to allow such fancies to break out into expression. Under all these circumstances, the ladies particularly, with a heroism that no words can describe, afforded to us the best examples of patience and fortitude.

We all joined in prayers, which tranquillized our minds, and afforded us the consolatory hope of bettering our condition: on these occasions we were all bare-headed notwithstanding the incessant showers. At noon St. John's bore W by N 3/4 N distant 148 miles. No observation.

Saturday, July 2. It rained hard during the night, and the cold became so severe, that almost every one in the boat was unable to move. Our hands and feet were so swelled, that many of them became quite black, owing to our confined state, and the constant exposure to wet and cold weather. At daybreak I served out about the third of a wine-glass of rum to each person, with a quarter of a biscuit, and before noon a small quantity of spruce beer, which afforded us great relief.

During the first part of this day, it blew strong from the southward and westward, with foggy weather; towards noon, moderate breezes from the northward and eastward.

At half past eleven a.m. a sail was discovered to the eastward, standing to the northwest. Our joy at such a sight, with the immediate hope of deliverance, gave us all new life. I immediately ordered the people to sit as close as possible, to prevent our having the appearance of being an armed boat; and having tied a lady's shawl to the boat-hook, I raised myself as well as I could, and, from the bow, waved it as long as my strength would allow me. Having hauled close to the wind, we neared each other fast, and in less than a quarter of an hour we perceived the jolly-boat. Our not having recognised her sooner, was owing to an additional sail having been made for her, out of one of my bed sheets, which had been accidently thrown into the boat, and was set as a bonnet to the foresail.

I cannot attempt to describe the various sensations of joy and disappointment, which were by turns expressed on all our coun-tenances. As soon as we approached the jolly-boat, we threw out to her a tow-rope, and bore away to the north-west.

We now mutually inquired into the state of our respective crews, after the late dreadful gale: those in the jolly-boat had suffered from swelled hands and feet, like ourselves, and had undergone great anxiety on our account, concluding us to have perished. The most singular circumstance was, their having steered two nights, without any light; and our meeting again after such tempestuous weather, could not have happened but from the interposition of Providence. Fearing a similar accident, we made a more equal distribution of our provision; and having received from the jolly-boat two bottles of wine and some biscuit, we gave them some rum in return.

Our hopes of deliverance had now been buoyed up to the highest pitch. The excitement arising from our joy began perceptibly to lose its effects and to a state of artificial strength succeeded such a despondence, that no entreaty, nor argument, could rouse some of the men even to the common exertions of making sail.

To the French Captain, and several of the people who appeared to have suffered most, I now, for the first time, served out a wine glass full of water. I had earnestly cautioned the crew not to taste the salt water, but some of the unhappy men had, nevertheless, taken large draughts of it, and became delirious; some were seized with violent cramps, and twitching of the stomach and bowels. I again took occasion to point out to the rest of them the extreme danger of such indiscretion.

Performed divine service. At noon St. John's bore W by N 3/4 N distant 110 miles. No observation of the sun.

Sunday, July 3. The cold, wet, hunger, and thirst, which we now experienced, are not to be described, and made our situation very deplorable. At eight p.m. having a strong breeze from the southward, we stood on under all the canvas we could spread, the jolly-boat following in our wake, and pulling her oars to keep up with us. The French Captain, who for some days had laboured under a despondency which admitted of no consolation, jumped overboard in a fit of delirium, and instantly sunk. The cutter at this time was going through the water so fast, and the oars being lashed to the gunwale, it would have been impossible to attempt to save him, even had he floated. One of the other prisoners in the jolly-boat became so outrageous, that it was found necessary to lash him to the bottom of the boat.

The melancholy fate of the poor Captain, whom I had learnt to esteem, affected me at first more sensibly, perhaps, than any other person; for on the day on which I was making the distribution in the boats, and was considering in which I should place him, he came to me with tears in his eyes, to implore me not to leave him to perish with the wreck: I assured him that I never had entertained such an idea; that as I had been the accidental cause of his misfortunes, I would endeavour to make his situation as easy as I could, and that, as we were all exposed to the same danger, we would survive or perish together. This assurance, and the hope of being speedily exchanged, if ever we reached the land, operated for a while in quieting his mind; but his fortitude soon forsook him, and the raw spirits to which he had not been accustomed, producing in him the most dreadful intoxicating effects, hurried on the fatal event.

We were all deeply affected by this circumstance; the most trifling accident or disappointment was sufficient to render our irritable state more painful, and I was seized with such melancholy, that I lost all recollection of my situation for many hours; a violent shivering had seized me, which returned at intervals; and as I had refused all sustenance, my state was very alarming: towards night I enjoyed, for the first time, three or four hours sound sleep, a perspiration came on, and I awoke as from a delirium, but painfully alive to all the horrors that surrounded me.

The sea continued to break over the boats so much, that those who had force enough, were obliged to bale without intermission. Those who sat in the stern of the cutter were so confined, that it was difficult for any one to put his hand into his pocket, and the greater part of the crew lay in water upon the boat's bottom.

The return of dawn brought us no relief but its light. The sun had never cheered us but once during the whole of our perilous voyage; and those who had a few hours of uninterrupted sleep, awoke to all the consciousness of wretchedness and misery.

A very heavy gale of wind came on from the southward, with so tremendous a sea, that the greatest vigilance was necessary in managing the helm, as the slightest deviation would have broached the boats to, and consequently must have hurried us on our destruction. We scudded before it, expecting every returning wave to overwhelm us; but, through the providence of Almighty God, we weathered the storm, which began to abate towards night. We had nearly run the distance we had supposed ourselves from St. John's; but, owing to the thickness of the fog, we were prevented from discerning to any great extent.

Towards evening we passed several pieces of rock-weed, and soon after Captain Thomas saw the wing of a Hackdown, an aquatic bird that frequents the coast of Newfoundland, and is much eaten by the fishermen. This event afforded us great hopes of our approaching the land; and all hands were eagerly employed in observing what passed the boats. About this time a beautiful white bird, web-footed, and not unlike a dove in size and plumage, hovered over the mast-head of the cutter; and notwithstanding the pitching of the boat, it frequently attempted to perch on it, and continued fluttering there until dark; trifling as this circumstance may appear, it was considered by us all as a propitious omen.

The impressive manner in which it left us, and returned to gladden us with its presence, awakened in us a superstition, to which sailors are at all times said to be prone: we indulged ourselves on this occasion, with the most consolatory assurances, that the same Hand which had provided this solace to our distresses, would extricate us from the danger that surrounded us.

There being every reason to conclude ourselves well in with the land, the few that were able to move, were now called upon to make a last effort to save their lives by rowing, and taking advantage of the little breeze we then had. It was strongly urged to them, that, if the wind should come off the shore in the morning, and drive us to leeward, all efforts to gain it might then be too late; as, independent of our feeble state, the provisions, with every economy, could not last more than two days; and that the water, which had as yet remained untouched (excepting in the instances before mentioned), could not hold out much longer. We had now been six days and nights, constantly wet and cold, without any other sustenance than a quarter of a biscuit and one wine-glass of fluid for twenty-four hours. The men who had appeared totally indifferent as to their fate, summoned up resolution, and as many as were capable of moving from the bottom of the boats, applied to the oars.

Monday, July 4. As the day dawned, the fog became so thick, that we could not see very far from the boat. During the night we had been under the necessity of casting off the jolly-boat's tow-rope, to induce her crew to exert themselves by rowing. We again lost sight of her, and I perceived that this unlucky accident was beginning to excite great uneasiness among us. We were now so reduced, that the most trifling remark, or exclamation, agitated us very much. I therefore found it necessary to caution the people against being deceived by the appearance of land, or calling out till we were quite convinced of its reality, more especially as fog-banks are often mistaken for land. Several of the poor fellows, however, repeatedly exclaimed they heard breakers, others the firing of guns; and the sounds we did hear resembled the latter so much, that I concluded some vessel had got on shore, and was making signals of distress: the noise afterwards proved to be the blowing of whales, of which we saw a great number.

Soon after daylight, the sun rose in view for the second time since we quitted the wreck. It is worthy to remark, that during the period of seven days, that we were in the boats, we never had an opportunity of taking an observation, neither of the sun, moon, or stars, nor of drying our clothes. The fog at length beginning to disperse, we instantly caught a glimpse of the land, within a mile distance, between Kettle Cove and Island Cove, in Conception Bay, fourteen leagues from the harbour of St. John's. Almost at the same moment we had the inexpressible satisfaction to discover the jolly-boat, and a schooner in shore standing off towards us.

I wish it were possible for me to describe our sensations at this interesting moment. From the constant watching and fatigue, and from the languor and depression arising from our exhausted state, such accumulated irritability was brought on, that the joy of a speedy relief affected us all in a most remarkable way: many burst into tears; some looked at each other with a stupid stare, as if doubtful of the reality of what they saw; several were in such a lethargic state, that no consolation, no animating language, could rouse them to exertion.

At this affecting period, though overpowered by my own feelings, and impressed with the recollection of our sufferings, and the sight of so many deplorable objects, I proposed to offer up our solemn thanks to Heaven for our miraculous deliverance. Every one cheerfully assented; and as soon as I opened the Prayer Book (which I had secured in the last time I went down to my cabin), there was an universal silence; a spirit of devotion was so singularly manifested on this occasion, that to the benefits of a religious sense in uncultivated minds, must be ascribed that discipline, good order, and exertion, which even the sight of land could scarcely produce.

The service being over, the people requested to have a pint of grog each; but, fearful of the consequences of such an indulgence, I mixed some rum and water very weak, and distributed to everyone a small quantity.

The schooner being now within hail, and having made our situation known, she hove to, and received us on board; our boats being taken in tow. The men could now with difficulty be restrained from taking large and repeated draughts of water, in consequence of which, several felt great inconvenience from the sudden distention of the stomachs; but, by being afterwards more cautious, no other bad effects followed.

The wind having blown with great violence from off the coast, we did not reach the landing place at Island Cove till four o'clock in

Reaching the Lifeboat. Saving shipwreck survivors, always a risky operation, depended upon the cooperation and humanity of entire outport communities. From *Canadian Illustrated News*, December 21, 1872. C58933, Courtesy of National Library of Canada/Bibliothèque nationale du Canada the evening. All the women and children in the village, with two or three fishermen (the rest of the men being absent), came down to the beach, and appearing deeply affected at our wretched situation, assisted in lifting us out of the vessel, and afterwards in carrying us up the craggy rocks; over which we were obliged to pass, to get to their habitations.

It was most fortunate circumstance for us, that we fell in with the land about Island Cove; a very few miles further to the northward, the coast is inaccessible, and lined with dangerous reefs of rocks, which, if we had seen them in the night, we should have pushed to; for our situation having become so desperate, I had resolved to land at the first place we could make: in that case we would have perished.

The different fishing-huts were constructed of pine logs. The three ladies, Colonel Cooke, Captain Thomas, and the Master, and myself, were conducted to the house of Mr. Lilly, a planter, who received us with great attention and humanity. This small village afforded neither medical aid nor fresh provisions, of which we stood so much in need; potatoes and salt fish being the only food of the inhabitants. I determined, therefore, to lose no time in proceeding to St. John's, having hired a small schooner for that purpose. On the 7th of July we embarked in three divisions, placing the most infirm in the schooner; the master's mate having charge of the cutter, and the boatswain of the jolly-boat; but such was the exhausted state of nearly the whole party, that the day was considerably advanced before we could get under weigh.

At two p.m. we made sail with the jolly-boat in tow, and the cutter in company, and stood along the coast of Newfoundland with a favourable breeze. Towards dusk it came on to blow hard in squalls off the land, when we lost sight of the cutter, and we were obliged soon after to come to anchor, outside of St. John's harbour. We were under great apprehensions for the cutter's safety, as she had no grapnel, and lest she should be driven out to sea: but at daylight we perceived her and the schooner entering the harbour; the cutter, as we afterwards learnt, having had the good fortune to fall in with a fishing vessel, to which they made fast during the night.

The ladies, Colonel Cooke, Captain Thomas, and myself, conducted by Mr. Lilly in the jolly-boat, having left the schooner when she anchored, notwithstanding the badness, as well as extreme darkness of the night, reached the shore about midnight. We wandered for some time about the streets, there being no house open at that late hour; but were at length admitted into a small house, where we passed the remainder of the night on chairs, there being but one miserable bed for the ladies.

Early on the following day, our circumstances being made known, hundreds of people crowded down to the landing place: nothing could exceed their surprise, on seeing the boats that had carried nine-and-twenty persons such a distance over a boisterous sea; and when they beheld so many miserable objects, they could not conceal their emotions of pity and concern. I waited on Brigadier-general Skerritt, who commanded the garrison, and who immediately, upon being informed of our situation, ordered down a party of soldiers to take the people out of the boats, and with the utmost kindness and humanity directed beds and every necessary article to be prepared for the crew.

The greatest circumspection was found necessary in administering nourishment to the men. Several of the crew were so much frost-bitten, as to require constant surgical assistance; as it was determined they should continue at St. John's, until they were in a fit state to be transported to Halifax: I hired a schooner for that purpose.

Being anxious to return to England, I engaged the cabin of a small vessel bound to Oporto; and on the 11th of July I embarked with Mrs. Fellowes, Colonel Cooke, and Captain Thomas, Mr. Bargus the master, and the Colonel's servant, who, during the voyage home, lost several of his toes, in consequence of what he had suffered. The master's mate was left in charge of the ship's company, and was direct-ed to conduct them to Halifax; whence they would be enabled to return by the first opportunity to their own country.

After taking leave of our hospitable friends at St. John's, and after recommending to their protection the companions of our hardships, we put to sea with favourable weather. During a voyage of fifteen days we had a few difficulties to encounter, such as pumping continually, the vessel having sprung a leak in a gale of wind; and we were obliged to throw overboard a considerable quantity of her cargo of salt-fish.

On the 26th of July we fell in with an American ship, the *Bristol Trader*, of New York. The owner, Mr. William Cowley, being told our distressed situation, and that we had been shipwrecked, immediately hove to, and with a benevolence and humanity that will ever reflect the highest honour on his character, received us on board, and brought us safe to Bristol; where we had the happiness to arrive on the 3rd of August.

NAMES OF THE SHIP'S COMPANY, &C.
OF HIS MAJESTY'S PACKET
LADY HOBART, SAVED BY THE BOATS

Names	*Station*
William Dorset Fellowes, Esq.	Commander
Mr. Samuel Bargus	Master
Mr. Robert Jenkins	Master's Mate
Peter Germain	Gunner
Benjamin Saule	Boatswain
John Gard	Carpenter
Francis Lambrick	Sail-maker
Thomas Bell	Ship's Cook
Edward Roberts	Captain's Steward
Richard Harris	" Servant
John Harris	Seaman
John Andrew	"
John Anderson	"
P. Martin	"
John Tipper	"
William Trigido	"
Christian M'Cleaver	"
John Watson	"
Timothy Donohough	Invalided Seaman
Richard Pierce	"
Charles Roffe	French Prisoner of War, afterwards drowned
G. Goslin	"
V. François	"

Passengers

Mrs. Scott, Miss Cotenham, Mrs. Fellowes, Lieutenant-Colonel Cooke, and Captain Richard Thomas of the Navy.

INTRODUCTION
On his Majesty's Service
St. John's, Newfoundland, July 9, 1803

Sir,

It is with extreme concern I have the honour to inform you of the total loss of his Majesty's Packet *Lady Hobart*, under my command, on the morning of the 28th of June, at sea, in lat. 46° 33' north, and long. 44° 00' west from Greenwich, on an island of ice.

The accompanying Narrative of our proceedings, from the time of the ship's foundering, will, I trust, be a sufficient testimony to their Lordships, that no exertion on my part, or that of my officers and ship's company, was wanting, both as to preserving the ship from sinking, as well as the total impossibility of saving the dispatches.

The sufferings and hardships undergone by us all, have been indeed greater than it is possible for my pen to describe.

After remaining three days at Island Cove, the place where we first made the land, there being no medical assistance for the people, I embarked in a small vessel I hired for the purpose, and arrived here yesterday.

With the exception of two women and myself, they are still in a most wretched condition, and several it is feared will lose their toes and fingers. As soon as they are in a state to be moved, I intend proceeding from hence in a schooner to Halifax, with a view to obtain a passage in one of the Packets, as there are no vessels about to sail from hence for England, and none that could accommodate so great a number.

I trust their Lordships will approve of what I have considered it my duty to do by these unfortunate men.

Brigadier-general Skerritt has been so kind as to give us quarters in the garrison, and has issued rations for our support, as well as maintenance to Halifax, at the expense of Government, for which I shall give receipts.

I should be wanting in gratitude were I not to make particular mention of the kind and humane attentions we have all experienced from General Skerritt, the officers of the garrison, and many of the inhabitants of St. John's.

I have the honour to remain
Your most obedient Servant,
WILLIAM DORSET FELLOWES

F. Freeling, Esq.

General Post Office, 18th August 1803

Dear Sir,
Having laid your affecting and interesting Narrative before my Lord
the Postmaster General, I am commanded to send you a copy of their
Lordships' minute thereon.

I assure you I enter fully into all their Lordships' feelings for
your past sufferings, and entertain the same sense of your patience,
fortitude, and perseverance; and I beg you to believe I have pleasure
in witnessing the promotion which has so quickly succeeded the
moment of your difficulties and dangers.

My Lords cannot fail to take into their favourable consideration
the very meritorious conduct of your officers and crew.

Believe me with great regard,
Dear Sir,
Yours most faithfully,
F. FREELING

Captain Fellowes

We have perused this Report with a mixed sentiment of sympathy
and admiration. We are satisfied, that in the loss of the Packet and of
the public correspondence, no blame is imputable to Captain
Fellowes, to his officers, or to his seamen. In their exertion after the
ship had struck on the floating mass of ice, and in their subsequent
conduct, they appear to have shewn all the talents and virtues which
can distinguish the naval character.

Let a proper letter be written in our names to the friends and
family of the very worthy French officer who perished. And we shall
be solicitous to learn the entire recovery of the other passengers,
who met such dangers and sufferings with the most exemplary
fortitude.

Mr. Freeling will return the Narrative to Captain Fellowes, with
our permission to him to communicate it to his friends; or, if he
shall think proper, to give it to the public. It cannot fail to impress
on the minds of all who may read it, the benefit of religion and the
consolation of prayer under the pressure of calamity; and also an
awful sense of the interposition and mercies of Providence, in a case
of extreme peril and distress. To seamen it will more especially show
that discipline, order, generosity of mind, good temper, mutual

benevolence, and patient exertion, are, under the favour of Heaven, the best safeguards in all their difficulties.

With respect to Captain Fellowes, we feel highly gratified in having it in our power so immediately to give to him a promotion, which we have reason to believe will be particularly acceptable.

(Signed)   Auckland
August 16, 1803

C. SPENCER

NOTES

1. *A Narrative of the Loss of His Majesty's Packet The* Lady Hobart *on an Island of Ice in the Atlantic Ocean, 28th of June 1803: Spectacular Account of the Providential Escape of the Crew in Two Open Boats By William Dorset Fellowes, Esq. Commander. Dedicated, By Permission, to the Right Hon. The Post Master General* (London: John Stockdale, 1803), CIHM 35106.

2. *Shipwrecks and Disasters at Sea or Historical Narratives of the Most Noted Calamities, and Providential Deliverances from Fire and Famine on the Ocean; to which is annexed, A Sketch of the Various Expedients for Preserving the Lives of Mariners in Cases of Shipwreck, by the Aid of Life Boats, Life Preservers, &c.* (Manchester: S. Johnson, 1837), 360-66.

3. Robert Sands, *The Shipwreck; or The Stranding of The Warrens, of London, On the Coast of Labrador, on the morning of the 25th October, 1813; with part of the 70th Regiment on board, bound from Cork to Quebec* (Quebec, 1814). See Appendix.

4. A popular rendition of the *Harpooner* narrative is contained in Michael Harrington, *Sea Stories from Newfoundland* (St. John's: Harry Cuff Publications, 1986), 61-69; also Frank Galgay and Michael McCarthy, *Shipwrecks of Newfoundland and Labrador* (St. John's: Harry Cuff Publications, 1987), 7-12. See Appendix for a poem published in the *Montreal Herald* and dedicated to one of the survivors of this shipwreck.

5. A subsequent version of this narrative is "The Distressing Account of The Loss of the *Lady Hobart* Packet," *Wonderful Escapes!* (Dublin: Brett Smith, 1818), 77-105.

6. Olaf Janzen, "The Royal Navy and the Defence of Newfoundland During the American Revolution," *Acadiensis* 14, 1
   (Autumn 1984): 28.
7. Shannon Ryan, "Fishery to Colony: A Newfoundland
   Watershed, 1793-1815," *Acadiensis* 12, 2 (Spring 1983): 34-52.

7

EXTREME PERSONAL SUFFERINGS:
THE *REBECCA* (1816)[1]

NEIL DEWAR

According to *Lloyd's Lists*, there were fewer wrecks in 1816 than in the two years that followed, and 50 percent fewer wrecks than in 1836. Nevertheless, 1816 saw 343 stranded or wrecked vessels, 19 missing or lost vessels, and 15 vessels in which the entire crew drowned, for a total mortality at sea of 945 persons.[2] Neil Dewar, the Scottish author of the following grim narrative, was one of the lucky survivors. His narrative went through three editions, and the information on his experience differs slightly from one text to the other. The second edition, which follows, was an expansion of the first edition published in 1818. Changes found in the third edition of 1843 appear in parentheses.

After serving in the Royal Navy during the Napoleonic wars, Dewar returned to his native land. He decided to ship out with four other crew from the then important port of Greenock, near Glasgow, aboard a vessel that brought him to Montreal. By then Glasgow had become associated with a dramatic increase in the timber trade with British North America.[3] From there he went on to Quebec City to work aboard a ship engaged in the flourishing saltfish trade between Newfoundland and Spain. The Peninsular War, also known as the Spanish War of Independence, resulted in preferential tariffs on British goods and an expansion of this trade. Saltfish exports to Spain peaked in 1815, then declined steadily, with eventual "catastrophic" results for the colony's economy.[4] The *Rebecca*, in taking fish from Cape Charles to Europe, participated just after this trade had reached its historic height.

It is not surprising that the ship, sailing late in the season, met with inclement weather before it was wrecked off Cape Norman in the Strait of Belle Isle. Four survivors, including Dewar, got on board a jolly-boat with only one oar and managed to make it ashore to Duck Island in the middle of a late-November snowstorm. After a land trek of 11 days, a full two weeks and a 50-mile journey from their wreck, they came upon Nady Bay Head at Cape Carpoon (Quirpon) on the Northern Peninsula of Newfoundland, where they were rescued by "two Indians," probably migrating Inuit or Montagnais who were employed in the schooner trade by local merchants,[5] who brought the survivors to Mr. Isaac Isaacs. This benefactor, who proceeded to care for his charges for roughly ten months, not only cared for them but saved Dewar's life by amputating his frost-bitten and gangrenous legs, using a finely honed seal-knife. Isaacs was likely one of the first English settlers in these parts, a "liveyere" [livyer] in charge of a winter crew, who combined the trades of fisher, sealer, and furrier, and worked with either a British merchant company or the Labrador company.[6] Dewar had been fortunate to have stumbled upon a layperson with some knowledge of folk medicine and obviously some practical experience, who managed to save his life.

This surgical intervention was however only the first of three amputations suffered by Dewar, the final one taking place at the Glasgow Infirmary in Scotland, leaving him "in a state of great debility ... a helpless object, dependent on the bounty of the humane." He was apparently still alive in 1843, when the third edition of *Affecting Narrative* ..., appeared. His condition, while lamentable, was not unusual or necessarily the worst possible. A study of nineteenth-century Newfoundland indicates that west coast mariners received, when available, medical treatment from surgeons of the French fishing fleet or doctors on British warships probably trained in the tradition of Dr. James Lind, whose *Essay on the Most Effectual Means of Preserving the Health of Seamen in the Royal Navy*, was first published in 1757. The very workplace of the sailor was an occupational hazard. Besides the injuries sustained from shipwreck and accident, one risked incurring smallpox, berri-berri, scurvy, typhus, lice, nervous exhaustion, venereal disease, blood poisoning, influenza, and a host of other diseases during sojourns at sea.[7] In short, the conditions of hypothermia, frostbite, and gangrene were among a variety of possible health concerns, though the plight of shipwrecked mariners and fishers was indeed often and particularly bleak.

⚓

HAVING BEEN FREQUENTLY ASKED what part of the kingdom I belong to, and other particulars respecting my life and parentage, I think it proper here to state, that I was born at Lochgilphead, Argyllshire, in the year 1793. My father was a wright to trade, and chiefly in the employment of Mr. M'Neill of Oakfield. After having received the usual education of a tradesman's son in Scotland, my father, when I was about twelve years of age, intended to teach me his own trade, but after a few months, I thought of trying the sea, and bound myself an apprentice with Captain M'Lachlan of the brig *Lord Collingwood*, belonging to Greenock. Having served my apprenticeship, I engaged in the *Robust*, Captain Landales, for Jamaica, at which place I was impressed into the Navy, and put on board the *Cleopatra* frigate, off the Spanish Main. This frigate was ordered home, and for two years after I served in several others of His Majesty's ships, when I was at length paid off from the *Sophia* sloop of war at Deptford. Having again returned to Greenock, I embarked on board the *Montreal*, Captain Reside, of that port, for Montreal in Canada.

Here I and four others of the crew went to Quebec, and embarked on board the *Rebecca*, Captain Maxwell, for Cape Charles, on the coast of Labradore, for a cargo of fish. Having returned to Quebec, we took in some other goods, and on our voyage to Cadiz, the *Rebecca* was wrecked on the coast of Labradore, where my painful and unfortunate disasters, from the inclemency of the season, it being winter, and the inhospitable climate, commenced.

For a more particular account of what followed, and my great sufferings and present helpless situation, I refer the reader to my Narrative, and trust to meet with the charitable assistance of a humane and generous public.

We sailed from Quebec on the 8th day of October, 1816, in the *Rebecca*, Captain Maxwell, bound for Cadiz, intending to call in at Cape Charles for some more fish, to make up the cargo, for it consisted chiefly of fish. Our voyage was prosperous, till the 17th of November, when being off the harbour of Cape Charles, on the coast of Labradore, it came to blow so very hard, that we had to carry very low canvas. The wind was about north by west, and the harbour lying about north and south; [*but a heavy gale coming on, blowing right out of the harbour, and the entrance being very narrow, we could not carry sail to beat the vessel in, we hoisted the Ensign, Union down, as a signal of distress, but the inhabitants made us a signal to reply, that they could afford us no assistance; and being on the larboard tack, we ran along shore ENE a few leagues farther; the gale increasing, we were obliged to heave the vessel to, about six o'clock, the same evening. We lay to for the long space of three days, the gale blowing tremendously, accompanied with heavy falls of snow. On the 20th, the wind shifted from NE to NW and it became necessary to bear up, for the purpose of clearing the land; we bore up, accordingly, about seven in the evening, and ran under bare poles till near midnight. The night was completely dark, and the gale continued with unabated fury, with heavy showers of hail and sleet.*

Being now off Cape Norman, in the Straits of Belleisle, the starboard watch being now on deck, the man who was keeping a look-out forward, was heard cry to the watch below, "Bear a hand upon deck men, for we are close upon a rock."]* No sooner had he uttered these words, than the vessel gave a tremendous crash; she then recoiled, and on striking again, both masts fell over the side, close by the deck; the boltsprit followed, leaving the whole forecastle completely torn up. Here our miserable situation was extremely distressing; no tongue can describe this awful scene in its true colours; nothing but present death was presented to our view; our vessel being full of water, and the sea breaking over her to such a degree, that she was in danger of breaking up in a thousand pieces every moment.

We now remained motionless, surrounded with all the hideous terrors of unavoidable destruction. By this time two of our crew, James Allan and Daniel Morrison, with Mr. Thomson our only passenger, got upon the boltsprit to make for the island, which was distant about a gunshot, but were all instantly whirled to the bottom, there being six of us remaining to meet our doom; to stay we could not, to proceed was death. At last finding our tempest-beaten vessel beginning to give way, uncertain of our doom, we took to the long boat, as the only resource for the preservation of our precious lives, and, under the sole protection of the Divine Being, reached the island about one hour after we first struck.

---

* All text in [ ] and italics is from the third edition of *Affecting Narrative* ..., published in 1843. R.B.

On attempting to land, the boat upset, and I, Neil Dewar, the most unfortunate, was precipitated on the rugged face of a rock which was naked by the percussion of the surge: then dashed prostrate on the beach, where I lay for some time insensible, and on recovering a little, found both my knees and elbows severely wounded by the fall. Here we remained for three days, destitute of a morsel to eat, or any thing to cover us from the inclemency of the tempest, which, with frequent showers of snow and hail, kept pelting at us with redoubled violence. Meanwhile, our mate and one seaman died from fatigue and hunger. The bodies of the two men who leaped with Mr. Thomson on the boltsprit were washed towards us; and having no method to bury them, we covered them with the others in the snow, out of our sight. On the 24th, the tempest being now greatly abated, Capt. Maxwell, Charles Donaldson, Richard M'Fie, and myself, the only survivors, agreed to leave this island, and steer for the main-land. Accordingly, about nine a.m., we set sail in the jolly-boat, which had driven from the wreck, steering her with an oar, and bailing her all the way till about one p.m., when we reached the land, being a distance of two leagues. On preparing to land, the surf which ran very high, took the boat in the stern, filled her with water, and swept Captain Maxwell into the tide. Donaldson and M'Fie hastened to his assistance, but I, from the effects of my similar fate, was incapable of rendering him any aid. They however succeeded in bringing him to the strand, where he remained speechless for a few minutes, then dropped down, gave a deep sigh, and bade a long adieu to us, his fellow sufferers.

In vain did we lament our helpless condition; in vain did we look in every direction for an asylum to our houseless heads, bounded on one side by a barren wilderness, and on the other by inland lakes and rivers. Donaldson and M'Fie, compelled by hunger alone, left me in the evening, while they went in search of some subsistence or place of refuge, promising to return, if in life, the following day. Being unable through my wounded knees and elbows to go with them, I sat down by the remains of my Captain, brooding over my helpless situation; the night freezing very hard, with a strong easterly wind. Now again the day appearing in the east, after passing a long and dangerous night, expecting every moment to be devoured by some wild beast, I then got upon my feet, and looking round me, I saw the jolly boat tossing among the surf, upon the beach. I then thought upon my shipmates who had left me the night before, what might have become of them, thinking that they had been killed by the wild animals that inhabit this country. At a loss what to do, I considered it best to follow. Accordingly I set out, and crawled to the top of the cliff, and steered my course to the westward along the shore, following their feet marks [*footsteps*] in the snow [*for three miles*]. I continued my journey till night, and betook myself to rest under a leafless tree. I passed a very restless night, being frequently disturbed by the howling of a wolf, and I imagining by the sound, that the animal was approaching me, I climbed up the tree for safety. Daylight coming on, I looked round me, and found I was, as it were, completely blockaded, for the snow which had fallen through the night, had filled up their feet marks. Being now without any guide whereby I could trace the course of my shipmates, I resolved on my departure from the tree, and steering my course back towards the place where I left my Captain's remains under the cliff, where I arrived about eleven a.m., I sat myself down by the back of the cliff, and soon fell fast asleep. My companions returned about noon that day, with the intelligence of their having fallen in with the vacant hut of an Indian, to which place they conveyed me, supporting me between them; we reached it about six in the evening, and next morning determined to travel in one direction, till we should meet either death or remedy [*assistance*].

    We accordingly set out on the 26th of November, about eight in the morning, and continued journeying for ten days without seeing a human being, subsisting all the time, on the frost-withered fruit of the rowan tree, which we casually fell in with, and reposing in the night close to each other, under the shelter of a leafless thorn [*tree*]. On the eleventh day of our journey, and fifteenth of our calamity, we came to a place called Nady Bay Head, the hill being so high and steep, and covered with snow, that we thought we should never get up to the top, and I being lame, was unable to keep up with my shipmates; the snow giving way under me, I came down to the bottom of the hill. However, I tried it again, taking care of my steps. By this time Donaldson and M'Fie had reached the top, and began a shouting and waving their hats, for joy that they had seen a house. I hurried up towards them with enlivened speed. We then sat down on the top of the hill to rest ourselves, uncertain whether it was a house or not. We then saw a person coming down towards the beach;

we shouted to him, thinking that he might hear, and come across the bay with a boat to us, the distance being about two or three leagues; however he did not hear us. We then set off again, and sliding down the west side of the hill to the bottom, and began journeying round the head of the bay, till we came to a narrow part that divided the island from the mainland; here we saw the mark of men and dogs' feet in the snow, and a small boat hauled up on the ice. We [*overcome with fatigue*] sat down on the snow to rest a little [*in hopes some of the inhabitants might come to our assistance*], when presently [*in a short time*], from the woods, started four large dogs, who began a growling and barking as if they would have devoured us. Presently followed two wild savage looking fellows [*two Indians*], dressed in hairy clothes, and each of them having a gun on his shoulder. We first addressed them by a recital of our misery, humbly imploring admission to their habitation to die, as we said, by their fireside. However barbarity over-ruled their humanity, and at our misery and solicitations they smiled with contempt. At last they consented to our request. It was at a place called Cape Carpoon [Quirpon], about fifty miles from the wreck. I was by this time so far spent, that I could hardly draw one foot after the other, they being swelled to an unwieldy bulk. We at last reached the hut, this being the fourteenth day from the wreck.

Upon entering the hut, Mr. Isaac Isaacs, (this was the fisherman's name the hut belonged to) placed us by a good fire side, and treated us with some bread and spruce beer. He then ordered one of his Indians to bring a tubful of ice water to soak our boots, and with a knife, he ripped down the back part of our boots, and turned them over our feet, and in drawing off the stockings, the skin and toe nails came off along with them. He next applied a poultice of fish blubber and Castile soap, and laid us by the fire, with a boat's sail over us. Our situation now began to thaw the cruelty of our host, and he endeavoured to show a great deal of commiseration. Donaldson in a few days was seized with a mental derangement, and died in a fit of delirium. M'Fie and I were now looking to meet with the same fate as poor Donaldson, both our arms and legs having mortified, and our host told us, that to save our lives, we must lose our limbs. Poor Richard, with a regardlessness of his doom, said, I will willingly risk my fate, hoping either of us may be left to tell our friends what we experienced. The mortification was rapidly spreading, and from my natural timidity, I begged Richard to suffer first, which he did, but no stoppage could be made of the great effusion of blood, till death in a short time terminated his agonizing existence. I then was placed for the awful operation, which was performed on Christmas morning.

The surgeon being a fisherman, first began with a large seal-knife, by carving the flesh off both legs about an inch above the ankle, then breaking and severing the bones, and afterwards applying a preparation of hot pitch and rosin, as the only remedy to stop the sanguinary discharge, which happily succeeded. He then proceeded to my arms, which he treated in a like manner. During this torture, I was lulled as it were into the arms of death, insensible to every act, save the amputation of my left hand, which with my right hand, was cut off by the wrist. Next morning, the reflexion of my extreme personal torture, unable to convey a particle of food to my lips, lying at once a complete object of sympathy and disgust, the prospect of a lingering death, in a desolate region, far from the consolation of a friend, and enduring the most excruciating pain, drew around me a combination of ideas which filled my mind with all the images of relentless despair. In a few days after the amputation of both my legs and arms, I was carried on a sledge drawn by twelve dogs [*and did not feel any bad effects from the journey*], twenty miles in the thickest of the forest, where they erected a hut to pass the severest of the winter. [*Our winter quarters consisted of a large hut built of logs, which was so completely buried in the snow, that, on approaching it, nothing could be seen but a flag-staff erected on the top of a chimney. It was entered by a large covered porch which protected the entry from cold; and, as the windows were blockaded up with snow, it was only lighted from the chimney, which was made large on purpose. I was placed near the fire on a bench, and covered with a boat's sail.*

The winter party consisted of Mr. Isaacs, three Englishmen, one Dutch sailor, and the two Indians already mentioned. They employed themselves, during the day, in cutting wood, and setting traps for deer, beavers, and other kinds of game; and in the evening, in making mokassons, or Canadian boots. As the season advanced, I began to recover my strength, and to be able to move from my bench, rolling myself upon an empty flour barrel, placed under my breast. Upon one occasion, I ventured a few paces beyond the porch, when the whole party were out; the cask unfortunately gave way, and I fell to the ground, but, by dint of exertion, I was able to creep back to the hut.]

Now the fishing season coming on, it was proposed to move back to our former residence. Accordingly on the 20th of May, we moved to the island of Carpoon, where I was placed in my old berth by the fire side, with a boat's sail over me, and was pretty well taken care of by Mr. Isaacs. Being an old man [*seldom absent with the others, and who dressed my sores in the best manner he was able*], he partly kept the house or hut, while the others were employed at their work out of doors. I began gradually to gather strength, and was able to crawl about the hut. In this affliction I lived eight months, but by the interposition of Divine Providence, I was conveyed on board of a vessel called the *Lilly* of Quebec, Captain Stewart, [*who received me on board, and who treated me with a kindness I can never forget. He had a medicine chest, and dressed my sores daily; he even gave up his own bed in the cabin to me, and cut his pillow in two to make cushions for my knees, bring me on deck every favourable day, and by this kind treatment, my health was restored*], and [*we*] reached Quebec on the 23rd of September, 1817. I was sent to the general hospital [*at St. Roque, and attended by Nuns, by whose care the sores in my arms were healed; but it was found necessary, to have both my legs amputated again*], and [*I*] underwent a second operation by Doctors Hicket and Holmes. I was well attended by the nuns. So I began slowly to recover, and was advised by the Doctors to go to Britain. Accordingly on the 28th of June, I took a passage in the *Robert*, Captain Neil, from Quebec, and reached Greenock on the 7th of August, 1818. I was conveyed to the Royal Infirmary in Glasgow, where I underwent a third amputation by Doctors Corkindale and Cummin [*and, thank God, my limbs are at length skinned over*].

The painful remembrance of my past miseries, with a constitution brought down to the utmost debility, and the idea of a sorrowful pilgrimage, represented to me the necessity of being with one who must treat me as a nurse doth a child. All that I now pray for is, that which may yield me a little earthly happiness, as it alone can secure a temporal alleviation of my destitute state, but I look for it only from those whose generous feelings this narration may affect. [*I am still, however, in a state of great debility, and must remain for life a helpless object, dependent on the bounty of the humane.*]

NEIL DEWAR

NOTES

1. *Affecting Narrative of the Extreme Personal Sufferings of Neil Dewar, (Who has lost both his legs and arms,) Sometime Seaman out of Greenock, but late of the Schooner* Rebecca *of Quebec, Wrecked on the Coast of Labradore, 20th November, 1816, and of the Painful Enterprises and Death of Captain Maxwell and Crew, Belonging to the said schooner* Rebecca. 2nd edn., with additions. (Glasgow: William Lang, 1822), CIHM 50246. Supplementary information (in brackets [ ] and italics) comes from the 3rd edn., printed in 1843, ed. James Smith.

2. *Report From The Select Committee Appointed To Inquire Into The Causes Of Shipwrecks: With The Minutes Of Evidence, Appendix and Index*, Great Britain, House of Commons, 15 August 1836, iii. The average annual loss to Lloyd's for these years was estimated at over two million pounds.

3. Gordon Jackson, "New Horizons in Trade," in *Glasgow, Volume I: Beginnings to 1830*, eds. T.M. Devine and Gordon Jackson (Manchester and New York: Manchester University Press, 1995), 221-22.

4. Shannon Ryan, *Fish Out of Water: The Newfoundland Saltfish Trade, 1814-1914* (St. John's: Breakwater Books, 1985), 101-13. This economic collapse marks the transition of Newfoundland from a British migratory fishery to a British colony. See S. Ryan, "Fishery to Colony: A Newfoundland Watershed, 1793-1815," *Acadiensis* 12, 2 (Spring 1983): 34-52.

5. See Charles A. Martijn, "The Inuit of Southern Quebec-Labrador: A Rejoinder to Garth Taylor," *Études/Inuit/Studies* 4 (1980): 194-98; also, his "Innu (Montagnais) in Newfoundland," in William Cowan, ed., *Papers of the Twenty-First Algonquian Conference* (Ottawa: Carleton University, 1990), 227-46; Ralph T. Pastore, "Fishermen, Furriers, and Beothuks: The Economy of Extinction," *Man in the Northeast* 33 (Spring 1987): 47-62.

6. See Patricia A. Thornton, "The Demographic and Mercantile Bases of Initial Permanent Settlement in the Strait of Belle Isle," in John J. Mannion, ed., *The Peopling of Newfoundland: Essays in Historical Geography* (St. John's: ISER, 1977), 168; also, her "The Transition from the Migratory to the Resident Fishery in

the Strait of Belle Isle," in Rosemary E. Ommer, ed., *Merchant Credit and Labour Strategies in Historical Perspective* (Fredericton: Acadiensis Press, 1990), 138-66.

7. See Raoul Anderson, "Nineteenth Century American Banks Fishing Under Sail: Its Health and Injury Costs," *Canadian Folklore Canadien* 12, 2 (1990): 102-21; Albert B. Perlin, "History and Health in Newfoundland," *Canadian Journal of Public Health* 61 (1970): 314; F.N.L. Poynter, ed., *The Journal of James Yonge [1647-1721], Plymouth Surgeon* (New York: Longman's, 1963); Nick Nyland, *Skørbug, beskøjter og skibskirurger; Traek af søfartsmedicinens historie* (Esbjerg, Denmark: Fiskeri-og Søfarsmuseet, Saltvandsakvariet, 1994), esp. 84-86 [includes an English summary].

8

THE H.M.S. *DRAKE* (1822)[1]

WILLIAM O.S. GILLY

The *Drake* was a frigate of Her Majesty's Navy,[2] capable of a maximum speed of 11 knots with wind abaft, and 2 1/2-3 knots into a head wind. In a top-gallant gale the ship proved itself "very weatherly," and in a top-sail gale, its double reef topsails were "very stiff."[3] In a gale, the vessel could run 6 knots and 6 fathoms with all sails set. The *Drake*'s steering and stability were notable and, as its assessors wrote, she "answers her helm quick, wears and stays well." In the water, it sat afore at 9'7" and abaft at 11'10", with the lowest gundeck sitting only 4'9" above the surface. While the *Drake* rode "very well," being "very heavy," it also tended to roll a great deal. Consequently, the vessel was "very wet," and shipped "a great quantity of water with the wind," for it plunged very deeply into the sea. So, despite its obvious seaworthiness, the *Drake*, on its way to Halifax from St. John's, smashed into the coast at an estimated 91 miles from Cape Race and 51 miles from Cape St. Mary's.

In 1851 William O.S. Gilly, who had been supported in his research by the Lords Commissioners of the Admiralty, wrote *Narratives of Shipwrecks of the Royal Navy*, and the narrative of the *Drake* was included in his collection. The main purpose of this volume was to illustrate "the discipline and heroism displayed by British Seamen under the most trying circumstances of danger." The fate of the *Drake* and the heroic conduct of Captain Charles Baker and his crew, an account of which follows below, was cited among seventeen other stories as an example of "perfect discipline."[4] Their action, Gilly argued, was in the tradition of the most famous examples of "good conduct," and reflected "calm and resolute endurance" and "admirable discipline," like that of the heralded *Alceste* in 1816. Baker, for reasons that are readily apparent upon any reading of the narrative, and at his own crew's request, had a monument erected to him at the Royal Dockyard chapel of Portsmouth, England.

A sharp contrast to the *Alceste* and the *Drake* was the case of the ignominious French ship *Medusa* and its crew. This notorious incident of the same year came to represent in marine culture broad confusion, cowardice, and ultimate selfishness, for the crew placed 150 persons on a make-shift raft with few provisons and then abandoned them, though against all odds there were survivors. The *Medusa*'s captain, though casting off his charges, had by then ensured his own survival and that of select crewmen by seconding a small boat. His action precipitated a scandal of national and international scope and prompted the famous French artist Géricault to paint "The Raft of the *Medusa*." Interestingly, Géricault removed all traditional ideological content from his canvas to convey "an image of human isolation and helplessness" beyond the powers of church and state; on the other hand, Gilly clearly did not do so.[5]

The British naval record, however, as Gilly points out, was not entirely above reproach. In contrast to his glowing commentary on the *Drake*, Gilly was highly critical of naval behaviour witnessed aboard the *Penelope*, which had been wrecked seven years earlier, near the Magdalen Islands. After encountering fog, ice, and strong winds off the Banks of Newfoundland, the ship crashed on 31 March 1815 off Cape Rozier, near the mouth of the St. Lawrence River. Upon impact, the survival of all crew and passengers was jeopardized by inebriated and insubordinate crew members. Gilly writes, "Their behaviour was not in the character of British seamen in general; they had neither principle nor humanity; some, in consequence, have suffered severely, and several died from drunkenness." This episode represented "one of the most disgraceful" cases in British naval history. Gilly's condemnation was a warning to all sailors to heed the code of naval discipline and honour,[6] while his praise of the *Drake* offered an inspiration and a model of behaviour to future generations of mariners.

⚓

THE *DRAKE*, 10-GUN BRIG, under the command of Captain Charles Baker, had been despatched by the commander-in-chief of the Newfoundland station, upon special duty to Halifax.

Having accomplished the object of her mission there, she set sail again for return to St. John's, on the morning of Thursday, the 20th of June, 1822. The weather was unusually fine, the wind favourable, and everything promised a short and prosperous voyage.

Nothing occurred to retard the progress of the vessel until Sunday morning, when the increasing thickness of the atmosphere betokened the approach of one of those heavy fogs which so frequently hover over the coast of Newfoundland.

There are few things more perplexing to the mariner than to find himself suddenly enveloped in one of these mists: it is impenetrable gloom; night and day are both alike; the sails, saturated with the watery vapour, hang heavily, and flap against the masts with a sad foreboding sound, whilst every heart on board feels more or less oppressed by the atmospheric influence, and every countenance expresses languor or discontent. But these discomforts are minor evils compared with other attendants upon a Newfoundland fog.

It often happens that, in spite of every precaution on the part of the men on the out-look, the bows of the vessel run across some unfortunate fishing boat; and before a single voice can be raised in warning, a sudden shock, a smothered cry, a gurgling of the waves, tell the sad tale! One moment, and all is silent; the ship pursues her course, and no trace is left of the little vessel and her crew, for whom many days and nights will anxious love keep watch; but those objects of a mother's tenderness and of a wife's affection will never more gladden the eyes of the watchers, till "the sea shall give up her dead."

Would that such calamities were of less frequent occurrence. There is one curious characteristic of these fogs, which in some degree mitigates the evil of them; they sometimes do not extend beyond a few miles, having the appearance of a huge wall of dense cloud or mist. A vessel, after beating about for hours, will suddenly emerge from almost total darkness, the clouds break away, and all hearts are gladdened by finding themselves once more beneath the rays of the glorious sun.

Captain Basil Hall gives an amusing instance of such an occurrence:

The *Cambrian* had run in from the sea towards the coast, enveloped in one of these dense fogs. Of course they took it for granted that the light-house and the adjacent land, Halifax included, were likewise covered with an impenetrable cloud of mist; but it so chanced, by what freak of Dame Nature I know not, that the fog on that day was confined to the deep water, so that we who were in the port could see it at the distance of several miles from the coast, lying on the ocean like a huge stratum of snow, with an abrupt face to the front the shore.

The *Cambrian*, lost in the midst of this fog-bank, supposing herself to be near land, fired a gun. To this the light-house replied; and so the ship and the lighthouse went on pelting away gun for gun during half the day, without seeing one another.

The people at the light-house had no means of communicating to the frigate, that if she would only stand on a little further, she would disentangle herself from the cloud, in which, like Jupiter Olympus of old, she was wasting her thunder. At last, the captain, hopeless of its clearing up, gave orders to pipe to dinner; but as the weather, in all respects except this abominable haze, was quite fine, and the ship was still in deep water, he directed her to be steered towards the shore, and the lead kept constantly going. As one o'clock approached, he began to feel uneasy, from the water shoaling, and the light-house guns sounding closer and closer; but being unwilling to disturb the men at their dinner, he resolved to stand on for the remaining ten minutes of the hour. Lo and behold! however, they had not sailed half a mile further before the flying gib-boom end emerged from the wall of mist, then the bowsprit shot into daylight, and lastly, the ship herself glided out of the cloud into the full blaze of a bright and "sunshine holiday." All hands were instantly turned up to make sail; and the men, as they flew on deck, could scarcely believe their senses when they saw behind them the fog-bank, right ahead the harbour's mouth, with the bold cliffs of Cape Sambro on the left, and further still, the ships at their moorings, with their ensigns and pendants blowing light and dry in the breeze.

But to return to our sad tale. Towards noon, the weather cleared up for about a quarter of an hour, allowing just sufficient time to get a good observation of the latitude, which, according to Captain Baker's reckoning, made their position to be about ninety-one miles from Cape Race, and fifty-one from Cape St. Mary's.

They continued to steer east till about six o'clock in the evening, when the breeze rather freshening, and the ship having run sixty miles since noon, she was hauled off to south-east.

The fog was then so dense that the men could not see more than twenty yards beyond the ship, but as Captain Baker's orders were to use the utmost dispatch, he determined to make the best of his way. Every precaution was taken, by using lead, and by keeping a vigilant look-out from every part of the ship. In this manner they proceeded, carefully feeling the way, until about half-past seven o'clock, when the look-out man shouted, "Breakers ahead! Hard a-starboard!" The ship was instantly hauled to the wind, but not being able to clear the danger on that tack, every effort was made to stay the vessel, but from the heavy sea, and whilst in stays, her stern took the breakers, and she immediately fell broadside on, the sea breaking completely over her.

At the moment the ship struck, every man was on deck, and there was such a universal feeling of confidence in the commander, that notwithstanding their extreme peril, not the slightest confusion ensued. Captain Baker's first order was to cut away the masts, so as to lighten the vessel, and perhaps afford means of saving some of the crew. The order was promptly executed, but unhappily without producing the desired result, for in a few moments the ship bilged, and the destruction of the whole crew appeared to be inevitable.

Captain Baker then ordered the cutter to be launched, but they had scarcely got her over the gangway before she sank.

It was a time of terrible anxiety for both officers and men, for, although the rocky shore appeared but a few fathoms distant, it seemed impossible that even the strongest swimmer could stem the raging sea that intervened, whilst the crashing of the masts, the strain of the vessel upon the rocks, and the roar of the waters as they swept over the decks, added to the horrors of the scene.

Yet, during this awful period, the crew, to a man, behaved with the most exemplary patience and fortitude. Each vied with the other for the general good, and when the repeated shocks of the ill-fated vessel upon the rocks warned them that unless some communication was formed with the shore, all must perish, then indeed, was a noble spirit of daring and self-devotion displayed.

Several of the crew volunteered to make the hazardous attempt of swimming to the shore; amongst them a man of the name of Lennard

Schooner Aground. The most common mode of transporting fish and all supplies to the outports was by coastal schooner. B12-93, Courtesy of the Provincial Archives of Newfoundland and Labrador

was selected, on account of his great strength and expertness as a swimmer.

This man, accordingly, having seized a lead line, was lowered into the boiling surf, but the current setting directly against him to the northward, his efforts were unavailing, and with difficulty he was dragged on board again.

It might be supposed that Lennard's failure would have damped the spirits of the men, and deterred them from a second attempt. But it seems to have had a contrary effect, and to have stirred them up to renewed exertion. A consultation was held as to the next steps to be taken. The only hope that remained was in the dinghy, (the jolly-boat having been washed away,) when Turner, the boatswain, as brave a fellow as ever breathed, volunteered to make the attempt. He secured a rope round his body, and was then lowered into the boat. The tackling was let go, the men gave a cheer, and the boat, with its occupant, was borne away by the current.

With intense anxiety the men on the wreck watched the progress of Turner, who had been carried in the boat to within a few feet of the shore; then the watchers saw it balanced upon the crest of a huge wave, and the next moment it was dashed to pieces upon the rocks; the boatswain, however, retained his presence of mind; he kept hold of the rope when dashed out of the boat, and succeeded in scrambling up the cliff.

In the meantime, the waves were making heavy breaches over the ship; the crew clung by the ropes on the forecastle; each succeeding wave threatened them all with destruction; whilst, at each surge of the vessel, it is related by one of the sufferers, that "the ship's bell tolled one, the funereal knell of many, and, as we fully expected then, of all, except the boatswain, who, though severely bruised, stood on the shore, and appeared in all probability to be the only survivor left." The brig continued to beat with great violence for upwards of an hour, when a tremendous sea lifted her quarter over the rock on which she had at first struck, and carried her close to a dry rock, which seemed to offer, for a time at least, a refuge from the present danger. The forecastle, which up to this time had been the only sheltered part of the ship, was now abandoned for the poop; and as Captain Baker saw no chance of saving the vessel, he determined to remove the people from her if possible.

Calling around him his officers and men, he communicated to them his intentions, and pointed out the best means of securing their safety. He then ordered every man to make the best of his way from the wreck to the rock. Now, for the first time, his orders were not promptly obeyed; all the crew to a man refused to leave the wreck unless Captain Baker would precede them. There was a simultaneous burst of feeling that did honour alike to the commander and the men. To the former, in that he had so gained the affection and respect of his people; and to the latter, inasmuch as they knew how to appreciate such an officer.

Never was good discipline displayed in a more conspicuous manner. No argument or entreaty could prevail on Captain Baker to change his resolution. He again directed the men to quit the vessel, calmly observing that his life was the least and last consideration. The men, upon hearing this reiterated command, took measures to leave the wreck, but this could not be done without much risk and danger; for, at each successive sea, the wreck surged upon the rock, and then again, as the waves receded, fell back. It was therefore necessary to spring from the wreck the moment she was close to the rock, and, unhappily, a few of the men perished in the attempt;

amongst these was Lieutenant Stanley, who being benumbed with cold, was unable to get a firm footing, and was swept away by the current; his companions, with every inclination, had not the power to save him; he struggled for a few moments, was dashed with irresistible force against the rocks, and the receding wave engulfed its victim.

When he had seen every man clear of the wreck, and not till then, did Captain Baker join his crew.

As soon as they had time to look about them, the ship's company perceived that they were on an isolated rock, separated from the mainland by a few fathoms. The rock rose some feet above the sea, but to their horror they perceived that it would be covered at high-water. It seemed as if they were rescued from one fearful catastrophe, only to perish by a more cruel and protracted fate. They watched the waters rise inch by inch around them, appalled by the feeling that those waters must sooner or later close over them for ever, and that nothing could save them except the outstretched arm of Him who could bid the waves be stayed, and say to the stormy winds, be still. Every man is more or less courageous under circumstances of danger, when it is attended by excitement, such as that of the battlefield. There is courage derived from the fear of shame; but the test of true valour is a scene like that we have described. *There* was no room for a display of the adventitious bravery which often becomes in reality the thing it strives to appear. No man *there* could reproach his neighbour if his cheek should blanch and his lip quiver; all were alike appalled, but the well-regulated mind rose superior to the rest. Such was the case with Captain Baker. Although he could not conceal from himself that their condition was almost hopeless, he continued with his voice to encourage the timid, and by his arm to support the weak.

Still the devoted crew, following the example of their commander, uttered no complaint. They were ready to meet death, yet they felt it hard to die without a struggle. The tide was rising rapidly, and if anything was to be done, it must be done instantly. The boatswain, who had never lost hold of the rope, went to the nearest point opposite the rock, and, watching his opportunity, he cast one end of the line across to his companions. Fortunately it reached the rock, and was gladly seized, but it proved to be only long enough to allow of one man holding it on the shore, and another on the rock, at arm's length. It may be imagined with what joy this slender means of deliverance was welcomed by all. The tide had made rapid advances; the waves, as if impatient for their prey, threw the white surf aloft, and dashed over the rock.

Would that we could do justice to the noble courage and conduct displayed by the crew of the *Drake*. Instead of rushing to the rope, as many would have done under similar circumstances, not a man moved until he was commanded to do so by Captain Baker. Had the slightest hesitation appeared on the part of the commander, or any want of presence of mind in the men, a tumultuous rush would have ensued, the rope, held as it was with difficulty by the outstretched hand, would inevitably have been lost in the struggle, and then all would have perished.

But good order, good discipline, and good feeling triumphed over every selfish fear and natural instinct of self-preservation, and to the honour of British sailors be it recorded, that each individual man of the crew, before he availed himself of the means of rescue, urged his captain to provide for his own safety first, by leading the way. But Captain Baker turned a deaf ear to every persuasion, and gave but one answer to all: "I will never leave the rock until every soul is safe."

In vain the men redoubled their entreaties that he would go; they were of no avail; the intrepid officer was steadfast in his purpose. There was no time for further discussion or delay. One by one the men slipped from the rock upon the rope, and by this assistance forty-four out of fifty succeeded in gaining the opposite shore. Unfortunately, amongst the six who remained, one was a woman. This poor creature, completely prostrate from the sufferings she had endured, lay stretched upon the cold rock, almost lifeless. To desert her was impossible; to convey her to the shore seemed equally impossible. Each moment of delay was fraught with destruction. A brave fellow, in the generosity of despair, when his turn came to quit the rock, took the woman in his arms, grasped the rope, and began the perilous transit. Alas! he was not permitted to gain the desired shore. When he had made about half the distance, the rope parted; not being strong enough to sustain the additional weight and strain, it broke; the seaman and his burden were seen but for an instant, and then swallowed up in the foaming eddies. At this moment the people on shore distinctly heard the words, "Then all hope is gone," and, indeed, it was so, for thus perished the last means of preservation that remained for Captain Baker and those who were with him on the rock. Their communication with the mainland was cut off; the water rose, and the surf increased every moment, all hope was gone, and for them a few minutes more must end "life's long voyage."

The men on shore tried every means in their power to save them. They tied every handkerchief and available material together to replace the lost rope, but their efforts were fruitless; they could not get length enough to reach the rock. A party was despatched in search of help. They found a farm-house; and while they were in search of a rope, those who stayed to watch the fate of their loved and respected commander and his three companions, saw wave after wave rise higher and higher. At one moment the sufferers disappeared in the foam and spray; the bravest shuddered, and closed his eyes on the scene. Again, as spell-bound, he looked; the wave had receded; they still lived, and rose above the waters. Again and again it was thus; but hope grew fainter and fainter. We can scarcely bring our narrative to an end; tears moisten our page; but the painful sequel must be told. The fatal billow came at last which bore them from time into eternity; all was over. When the party returned from their inland search, not a vestige of the rock, or of those devoted men, was to be seen.

> And is he dead, whose glorious mind
>   Lifts thine on high?
> To live in hearts we leave behind
>   Is not to die.

CAMPBELL

We feel how inadequate have been our efforts to depict the self-devotion of Captain Baker, and the courage and constancy of his crew. The following letter addressed to Lieutenant Book, formerly an officer of the *Drake*, will go farther than any panegyric we can offer, to display the right feeling of the ship's company, and their just appreciation of their brave and faithful commander.

SIR, Your being an old officer of ours in a former ship, and being our first lieutenant in H.M. ship *Drake*, leads us to beg that you will have the goodness to represent to our Lords Commissioners of the Admiralty the very high sense of gratitude we, the surviving petty officers and crew of his Majesty's late ship *Drake*, feel due to the memory of our late much lamented, and most worthy commander, who at the moment he saw death staring him in the face on one side, and the certainty of escape was pointed out to him on the other, most staunchly and frequently refused to attempt procuring his own safety, until every man and boy had been rescued from the impending danger. Indeed, the manliness and fortitude displayed by the late Captain Baker on the melancholy occasion of our wreck was such as never before was heard of. It was not as that of a moment, but his courage was tried for many hours, and his last determination of not crossing from the rock, on which he was every moment in danger of being washed away, was made with more firmness, if possible, than the first. In fact, during the whole business he proved himself to be a man whose name and late conduct ought ever to be held in the highest estimation by a crew who feel it their duty to ask from the Lords Commissioners of the Admiralty that, which they otherwise have not the means of obtaining, that is, a public and lasting record of the lion-hearted, generous, and very unexampled way in which our late noble commander sacrificed his life in the evening of the 23rd of June.*

The above letter was signed by the surviving crew of the *Drake*. We need not add that their request was complied with, and a monument erected to the memory of Captain Baker, in the chapel of the Royal Dockyard at Portsmouth.

*The verses on the loss of the *Drake*, the production of a friend, are omitted, because beautiful as they are, the addition of the poetical and the imaginative to a narrative of such pathetic reality, was found to give pain to the surviving relations of the lamented Captain Baker.

NOTES

1. William O.S. Gilly, *Narratives of Shipwrecks of The Royal Navy: Between 1793 and 1849. Compiled Principally from Official Documents in The Admiralty*, 2nd edn. (London: John W. Parker, 1861), 230-41.
2. The specifications for the class of military vessel to which the *Drake* belonged are laid out in David Lyon, *The Sailing Navy*

List: All the Ships of the Royal Navy, Built, Purchased and Captured, 1688-1860 (London: Conway Maritime Press, 1993), 146.

3. Admiralty Records 95/23-62, Ships: Sailing Qualities, Observations of the Qualities of Her Majesty's Ship, Piece 45, Folio 165, Public Record Office (Kew), London, England.

4. Gilly, *Narratives of Shipwrecks of The Royal Navy*, xix.

5. George P. Landow, *Images of Crisis* (Boston, London and Henley: Routledge and Kegan Paul, 1982), 195-96, 225-26 at n. 8.

6. Gilly, *Narratives of Shipwrecks of The Royal Navy*, 200-08.

9

TWO WRECKS ON THE PETIT NORD:
THE *BELLE-JULIE* AND THE *NATHALIE* (1826)[1]

CAPTAIN CLAIR-DESIRÉ LETOURNEUR
and GAUD HOUISTE (trans. Scott Jamieson)

The following narratives involving the French migratory fishery take place in the early nineteenth century on that peninsula near Conche and the Isles Groais (also Groays; Grey Islands). The importance and prestige of these merchant fleets is affirmed by the honours and considerable compensation bestowed on the survivors of these two ships. Shipwrecked in heavy ice, the *Belle-Julie*, "a huge vessel," had only 35 survivors among 106 crew, and the *Nathalie* only three survivors, from an unspecified crew list; both were part of the French fleet of 1826.

Economic interest in the region was generated almost entirely by the rich resource that abundant cod and other marine life presented. As Turgeon notes, it was "France's first great trans-Atlantic trade."[2] The annual French fleets to St. Pierre and Miquelon and the French Shore were often very large. The ports of Saint Malo and Granville outfitted roughly 8,800 ships employing 353,171 mariners for the North American fishing grounds, or an estimated two-thirds of the entire shipping fleet for the period 1713 to 1792.[3] The substantial French vessels carried a large number of crew, with roughly one person aboard per ton of ship, three times as many as did most merchant vessels. The reason is simple. Like those of the British merchant fleet, these expeditions were considered essential to national security as well as to the economy, for they served as a "nursery" of future naval seamen.

Since the sixteenth century French fishers and the French naval fleet had often been directly involved in major conflicts with Great Britain, including the War of the Spanish Succession, which ended with the Treaty of Utrecht of 1713. In theory though not in fact this treaty gave the British outright political and economic control over Newfoundland, but, as one historian has asked, "was France the actual beneficiary?"[4] Another phase in the dispute over jurisdiction came with the conclusion of the Seven Years' War and the signing in 1763 of the Treaty of Paris, in which British rights were again reaffirmed. Subsequently, with the exception of the islands of St. Pierre and Miquelon, with their mixed population of French, Acadians, and English, the chief supply station for the French Bank fishery and the Gulf of St. Lawrence fisheries, France retained the right to fish along the so-called French Shore, which more or less extended along the entire west coast of Newfoundland, and the Northern Peninsula, then referred to as the Petit Nord.[5] Because of the threat of piracy on the high seas and other possible hostile encounters, until 1783 cod-fishing vessels, especially those bound for Labrador, were not only larger than many merchant vessels but also heavily armed.

Between the time of the Conquest and the American Revolutionary War, this annual presence was estimated at 220 fishing ships and 8,000 crew. Interrupted somewhat by both the American and French revolutions and then the wars against Napoleon and the United States, the French North Atlantic fishery revived and flourished even after 1815, when Newfoundland's own colonial economy went into a tailspin because of custom duties and falling prices. Between 1817 and 1829, when the wrecks of the *Nathalie* and the *Belle-Julie* occurred, the bounty paid by France for fish dried and exported from the colony rose more than tenfold, and the fleet had grown to between 300 and 400 vessels manned by upward of 12,000 mariners. The continuing tenacity with which France maintained its treaty fishing rights is indicated by the fact that in 1829, when the British government sent the *Hannah* to Quirpon on the Northern Peninsula to establish equal rights of its fishers alongside the French fleet, the ship was refused entry, and told by French authorities that it risked eviction for trespass.[6]

French authorities had long recognized that ship safety could be jeopardized in Newfoundland waters by below freezing temperatures, ice fields, fog, and storms.[7] Though difficult to enforce, French royal regulations governing safety at sea, including an obligation to have present at least one ship's surgeon on all vessels over 19 tons, had existed since 1681. Naturally, these were not surgeons in the modern sense, more like "barbers," persons adept at performing the occasional life-saving amputation. One cannot help but wonder, however, if the judgment of French mariners, as the British jack-tar, was not sometimes adversely affected by their rations. The average modern individual requires between 3,500 and 4,500 calories per day; the basic daily diet of British and French mariners, according to sixteenth-century records, was 750 to 900 grams of biscuit (for an estimated 2400-3200 calories) and 2.5 to 3 litres of of wine![8]

Yet despite this environment and diet, shipwreck within the eighteenth-century French fishery was apparently less common than in the British fleet. The incidence of shipwreck of ships cleared from the ports of Saint-Malo and Granville was 2.2 and 1.5 percent respectively, with one-tenth of the mortality of French crews occurring on slave ships to the West Indies.[9] Nevertheless, there are numerous recorded shipwrecks around St. Pierre and Miquelon, and the French Shore, though not all, of course, of French origin.[10]

⚓

A. THE LOSS OF THE *BELLE-JULIE*

1. Report, Captain Clair-Desiré Letourneur to the Commandant of the French station in Newfoundland

Havre de Fichot, Terre-Neuve

Commandant,

I respectfully submit the present report. On 2nd June past, we were navigating by sight in the ice with two other ships from Granville, the *Comte d'Estourmel* under Captain Alix and the *Élisa* under Captain Gallien. Our course was NW toward Belle Isle and Groais [the Grey Islands]; we estimated our position at 13 leagues E. There were 10 other ships ahead of us and 5 more behind, separated by several leagues, and all following the same course. The winds were strong from the SSW and the seas were heavy. A few minutes before five in the evening, we struck a small ice pan, whose impact we hardly even felt on board. Moments later, I noticed that the *Belle-Julie* had become difficult to steer and had slowed down considerably compared to the other ships. I immediately gave orders to sound the depth and to man a pump. We learned that there were 12 feet of water in the aft hold. There were terrified cries from below that the hull was pierced, and that there was water knee-deep in the storeroom. So at once I gave the order to furl the sails, to manoeuvre to the other side and to set the flag at half-mast, but it could not be found. Since the ship now had water up to her hawse-holes, I ordered part of the crew to climb the shrouds to signal the *Élisa* and the *Comte d'Estourmel* that we needed immediate help. They changed direction and headed toward us but my poor ship was sinking faster and faster and I realized that nothing could prevent it from going down. I ordered the mast to be cut down and the boats launched in order to save as many lives as possible.

At this point words fail me; I cannot fully convey what a terrible situation the unfortunate men aboard the *Belle-Julie* found themselves in. It was the height of confusion. The rough seas, the bitter cold, everything indicated the impossibility of our being saved from certain death. I succeeded in having the mizzen cut down, but this did not help in any way. When I saw that the water had reached the level of the capstans, I had no other choice but to instruct the officers and crew to take to the water in an attempt to save themselves. In order to do this, I had them cut lashing which secured the small boats to the deck, and ordered them to throw everything overboard: the hens' cages, compartment hatch covers, empty barrels, whatever could float and that the men could hold onto. I urged them to remain calm and pointed to the *Élisa* and the *Comte d'Estourmel* sailing to our rescue. At that moment, those who knew how to swim jumped into the water, but nearly all were paralyzed by the cold and disappeared beneath the waves. Those still on board felt their courage somewhat buoyed up by the sight of the skillful manoeuvring of the two ships heading our way. In spite of the violent winds and waves, they had put their boats in the water to save as many of the shipwrecked seamen as they could.

I remained on board with 80 men and appealed to them not to lose hope and to cling to whatever floating objects they could find. The first mate and I, along with the ship's boy, climbed the shrouds.

The next moment, only about 10 or 12 minutes after we had become aware of our terrible plight, the *Belle-Julie* went down. One hundred and six men drowned, 31 were saved by the *Élisa*, and six

by the *Comte d'Estourmel*, of whom two died later. The terrifying
catastrophe happened in less than a quarter of an hour.

In the name of all the shipwrecked seamen, and especially myself,
I must express how much we owe to the captains and crews of the
Élisa and the *Comte d'Estourmel*. May their courage be made known
to all, especially to all sailors. It would be impossible for me to list in
detail all they did for us. I will not tell of the sailors who manned the
rescue boats, manoeuvring amid the floating debris, who did not
return to their own ship until there was no longer a man left on the
surface. They were forced to return to look after the ships, which were
in grave danger themselves because they had come to our aid; there
was a huge ice-field to the lee side where they ran the risk of being
driven by the strong winds and currents. I will describe this one fact
only: the *Élisa* had hove to at about one cable-length from us. Mr.
Gallien, her captain, made sure any man in sight was pulled out of
the water. Mr. Jourdan, the ship's owner and first mate, was on watch.
He had considerable influence over the crew and noticed that the
boats were unable to rescue very many people, and moreover, our
mizzen was down. He let his ship bear down upon the *Belle-Julie* and
approached our quarter so that as many ship-wrecked men as possible
could jump onto his vessel. He was soon 10 or 12 fathoms from us
and as soon as the *Belle-Julie* had disappeared, Mr. Jourdan had his
vessel brought to, in the eddy left by its sinking. Mr. Jourdan could
have saved 80 men by this brave manoeuvre if my ship had stayed
afloat one minute more. He did save 20, while the courageous and
skilled seamen in the small boats were able to pull only 11 others to
safety. I myself, and 12 of my crew, owe our lives to their efforts.

Approximately 40 widows with families have been reduced to the
most abject misery and deserve the attention of the Minister of the
Navy, who will undoubtedly obtain assistance through the generosity
of his Majesty the King. I will not cite any of the names of the crew
of the *Belle-Julie* for their courageous behaviour during these horrify-
ing circumstances. After the initial moments of terror, they performed
acts of unimaginable bravery, strength and selflessness. Every one of
them carried out his duty. As for me, I was holding on to the shrouds
and went down with the ship.

I remain, Commandant, your respectful, humble and obedient servant,

C.D. Letourneur

2. Letter from Mr. Clair-Desiré Letourneur, ex-Captain of the Belle-Julie *to Mr. Bajot, editor of the* Annales de la marine *concerning the best course of action to take during a shipwreck*

Dated at Granville, December 1st, 1826

Sir,

I feel it is my duty to share with you the following remarks concerning the sinking of the *Belle-Julie*, a huge vessel which was swallowed by the waves and disappeared along with her crew, save 35 men, in 10 minutes. What saved my life was the fact that I remained calm during that brief but most frightening of catastrophes. Since I do not know how to swim, I went down, as I should, with my ship. The only way seamen can save their lives is by acting calmly and not hastily.

As a general rule in such circumstances, on board a ship about to sink, one must remain on board as long as possible, because the ship itself is the largest and most suitable piece of floating debris. Secondly, one then does not have as long to struggle against the destructive elements.

If at all possible, a shipwrecked sailor must choose, from among the floating debris, the longest pieces of wood, such as masts, yards or oars. These are the best to hold onto, since shorter, round or square pieces turn over too easily in the water. When this happens, the man holding goes under also, swallows a considerable amount of water and becomes so weak that he loses his grip. The best of my crew members drowned in this way. I would advise any unfortunate person holding onto floating debris to use just enough strength to remain afloat. By doing so, he will not tire himself unnecessarily and will resist longer by preventing the object from turning over and dragging him under as well. That is what caused many of my men to die.

Let us consider the measures that are needed when a ship is fortunate enough to be called to help another during a heavy gale. In the tragic sinking of the *Belle-Julie*, many men perished right alongside the ships that came to help us. Only 35 were rescued because the others were unable to grasp the lines thrown to save them. To prevent this, the ship throwing the lines should attach a piece of wood to the end of each line to give the person something to hold with his hand, forearm or even by bending his leg. If it is impossible to do this, then at least they should tie as large a knot as possible so that the line will not slip easily out of the hand and the person will have a moment to grasp it with the other hand. You will notice that, when you are holding onto floating debris, as I have had the fateful experience to do, it is the weaker hand that reaches for the safety line, while the stronger grips the wood on which your life depends. For in such dire circumstances, the unfortunate victim is guided by a sort of instinct. This is why the precautions that I have indicated are of utter necessity.

In high winds and heavy seas, when shipwrecked men are holding onto floating debris, small boats are of little help in saving them. Rather, the captain of the ship must immediately bring his vessel to among the men in the water and begin hauling them on board. If Messrs. Jourdan, Alix and Gallien had not used this method so skillfully and pulled some 35 men from the angry sea, there would have been only 8 or 10 men saved by small boats.

If any of the above suggestions might save a man, my purpose has been served. That is my only intention in asking you to publish this letter.

C.D. Letourneur, Retired Naval Lieutenant, Knight of the Order of Saint Louis, ex-Captain of the *Belle-Julie*

B. THE LOSS OF THE *NATHALIE*

[Following comments of Mr. Bajot, editor of the *Annales de la marine*, in italics]

To describe a shipwreck, the sailors' courage, the constant struggle for their lives, one thinks of Seneca's words on man confronting adversity and, through his virtue, coming out victorious:

> *Ecce spectaculum dignum ad quod respiciat, intentus operi suo, Deus: ecce par Deo dignum, vir fortis cum mala fortuna compositus, utque si et provocaverit.*[11]

What an astounding sight it is to see those men, dedicated to an arduous life at sea, continually brave in all kinds of danger, and so often succeeding, thanks to the characteristic qualities of their noble profession: admirable presence of mind, calm fearlessness.

In another report, on the sinking of the Belle-Julie, *we witnessed the bravery of Captain Letourneur, whose duty required him to remain on board his ship until the last man was safe. He went down with her, but not without having attempted to provide safety for his unfortunate crew by every means that his authority, powers of persuasion and example were capable of in such a sudden disaster.*

In the account that follows, the first mate of the Nathalie *relates how, after his ship sank, he fought for his life for 19 days, battling ice floes, heavy seas, starvation, bitter cold and despair, and clawed his way back from the brink of death. Moreover, he saved the lives of two other sailors through his courage, devotion, and incredible perseverance, and returned with them to safety.*

COMMANDANT

On May 29th, 1826, at around 8 p.m., the *Nathalie* sank.

There were seven men left floating, holding onto debris of various sizes. The weather was overcast, with a fresh breeze from the NE. We were approximately 10 leagues from *l'île de Grouais* (Grey Islands). I will only include the details of what happened to me and to my unfortunate companions, Joret and Potier, seamen on the *Nathalie* who, like myself, lived for 19 days on almost nothing; they showed both resignation and courage in that awful situation. I have been a sailor all my life, Commandant, so I beseech you to excuse my clumsy language and to accept what I relate here as the truth.

As soon as the ship went down, I came to the surface and found myself, along with Potier, on two pieces of wood moored together. After much effort, we managed to climb onto a flat pan of ice. When we were finally in that cruel situation, and freezing cold, fog and darkness came over us, making our suffering and anguish all the worse.

The next morning, the fog lifted and we saw four men a considerable distance away and one other a cable-length from us. The fog moved in again until nine that evening. When it lifted, we sighted a three-masted ship where we had seen the four men that morning. Throughout the remainder of that day, we were unable to see the ship again, or to get any closer to the nearest man.

Until June 1st, a lot of rain and freezing rain fell, and we were overwhelmed with hunger, cold and exhaustion. At around mid-day,

Nathalie survivors on an ice-floe. "Deep in thought and reflecting upon Eternity, we awaited death, resigned to our fate."

"They took us into their arms to help us leave." The survivors from the wreck of the *Nathalie* are finally spotted and rescued. Both scenes from lithographs by C. Motte. Courtesy of the Department of Rare Books and Special Collections, McGill University Libraries

the weather cleared. We saw what was left of the debris of the Nathalie and spotted the man we had seen two days earlier. Among the floating debris, there was a hens' cage, about 20 fathoms away. I was able to climb onto a small pan of ice and use it as a dinghy, sculling with an oar I had saved from the shipwreck. I found four dead hens in the cage and cannot describe the joy I felt. I instantly devoured a leg, which restored a little of my strength. Feeling somewhat courageous, I headed toward Potier to give him some as well. The two of us ate the rest of the hen. Almost immediately, we saw a barrel of cider nearly full and, after a lot of effort, managed to get it onto our ice pan. Although the cider tasted salty from the seawater, it was quite drinkable.

Half an hour later, we spotted a rowboat a quarter of a league upwind from us. I then helped my unfortunate companion onto a smaller ice pan and headed toward it. It was incredibly difficult to make progress, but we finally arrived alongside the half-submerged boat.

I had previously taken the precaution of saving some small nails that I had removed from the hoops of the barrel we had found, so I devised a plan to make the boat seaworthy. I took hold of a length of cord from the boat and tied it securely to the middle seat, with the idea of capsizing it and repairing it with a barrel stave. We were never able to succeed in carrying this out and had to get into the boat with water up to our waists.

We then tried to make our way toward the man we had seen floating on the ice pan, a half a league away. It took nearly two hours of continuous effort to reach; it was Joret, and he was extremely weak. We made him eat some of the hens, and this gave him a little strength. The three of us together, after great pains, were able to get the boat floating properly and this made us all hopeful. I can assure you that the first day of June, even in such a dire predicament, was a happy day for us. The fact that we were together made us feel certain that we would survive. Our boat was no sooner afloat than we sighted land, which I recognized as Belle Isle and Grouais, some 10 leagues away.

June 2nd
We continued our course toward land until 10 o'clock on June 2nd, when the boat became jammed in the ice about four leagues from Grouais Island. All we had to eat were two and a half hens, and nothing to drink but ice.

June 3rd, 4th, 5th, 6th
At about five the next evening, the fog came upon us and we stayed
in the same position until the morning of June 6th at around 11
o'clock. The weather cleared and we sighted about 30 ships near the
ice fields two leagues to the east of us. With no more than half a hen
remaining, we agreed to abandon the boat, having left the oar stick-
ing up with a shirt tied to it, in case we were not rescued by one of
the ships and needed to locate it again. Though we were very weak
and the distance across the ice fields quite considerable, we walked
rapidly toward the ships. When we were nearly halfway there, a
strong wind arose in the north and separated the ice pans, making it
impossible to go further or to return to our boat. We were overcome
by deep despair and looked at one another without a word. So we
stayed for an hour and then gave ourselves up to God's mercy. We
were overwhelmed with exhaustion, weakness and lack of sleep; the
cold and dampness would awaken us the very instant we fell asleep.
This was even worse than hunger, which was already unbearable in
the extreme. For eight days, the only sustenance we'd had was dead
hens, and now even they were gone.

June 6th to 10th
The same day, at around 10 o'clock in the evening, the northwest
wind calmed down. The fog returned, brought rain with it and lasted
until around two in the morning on June 10th. Those four days
seemed like four centuries, filled with fear and dread of the worst
kind. For me to describe them would make your hair stand on end.

   Then we saw land. I realized that we had been carried at least six
leagues to the south. Seeing that the ice was tightly packed to the
land, I urged my companions to follow me. We took the two short
planks we had saved and set out on the ice toward land, at a distance
of some nine leagues.

June 10th to 13th
It is impossible for me to describe the torment that we suffered to
cover that distance. For three days, we struggled toward the safety of
dry land, exhausted and starving, sustained only by hope. However,
just when everything seemed to give us reason to believe that we were
safe, one of us would fall between the ice pans. The blood from our
wounds left behind us a trail of our passage and our pain.

June 13th

On June 13, we finally arrived within a quarter of a league of the shore, having lived through excruciating agony and overcome obstacles that are impossible to imagine. Seeing that we were now still separated from the shore by open water cast us into the depths of despair.

After a few minutes, I regained my senses and suggested to my unlucky companions that we should entrust ourselves to a small ice pan, which we could paddle with the two planks. We were about halfway to shore when the ice pan broke in two, causing more problems. Thanks to Providence, we overcame them and, that same day, finally arrived on land!

Because of the suffering, the utter exhaustion, the fear and the hope we had felt, that day was the most terrible we had experienced since May 29th.

We collapsed on the grass, but the sleep that should have brought us relief produced the opposite effect. Joret went blind, and all three of us were crippled with pain. I somehow managed to drag myself to the water's edge, where I filled my hat with mussels. I then realized that the bay where we had landed was inhabited, because I saw wood chips and pieces of biscuit floating by. This sight, combined with the excellent meal of raw mussels, raised our hopes enormously, without improving our poor health in any way.

June 17th

The anxiety we still felt remained with us until June 17th at four in the afternoon, when an English schooner, the *Brothers of Saint John*, and Captain Wilhelmy, rescued us and took us to the safety of Fousche Harbour nearby. For two days we were given the best possible care on board that schooner. On June 19th, at two o'clock in the afternoon, we were put on board the *Bonne-Mère*, bound for Granville.

There ended our troubles. We had the good fortune to be treated like brothers by Mr. Herain, the ship's owner. We are happy to say that we owe so much to those men.

Here ends the account of the events that happened to me, Potier and Joret, between the 29th of May and the 17th of June, 1826. You have learned how we survived 19 days of the worst possible suffering on four hens and a hatful of mussels.

My two companions and I are still in pain and perhaps may never fully recover our health. God willing, however, we will be able to resume work, for we know no other life than that of a sailor. Joret and I are married and place ourselves in your hands and under the benevolence of the Minister of the Marine. I enclose our medical certificates, signed by the doctors who have examined us.

Your humble and obedient servant,

Houiste

N.B. His majesty the King, by an ordinance dated December 3rd, 1826, made Houist and Jourdan (of the *Belle-Julie*) Knights of the *Légion d'Honneur*. The Minister of the Marine granted the sum of 6,000 francs to each of the families of Granville affected by the loss of the *Nathalie* and the *Belle-Julie*.

NOTES

1. "The shipwreck of the *Belle-Julie* from Granville in the ice off the Great Northern Peninsula of Newfoundland on June 2, 1826. A Report by Seagoing Captain Clair Desiré Letourneur, retired Lieutenant, Knight of the Order of St. Louis, addressed to the Commandant of the French station in Newfoundland. The loss of the sailing ship *Nathalie*, out of Granville in the ice off Newfoundland, May 29, 1826. A Report by Gaud Houiste, first mate, concerning the extraordinary events experienced by him and two other seamen following the sinking of the *Nathalie*, submitted to Monsieur Brou, Capitaine de frégate, Commandant de la Station de Terre-Neuve." From *Annales de la marine*, 1ᵉ partie, tome 2, 1826 (1ᵉ année, le série 28, Mémoires 2). Based, with thanks, on an unpublished translation by Dr. Scott Jamieson, Frecker Institute, Memorial University of Newfoundland.
2. Laurier Turgeon, "Towards a History of the Fishery: Marketing Cod at Marseilles During the Eighteenth Century," *Histoire Sociale/Social History* 14 (November 1981): 295; see also F.J. Thorpe, "The Cod Fishery in French American Strategy, 1660-

1783," Unpublished paper presented at an Annual Meeting of the Canadian Historical Association, June 1989, 1-2.

3. Jean-François Brière, "The Ports of Saint-Malo and Granville and the North American Fisheries in the 18th Century," in *Global Crossroads and the American Seas* (Missoula, MT: Pictorial Histories Publishing, 1988), 13.

4. Jean-François Brière, "Pêche et politique à Terre-Neuve au XVIIIe siècle: la France véritable gagnante du traité d'Utrecht?," *Canadian Historical Review* 64, 2 (juin 1983): 168-87.

5. For background on the rivalry between France and England and the extent of the French fishery, including St. Pierre and Miquelon, see D.W. Prowse, *A History of Newfoundland From The English, Colonial and Foreign Records* (London and New York: Macmillan, 1895), 564-74; F.J. Thorpe, "The Cod Fishery in French American Strategy, 1660-1783," Unpublished paper presented at an Annual Meeting of the Canadian Historical Association, June 1989; Brière, "The Ports of Saint-Malo and Granville," 9-18.

6. Frederic F. Thompson, *The French Shore Problem in Newfoundland: An Imperial Study* (Toronto: University of Toronto Press, 1961), 22-23.

7. Jean-François Brière, "The Safety of Navigation in the 18th Century French Cod Fisheries," *Acadiensis* 16, 2 (Fall 1987): 88.

8. Laurier Turgeon and Denis Dickner, "Contraintes et choix alimentaires d'un groupe d'appartenance: les marines' pêcheurs Français à Terre-Neuve au XVIe siècle," *Canadian Folklore Canadien* 12, 2 (1990): 61.

9. Brière, "The Safety of Navigation," 85.

10. Joseph Lehuenen and Jean-Pierre Andrieux, *Naufrage!: histoire illustrée des désastres maritimes aux Iles Saint-Pierre et Miquelon* (Beamsville, Ont.: W.F. Rannie, 1977).

11. "Behold the worthy sight that God sees, reflecting upon his creation: behold the one worthy of God: a strong man, calm in the face of misfortune, even when God has provoked him."

I O

SHIPWRECK AND SUFFERINGS OF THE CREW AND PASSENGERS OF THE BRIG *NEPTUNE* (1830)[1]

JOHN SMITH

The *Neptune* was wrecked during a significant transitional period in the history of settlers and native peoples of Newfoundland and Labrador, a mere five years after the creation of the colony's first Supreme Court, two years before the opening of the first representative assembly, during the beginnings of permanent settlement along the Strait of Belle Isle and northwestern Newfoundland, two years before the arrival of the Hudson's Bay Company in Labrador, and in the first year of the reign of King William IV. The previous year had seen the "extinction" of the Beothuks with the lamented death of Shanawdithit.[2] This event supposedly marked the end of indigenous occupation on the island, but such, of course, was not the case.[3]

A longstanding trade among Inuit, Montagnais, Beothuk, and Europeans had been initiated before the arrival of the Basque whalers and had lasted into the early nineteenth century. An eighteenth-century map designated an area between southern Labrador and the Northern Peninsula as "Passage of Savages."[4] Mi'Kmaq peoples had long ago established their presence along the southwest and west coasts from St. Pierre and Miquelon to Bonne Bay and probably farther north.[5] Some surviving Beothuk after Shanawditith may well have become integrated into existing native and settler communities, especially along the southern Labrador coast.[6] Many native peoples, then, existed in western Newfoundland and southern Labrador, and those shipwrecked on the *Neptune* and other vessels would not have survived without their humanitarian intervention.

Coming as he did from the United States, the narrator John Smith had been reared in the history and mythology of the "savage." The encounter between First Nations peoples and Americans had been much more violent than in British North America, certainly since the War of American Independence, and perhaps the divergence of attitudes was exaggerated as a result of the role of Tecumseh and his following, as British allies, during the War of 1812-14.[7] This helps to explain why Smith assumed from his readings that "the Indians of North America" were "of a cruel, revengeful, inexorable disposition," and that they would pursue their enemies and gain their revenge, experiencing "a diabolical pleasure from the tortures they inflict on their prisoners." There are documentary records of violent conflict between the different native groups and the European populations of southern Labrador and the island, but these had occurred almost entirely prior to the nineteenth century. It appears therefore that Smith's ponderings concerning the native population in the region of the shipwreck were based entirely on ignorance.

Nearly a month after the shipwreck, after having subsisted only on some food salvaged from the *Neptune*, Smith and a handful of survivors encountered an aboriginal person dressed in furs and holding a musket. Identifying himself as "Esquimaux," he told them in broken English that he was spending the winter hunting and trapping furs which he intended to sell to traders at Belle Isle, roughly eight or nine days away to the southwest. He then proceeded to provide food and shelter in his wigwam to the survivors. Though initially mindful of possible rape and robbery, Smith changed his mind wholeheartedly as a result of this experience, describing his "friend and benefactor" who provided the group a "peaceful asylum" as belonging to a people "who are social and humane to those whom they consider their friends and ready to partake with them of the last morsel, or to risk their lives in their behalf."

After caring for them, their Native benefactor took them to the nearest White settlement at Belle Isle. The presence of schooners and a handful of "wintermen" at this site during January suggests that these traders were associated with English rather than Jersey mercantile firms, which controlled northeast Newfoundland and Labrador. They were there because of an interest in maximizing the winter seal and fur economy of southern Labrador.[8] This pattern of merchant establishments, which was firmly entrenched by 1830, remained largely intact for the next 40 years.[9] This combination of a native and a settler presence as a result of this economy undoubtedly saved the lives of these shipwreck victims.

Apart from its historical content, this narrative is fascinating for its spiritual preoccupations. In a concluding section, "Moral Reflections," Smith develops one of the more complete arguments to be found in any shipwreck narrative on the nature and value of human existence and the impact that such an event has on the individual. For him, religion was "the balm that heals those wounds" suffered on life's "stormy sea of adversity" and its accompanying "ills, infirmities and disappointments." Later he adds, "Religion is the only balm for a wounded spirit." In metaphorical and literal terms, he regarded his faith as a form of protection from depression and despair; it was a source of hope, and it also influenced an individual's behaviour: "It purifies, it adorns, it ennobles our nature." For Smith, this experience and its ensuing narrative served the very important purpose of instructing and reforming "careless" non-believers who were "unconcerned, as regards the future welfare of their precious and immortal souls."

AFTER AN ABSENCE of nearly three years from my native country, on the 25th day of November, 1829, I shipped as first mate on board the brig *Neptune*, Captain Charles Mason, for a voyage from Bristol (Eng.) to Quebec; with the promise of there receiving my discharge, and with the intention of proceeding from thence to the city of New York, where, I supposed, I had an aged and widowed mother living. I had flattered myself with the prospects of a short and pleasant voyage, but so far from its being realized, it was my misfortune to experience a sad reverse, the most remarkable events of which, I must beg liberty to relate as they occurred, without ornament or art. I am but little used to writing; the reader must not, therefore, expect to meet with any manner of elegance in my stile [sic], in which he will find nothing, but the frank language of a sailor, which I hope, will be accepted as an apology for its incorrectness. We set sail about nine a.m. with 17 souls on board, including the captain's wife and two sons, one six and the other eight years of age. The wind continued with little variation favourable, and the weather not unpleasant, until late in the afternoon of the 2nd of January, when we experienced a shift of wind nearly ahead, which from its rapid increase, and beclouded and threatening aspect of the horizon, was considered as a sure indication of an approaching storm. At twelve at night, the wind increased almost to a hurricane; but having a staunch good vessel, and as we supposed plenty of sea room, we, at its commencement, apprehended but little danger; but in this we too soon found our mistake, for having now reached a cold latitude, in an inclement season, and the wind rather increasing than abating, in the morning of the 3rd, the sails and the rigging became so stiff with ice, as to render the brig almost unmanageable, and the sun being completely obscured and hidden from our sight by thick clouds, and preventing an observation, we were left to the mercy of the winds, which were driving us we knew not whither, but in the opinion of all, far out of our course, as it afterward proved. What we all suffered from the intense cold (particularly the wife and children of the poor unfortunate captain) can be best conceived by such of my seafaring brethren, whose fate it may have been to navigate these northern latitudes in mid-winter; several of our most able-bodied seamen became so frost bitten, as to be unable to stand on their feet, and to add to our misfortune, our water froze to a solid cake of ice, which we were obliged to cut off in small pieces and dissolve in our mouths.

Such was our situation from the second to the twelfth of January, when in the evening about nine o'clock, in as violent a snow storm as was ever probably experienced by man, and which so obscured every thing from our view, as to prevent our discerning an object of the brig's size twice her length ahead, amid the roar of the wind and waves, the unwelcomed sound of breakers were heard, and in twenty minutes after the brig struck; alas, what a scene of distress now ensued! And the lamentations of the poor unfortunate female, and her two helpless children, were sufficient to melt the hardest heart! They all clung to the husband and parent begging for that protection, which it was not in the power of any human being to afford them. The masts being loosened by the shock, quivered over our heads, and the sails were torn in a thousand pieces. Indeed, the fury of the storm, the darkness of the night, the dashing of the waves against our stranded brig, and the prospect of an immediate death, which we were all in momentary expectation of, created a scene of horror past description. But in whatever situation fate may place mankind, however distressing, it is an acknowledged fact, that life is sweet, and each one of us was endeavouring to preserve it by clinging or lashing ourselves to the wreck. But in this all were not successful, for at day's dawn it was discovered that four of our number were missing, whom it was conjectured became so frozen as to be unable to help themselves, and were washed overboard. Yet contrary to the expectations of every other soul on board, the captain's wife and two children were found among the living.

The day dawned, but only to present us if possible with a more melancholy view of our situation. Land was indeed discernible ahead, but without the appearance of being inhabited, and at so great a distance that an attempt to reach it with our boats or by swimming, appeared to promise nothing but the inevitable destruction of our lives, for the waves agitated by the winds rolled and broke with such violence against the rocks, which were not discernible above the surface of the water, that had any attempted it he must have run the risk of being launched back into the main ocean, or dashed to pieces against the rocks. Several hours passed thus, without our being able to conclude what was best to be done in our deplorable situation. To remain much longer in that in which we then were, all believed impossible, as the brig's stern was already stove in by the waves and there was no certainty that she would hold together from one minute to another; and should it have proved otherwise, and we had attempted to remain another night on the wreck, all must have perished, as our fire had become extinguished and without a possibility to rekindle it, and if enabled to resist the calls of hunger the cold was too piercing to be long endured.

In this awful dilemma, we could do nothing more than to huddle ourselves together on the quarter deck, and thus attempt to contract heat one from another, placing the unfortunate mother and her two wretched offspring in the centre. While thus situated, little expecting any other deliverance than that produced by death, every suppliant hand was raised in petition to Providence to afford us some unforeseen means of escaping to the shore. There never could be a more fervent petition. Heaven at length seemed to look down with pity and compassion on our miseries. Truly we could say the Lord is a prayer-answering God, for when we little expected it, of a sudden, the wind began to abate, and the agitation of the sea in a measure to subside, insomuch that one of our hands, who was supposed to be the best swimmer on board, having contemplated the distance to the shore, resolved to attempt the passage at the risk of his life, observing that he could but die in the attempt, and if such should be his fate he should conceive himself better off than to be doomed to pass another night on the wreck. Thus resolved he plunged into the sea, and we saw him for many minutes attempting to combat the waves, which sometimes hurried him forward almost to touch the shore, then washed back into the deep, disappearing for some minutes, and appearing again only to be seen dashed against the rocks. The poor fellow became at length exhausted and sunk to rise no more.

Our number was now reduced to twelve miserable souls, who could not but view themselves in a situation worse than that of their unfortunate companion, whom they had seen perish before their eyes, but whose sufferings were at an end. As we could now only look to Heaven for deliverance, we did not for a moment suspend our prayers and supplications, and I truly believe that we did not pray in vain, for the wind continued to abate and the sea became less boisterous, insomuch that at noon, we began to turn our attention to the boat, which although in a leaky condition, and so filled with ice as to render it extremely difficult to launch her, yet there was now but one alternative left us, either to attempt the passage at the hazard of our lives, or to remain where we were and perish together, for not one soul of us could have survived another night.

After much hard labour we succeeded in getting the boat over-board; and by casting lots, determined who of us should attempt the first passage. It fell to five, including myself and the Captain's wife and eldest son, which was all the boat would contain with any degree of safety. Before leaving the wreck a coil of spare rigging was put into the boat, one end of which was attached to the brig's foremast, with which it was the intention of those left on board to warp back the boat if we should be so fortunate as to succeed in reaching the shore, which with but very faint hopes of doing we at parting shook each of our shipmates by the hand, and bid them an affectionate adieu, expecting that if we ever met them again, it would in all probability be in another world; the separation of the captain and his wife and little son was affecting beyond description. All things now being in readiness, the word was given "cast off!" and in a moment our crazy bark [barque] was mounted on the white foaming surf to half the height of the brig's main mast. We yet however possessed sufficient strength with our oars to keep her head to the shore, and when but a little distance from the wreck a prodigious wave took us in an instant to more than half the distance, and a second in quick succession threw us with violence upon a sandy shore.

As soon as we were all so fortunate as to recover our feet, we displayed one of our hats in the air, which was extended upon the end of an oar, the signal agreed upon of our safe landing, before we quit the wreck. In a moment it was answered by the boat's shooting back through the foaming surf, by aid of the warp — and in about half an hour, we had the satisfaction to see the boat returning with those who were left on board the wreck. This was however a satisfaction which was but a few moments enjoyed. Fate had determined that these poor fellows should be less fortunate than ourselves, for when within about twenty rods of the shore, they were met and capsized by the surf! We now gave them all up as lost, as we conceived that no one could reach the shore unless by a miracle. In this we were however mistaken, for a great swell in an instant after threw the unfortunate captain within our reach, and we were so fortunate as to rescue him from a watery grave, and without his having apparently sustained very great bodily injury. But, destruction notwithstanding seemed to have selected this truly unfortunate man, as a victim! For no sooner did he behold his little son driven to and fro, and the sport of the foaming billows, than breaking from the hold of those who attempted by force to deter him, in a fit of desperation, he again threw himself into the sea and was himself soon compelled to yield to the unconquerable impetuosity of the surf, without being able either to afford protection to his child or to save himself. The lifeless corpses of both were a few moments after thrown upon the shore, and produced a melancholy spectacle for his surviving companion and child to behold, and whose feelings on an occasion like this may be better imagined than described! For more than one hour the wretched woman remained kneeling and weeping by the side of the lifeless bodies of her unfortunate husband and child, and could not be removed but by force!

By great exertion we were enabled to save the life of one more of our shipmates which the last boat contained. When nearly exhausted, he was so fortunate as to seize upon a rope which was thrown to him, and by which he was drawn on shore. The number of survivors now amounted to no more than six, among whom was the cook, who fortunately had been so wise as to secure fireworks in his pocket previous to leaving the brig, which had he failed to have done, our situations would have been no better than while on board the wreck, for as the day was now far spent and the night approaching, we must have all perished with the cold had we been deprived of the means of enkindling a fire.

For our better security for the night, we all retired to a thicket a few rods distant from where we landed, and where, although we were careful to keep up a large fire, we suffered very much from the sharpness of the wind, against which we had but an indifferent shelter. The trees by which we were encompassed were insufficient to protect us from the snow, which still continued to fall in immense flakes. While it seeped through our clothes on the side exposed to the fire, on our backs it formed a heap which we were obliged to shake off before it froze into ice; yet so anxious were my shipmates to render as comfortable as possible the situation of the wretched female and her helpless son, whom fate had deprived of a husband and parent, and now placed in a situation to demand their protection, that their own sufferings and deprivations produced not a murmur. We all spent the dark, gloomy and stormy night, as comfortably as could be expected for persons in our wretched condition, yet I think I may say it proved to all a sleepless one, although two nights had passed since we had enjoyed a minute's slumber.

The next morning we began to think more seriously on our condition, and what new difficulties would most probably attend us. We had esteemed ourselves fortunate when we succeeded the day previous in making our miraculous escape, but ceased to feel that degree of satisfaction, when we looked forward to our future safety. We were to all appearance cast upon a wild and uninhabited coast. We could perceive nothing before us but a thick and almost impenetrable forest, and the ground covered with snow of more than two feet in depth, and without any other sustenance than a small keg of beef, and a bag of hard bread, which was fortunately thrown into the boat in her first trip to the shore. Nor were we without apprehensions of being attacked by wild beasts, or with meeting with savages, not less to be dreaded, for in either case we were not possessed with any thing that deserved the name of weapon, with which to defend ourselves, and to add to our wretchedness, we had dependent upon us for support and protection an afflicted and helpless female, and her son, a tender youth not exceeding eight years of age! Indeed, the more we reflected on our miserable helpless situation, the more we were on the eve of being driven to despair.

As it was impossible for us at that inclement season, and with the ground covered with so great a depth of snow, to attempt to penetrate the thick forest in search of inhabitants with any possibility of success, it was by all agreed that our wisest plan would be to erect with rotten logs and branches of trees, as comfortable an habitation as our means would admit, and which might serve us for a shelter, until the snow should become so diminished in depth, either by rain or the rays of the sun, as to render travelling less difficult. In doing this we had a twofold object in view, for by encamping near the seashore, and in fair view of the wreck, which still lay stranded upon the rocks, exposed to tremendous surf, from her it was not impossible that we might obtain some necessary articles of food or clothing; as it was the opinion of all that she could not hold together much longer, her stern having nearly disappeared and the surf making a clear breach over her. In this we were all soon sadly disappointed, for in the course of the night of the 13th, the wind having shifted from south-west to a north-east point, early in the morning of the 15th, not a vestige of the wreck was to be discovered; nor were we able afterward to determine whether she was driven from the rocks by the strong winds from the NW to the sea, or sunk in deep water in the immediate vicinity of the reef on which she had foundered.

The dismal apprehensions we were under, in consequence of having our fondest hopes thus suddenly and unexpectedly blasted, can be better imagined than described. We found ourselves at mid-winter on a wild, and apparently uninhabited part of the coast, fatigued, sickly, and almost destitute of food and clothing. Nothing remained but to commit ourselves to kind Providence, and make the best of our situation. On the 16th and 17th, we were employed in scraping away the snow and in building a sort of hut, under a cliff adjoining the sea-side, to secure us from the inclemency of the weather. Here we remained four days, in as comfortable a situation as could be expected, as we did not want for fuel; the piercing keen air was in a great measure expelled from our hut, by the means of a great fire which we kept constantly burning night and day. As our only food was salt beef and hard bread, we contrived to freshen the former by removing to our hut a hollow stump, closed at one end and about four feet in length, and by filling it with snow and ice, which was dissolved by means of hot stones obtained from the shore, and into which after the ice had become so dissolved, we deposited our beef, cut into small slices, which were afterward broiled on the coals.

The situation of our unfortunate female companion, and her little son, was rendered as comfortable as our means would admit of, nor ought I to omit mentioning, that they both exhibited that degree of fortitude, and resignation, amid their afflictions, that I should have supposed hardly possible had I not been an eye witness thereto. While we were employed either in repairing or improving our hut or in devising means to render our food more palatable, their time was almost wholly occupied in solemn devotion in prayer to the Almighty, supplicating his mercy and kind interposition in our favour! And I am not now ashamed to say to the world, that as regards the welfare of my own immortal soul, the prayers of the pious mother, and her little son (particularly the latter, but eight years of age) were productive of the most happy effects. It sent arrows of conviction to my soul, and caused me to cry aloud "Lord have mercy on me, the chiefest of sinners!" Yes, reader, of whatever persuasion you may be, permit me to declare to you, that that important happy moment, will never be forgotten by me, when the Almighty in his infinite goodness, was pleased to speak peace to my soul! When I met with conviction and conversion in the wild wilderness, through the instrumentality of a child! And who, permit me to ask, can for a moment doubt the goodness, the omnipresence of the Almighty? To Him we have the promise that we shall have free access, whatever may be our condition, or in whatever situation fate may have placed us, if we come to Him with a contrite and penitent heart!

Early in the morning of the 20th, discovering that the snow had become sufficiently encrusted to bear us, it was by us resolved that three of our number should set out on a tour of discovery, leaving one to remain with Mrs. Mason and her son, until our return, which we promised should be in four days, should we be so fortunate as to make or should we not make any discovery of inhabitants. Providing for ourselves a sufficient quantity of food to which we had been confined for several days, about 10 a.m., we took an affectionate leave of those we left behind (having requested their prayers in our absence); we set forth with heavy hearts, taking a course westward, as nearly as we could judge by the points of the compass. We found our course frequently impeded in the first day's travel, by thick underwood, and almost impenetrable swamps; to avoid which, in some instances we were compelled to take circuitous routes of some miles. Nearly an hour before sunset we became so exhausted as to compel us to seek a shelter for the night, beneath a shelving rock, where, with a comfortable fire, we were enabled to repose until morning.

We early arose, and after partaking of our humble repast, we again put forward, still bending our course to the west, but without meeting with any thing to encourage us that we should be so fortunate as to discover the object of our pursuit. We this day as in the former, met with many obstacles in our journey almost of too difficult a nature to be surmounted by us, in our weak and debilitated state. Sometimes high and impassable ledges would present themselves in our course, and then a wide extending miry marsh, thickly covered with small brush, and creeping briars, and through which it is not improbable that no human being ever attempted to pass.

Having about noon arrived in an exhausted state, on the summit of a very high hill, and beholding nothing around us on either side but a boundless forest, as far as the eye sight could extend, we came to a halt, and held a consultation among ourselves whether it would not be more prudent for us to return, than to attempt to proceed any further in the course we had been travelling, and without the most distant prospect of meeting with deliverance; as in our whole journey, we had not met with any thing that could satisfy us, that the country was inhabited by human beings; but not improbably abounded with wild animals, peculiar to a cold climate; as we several times saw at a distance what, from information, we have since received, we suppose might have been bears, moose, and deer. There was indeed another very great reason why we should return, for by penetrating further into the country, we possibly might meet with insuperable difficulties, in our attempts to find our way back again to what we now called our home. It was therefore concluded by all that it was most prudent to retrace our steps, while our tracks still visible on the surface of the snow, would serve us for a guide.

Without meeting with any thing remarkable, or worthy of notice, we succeeded in reaching the hut late in the afternoon of the 23rd, and found our companions in the same condition as when we left them. We had no occasion to inform them of our ill success, as regarded the flattering hopes that we had entertained of meeting with inhabitants; they too plainly saw it depicted in our countenances, and for the moment, caused in all a very great depression of spirits, and how could it be otherwise? We had thought ourselves peculiarly fortunate in reaching the shore, but we began now to think ourselves less so, than those of our shipmates who had found a watery grave, and whose troubles were at an end! Our prospects were indeed gloomy beyond description! We had food sufficient but for a few days longer, and without arms and ammunition with which we could procure subsistence. Our only clothing was that which we wore on our backs, and at that inclement season of the year, the ground being covered with snow, of more than twenty inches in depth, prevented our obtaining any thing calculated to sustain us; nor did the shore afford shell-fish of any kind that we could discover, so that we could not but view ourselves the most wretched and miserable of all human beings! In a state of wretchedness from which death alone could deliver us!

But in this we were mistaken. There was one, blessed be God, that was able and willing to deliver us in his own good time. Truly may it be said, that

> God moves in a mysterious way
> His wonders to perform;

on an uninhabited coast, in the midst of a wild wilderness, and amid all our afflictions and deprivations, the Almighty in his tender mercy was pleased to visit us in a manner we little expected. And there wrought a good work for us, which no man without His aid could have accomplished — even that of the conversion of our precious souls! Yes, through the instrumentality of a lad, yet of infant years, we were brought to see how unprepared we were to meet death, which we could not but believe fast approaching in its most horrid forms. It was a subject which probably had never previously occupied our minds, for a moment. For myself, I can say, that until within a few days, the necessity of a preparation of my soul for eternity, was a subject so foreign from my mind, that I had scarcely taken pains to acquaint myself with the meaning of the word "immortality." Nor do I think that my shipmates, who had been my companions in misery, had been less careless, in this respect. But I do indeed rejoice, that I have it in my power to say, that they too became so sensibly affected, and their feelings so powerfully wrought upon, by the prayers and pious exhortations of the youth, that they required little urging to unite with myself and the afflicted mother and son, in our supplications for mercy! It was from Heaven alone that we could expect relief, and such was now the state of our minds, that it became a pleasing devotion for us almost every hour to kneel down, and to pour out our souls to God. And when not thus engaged, in listening to the pious admonitions of the dear youth, who, like an angel commissioned from on high, to administer peace and comfort to our souls, ceased not to exhort us to put our trust in one, who was both able and willing to save all who could come to him, humble and penitent, confessing their sins.

Nor ought we to doubt a moment that our prayers were heard and answered, for when on the very brink of despair, doomed, as we could not but suppose ourselves, to end our days and to remain undiscovered and unburied in a wild and unfrequented wilderness, crowded and immured in a wretched hut, scarcely sufficient to shelter us from the piercing cold, the whole inside of which became lined with a crust of ice. And although on an allowance of one biscuit and two or three ounces of salt beef each, per day, yet of this there was not a sufficient stock to sustain us twenty days! Such, indeed, was our wretched condition, and such our awful forebodings, when there was experienced by all a sudden and unexpected transposition in our minds, from the most gloomy and desponding reflections, to that of the most cheering sensations; to which nothing can bear a comparison, but a mind agonized in sleep by frightful apprehensions of approaching danger, and suddenly awaking and finding it but imaginary, a dream! All complaints and murmurs from this moment ceased, as not a doubt remained on the minds of any one of us, but that the Almighty would deliver us, and that the hour of our deliverance was not far distant.

It was on the morning of the 29th (having previously concluded it best among ourselves, that another tour of discovery should be made) three of us, who were considered in the best condition, set out for the purpose. We concluded to bend our course as before, westward, and as it was natural to suppose that there might be a less depth of snow near the sea coast, we thought it most advisable to follow that, as near as the surf would admit of. In doing this we were encouraged with a hope, that we might possibly fall in with the wreck of our own, or some other vessel, from which something that might serve for food, or clothing, might be obtained; which, if in the most perishable state, would have been very acceptable to us, in our then destitute condition. Our hopes in this respect were not however realized, and we had travelled all the day of the 29th, and a part of the 30th, without meeting with a single object, or witnessing a change of scene to encourage us. About noon, having come to a halt, on an eminence, and while in the act of sharing to each his allowance for the day, the report of a gun, to our inexpressible joy, was heard, and so distinctly, as to render it certain that it could not have been discharged at a very great distance from us.

The report appearing to have proceeded from a direction south west, we immediately started in that direction, united our voices and raising a loud halloo, every now and then, as we proceeded, which was finally answered by a loud shrill screech, or what is more properly termed, an Indian yell! Regardless from whom or what it might proceed, whether friend or foe, we redoubled our pace, and were soon brought in view of one of the tawny sons of the forest, clad from head to foot in a garment of fur, and armed with a musket. We now came to a halt, and for a moment paused, fearful that by too sudden an advance, the Indian (who stood as motionless as a statue, with his eyes fixed steadfastly upon us) might become alarmed, and hastily fly from our presence, and thereby deprive us of the much desired interview. Recollecting at the moment, of having heard that among some of the savages of North America, a green bough was an emblem of peace, and of a pacific disposition, I seized a branch of pine, and with it advancing a few paces ahead of my two companions, exclaimed "fear not, we are your friends," which, to our great joy, appeared to be well understood by our new discovered friend and benefactor (as he afterward proved himself) who instantly replied in very broken English, "you no fear, me friend!" on which, without further parley, we fearlessly approached each other; when presenting our hands, they were good naturedly grasped and shook by the savage, as a token of friendship.

Having seated ourselves upon a dry log, we gave him a brief account of our shipwreck, and the manner in which we had been enabled to subsist since that unfortunate event, to which he listened with much apparent attention, we communicating by signs what he was unable to understand by words. In turn, he gave us as intelligent an account of himself, as his imperfect knowledge of the language would admit of; he represented himself to be one of the Esquimaux tribe, and pointing to the north, observed that "he came from a country as far that way, as the great island [Newfoundland] was that way," pointing west; that for several winters he had made these his quarters, for the purpose of hunting the bear and deer, for their skins, which in the spring, he conveyed and disposed of to a company of fur traders, who resided in a white settlement eight or nine days travel south-west [Bellisle]; that he had built him a comfortable cabin, or a wigwam, in which he reposed nights, and which he represented as situated but a few hours' travel distance from where we then were; that his only companion was a faithful dog, and that his hut was sufficiently spacious to hold us all; that he had provision in plenty, his dog and gun never failing to keep him supplied with fresh meat in abundance, and concluded by assuring us that we were welcome to make this our home, until we could provide ourselves with another and better.

Having informed him of the situation of our unfortunate companions, whom we had left behind, he readily agreed to accompany us to where they were, and to assist us in their removal, but stated that it would be first necessary for him to return to his cabin, to provide himself with some few necessaries, and to which we willingly accepted of his invitation to accompany him. We found it as he had represented, a comfortable dwelling in every respect; and comparatively a palace to our own miserable shelter. We were presented with a well cured ham of venison (of which he had several) and of which, as the reader may suppose, we made a delicious meal; nor did we forget to return thanks to God, for this remarkable manifestation of his kind and tender mercy, in sending that relief which we had so fervently prayed for.

Having sufficiently satisfied our appetites, we set out on our return, to bear the joyful tidings of our good fortune to our friends, accompanied by our kind benefactor, whom we found very serviceable as a guide, as well as for the important information that he was enabled to impart to us, as regarded the best mode of travelling. With revived spirits, we reached the spot of our destination about noon of February the second, and communicated to our friends the particulars of our adventures, and the good success which had attended us — which was received with a transport of joy. The grotesque appearance of our Indian friend, garbed as he was, in skins, on his first introduction, produced rather an unfavourable impression on the minds of our female companion and her little son, but a moment's interview, was sufficient to remove all apprehensions as regarded their personal safety; and preparations were not delayed for an immediate remove from a place where we had suffered too much, for which to feel any degree of attachment.

Our greatest fears now were that Mrs. Mason, and her son, unaccustomed to hardship, would not be able to perform the journey, but in this we were very much encouraged by our Indian friend, who engaged to go forward, and at the distance of every mile to build fires. Having supplied each with such garments of our own as we could spare, we set out about the middle of the afternoon of the same day, our Indian guide preceding us at the distance of about one mile ahead, and failed not in his promise in preparing for us a good fire at the distances mentioned; which was found not very uncomfortable, particularly as regarded our female companion and her son, who although the air was piercing, uttered not a complaint. Ah, true it is, that the Almighty will "temper the storm to the shorn lamb"!

The knowledge which our guide fortunately possessed of the shortest and best route, enabled us without being much fatigued, to reach the place of our destination early in the evening of the 3rd. So happily disappointed were my companions, (to whom I had attempted to give a faint description of the habitation of our Indian friend) to find it so much more convenient and comfortable than what they had anticipated, as to cause them almost to conclude that their troubles were at an end, and their deliverance complete. The wigwam was of simple construction; three or four poles, of ten or twelve feet in length, were stuck in a circle with their tops gathered to a point, and secured by a few strips of green hide. The whole was covered with skins, of which there was a sufficient number to exclude effectually the cold; at the top was an aperture to let out the smoke, the fires being always built in the centre; near the aperture were hung hams of venison to smoke for summer's use. The hut was of sufficient size to shelter eight or nine persons, very comfortably, the internal part of which was well lined with fur skins, and which also afforded comfortable bedding.

We were treated kindly by our Indian friend and benefactor, who spared no pains in rendering our situation (during our two

days' residence, at his hut) as comfortable as possible. The greatest inconvenience that attended us was the difficulty of conversing with him with that facility that we could have wished; he possessing no greater knowledge of the English language, than what he had obtained in his intercourse with the fur traders and fishermen.
In his person, there was nothing very disagreeable or unprepossessing. He was of small stature, inclined to corpulency, and of a tawny complexion, his face very broad, with a large mouth, and with black hair and eyes. His only companion was a faithful dog of the Newfoundland breed, and to whom he appeared much attached. He possessed a good rifle, and appeared well supplied with ammunition. His opinions of the immortality of the soul, or of the existence of a Supreme Being, appeared very restricted, yet when we explained to him the object of our religious devotions, he appeared much pleased, and manifested a disposition to take part. For the welfare of the unfortunate mother and her little son, he manifested an interest, that would have done honour to one of more civilized origin, having humanely presented each with a pair of moccasins, and a blanket of deer skin, the better to protect them from the cold.

Although authors in most instances may be correct, in their opinions of the Indians of North America, that they are of a cruel, revengeful, inexorable disposition, that they will watch whole days unmindful of the calls of nature, and make their way through pathless, and almost unbounded woods, subsisting only on the scanty produce of them, to pursue and revenge themselves on an enemy, that they hear unmoved the piercing cries of such as fall into their hands, and receive a diabolical pleasure from the tortures they inflict on their prisoners, yet by what I have myself experienced and been an eye witness to, I well know that there are exceptions, that there are some of a much less unfeeling savage disposition, who are social and humane to those whom they consider their friends, and ready to partake with them of the last morsel, or to risk their lives in their behalf. Such a one indeed proved our friend and benefactor. Nor could we but view it, as an instance of the interposition of kind providence, in our favour, in delivering us into the hands of one, so generous and benevolent, whose kindness we experienced in every instance; how different would have been our situations had we met with one, who, more in the character of a savage, might not only have withheld that aid which we so much stood in need of, but might have robbed us of the few articles of clothing which we had left, and then left us to perish.

Early in the morning of the 6th (having become much recruited, and made every necessary preparation for the journey) we left the peaceful asylum of our Indian friend, who, for a promised reward, had consented to accompany us to Bellisle, which he had told us that with moderate travelling, we might reach in eight or nine days. The arrangements made for this journey, were, our Indian guide and one of our people were to lead the way, at the distance of about one mile, carrying with them such articles as were necessary to enable them to pitch a tent at the close of each day, for our accommodation at night. Fires were likewise to be enkindled by them at very short distances. The remainder of us were to follow in a body and to afford all the assistance we possibly could to our female companion and her son; for the better accommodation of whom, we had constructed a kind of sled, on which they were to be drawn where the woods and precipices did not prevent. In this manner we traversed a country, the very appearance of which, was sufficient to satisfy us that we could never, at that season of the year, have passed without the assistance of our guide. Obstacles would have presented that it would have been impossible for us to surmount, and we must have perished with hunger or fatigue, in making the attempt.

Through the mercy of God, (meeting with a favourable conveyance from the mainland) we were enabled to reach Bellisle, in the afternoon of the 15th, alive, although nearly overcome with fatigue; which, so far from being unexpected, the reader will no doubt be surprised that we were so long able to support ourselves, under such severe trials, as we had experienced for the three weeks preceding. We found at Bellisle but a very few white inhabitants, and but two small fishing schooners, one bound to St. John's, and the other to Halifax. From the master of one I obtained on credit half a dozen jack-knives, and as much powder, as probably might be purchased for four dollars, which I presented to our Indian guide and friend, as a reward for his kind services; and to whom I feel that I yet owe a debt of gratitude, which I fear it will never be in my power to repay in the manner I ought. I can never reflect without the most grateful sensibility, on the kind offices of this humble son of the forest.

As Bellisle could afford us but a very few of the necessaries, which our enfeebled situations then required (the inhabitants having mostly left it, as they were in the habit of doing, at the commencement of winter) we concluded it best to improve the only opportunity which presented, or probably would present for some weeks, to leave the place. Accordingly myself and surviving shipmates took passage for Halifax, and Mrs. Mason and son, were received on board the schooner bound to St. John's (Newfoundland) with the intention of proceeding from thence to Quebec, where she had relatives living. Of this unfortunate lady and pious little son, we took leave with mutual regret; they having been for more than three weeks our companions in misery, as well as for their religious counsel, so infinitely important as regarded our spiritual welfare, had bound us in the tenderest ties of friendship. But we parted with the happy reflection that our miseries were at an end, and on which account, no further anxiety remained as regarded our personal welfare.

After a somewhat boisterous passage, I in safety reached Halifax, where I had the good fortune the same day to obtain a passage direct to New York, leaving the remainder of my shipmates in Halifax, awaiting a passage to Europe; I landed at New York in the afternoon of the 28th, where, after much enquiry, I found that my mother was still living, and was then residing in the country, about five miles from the city. Thither I repaired without delay, and feel thankful to God, for his kind mercy in restoring me (although penniless) to the arms of a kind and affectionate mother. In my three years' absence from the land of my nativity, and from the presence of an affectionate parent, the ocean has been principally my home; in which time I have been made the subject of, and experienced many of the disasters peculiar to those who navigate the deep: once I have been brought near the grave by pestilential disease, once miraculously preserved from drowning; twice from necessity put on an allowance barely sufficient to support nature; and finally, shipwrecked in mid-winter upon (to me) an unknown and unfrequented coast, with the loss (my life excepted) of every thing but the clothing upon my back. But, although it has been my hard fortune to be thus deprived in an unexpected manner of the fruits of many months' hard toil, of earnings which it was my ardent desire and intention to apply to the relief and support of an aged and infirm widowed mother, yet, I feel that I have thereby obtained a blessing, which I ought and do conceive of infinitely more value. If it has, as I trust it has, been productive (through the instrumentality of a pious female) of the conversion of my precious soul (for "God moves in a mysterious way His wonders to perform"!) I ought, and do view it as one of the most fortunate circumstances of my life, and feel that I can say with the Psalmist, "I know, O Lord, that thy judgements are right, and that thou, in faithfulness hast afflicted me."

MORAL REFLECTIONS

As the foregoing interesting narrative, will probably receive an extensive circulation, and it is not improbable may fall into the hands of some, who may yet remain careless, and unconcerned, as regards the future welfare of their precious and immortal souls, a few closing moral reflections are, by another hand, hereunto annexed, which, while they may not prove unprofitable to any, should they be the means of awakening and reforming a single individual of the class alluded to, the writer will consider himself amply repaid, for his trouble in penning them.

The melancholy events which attended Capt. Mason, and his crew, in their late voyage (as related in the preceding pages) were such as should teach all the uncertainty of life, the danger of delay in the great concerns of immortality from day to day. Human life is "but a vapour that appeareth for a little time, and then vanisheth away!" Time, like a long flowing stream, makes haste into eternity, and is forever lost and swallowed up in there; and while it is hastening to its period, it sweeps away all things which are not immortal. There is a limit appointed by providence to the duration of all the pleasant and desirable scenes of life, to all the works of the hands of men, with all the glories and excellencies of animal nature, and all that is made of flesh and blood. Let us not therefore dote upon any thing here below, for heaven hath inscribed vanity upon it. Mysterious are the ways of Providence; the same wheel which raises us to day, on the smooth, unruffled ocean of prosperity, may, before the morrow, roll us in the stormy sea of adversity. Mankind in this world are ever subject to ills, infirmities and disappointments. Pains and perplexities are the long lived plagues of human existence, but, religion is the balm that heals those wounds. It was this, no doubt, that preserved and supported the unfortunate Mrs. Mason, and her little son, when doomed to experience one of the severest trials of this life, when doomed to witness the melancholy fate of an affectionate husband, and parent,

and a beloved child and brother! It was at this trying moment that he
sent Religion and reason to their aid, and bid them not to grieve for
them whom they could not, and ought not wish to recall to this
troublesome world. The consideration of the sorrows of this life, and
the glories of the next, is our best support. Dark are the ways of
providence while we are wrapped up in mortality; but, convinced
there is a God, we must hope and believe, that all is right.

Kind reader, whatever may be thy rank in life, if thou would wish
to be happy in this world, and to secure a certainty of being infinitely
more so in the world to come, I pray thee cherish Religion. Where
can any object be found so proper to kindle all the benevolent and
tender affections as the Father of the Universe, and the author of all
felicity? Unmoved by veneration, can you contemplate that grandeur
and majesty which his works every where display? Untouched by
gratitude, can you view that profusion of good, which at this pleasing
season of life, his beneficent hand pours around you? Happy in the
level and affection of those with whom you are connected, look up to
the Supreme Being as the inspirer of all the friendships which have
ever been shown you by others; himself your best and first friend; first
the supporter of your infancy, and the guide of your children; and
next the guardian of your youth, and the hope of your coming years.
View religious homage, as a natural expression of gratitude to Him
for all his goodness. Consider it as the service of the God of your
fathers; of him to whom your parents devoted you; and by whom
they are now rewarded and blessed in heaven. Connected with so
many tender sensibilities of soul, let religion be with you, not the
cold and barren offspring of speculation, but the warm and vigorous
dictates of the heart.

The world which we now inhabit is a world of trials and
temptations; sad if we suffer our passions to take possession of us.
It is no easy matter to break their force. If we once give a loose to our
appetite, we know not when to hold the rein: nor is it in our power
always to stop short of vice; so frail is human nature, so strong the
force of habit, that "it is easier to suppress the first desire than to
satisfy all that follow it," is a maxim, the truth of which, many
unthinking of you has, too late, been forced to acknowledge. Religion
is the only balm for a wounded spirit. It is the only sure staff for the
weary traveller through this wilderness of misery and sin. What an
inexpressible grace does it throw over the countenance and actions of

its sincere votaries! It purifies, it adorns, it ennobles our nature, and as without the aid of a telescope, the shipwrecked sailor could never discern in the far off horizon the vessel that is to bring him relief, but might abandon himself to despair; so without religion man's views would be confined to a narrow circle of melancholy. Reflect much on the excellency and glory of religion. It is a friend in adversity. When every earthly hope fails, and the soul is ready to say of all human helpers, "miserable comforters are ye all," then religion is a friend indeed. Are not those blessed, whom God blesses; safe whom he protects; and strong whom he strengthens? Can any one say with David, "The Lord is my refuge, I will not fear, though the earth be removed, and the mountains cast into the midst of the sea"; or with Paul, "Neither death, nor life, nor angels, nor principalities, nor powers, nor things present, nor things to come, nor height, nor depth, nor any other creature, shall be able to separate us from the love of God, which is in Christ Jesus our Lord" — can any one say this, without being unspeakably happy?

> Oh, thou! who sit'st enthroned on high,
>   In viewless splendour rayed;
> Before the lustre of whose eye
>   The brightest glories fade.
>
> Though thou art high, yet thou dost hear
>   The lowly suppliant's moan;
> Though thou art great, each secret tear
>   Begems thy radiant throne.
>
> When shafts of anguish wound the soul,
>   The healing balm is nigh;
> When tempests rise, and billows roll,
>   To thee, alone, we fly.
>
> Then hush! dark sorrow's weeping child,
>   Tossed on this troub'lous sea,
> In strains of peace he whispers mild,
>   "Fear not! for I'm with thee!"

NOTES

1. John Smith, *Narrative of the Shipwreck and Sufferings of the Crew and Passengers of the English brig* Neptune *Which was wrecked in a violent snow storm on the 12th of January, 1830, on her passage from Bristol to Quebec* (New York: J. Smith, 1830), CIHM 48082.
2. Ingeborg Marshall, *A History and Ethnography of the Beothuk* (Montreal and Kingston: McGill-Queen's University Press, 1996), 438-45; Ralph Pastore, "The Collapse of the Beothuk World," *Acadiensis* 19, 1 (1989): 52-71.
3. A full historical and legal discussion of this matter can be found in Michael G. Wetzel, *Decolonizing Ktaqmkuk Mi'kmaw History*, Unpublished LL.M. thesis, Dalhousie University, 1995.
4. "His Majesty's Commission For The Well-Governing of His Subjects Inhabiting In Newfoundland (1708)," 785. See this map on page 12, this volume. For background see Ralph Pastore, "Fishermen, Furriers, and Beothuks: The Economy of Extinction," *Man in the Northeast* 33 (1987): 47-62; François Trudel, "The Inuit of Southern Labrador and the Development of French Sedentary Fisheries (1700-1760)," in *Papers from the Fourth Annual Congress, 1977, Canadian Ethnology Society*, ed. Richard A. Preston, Canadian Ethnology Service Paper No. 40 (Ottawa: National Museums of Canada, 1978), 99-121.
5. Selma Barkham, "A Note on the Strait of Belle Isle During the Period of Basque Contact with Indians and Inuit," *Études/Inuit /Studies* 4, 1-2 (1980): 51-58; Charles Martijn, "An Eastern Micmac Domain of Islands," *Actes du vingtième res des Algonquinistes* (Ottawa: Carleton University, 1989), 208-31; his "Innu (Montagnais) in Newfoundland," *Papers of the Twenty-First Algonquian Conference* (Ottawa: Carleton University, 1990), 236-37; Dorothy Anger, *Noywa̓mkisk (Where the Sand Blows ...): Vignettes of Bay St. George Micmacs* (St. John's: St. George Regional Indian Council, 1988).
6. Marshall, *A History and Ethnography of the Beothuk*, 224-26. This suggestion that Beothuks assimilated into Montagnais (Shaunamunc) society was also made by Joseph Jukes, who travelled around the island in 1839-40. See Robert Cuff and Derek Wilton, eds., Jukes' *Excursions* (St. John's: Harry Cuff, 1993), 199.

7. Olive P. Dickason, *Canada's First Nations: A History of Founding Peoples from Earliest Times* (Toronto: McClelland and Stewart, 1992), 216-24.

8. Patricia A. Thornton, "The Transition from the Migratory to the Resident Fishery in the Strait of Belle Isle," in Rosemary E. Ommer, ed., *Merchant Credit and Labour Strategies* (Fredericton, NB: Acadiensis Press, 1990), 145.

9. Patricia A. Thornton, "The Demographic and Mercantile Bases of Initial Permanent Settlement in the Strait of Belle Isle," in John J. Mannion, ed., *The Peopling of Newfoundland: Essays in Historical Geography* (St. John's: ISER, 1977), 191.

I I

A NEWFOUNDLAND MISSIONARY'S JOURNAL:
THE *DESPATCH* AND OTHERS (1835)[1]

EDWARD WIX

Edward Wix was a missionary for the Society for the Propagation of the Gospel (SPG)[2] and an Archdeacon of the Anglican Church, only the second clergyman in Newfoundland to hold this title. He traversed the island between February and August of 1835, baptizing, marrying and burying outport inhabitants. Wix's diary of his travels, which was written on material taken from "some boxes of paper, which had been dispersed along the shore from different wrecks," makes numerous references to shipwrecks and wrecking. To some degree, he wrote his diary with these very wrecks in mind, as they became central to his overall observations of the poverty, morality, and humanity of the outport peoples.

In his journey, he met several individuals who were involved in wrecking. At Bay Chaleur, for example, he met Reuben and Sarah Samms, "a poor but worthy couple." They had taken into their home 15 crew and passengers of the *William Ashton*, wrecked at nearby Lance Cove on August 9, 1830 while en route from Dublin to Quebec. The accident was "said to have been occasioned by intemperance." The couple provided provisions for all the remaining passengers and crew and built a tilt, a crude shelter, for 48 survivors. On previous occasions, Reuben and his brother had saved victims of five wrecks, including survivors from the *Mary*. In that instance, the Samms followed a three-day old trail into the interior until they came upon a starving and lost crew. The encounter between rescuers and survivors was "most affecting," and it reminded Wix of "the experience of the lost sinner, when he first makes discovery of a Saviour!" Reuben's conduct, Wix concluded, contrasted "well" with the "less creditable conduct of many upon this shore."

Upon entering Seal's Cove, Dead Island (Isle aux Morts), Wix held a service for his host George Harvie (Harvey) and his family, already well known for their daring rescue in 1828 of 180 passengers of the emigrant brig *Despatch*, wrecked while on its way between Londonderry and Quebec. For his efforts, Harvie and his daughter had received a Gold Medal from the Royal Humane Society of London and £100 from Lloyd's subscribers, which Wix had presented to him on an earlier visit. Such rewards to heroic wreckers, Wix believed, heightened pride in a liberal and parental mother country and demonstrated the crown's interest to inhabitants of the most isolated and distant settlements of its empire. These forms of recognition also fostered selflessness and humanity to combat "selfish apathy" during wrecking. Incidentally, in 1838 Harvie personally saved another 25 crew of the shipwrecked *Rankin*, for which he received no compensation.[3]

During his brief stay at Dead Island Wix saw further evidence of other recent wrecks, including a 300-ton ship that had gone aground the previous fall and a 70- or 80-ton vessel built by "Basques" (probably Acadian settlers) from the Codroy valley, which sank during his visit. The presence of wrecks in these parts was inescapable. When Wix visited the west coast of the island, he noted how "wreck-wood" was strewn all along the Little Codroy River. At First Barisway he was told of George Green, a wrecked seaman from the barque *Fanny*, which had gone aground off Red Island, Port-au-Port, on its voyage from Quebec to Greenock in October of 1833. He observed approvingly that through the winter and spring this "hospitably entertained" shipwrecked mariner had immersed himself in the Bible before returning home. When Wix went south again in July to Port-au-Basque, he saw new wreckages of the *James* and the *Nathaniel Graham*, the latter resulting in 40 deaths.

Wix used his diary to reinforce public support for the SPG and its missionary activity in the colonies. Bibles were at a premium, and competing secular American publications, which Wix despised, were not uncommon. He related happily that various religious tracts and books survived the most recent wrecks, and he planned to put them to good use. Religious writings he found scattered in planters' houses throughout this isolated region, where they were "highly prized" as a resource for religious devotions.

The excerpts from Wix's diary reprinted below relate to aspects of his observations on wrecking: his meeting with an unidentified fisher and wrecker at La Poile on May 3, 1835, and four days later his encounter with Miessau [Mousseau?], a French Canadian and "a worthy man," who lived near Cape Ray (known locally as Cape South), at Gale's Harbour. Miessau had been instrumental in aiding survivors of the *Nathaniel Graham*. These descriptions highlight two different personalities and some important aspects of wrecking: one, the influence of "awful wrecks" on "character," and two, the oft-noted and indispensable role that Newfoundland dogs played in saving shipwreck victims.

⚓

SATURDAY [MAY] 2: Off before seven a.m. and, to my great regret, passed the Burgeo Islands, with the respectable inhabitants of which place I had kept up a correspondence, and supplied them with books, since my visit to them in 1830. We anchored at eight p.m. at Duck Island, Cutteau Bay, fourteen leagues. There, by the blaze of a cheerful fire, made from the wreck wood, so common on this coast, I held full service in a neat planter's cabin, and baptized six children.

Sunday, [May] 3: Off at half-past five a.m., struck, for an instant, upon a rock in working out with our deckboat. Got, by one p.m. to Burnt Islands. We passed La Poile. This part of the shore is so fatal to European vessels which are outward bound to Quebec in the spring, that it is much to be regretted that the legislatures or Chambers of Commerce of Nova Scotia, New Brunswick, and the Canadas, do not unite with the government and merchants of Newfoundland, for the erection of light-houses here and at Port-aux-Basques, and at Cape Ray. Many vessels and many lives might, each year, be saved from destruction by such a measure. Mr. Anthonie, indeed, a humane Jersey merchant, resident at La Poile, has erected, upon a rock off La Poile Bay, a small observatory. This is of some service to a few who know its situation; but the shore in this neighbourhood is so very low, and the ledges of rock extend so far out to sea, that a vessel may be in danger before the little beacon is discovered.

At the cabin in which I stayed at Burnt Islands, the playthings of the children were bunches of small patent desk and cabinet keys, which had been picked up from wrecks. Beautiful old China plates and pieces of a more modern elegant breakfast set of dragon china, which had been washed ashore in the same way, were ranged upon the shelves alongside the most common ware; and a fine huckabac towel, neatly marked with the initial letters LCD, was handed me on my expressing a desire to wash my hands. This had been supplied from the wreck of a vessel in which were several ladies. To some hearts those letters, doubtless, would renew a sad period of anxiety, which preceded the intelligence of the melancholy certainty of a sad bereavement. I could not look at this relic of a toilette, now no more required, without emotions of deep interest, although I had no clue by which I could attach recollections of brilliant prospects early blighted, or pious faith exemplified in death to these three letters. Indeed, the scenes and circumstances, the very people by whom I was surrounded, roused within me a train of deeply melancholy sensations. My host may have been a humane man; his conduct to me was that of genuine hospitality; but it had been his frequent employment at intervals, from his youth till now, to bury wrecked corpses, in all stages of decomposition. There had been washed on shore here, as many as three hundred, and a hundred and fifty on two occasions, and numerous in others. This sad employment appeared to have somewhat blunted his feelings. I would not do him injustice; the bare recital of such revolting narratives, unvarnished as such tales would naturally be, in the simpler expression of a fisherman, might give an appearance of a want of feeling, which nature may have not denied to him, and of which the scenes and occupations of his life may not have wholly divested him. I remember well my expressing my reluctance to allow him to disinter a delicate female foot, the last human relic, which the waves, or the wild cats, or the fox, or his own domestic dog, had deposited in the neighbourhood of his cabin. He had recently picked it up to his door, and had buried it in his garden, and was very anxious to be allowed to shovel away the lingering snow, that he might indulge me with a sight of it. I suppose my countenance may have betrayed some feeling of abhorrence, when he said, "Dear me, Sir, do let me; it would not give me any concern at all: I have had so much to do with dead bodies, that I think no more of handling them, than I do of handling so many codfish!"

I have said, that I believe him humane; yet wrecks must form his
chief inducement to settle in a place so barren and bleak, and to live
through the winter out upon the shore as he does, contrary to the
usual habit of the people, which is to retire into the woods until late
in the spring. But humanity might prompt a man to live where his
services may occasionally be exerted usefully for the preservation of
human life. Yet, did I wrong him in the judgment of charity, when
I saw his quick eye kindle with the gale, as he watched the stormy
horizon? Was I wrong when, as he went in the early dawn and dusk
each evening, while I was there, to a hill a little higher than the rest,
with his spy-glass, I thought his feelings and my own on discerning
that a vessel had, during the night, struck some of the numerous
rocks which abound hereabouts, or was on her way to do so, might
be of a very different character? This man is only a sample of many
whom I saw on this part of the coast.

Thursday, [May] 7: The gale so strong that I could not proceed; held
full service and baptized four more children. I stayed here at the
house of a French Canadian, whose simple recital of the efficacy of
his prayers, in a certain season of imminent peril at sea, and intimate
acquaintance with the scriptures, which he knew just sufficient of
English to read in our tongue, pleased me very much. Within a few
days of my leaving his house, the courage and humanity of this man
of faith were called into exercise by the appearance in his neighbourhood, of a boat with a portion of the exhausted crews from a wrecked
vessel in her. The breakers made it impossible that the people in the
boat should effect a landing; he leaped into the sea at the peril of his
life, to give them a rope: a favourite dog, which I had admired while
there, was with him; and on the boat's swamping, when Miessau
swam with one man in his protection, his faithful dog seized another
to draw him to the shore. The southwester cap, however, which the
drowning seaman wore, on which the dog had seized his hold, came
off in the water, and the dog not observing the diminution in the
weight of his burden, was proceeding to the shore with the cap alone,
when the sailor seized the tail of the dog, and so was towed to shore.
The master of the wrecked vessel, who was one of the boat's crew, was
taken in a state of insensibility into Miessau's house, and some hours
elapsed before he became conscious of any thing which was passing
around him. This late instance, which I have quoted above, of the

sagacity of the dog of Newfoundland, may be classed with many of
the same kind, which I have heard well authenticated, and indeed
have witnessed many since my residence in the island.

NOTES

1. Edward Wix, *Six Months of a Newfoundland Missionary's Journal,
   from February to August 1835* (London: Smith, Elder and
   Company, 1836).
2. Information concerning this missionary organization is provided
   in Ruth M. Christensen, "The Establishment of S.P.G. Missions
   in Newfoundland, 1703-1783," *Historical Magazine of the
   Protestant Episcopal Church* 20 (1951): 207-29.
3. Jukes' Excursions, ed. Robert Cuff and Derek Wilton (St. John's:
   Harry Cuff Publications, 1993), 83. Revised edition of Joseph
   Bette Jukes, *Excursions In and About Newfoundland During the
   Years 1839 and 1840.*

12

THE LOSS OF THE BARQUE *MARSHAL M'DONALD*, OFF NEWFOUNDLAND (1835)[1]

THOMAS GOODWIN AND JOSEPH SHEARER

The transcriber of this narrative, Moses Pumfre, was not a victim of the wreck of the timber ship *Marshal M'Donald*. As he explained in his advertisement of this "pamphlet for the press," he had prepared its contents from notes taken at the request of the survivors Thomas Goodwin and Joseph Shearer. Describing himself as motivated by Christian benevolence and as a person "anxious at all times to assist the child of misfortune," Pumfre was moved by their "truly forlorn and destitute condition," having "never witnessed any scene that impressed my mind more deeply, or that moved the sympathies of my heart so powerfully as these deplorable objects of commiseration." Their narrative, he claimed, was not exaggerated to elicit public support: "I have confined myself to a simple detail of their statement, and am perfectly unconscious of having exceeded the truth, or that I have given it the gloss of fiction."

The shipwreck ordeal of Thomas Goodwin and Joseph Shearer had been compounded by their reception in Newfoundland. Magistrate Syms of Trepassey refused to provide them with housing and sustenance. While Syms was legally entitled to his actions and constrained by law in providing them state relief, the narrators characterized his failure to assist as "cruel," unchristian, and contrary to "the law of nature." By neglecting "to afford protection and assistance to his fellow men in their distress," Syms was "a disgrace to the poorest or meanest person in the village." Moreover, where he could have helped as a private citizen, he chose to do nothing to alleviate their condition. Without the help of the private charity of "a respectable and benevolent fisherman," and then again by "a few poor fishermen," Goodwin and Shearer would have died in Newfoundland, especially as their frost-bitten limbs had started to rot with gangrene. After a forced stay of over four months, the survivors were taken on board a sealing vessel en route to St. John's, where a surgeon amputated their limbs. They were then delivered to Portsmouth aboard a military transport vessel.

In Portsmouth, local authorities temporarily relieved them as "helpless cripples." They did not have legal residence in England, their homes being Scotland and Ireland. Afterwards, Goodwin and Shearer's only recourse, in the wake of the Poor Law Amendment of 1834, was to apply to the local workhouse, where they remained. In light of these events, Pomfre called on "a humane Christian Public" to buy this pamphlet and assist these "destitute yet deserving" sailors.

The many sufferings of shipwrecked timber ship crews were finally documented by the Select Committee On Shipwrecks Of Timber Ships of 1839. Influenced by "advancement in science," such official inquiries into shipwrecks now contributed to improvements in ship building, the construction of life boats and life preservers, and the identification of shipping hazards.[2] What is clear from the evidence is that these measures were only beginning to be addressed. Moreover, there remained great shortcomings of "humanity, philanthropy and national interests" in adequately preserving the lives and wellbeing of sailors and ship passengers associated with the timber trade (see Appendix).

The fate of the *Marshal M'donald* was not unique, rather far too common. In the 1840s, there were hundreds of non-resident shipwrecked and ailing sailors forwarded by the Lord Admiralty's Office from St. John's to Great Britain (see Appendix, Table 3). Under the Navigation Acts, those merchant mariners like Goodwin and Shearer who crewed in the empire were generally severely disadvantaged, particularly with respect to money, in the event of a shipwreck. Legally, shipwrecked sailors did not have to be paid their outstanding wages, though they could demand to be compensated in the event of a successful salvage. Furthermore, imperial and colonial sailors had to find a way home to qualify for long-term hospital or out-relief as the "deserving poor," or to receive benefits from the society to which they had contributed money.

To meet existing needs, many sailors' societies were founded in the early nineteenth century. Before 1839 relief to mariners who worked on British ships was provided by the local parish or by shipowners and registered seamen who contributed funds to a few local societies, which existed primarily in the major ports. Described as "a large tax on the wages of the seamen," this funding supported organizations like the Port of Newcastle Association, for the preservation of Life from Shipwreck, in aid of the Royal National Institution, established in 1825. Newcastle set up its first Society for the Relief of Widows and Orphans of Shipwrecked Mariners only in 1831.[3] To meet the growing demands of shipwreck victims, and to preserve the morals of the Jack-a-tar, the Select Committee on Shipwrecks of 1836 urged the establishment of saving banks, an innovation of the age designed to promote forced savings among the labouring classes, and of asylums for the reception of shipwrecked mariners.[4] The first national organization, a private charity called the Shipwrecked Fishermen and Mariners Royal Benevolent Society, began in 1839, enrolling 50,000 fishermen; it claimed that in its first 50 years it had provided assistance to 406,817 individuals and their families. This figure includes an estimated 11,000-12,000 persons in the colonies through 1,000 affiliated agencies.[5]

The immediate health needs of shipwrecked sailors in British North America were met at least in part within the colonies. The Kent Marine Hospital of Saint John, New Brunswick, which opened in 1821, provided an alternative to placing mariners in the local poorhouse. In Halifax, sick and infirm mariners had the choice of a private hospital or the house of industry. The Quebec Marine and Emigrant Hospital, founded in the 1830s, also operated on a congregate basis by accepting a variety of patients.[6] Only after 1867, when transportation became a federal responsibility, was a system of marine hospitals established. Newfoundland, not having joined Confederation, was of course excluded.

Few charitable societies operated independently in Canada. A sailors' home in Saint John operated briefly at mid-century. Also in these years, two small homes and various missions opened in Halifax, and late in the century a Ladies' Seamen's Friends Society was founded there. These were mostly church-run charities, although they received some state support. For Newfoundland, Shannon Ryan writes, "there were no specific provisions made under the government's health and welfare schemes to assist the survivors and the widows and orphans left

without means of support by disasters and misfortunes."7 How many
colonial sailors were aided under the auspices of the Shipwrecked
Fishermen and Mariners Royal Benevolent Society remains as yet
unknown.

⚓

THE AGE IN WHICH WE LIVE is eminently distinguished for its
advancement in science. But for the calamities that attend mankind,
we might cherish the belief that human ingenuity had attained
the highest summit of perfection. The laudable efforts of the
philanthropist have been incessantly directed to lessen the aggregate
amount of human woe. There can be no greater or better evidence
offered in proof of this remark, than the constant attention that
within these few years past, has been paid to the numerous
emergencies and dangers that attend the sailor in his perilous passage
through the voyage of life, on the boisterous ocean. The British
Government has paid a regard to the interests of seamen which is to
their credit, and to the high honour of our national character; they
have exhibited benevolence as our principal and prominent feature,
and as an object of peculiar importance among Britons. Every
improvement which science could suggest, has been adopted in the
erection of British vessels; whether such improvements tend to secure
their inhabitants from danger in tempestuous weather, by strengthening the ship to bear the violence of the storm, or facilitate their
progress on the briny wave. While the structure of vessels has become
an object of serious attention, premiums have been awarded to the
skilful and experienced mariner, who has also been promoted in the
Navy for any improvement in the art of Navigation. For the benefit
of seamen on our own coast, additional landmarks have been erected;
and to give further security to shipping, the greatest undertaking in
England, the Plymouth Breakwater, has been accomplished.

It is remarkable, and worthy of observation, that with all the
advantages offered to the mariner, the general dangers and hazards of
a foreign voyage have not been proportionably diminished, nor has
individual misfortune been lessened. The events of the last few years
have brought under public observation, a series of disasters at sea, in
which the sufferings of the survivors have exceeded the troubles of
many of their predecessors in peril and danger. We have read of the
numerous misfortunes of the crew of the *Victory*, under Captain Ross;

of the loss of the *Sir James Spreight*, and of many others that could be very easily enumerated; but in few instances do we remember that men have undergone more protracted misery, than the unfortunate subjects of the subjoined narrative.

On the eighth day of November, 1835, the Barque, *Marshal M'Donald*, of about 350 tons burden, sailed from Quebec with a crew of fifteen hands, and one passenger, laden with timber, for the City of Limerick. She proceeded on her voyage till the 21st. At several periods she admitted the water, and the fears of the crew were excited as to the safety of the vessel: these fears, however, were allayed by the confidence which the seamen reposed in the superior knowledge, maturer judgement, and greater experience of their Captain, so that nothing, either very singular, or remarkably interesting, occurred till the 21st of November.

Proceeding on our voyage, while we were in the Gulf of St. Lawrence, off the Island of St. Paul's, on the 21st of November, a heavy storm arose, the wind blowing very fresh from the north west. The storm raged with uncommon violence, carried away our main-top-sail, and did serious damage to our leaky vessel. We entertained a pleasing hope that on the succeeding day the weather would abate, so that we might repair our loss, and prosecute our voyage. In this we were however disappointed, as each succeeding day increased our privations, and added to our sufferings.

The morning of another day began to dawn upon us, after a long and tedious night of fear, anxiety, and suffering. The sun appeared reluctantly to dispel the darkness of the night. All seemed dreary. Every heart was filled with the deepest gloom and sorrow. The conflicting passions of the mind responded to the awful scene before us. Awful is that scene which is presented to the observation of the unfortunate mariner. No friendly assistance within his reach, he looks on the melancholy prospect before him in all its horror. The swelling ocean omnipotent in power, bursting its violence on his shattered vessel, the winds also blowing a perfect hurricane, tremendous in strength, and when united with the mighty and mountainous sea, depriving the seaman of all control over his bark. The very sun of heaven involved in such darkness, that its light is all but totally denied; at such a trying and painful moment what heart can refuse its sympathy to human beings in such a situation, witnessing the most awful convulsions of nature, and contemplating all the dangers to which they were inevitably exposed from the storm. Dangers from which there is no hope of escape, however faint and glimmering.

The morning dawned in gloom upon us. Fresh dangers seemed impending, and we were doomed to encounter fresh difficulties. The storm continued unabated, and the vessel sustained a further loss, the loss of her fore-sail and fore-top-sail; the force of the sea carried away also the bulwarks, the stanchions, and the long boat. The vessel was still in a very leaky condition, and while most of the hands were on deck working the pumps, she shipped a heavy sea, and became completely water-logged. Twelve of the crew were washed overboard. Thus was our future progress impeded, and thus was our crew reduced to a state of misery which the pen can but feebly describe. Our trouble increased at this awful moment. Three of our companions, unable to reach the ship, perished, leaving an unmanageable wreck to the mercy of the tempest with a crew reduced in number by this calamity, and in strength by their continued exertions at the pump, and in performing other duties during the earlier part of the storm. When we needed an increase of hands, we felt a diminution in our number to be a loss which nothing could supply.

When the sea struck the vessel, the mate was driven by the force of the water between the lee-rigging and the deck cargo. It was midnight, and he called, but for some time he called in vain on the crew to extricate him from his perilous situation. The crew were anxious for their own safety; yet while they deplored the fate of their companion, they hesitated for awhile to expose themselves to the danger of immediate death. His cries were repeated till the Captain and one of the crew took a lanthorn and went to his assistance; they took him to the cabin, and put him in his berth; in about an hour he called again for help, declaring that he was likely to be drowned even in the cabin. All hands being now below, a more prompt attention was paid to the second call of the mate, when the sad discovery was made of the real state of the ship. The most timid on board had no apprehension of our danger, or that the vessel was filling so quickly with water.

On the discovery of the danger that was inevitable to the whole of the crew if they remained below, we all took to the main-top. Uncheering indeed was our prospect, and melancholy were the sensations felt in every breast, expecting that every hour would terminate our lives, as the tempest still raged with unabated and

irresistible violence and fury. We clung however to the rigging with
that ardour to which the love of life could alone give birth. Our
situation was hopelessly forlorn; our nerves, which were enfeebled by
labour and the scene before us, were strengthened, and we were
stimulated again to renewed exertion, with renewed vigour, when we
thought on our homes, and of those persons whose future bliss or
woe depended on, and would be powerfully influenced by our
destiny. For these of our kindred did we principally value life and
desire to live.

The mate was either too much exhausted, or had been too
severely injured to ascend the rigging, and day-light presented him to
the notice of his companions, a clay-cold and stiffened corpse! We
looked on the fate of our companion as if expecting at a period fast
approaching us, a similar death. On discovering the death of the
mate, before consigning the body to the deep, it was stripped of its
clothing, and two of the men who were most deplorably destitute
of clothes, and therefore exposed to a state of greater suffering from
the bitter severity of the cold weather, appeared pleased at his death,
and actually entered into a pugilistic combat for the dress of the
unfortunate fellow companion. We were reduced to that state of
misery that the fine feelings of humanity, or of mutual sympathy,
were completely extinguished by the severity of individual suffering,
and a love of self predominated in every breast to the entire exclusion
of every other principle.

Early on the 23rd the carpenter, who had sustained a previous
injury from being washed overboard the day before, was also
discovered dead. The Captain had ordered the masts of the vessel to
be cut away at the commencement of our disasters; the carpenter was
too much injured to obey the command of the Captain, and as the
crew were unable to get at the carpenter's tools, the masts were
unwillingly permitted to remain; this was one day deeply deplored as
a most unfortunate event, but a few hours afterwards exhibited our
short-sightedness, for had we cut away the masts as we desired and
hoped to do, instant and certain death must have been the inevitable
portion of all on board. The carpenter like the mate was thrown into
the sea but without being deprived of his clothes.

The same day death released another of our companions from
his sufferings. The cook, a man of colour, was seen to be in a dying
condition; when we ascended the rigging, the Captain took with him

a bottle, containing a little rum, and with this he endeavoured to allay the pain of the unfortunate sufferer. While however he was pouring the spirits down the throat of the cook, the vital spark became extinct, the spirit was called before its judge, and the body fell (frozen to death), from the main-top in a state of lifeless inanimation on the deck, and was washed overboard. Thus our number seemed hourly diminishing.

In this situation we continued in the depth of winter, for a period of fifteen days, exposed to all that human beings could possibly endure. Many of our companions, although possessing equally with their survivors the advantages of youth and bodily strength, unable to bear the intense cold or to exist under such privations as a want of food and clothing, died before our eyes.

Who can expect a correct description of our misery. It would be altogether impossible to depict in proper or just colours the horror of the scene before us, or the deep state of mental gloom and despondency which had taken full possession of every bosom. The swelling of the boundless ocean continued unabated; we saw its awful commotions from the height in which we had sought safety, and to which we had ascended for better security from the danger of the storm. We looked on the waves in which (and that ere long) we expected to be engulfed, with emotions of indescribable agony. What a dreary prospect lay before us. The rain too descended, and so severely cold was the air, that as it fell it froze upon our persons, and we thus assumed the appearance of living masses of ice. The tempest drove our vessel, of which we had no knowledge. Human skill was of no benefit, and we looked to Heaven only for succour. We became entirely dependent on that omnipotent power who rules alike the wind and the sea, who could alone say to the storm "*peace, be still,*" and lay at the mercy of the waves, under the control of our only friend and refuge in trouble.

The main-top afforded us no shelter; our clothes were insufficient to preserve animal warmth through our bodies, and our water being inaccessible to any of the crew, we were painfully reduced to the necessity of drinking each other's urine. Our stock of food was so slender, that we might be almost described as destitute of provisions also.

When we took to the rigging, immediately after our greatest calamity on the 22nd, we had preserved for our support a handkerchief of bread, weighing, perhaps, about twelve or fourteen pounds. A portion of this bread was daily distributed among the crew, each man's share amounting to no more than half of a biscuit; this stock of bread divided so sparingly among us was soon exhausted, and on the tenth day we had but three quarters of a biscuit to share among ten men who were starving with hunger. We had foreseen that unless very speedily delivered by the hand of Providence, our stock of provisions would fail, and the misfortune which we dreaded, we were apparently now to encounter. One of the crew, however, at the risk of his life descended into the cabin, to procure if possible a further supply of food. He discovered no trace of the bread locker, which had been washed away, but observing a few pieces of pork floating in the cabin, he made these his prize, and ascended again to the main-top, and on these pieces of pork we subsisted for a period of five days longer. There was a strong feeling prevalent among some of the crew, horrid as it may appear, towards preserving the bodies of the mate and carpenter for human food! Indeed our emergencies were so pressing as to drive us to any resource. The hope of a deliverance (although we had no reason or prospect to induce such a hope), enabled the crew to bear their sufferings, and encouraged them to prolong by all the means within their power, the term of their existence.

On the third day we saw a vessel to windward bearing down upon us. We made signal of our distress. At the sight of this vessel, joy was visible in every countenance, and pleasure gladdened every heart. We considered our misery brought to a termination, and could not refrain from returning thanks to God, with tears of gratitude streaming from every eye, for a deliverance so unexpected and providential. How transitory is human happiness, how fallacious are our fondest hopes. While we considered ourselves as safe from danger on board the vessel sent by God to relieve us from our sufferings, and to preserve our lives, she saw our forlorn and destitute condition, she witnessed our distress, and she took in her studding-sails, hauled upon a wind, and sailed again from us. We were thus left to encounter misfortunes which we could neither foresee nor prevent. The cup of disappointment and sorrow was again raised to our lips, and deeply were we doomed to drink of its bitter contents, even to the very dregs.

A greater degree of human misery has been scarcely ever meted out to mortals, than that under which we were suffering, and we found it difficult to suppress our feelings of resentment and indignation at the cruelty exhibited towards us by the crew of the vessel by whom we had been so unfeelingly neglected. If our distressed condition could not procure us their sympathy, it would be in vain to look among such people under any other circumstance for aid or consolation. The atrocity of such an act is increased by the fact of seamen being equally exposed to danger, who have escaped the perils of the storm, and who can witness without emotions of pity the sufferings of their fellow men, and cruelly resign them to the hardships, privations, and dangers of such a situation as ours, possess nothing human but the human form, dispositions that debase such wretches far below untutored savages! Who can envy such men their feelings in the moment of calm and deliberate reflection.

On the 6th of December we saw land to the leeward, which we have since conjectured to be Cape St. Mary's; we seemed again to enjoy all the pleasures of hope. The swelling and boisterous sea drove us however from the land, and despair seized every breast. The steward saw our situation with all its horrors and became a helpless and pitiable maniac, but happily sometime after his reaching land his reason was restored.

On the morning of the 7th of December we again saw land, the current drifted us towards it, and then a heavy sea drove us on shore at St. Shotts, which is justly dreaded by every mariner as a place of danger and death. The vessel was dashed to pieces, and the masts fell towards the shore, and three of the crew who endeavoured to reach the shore by means of the masts perished in their attempt, while the remaining portion of the crew, seven in number, succeeded after many difficulties, in getting on the Island of Newfoundland.

When we landed, we observed but one dwelling house, which was occupied by a respectable and benevolent fisherman; we made towards this house, and were kindly received with all the generous hospitality which characterizes Britons. After three days' rest and refreshment we proceeded on to Trepassey, a small village 15 miles distant, containing a population of about 300 persons. The Captain having been frost-bitten kept behind while means were adopted to produce a cure. The Captain had money, but those who were destitute though more severely afflicted, could command no kindness to administer to them the relief they needed. The narrators being also severely frost-bitten in their feet and legs, and therefore unable to perform the journey on foot, were provided with horses for that purpose.

On reaching Trepassey, we went immediately to the house of Mr. Syms, but learned that that gentleman and his lady were both at St. John's on a visit. His wife's mother made her appearance; she listened to our tale without betraying the least emotion or feeling on our account. She refused us the shelter of a house, and permitted us to lie down on the snow, till the hearts of a few poor fishermen were moved towards us. While they expressed their just indignation at the unfeeling conduct of Mr. Syms' mother-in-law, they took us to their homes, and humanely did all in their power to contribute to our comfort.

We remained with these poor but hospitable people about a fortnight, till after the return of Mr. Syms from St. John's. Mr. Syms on his arrival refused to provide any place for our accommodation. The inhabitants of Trepassey appeared deeply interested in our welfare, as our feet and legs were so severely frost-bitten as to require surgical attention. The season of the year would not permit the fishermen to follow their calling, and their boats were hauled up and removed some distance from the sea, to preserve them from injury during the storms and tempests incidental to the winter season. The fishermen proposed to Mr. Syms that if he would allow them the use of his boat, which was the only one fit and ready for sea, they would find themselves and us in provisions, and take us the distance of 90 miles to St. John's, where we could be properly attended to. To this proposal Mr. Syms would not listen, and while we live we shall feel the effects of Mr. Syms' refusal of the request of the fishermen. The legs began to rot from our bodies, and emitted a stench that it was almost impossible to bear. The fishermen appealed, but they appealed in vain to the inhumane Mr. Syms on our behalf. They threatened to put us out of their houses, and asked for a place of shelter for our reception. We were removed to a house in ruins, the snow penetrated through the dilapidated sides of our wretched habitation. We lay in one corner of the room upon a bed, if a heap of hay without either a blanket or a sheet, could merit that appellation; a hearth-rug, so stiff with frost as to stand in an erect position, was the only covering allowed such men and in such a situation as ours. Our destitute condition moved the sympathy of our ship-mates, who went begging for us, and procured a supply of blankets for our use; still we were permitted to remain in this place, without any attention being paid to our legs from the 10th of December to the 17th of April, a period of four months and seven days! And during that time, our feet became so putrid as to fall from our legs. The pain this occasioned was so severe that for some time we lost our sight and faculty of speech. One of the ship's company was kept in Trepassey to wait upon us, and the others went on to St. John's by land.

While we were in Trepassey, in our unenviable and horrid abode, our legs would continue to swell, and blisters would frequently appear visible; we broke these blisters with a pin, but being detected at this, the pin was taken from us, and afterwards we inserted the end of a piece of hay into the blisters on our legs for the purpose of procuring a discharge of the watery matter. Little does Mr. Syms know, or indeed, perhaps, little does he care, what we are likely to suffer in our future life, through his unkindness of disposition towards us.

Had we been cast on a dreary or desolate island without an inhabitant, we could have expected no friendship or assistance. Had we run ashore on an island inhabited by uncultivated heathens or brutalized hottentots, we should have expected no friendship or assistance. Although it is likely, that the natural sternness and cruel dispositions of such people might have been subdued into benevolence by the sad recital of our woe. To say nothing of Christianity, should not human kindness have taught Mr. Syms a lesson of humanity, "To feel another's woe"?

He was bound by the law of nature to afford protection and assistance to his fellow men in their distress; the law of God is still more imperative, and enjoins the discharge of this duty. These laws, however, and their mandates he equally disregarded, and although filling a high official station in society, he steeled his heart against the piteous supplications of men reduced to the lowest abyss of human wretchedness. We paid dearly for life, by the suffering in which our lives were preserved and protracted while we were on the wreck. Was the sympathy of Mr. Syms in accordance with his duty as a magistrate, or creditable to his reputation as a man? Or could he suppose that, although we were in a state of perfect misery, that we were unworthy of his protection, or deserving such stern severity, such unexampled, and unpardonable cruelty? Happily for our national character, happily for mankind too, there are but few such persons as Mr. Syms vested with magisterial authority. In England Mr. Syms would be compelled to retire from the bench in compliance with the powerful and united voice of a humane people, who would despise and condemn such a character as unworthy of their respect and attention. Wealth may have placed him above many of the inhabitants of Trepassey, but the conduct of Mr. Syms would be a disgrace to the poorest or meanest person in the village.

On the 16th of April, a seal-fishing vessel put into Trepassey, wind-bound; on the following day we were taken on board, and sailed for St. John's, where we arrived the next day, the 18th of April. On reaching St. John's, and going on shore, we were immediately visited by the surgeons of that place. One leg was first amputated from the person of Thomas Goodwin, whose sufferings were so excruciating, that it was six weeks before he could be prevailed upon to undergo a second operation, when the other leg was taken off. His companion and fellow sufferer Joseph Shearer, was not in so bad a situation, having but one leg that it was necessary to remove, although the other is rendered entirely useless, the contracted nerves having drawn it out of its natural posture. We remained in St. John's till the 5th of August, when we were put on board the *Arab Transport*, and sailed for Portsmouth, where we arrived after a pleasant voyage of seventeen days, on the 22nd.

We can present the reader with no correct idea of our feelings of pleasure on landing at Portsmouth. Denied the friendly assistance of Englishmen in foreign countries, to whom we looked for succour; denied surgical assistance at a time when our limbs were actually perishing from our bodies, and permitted to remain in this pitiable situation during a severe winter, in a habitation that none of the inhabitants considered habitable, with scarcely any fire, while the snow penetrated through our ruinous building, even to our very bed. We were compelled by a British Magistrate to remain in this unenviable state of bodily suffering and mental agony for a period of four months and seven days! A remembrance of past sorrows, and a feeling of most excruciating pain, embittered our anticipations of the future. A remembrance of the past impressed on the memory never to be obliterated, we looked forward to our succeeding days with the gloomiest forebodings. We endured all the dangers of the storm, we partook our full share of the perils of the perilous deep, under which, more than half the number of our companions sank into the arms of death. Reduced to a state of unutterable woe, we landed with our lives only, on a British island. We told our melancholy tale to an English magistrate, but we were disregarded. We survived the dangers of the deep, but through the cruellest neglect of people professing Christianity, who had the means of relieving our suffering by expelling the frost from our legs, we are prevented while we live from procuring for ourselves the commonest food. Incapable of exertion, we are thrown on the community as helpless cripples. Impressed with these sentiments, who can conceive our joy when we were taken on shore at Portsmouth, where, as in most other parts of England, are Christians to commiserate with the sufferings of the unfortunate child of misery; where, when distress is seen, the tear of sympathy as well as the hand of benevolence is ready to soothe at once the mental grief, and alleviate the bodily pain of the sufferer, requiring such consolation or assistance. On landing at Portsmouth, we were taken to lodgings provided for us by the parochial authorities, whose kindness and humanity as well as of the governor of the poor, we can never forget, while we have the use of reason, or while memory is faithful to her office, [afterwards they were removed to the Workhouse where they still continue]. May the God of Heaven reward our benefactors.

NOTES

1. *An Authentic Narrative of the Loss of the Barque* Marshal M'Donald, *Off Newfoundland, On her passage from Quebec to Limerick, On the 7th of Dec. 1835: Including Interesting Particulars of The Sufferings of the Crew, as related by Thomas Goodwin and Joseph Shearer, two of the Survivors, who were landed at Portsmouth, by the* Arab Transport, *August 22nd 1836* (Bath: W. Browning, 1836).
2. "Life Boats, Life Preservers and Expedients for the Preservation of Shipwrecked Mariners," in *Shipwrecks and Disasters at Sea* (Manchester and Liverpool: Samuel Johnson and T. Johnson, 1838), 367-83.
3. Select Committee on Shipwrecks of Timber Ships (1839), 124, 129.
4. Select Committee on Shipwrecks of Timber Ships, ix.
5. *Shipwrecked Mariner*, vol. 36 (London: Shipwrecked Fishermen and Mariners' Royal Benevolent Society, 1889).
6. Judith Fingard, *Jack in Port: Sailortowns of Eastern Canada* (Toronto: University of Toronto Press, 1982), 117-26.

7. Shannon Ryan, *The Ice Hunters: A History of Newfoundland Sealing to 1914* (St. John's: Breakwater Books, 1994), 317-18. Another development of the 1890s was the arrival of a British-run charity, the Mission to Deep Sea Fishermen, which had worked with the North Sea fleet since 1881; it now became interested in the fate of fishers in Newfoundland after the colonial economy fell upon hard times. Primarily religious in orientation, this charity also provided medical care. For this purpose, Dr. Wilfred Grenfell (late "Sir") was sent in 1892 to assist men and their families in the Labrador fishery. See Ronald Rompkey, *Grenfell of Labrador: A Biography* (Toronto: University of Toronto Press, 1991), 31-47.

13

THE PASSAGE OF THE *PIQUE*
ACROSS THE ATLANTIC (1835)[1]

LADY LOUISA ANNE WHITWORTH-AYLMER

One vessel that escaped wreckage despite grounding on a rock on the south Labrador coast was the *Pique*. It represents one of 1,702 wrecked or missing ships between 1833 to 1835 recorded by *Lloyd's Lists*. This military ship carried a distinguished vice-regal entourage, Lord and Lady Aylmer, the recalled Commander of the Forces and his wife, who were returning to England.[2] Born Louisa Anne Call, Lady Aylmer was 34 years old and childless when the voyage was made. Reared among a family of lesser nobility, she had spent the previous five years engaged in a variety of philanthropic causes, as was the custom of many gentle-women imbued with a sense of civic duty and evangelical reform, including the Female Orphan Asylum, of which she was a patroness while she lived in Quebec. Though we know little about her, there does exist a visual record. In 1831 she sat for James Bowman, a well-known American artist, who painted her portrait.[3]

Lady Whitworth-Aylmer's narrative is dedicated to the young Queen Victoria, who ascended the throne in 1837; it would not have been so dedicated without the monarch's own permission, which is gratefully acknowledged by the writer. Preoccupied with the social position and place of women and issues of morality, Aylmer's lengthy story is far more than a personal account of near-catastrophe. It is as a cultural artifact of the emerging cult of domesticity, "the power of virtue," and the sharply defined spheres of gender that came to dominate the

Victorian era. This "spirit of society," which affirmed and deepened "the proper sphere of woman" as the private sphere, had begun to make itself felt by 1820, in Louisa Anne Call's formative years, under the influence of Queen Caroline.[4]

Describing herself as "a weak, a helpless woman, who would have been less than useless in the dreadful trial had she not breathed out her prayers to Heaven for mercy," and dependent on her maid and other servants, Lady Aylmer symbolizes her gender and her era.[5] While immersed in moral earnestness and religious piety, her account also reflects shifting relations between men and women.[6] She writes, "It is a woman's part and portion to suffer, not to act.... Man! noble man! is born to resist, and in resisting to overcome." This narrative is thus far more than a private account of a voyage. While she never rears a family, Lady Aylmer contributes to the public good by writing about morality, providence, and, a common theme of Victorian literature, a woman's duty and powers; she hopes, she says, that her account will "prove useful" to younger readers. In the words of her contemporary, the English writer John Ruskin, her responsibility was "to assist in the order, in the comforting, and in the beautiful adornment of the state."[7]

That the *Pique* survived its grounding was regarded as providential by Lady Aylmer, who recorded the tumultous crossing home. Though great luck played a significant role in keeping it afloat, the ship's architecture was largely responsible for keeping it initially from sinking outright. A model of the *Pique* was used in witness testimony given before the Select Committee of Shipwrecks in 1836.[8] Commonly, merchant ships did not have solid timber bottoms, and the ceilings above their holds were uncovered. This design resulted in an average life-span without refitting of six years. In contrast, the timbers of the *Pique* were filled in solidly from the load-water line to the light line, and it had a caulked ceiling above the hold. Even though the rocks had penetrated 4 to 5 inches, there remained 11 to 13 inches of floor timber with a filling of felt, which allowed for free circulation of air to prevent rot; this construction saved the ship from immediate wreckage. Moreover, according to Richard Bonniwell, employed in the Admiralty Office and a witness of the committee, this vessel could have lost its stem and keel and remained afloat. He recommended that steam-vessels be constructed, like the *Pique*, with air-tight compartments; not merchant sailing vessels, however, because this design would interfere with stowage.

⚓

DEDICATION
THE QUEEN'S MOST GRACIOUS MAJESTY

MADAM,

Having received your Majesty's gracious permission to dedicate to you a little narrative of the passage of your Majesty's ship the *Pique* across the Atlantic, as drawn up by me partly during that passage, and finished since, from memory, it becomes my duty to express my gratitude for such gracious permission.

Your Majesty's indulgence will secure my narrative being read by the younger part of your subjects, to whom its perusal may prove useful, by showing them how wonderful the interposition of Providence is, in occasions of the most awfully impending danger.

The humble testimony I am thereby enabled to give of the gallant conduct of the *Pique*, will render my short account agreeable to your Majesty; and I need only to add, that I put an entire reliance, on your Majesty's goodness to excuse those defects and inaccuracies which my determination not to admit of any corrections from any other hand or memory, must render myself alone answerable for, as I have the honour to venture to lay before your Majesty my original feelings, such as they were noted down in the moment of our danger, from

> Your Majesty's
> Very Faithful Subject,
> and Devoted Servant,
>
> L. AYLMER
> Carlton Hotel,
> Oct. 2, 1837

While the hoarse Ocean beats the sounding shore,
Dashed from the strand the flying waters roar,
Flush at the shock, and gathering in a heap,
The liquid mountains rise, and overhang the deep.

But when "the Almighty" from his throne surveys,
And calms at one regard the raging sea,
Stretched like a peaceful lake the deep subsides,
And pitched vessel o'er the surface glides.

ANSWER TO THE FREQUENT CALLS ON ME TO NARRATE THE PARTICULARS OF OUR EVENTFUL PASSAGE ACROSS THE ATLANTIC

Yes, I will write! And it shall be a simple narrative of our passage across the Atlantic, not technically described, as a sailor would describe it; I could not attempt that. No, my account can only be such as the voyage was to me, a weak, a helpless woman, who would have been less than useless in the dreadful trial had she not breathed out her prayers to Heaven for mercy: but what human being shall dare to say, that such prayers are worthy to be heard by the high Power who alone rules our destiny? Yet, we are permitted to pray: and if God gives me now the power to tell his goodness to us, my memory ought not to fail me, for how can I forget such scenes? They need not the aid of tablets; gratitude should engrave them deeper on our hearts, than the terrors of which I shall have to speak.

I can only undertake to recall my own feelings as the events passed; may they prove useful to others who may learn by this narration, how good the God of winds and waves is, and that even "in his wrath he thinketh on mercy." I speak here to hearts where feeling and religion dwell: to such, there is poetry in the storm, and love in the refuge which was given us. Who are those to whom I address myself when I write? First, to many dear to my friendship; to those who, I know, in following my narrative will feel with me: there are such in America, in France, in England! Many whom I could name, but, that I should seem to boast of what the heart alone gives to the narrator of facts, the kindest sympathy. I feel that I have possessed this, and I shall again possess it; I therefore comply with the wishes so often expressed that I would let others know what passed in a woman's trembling heart during so long a suspense between life and death. I cannot so often repeat these events. Let them become a lasting record. I owe it to the Almighty hand, who graciously guided our frail vessel, without a rudder, through the tremendous deep of waters.

NARRATIVE

After receiving every demonstration of kind regret at our departure from Canada, which kind hearts could bestow, we embarked on the 17th of September, 1835, on board the *Pique* frigate, commanded by the Hon. Captain Rous, and sailed for England, from Quebec, which for five years had been our home. There is a feeling in leaving those whom you look on, probably, for the last time, which admits of more than seriousness, and which, not all the gratifying proofs of respect (however the heart may answer to them) can lessen. The only thanks I could give were tears: and they were with difficulty restrained and concealed. Of Lord Aylmer I say nothing; with a conscience free from offence, he ended his government of Canada; and left, of course, some friends behind, who will not forget him.

Wind and weather befriended us on our passage down the beautiful St. Lawrence, and across its often-to-be-dreaded gulf. It was decided about three o'clock on the fourth day of our voyage, (the 21st,) that we should pass through the Strait of Belle Isle: Captain Rous had very good reasons for this decision, and I only mention my feelings on seeing a cloud coming after us (as I may term it), because they were very remarkable at the time: an officer, who was then walking on the deck, said, "Yes, that cloud is one which will envelope us in a thick fog very soon." We went below to dine, and not long after, the fog enclosed us as in a veil; it brought with it a fearful destiny, for, owing to the darkness which it spread around, was our striking on the rocks that night, off the coast of Labrador.

Captain Rous had on every previous evening played whist, with the other gentlemen of our party, but on this eventful evening, he had remained on deck, and till ten o'clock I had taken his place at the card table. I had been seriously unwell before our leaving Canada, and as the usual noises on board the best regulated ship are always sufficient to disturb an indifferent sleeper, I had not enjoyed one good night's rest since embarking; and excusing myself from remaining longer up, was determined to take advantage of some arrangements which had been kindly made to ensure me a calm and quiet night, and was just composing myself to sleep, when the tremendous crash occasioned by the ship striking forcibly against the rocks instantly roused me: as the ship was going her smooth and even course, eight knots an hour, with scarcely any motion, the shock was the more alarming. I jumped up, and rushed into the cabin I had left: my maid, who was undressing in the cabin next to mine, hurried in, and throwing herself on her knees beside me, tried immediately to comfort me, thereby bringing my scattered senses under control. Lord Aylmer had rushed on deck to discover, if possible, the extent of our danger; it was of a pitchy darkness, and none could judge where we had struck. One of the lieutenants came into the cabin, and tried to reassure those he found there, by saying the ship would soon be off; and with this attempt at inspiring hopes which probably were felt by very few on board, he left us, to attend to his anxious duties. All the male part of those on board were soon engaged in what seemed to be the first object, namely, to lighten the ship, by throwing the guns overboard. All were soon employed in obeying the orders which our captain gave, in that manly and distinct way, which probably was the chief cause of that admirable discipline, which was never for one moment during our more immediate danger, or afterwards, relaxed: and I have pleasure in giving my humble testimony, here, to the conduct of these brave men, during that night of awful trial. When they came to obey the orders they had received to go into the various cabins to examine the state of the ship, they never passed me, when they had occasion to disturb me from the only quiet corner, where I was seated on a chair awaiting our destiny, without the ceremony and civility they would have used under happier circumstances. I remembered it then, and such conduct strikes me more, now I reflect on it. How often I envied these men their activity and occupation: all was bustle and effort, but not confusion; the exertion necessary towards throwing over the guns, and the necessity for using pumps, occupied all hands.

Anxiously did we, who sat in the cabin, await the smallest glimmering of daybreak. Alas! it seemed awfully long in coming; and yet, as I look back, the eleven hours and a half so spent seem short. After coming a little to our senses, myself and my maid dressed ourselves, so as to be ready for any attempt which might be thought best to make to reach the shore, should daylight present any such chance of escape for us. We then employed ourselves and our menservants, in putting together such things as might be useful, if landing was accomplished. I have before said that all the gentlemen were working at the guns, the grand object being to get them overboard, to ease the ship, while we females found relief in the

occupations of such preparations as my state of nerves would permit
me to think over, by getting together articles of clothing likely to be
most required on the inhospitable coast on which our fate might
throw us; and a variety of articles of utility, which I tried to think
over, such as candles, coffee, a tinderbox, a coffee boiler, our bedding,
ready tied up, and a small trunk or two, of the warmest clothing;
forbidding the servants to think of saving trinkets or jewels, and to
keep their attention fixed on necessaries for ourselves and them: in
such preparations I found certain relief of occupation. And between
the interval of a few seconds of horrid striking of the ship, which
never failed to inspire fresh terror, we were calm, and generally alone;
I mean myself, my maid, the steward and his boy, and now and then
Lord Aylmer, or one of the officers, who as well as himself, I need not
say, on all occasions did their utmost to support and encourage hope
of final release from our awful position: though we often heard
lamentations from the lips of the midshipmen and other officers, not
for their own fate, but that the beautiful *Pique* should "lay her bones"
on the rocky coast of Labrador. How curious, at such a moment of
danger, was the unselfishness of such a regret! The fate of the *Pique*
occupied those whose too certain destruction would have followed
hers. There was something very fine and sailor-like in this; and it had
its effect on us at the time.

As I am writing in the desultory way which such an unusual
detail from a female pen may excuse, I shall just remark on what
struck me at intervals during the night. With that instinct which all
believe to be preeminent in dogs, the one belonging to Captain Doyle
was very uneasy that night; he had attached himself to me, probably,
as being the most considered in the way of comfort, and as I was not
permitted to go into our own cabin, as it was feared the ship might
strike harder there, I sought relief by stretching myself on the mattress
laid on the floor of Captain Doyle's cabin, where his favourite bulldog
terrier shared this convenience with me, which kept him more quiet.
His master complained of fatigue, from hard labour at the guns, and
no wonder; for, as he had the key of the only box among Lord Aylmer's
luggage, containing money, he had the precaution, immediately on
striking, to tie round his waist, after partially dressing himself, two
bags of sovereigns and dollars containing $100 each, and with this
weight about his limbs did the poor man uncomplainingly work away
at throwing over the guns. I entreated him to lay aside his burden,

and promised that the dog and I would guard the treasure. My brave attendant was planning her arrangements for convenience on landing, and though I sighed when I answered her, yet, I could not find in my heart to discourage the buoyance of spirits, which could take pleasure in anticipations which promised so little less than despair.

She arranged with any of the young officers who came to give and receive comfort, a hundred plans for bivouac on shore, and in such attempts at encouraging each other we banished unavailing complaints.

When, at last, daybreak came, this young woman added her entreaty to Lord Aylmer's that I would just go and look at the shore, by way of comforting and reassuring me. I can only remember how dreadfully it had a contrary effect on me, and for once my imagination had fallen short of the reality; for I own I saw no happy prospect of a landing when my eye rested on irregular and rocky coast so near to us, where the sea was beating against it, and I turned from it, and retreated in more hopelessness than I had allowed myself before to entertain.

Whether it seems to creep or fly, time passes, and daybreak soon became daylight; and I now look back with regret, that I did not see the sun rise on that beautiful morning, on that coast which my eyes shall never look on more: but I was below, and by orders confined to our dining cabin, and the one next to it. There was one fearful circumstance which I now call to mind, as I look back on these events: fearful, because it seemed unnatural; it is this: each time that the ship struck against the rocks, it caused a perpendicular motion of the lamp which hung over the table in the cabin, and, which was occasionally nearly extinguished by this up and down vibration. I could not support this patiently, and the steward's boy was much occupied in getting on the table to stop the motion, till the lamp was again disturbed by the next awful blow, which each time wounded the poor *Pique's* keel. The ship being wedged, as I may say, in a bed of rocks, she continued nearly in an upright position throughout the night.

The wind was freshening, the pumps constantly going, and increasing alarm prevailing, when, preceded by a brilliant aurora borealis, day at length dawned, and our position on the coast of Labrador was ascertained.

At the usual hour they piped for breakfast. What an inspiring sound was that! That anything should be going on in its usual course, was of more value to the alarmed feelings, than those who cannot follow our terrific position can conceive. I knew the necessity for these poor men having their accustomed refreshment; they had laboured hard all night, and as theirs is usually a life of labour, they could the less spare their accustomed sleep: the steward saying, therefore, "The men must have their breakfast," had its full value on reflection, and when Captain Rous came down to the cabin for a moment, and stood drinking the cup of tea which the steward held to him, I thought I saw that sad anxiety on his manly face, which brought those tears into my eyes, which I should not have thought weakness at such a moment in his. I spoke for one moment to him, because I wished him to know that I could speak. He had few words to bestow; his time was too precious for words, and he was never from his post. But I must not dwell, even on such details. About a quarter past nine, I called the attention of the few in the cabin to a difference in the manner of the ship's striking; and I observed a greater distance of time between the blows: this circumstance, as the tide was now flood, inspired hope; and I called out that I thought she was moving. There was nobody to answer questions: women were not allowed to go on deck, as every person not at work was in the way, and danger from the expected fall of the masts was too apparent to all there. At last confusion and noise on deck increased, and shall I ever forget, will any one on board ever forget, the sound of the words, "She's off! she's off! hurrah! hurrah!" one long simultaneous hurrah: in which with clasped hands I joined, and tears flowed fast, and relieved me!

I think at this part of my narrative I cannot do better than turn to such extracts as I may have written on board, and which will, at least, be original and actual feelings of the moment. Where they are not sufficiently explanatory of our state, I will add such details as may serve to render this sort of journal of our voyage satisfactory to those who may wish to follow us through our perils.

EXTRACT FROM MY JOURNAL WRITTEN ON BOARD

Wednesday night, Sept. 23. God be praised that I am permitted once more to sit at peace in my cabin, and write in my journal, to my dear friend, after such a terrific eleven hours as the last have proved: it is indeed a luxury, to sit again in peace, and I cannot resist the sharing of it with you. We are anchored in a little bay called L'Anse-au-Loup, in the Strait of Belle Isle, about twelve miles from the spot where the ship had struck, and not far from the Labrador coast: look at your map: there lies the dear good *Pique*, and God in his mercy grant that the injury sustained by her may not be fatal to your friends! If this letter ever reaches you, we shall have arrived probably safely in England: but, after eleven hours on a ledge of rocks, buffeting and thumping every second minute against them, the ship seeming, by her remaining nearly in an upright position, to be wedged in between the rocks. After this, God only knows what we have to expect.

The ship struck at half-past ten. I will not dwell on the past: I fear I was not half so self-possessed as I might have been and wished to be. Who that is a sinner can at such times be quite at ease? Innocence and goodness then tells: at such awful moments the soul looks at her own real state: and the hours passed heavily last night, in momentary expectation of worse, were, I pray my God, not unprofitable. I saw noble men acting like men; I saw none weak, or wanting in moral courage; I admired these, as I should have pitied, without condemning the reverse. I saw a woman, younger than myself, yet surpassing me far in courage, her mind rising to the circumstances, and I felt humbled and abashed, and said, inwardly, "This comes of fearing death: shall I not grow better if permitted to arrive in England?" I thought also of those we had left behind, and rejoiced they had not been with us, and that they were ignorant of our danger. Other details you will get hereafter; I cannot now give them.

No one can tell the injury the *Pique* has sustained, either in her ribs or keel: the latter is the most to be dreaded, as she never took in water before, and now seventeen inches of water is pumped every hour: this quantity they do not fear, but the prospect of crossing the Atlantic in this uncertainty is fearful, I confess. I heard the orders given for sailing at four in the morning. It blows fresh, even in the bay, and God speed us on our voyage.

A consultation has been held, and it is decided as best, that we should cast to St. John's; if necessary put in there, and either by communication with Halifax, procure some vessel to convey us to England, or consent to winter at St. John's. If the *Pique* is considered safe, we are to proceed in her: a trial of nerve this, is it not? But now I feel satisfied that all has been well considered: we must abide the rest as bravely as a nervous being can do. Would to God that we were landed in dear old England! And now that I have indulged in this communication, while all who can, or may sleep, are fast asleep after their great fatigues, I can go more calmly to rest; for this night, at least, we are safely at anchor; when we shall be so again, God alone knows; for in the midst of our glory yesterday, we fell, and now are humbled; we may rise. It is no small addition to my comfort, as I sit writing, to have the luxury of a fire, while Eliza is trying to dry all our wet clothes, a very difficult thing, having been wetted with the saltwater last night. We have been really in comparative comfort this evening, and I would not exchange this luxury for an attempt at sleep.

Friday, Sept. 25. We are going on well towards dear England; have accomplished more than a third of our way, a straight course now, and if this delicious southwest wind lasts ten days longer, may see us please God, safely landed at Portsmouth: but we must not expect this good fortune.

I here remark how far ignorance is often happiness, for on referring to the naval account, written long since my journal at sea, from which I have extracted what goes before, I see this remark:

"*22nd.* The leaks increased to two feet an hour: one was got at in the junkroom, under the gunner's storeroom, and some attempts made to stop it: the cutwater bolts were found driven up a foot or more. Several icebergs were seen. The wind still fair, with a heavy NW swell. The foremast was discovered to work in the step, or, rather, the step itself was loose."

So far, the difference between my calculations and the truth; which truth, I need not remark, whenever evil, could be kept from my knowledge, it was invariably done, and when we assembled at dinner, the best report was always given, to keep up my spirits.

I had with me one, whom, however ill he might have thought of our position on that night of trial, I had rather to find fault with for not seeming to appreciate the danger of our position, the rocky coast before us as our only resource, and the awful alternative of struggling to land there, in boats, during a swell; he smiled at seeing all the goods collected together in preparation for our landing: such ridicule served much at the time to reassure me, and I never could have guessed how justly he appreciated the extent of our danger, till we were off the rocks. Who can ever forget the hurrahs, the shouts? How heartrending! And how unlike the hurrahs on that day week, when we were sitting, surrounded by brilliant decorations and a blaze of light, at the ball given to us by the citizens of Quebec on our departure!

Can any of us ever forget the contrast? One of the young lieutenants, I remember, observed to another, "Oh! how I wish I was where I was last Tuesday, waltzing with that pretty girl, at that beautiful ball!" Well might such recollections come across the youthful sailor in our dark hours of horror on that night of danger, when all behaved so well! My husband, all manly feeling, yet calm: Captain Doyle worked hard, and was always good humoured: Colonel Craig also assisted, but he had been unwell: Captain Rous quite self-possessed, only once a little moved, when I saw him, but soon recovered himself. But I am repeating myself.

Here there is a lapse in my journal from the 26th of September, to the 6th of October, and I now take it up to account for that lapse.

October 6, Tuesday evening. To sit down again at ease is indeed a luxury, which none, perhaps, but those who have undergone what we have, during the last ten days, can duly appreciate.

On Sunday, the 27th of September, having been much confined by weather for some days, I was walking on deck with Captain Rous: the weather was fine, the wind fair, and the ship, under a press of canvas, was making her way rapidly through the water, the officer's dinner going on, Lord Aylmer below asleep in his cabin, as also was Captain Doyle. Divine service was to be performed at three, and being then half past two, I proposed remaining on deck, and joining with the other passengers, and with all the ship's company, in thanksgiving to Heaven for our deliverance from the peril we had been in, off the coast of Labrador, on the preceding Tuesday.

I was enjoying the air, and the pleasure of being again on deck, when suddenly Captain Rous, on whose arm I was leaning, loosened my arm from his, and I tottered back to the gun carriage on which I had been sitting; the officer on watch had whispered something to Captain Rous in passing us. I did not hear what he said, but Captain Rous immediately called out, "All hands on deck! Shorten sail!"

I felt faint, and felt thunderstruck. I knew something serious must have happened, though I knew not what. One of the lieutenants came up, and sat down by me; he said, "I really don't know what has happened. I suppose the captain thinks a squall is coming on," he added, addressing another; "Send for Captain Doyle." I looked round; there seemed no appearance of a change of weather. All was bustle on deck obeying orders. I sat still, and as they passed heard one of the sailors say to another, "A sad job this!" Another said, "What is to become of us now?" These words sounded awful to me then, and I had my anticipations that we were sinking, and the leaks past management. Captain Doyle had been wakened; and came up to me to support me down. At last we learnt that the rudder had broken short off at the head, and was gone clean away, and we on deck had never remarked it; the day we were on the rocks it had been injured, and now it had failed us. Here the officer's journal remarks that "the ship came up right to the wind"; he adds, "a severe trial for the tottering foremast." I only now, as I copy out this in looking back, remember how quickly Captain Rous caused them to shorten sail, and how instantly he began to steer the ship by the sails. It was vain to seem anything but discouraged. What was to be done? Merciful God befriended us, and a fair wind enabled Captain Rous to steer by the trimming of the sails. A temporary rudder was to be attempted, and day and night was employed in its fabrication. An awful time, while waiting for its being put down! It blew so hard, the ship's leaks had increased, but I know not to what amount, and on the 28th the new contrivance for a rudder was shipped in the evening. A brig had appeared in sight, signals of distress were exhibited; which I here remark, is done, by lowering the colours and turning them upside down, I believe: but the cruel brig, whether by accident or design, made all sail, and left the poor *Pique* to her fate.

Captain Rous became at this critical time extremely anxious to take advantage of any vessel which might approach us (wherever bound), to get rid of his passengers, and all the useless hands. One of the boats was lost, being stove; but I was at this time ignorant of this untoward accident, as well as of the extent of our danger, or of Captain Rous's proposal, that if any opportunity presented itself we should at any risk quit the *Pique*.

On the 29th another brig was seen and hailed: she approached us; and it was decided, that if she would receive us on board, ourselves and suite, with the few passengers, and useless hands, should seek our safety there. Captain Doyle, the carpenter, and two men, I think, went toward her, to make the necessary arrangements, should our quitting the *Pique* be possible: her condition was becoming, in Captain Rous's opinion, every moment more critical; and as I now look back, I can justly understand his anxiety on this point at the time. I was very unwilling to make the attempt; the sea was tremendous, and the gale was expected to increase; the rudder was little to be depended on, and the increase in the leaks, added to the state of the foremast, altogether our situation was, to those who could weigh the danger, very awful. Here Captain Rous's character rose; he gave all the necessary orders preparatory to our quitting him; provisions were prepared, sheep killed, and a proper quantity of spirits, wine, &c., to send on board the brig; no very easy task was before us to accomplish, should it be feasible.

I hardly knew at the time, and on reflexion since, I hardly know, what were the nature of those feelings which made me rather averse than otherwise to the prospect of quitting the poor *Pique*; it could not be that sort of affection, if I may so term the predilection, which we often feel towards an inanimate object, and which I readily conceive sailors feel for the ship to which they belong, feelings so useful, I imagine, that they should be respected and encouraged, by not moving men who have so much hardship to support, from the local habitation which these interesting sympathies of our nature makes a home; their home indeed it is, for there they live, and act, and suffer, or enjoy. These are the associations that form home everywhere. Mine did not bind me to the *Pique*: yet, as I sat opposite to Captain Rous, while I read in the manly seriousness of his countenance that he was engaged in writing what he might consider as his last dispatch to the Admiralty; words were few that passed between us. We were alone, excepting indeed one of our servants, who was engaged in collecting such things as we had ordered to be put up ready for our quitting the *Pique* to go on board the French brig; when I saw Captain Rous closing this letter, I ventured to address him. I named some boxes with letters, valuables, &c., &c., what I wished done with them, should he reach England, which I hoped he would, before us. I added, "Remember, Captain Rous, it is much against my inclination that we leave you." He answered, "You have no choice left, for I would not keep you here five minutes if I could get rid of you; besides, you are not aware that we have lost one of our boats, and if it should be necessary to take them, the fewer we have to fill them the better." The footman who attended me, had offered to remain, could he be useful in working the ship: Captain Rous thanking him for this offer, answered with a decided negative: and on my naming my determination not to quit the ship, unless, besides Lord Aylmer's suite, the few other passengers were included, he said that all this had been contemplated and provided for by Lord Aylmer and himself. After these few words I rose, and went round to take leave of him; he then said, "If you reach England before me, you will go and see my mother." I need not add my reply. I made him some similar request, and then adding a few directions about other things, put into his hands a little book, which I held in mine, and this most awful conversation ended! Nothing could have been better devised to reconcile us to leaving the *Pique.* Remaining was adding to Captain Rous's difficulties and anxiety: his duties, and ours, were in this case opposite: ours to go, his, of course, to remain. But we were doomed to stay. I had watched, from my cabin window, for the return of the boat: it blew very hard and the reaching the brig had not been without danger to those, who were making the effort. Captain Doyle was nearly drowned in getting on board. The appearance of the little boat, now visible and now lost to sight between the mountainous waves, was an intensely interesting object. Lord Aylmer had watched her motions from the deck, and on their return from their unsuccessful mission, requested Captain Doyle and the carpenter to report the cause of the failure to me; fearing that I might be terribly disappointed at the prospect of escape being at an end. They found those in the cabin waiting the result of their treaty quite reconciled, and even relieved, by the decision. This reception of their mission was a great relief, I doubt not, to all parties, for, had we been building on this hope of going on board a safer vessel, the disappointment experienced by the wider part of the passengers would have added to the anxiety of the braver sex. The carpenter's account of the unsafe and leaky state of the vessel, which proved to be a merchant vessel of about 200 tons, and in the most disgusting state of uncleanliness, having been engaged in the illicit trading for cod fish off the coast of Labrador, seventeen men on board, crowded, and all inhabiting the only cabin there was, their habits! Imagine what a prospect for females in any position of life: and without the least claim to heroism, for I am a great coward, I may safely aver, that when I think of the two evils, the least appeared to me then, as it does now on calmer reflection, to be obliged to the alternative of remaining on board the *Pique*, with our brave, and well-conducted crew, rather than to be condemned to the horror and inconvenience of such an association. The crew on board the French vessel were, besides this, decided against changing their course for any sum offered them; they were bound to Marseilles, and were averse to taking us at all on board. The risk in attempting to board her would have been very great: we had two soldiers' wives, and three children on board to be saved, and altogether there was little chance, considering the weather, of our ever being put safely on board. So ended this attempt for saving ourselves from the impending danger; and this was the only attempt ever made for quitting the *Pique*, till our landing at Portsmouth.

On the 29th, the temporary rudder, which had proven anything but useful, was cut away: our situation increased in discomfort; all the officers' cabins constantly wet, and hardly habitable. But no complaints were made, and all was submitted to with good temper and good feeling. Captain Rous spared the men when he could, and when he could not he seemed to have no cause for complaint. Officers, marines, and seamen, did their duty cheerfully.

The 30th, a heavy gale, and the ship's head the wrong way; the leaks increased to thirteen inches and all looked gloomy enough. I seldom had any lengthened sleep, and the nights were consequently more horrid than the day. I changed my cabin, and would not be separated from Lord Aylmer during the long night, but had recourse, after much effort, to the swing cot, which, from the nervous feeling of the 30th can never be forgotten by me; though every effort was made by Lord Aylmer and Captain Doyle, aided by the medical gentleman on board, to calm my agitated nerves, yet I seemed awfully aware of the danger of our position on that fearful night; and I may note down here, from my few remarks written while on board, what these horrors were.

On the night of the 30th of September, we had been what was called laid to for the night; the topgallant mast taken down, and I believe two more guns thrown overboard, the trysail, a name I can never forget, set,* and I was assured we were as snug as if we were at anchor.

---

* Since writing this I have been assured by an officer on board that there was not on that awful night, to use his words, "a stitch of canvass up."

Alas! I could not be brought to be satisfied of the assumed fact, and the tremendous sea, while I could hardly preserve myself from being thrown out of the standing cot which I had till then occupied, was not calculated to reassure me. The timbers of the vessel creaking under the stroke of each billow, making a fearful noise, to which nothing singly could be compared. It was like the shrieks of wild birds, the dying groans of animals, the roaring of the only lion I ever heard roar, and the howling of the only wolf I ever heard howl, joined to the cracking kind of noise peculiar to the heaving of a ship in a gale of wind, and which is caused by the separating of the boards termed "bulkheads": then the creaking of the masts, the whistling of the wind in the sails, the spray of the foam, which being thrown with violence over the deck, hissed as it fell: let imagination try to mix all these opposing and terrible sounds, not any one of a pleasing nature, and then it may yet fall far short of the tremendous crash of inharmonious and unnatural noises, which overpowered the senses and irritated the nerves to a frightful degree of suffering.

I was distracted by these at the time, and as I look back, they form a very prominent part in the distressing circumstances of our eventful three weeks of danger.

On Thursday, the 1st of October, the weather was more moderate, but alas! the ship's head the wrong way still, and no chance of reaching England while that was the case. The Pakenham rudder was completed, which had night and day occupied the carpenters. But the sea ran too high to attempt fixing it. A brig was seen, and hailed: she approached, and the wind moderating, at length a hawser (a rope) was sent on board, which broke in an attempt to wear (turn) our ship. The friendly brig proved to be the *Suffrien* of St. Malo, from Cape Rouge, in the Strait of Belle Isle, employed also in the cod-fishery carried on by the French to the injury of our commerce. This may be one reason for the averseness of these small vessels to approach an English frigate; and the *Suffrien*, having done so, was the more praiseworthy in her. She did her best to aid us. Some think the *Pique* wore round at length by the management of the sails, and by sending the whole ship's company to one end of the ship. What joyful acclamations when her head was the right way and Captain Rous relieved from the wretched feeling that we were losing ground and had no help for it! During the 1st, 2nd, 3rd, 4th, and 5th, the ship was steered by the sails, assisted by cables astern, and we were within five hundred miles of the Scilly Islands. At length the effort was to be made, and the Pakenham rudder fixed.

October 7. It is woman's part and portion to suffer, not to act; she therefore requires to be patient in order that she may endure with calmness. Man! noble man! is born to resist, and in resisting to overcome: active, he braves the danger; his first thought is not only how to meet it, but to overcome it. Happier lot, I thought, as I sat below, with clasped hands, and painfully attentive ear, listening to the united efforts of every male on board towards the accomplishment of our vitally important object of getting down, and fixing the Pakenham rudder before evening, for the weather was at last favourable, and God only knew how long it might remain so. With that false estimate of human power, which the will is apt to give, I had been told that a few hours would be sufficient to fix this much-desired rudder. Oh! how I longed once to change my sex: how I wished to be bodily, actively employed! Alas! it was fearfully painful to sit and listen. I could only pray: my heart alone could bow, my body could not. I was not sufficiently at ease to kneel. But time passes, however heavily. It took nearly the whole day to complete the placing of this rudder; the greatest anxiety prevailed: it was at last fixed, and pronounced to work well. None but those situated as we were could judge of how important a relief the certainty of success proved. The night was more tranquilly passed by all, and I dare say sleep visited my eyes more favourably than before. Seldom indeed could I be said to have slept profoundly during the whole voyage, for I well remember, whenever the watch was changed, I was awake to note it, and to hear every word that passed, when the report was made to Captain Rous, whose cot was slung in the only habitable cabin, the dining, next to ours; his own being, as the others were, under water, whenever the pumps were at work, which was every hour during the day and night.

Extract from notes made on board, which as the weather permitted writing, I occasionally made, and conceive more interesting as written at the time and on the spot:

"Yesterday our rudder was put down, being the first day since its completion on which it could have been shipped; you would be horrified could you peep at us now to see the state of the beautiful *Pique*, every cabin's separating walls destroyed. We are sitting in the cabin, the ropes quite round it, so that, as the ship is always rolling awfully, in consequence of her lightness, it is difficult to get across the cabin, without danger of being thrown down by some impediment, not to mention the carpenter's tools, which have been lying about; and whenever the ship rolls, the whole apparatus comes rolling from one side to the other, at the risk of breaking shins, or crushing feet, should an iron crow, or other implement, come in contact with any unfortunate leg or foot. How we have hitherto escaped fractures I know not; but, God be praised, we have little sickness or serious accident on board, and I here remark that none of our party have ever suffered from seasickness. Colonel Craig has been very unwell, but from other causes, and confined to his cabin, which must be truly uncomfortable; and I have not been able to see him, or afford him any consolation for many days, but he bears all this suffering very patiently. The chaplain is also indisposed. To proceed, all the carpets, sofas, and elegancies, gone; our cabins, when the men are at work at the pumps, are generally more or less wet every day, and our meals taken as we best can, holding on.

I only touch on these comparative trifles *en passant*: here, they are hardly thought of and never discussed, though the officers and myself do compare notes as to the variety and additional horrors of the noises, which each night do increase. It does my heart good to be sitting now, at the dining table, writing, while the rest are playing whist, laughing, and really joyous. Wind in our favour, rudder succeeding, and three hundred and nine miles from Scilly.

Seven knots an hour is as much as Captain Rous wishes to go, for fear of wearing the rudder or straining the ship in her present leaky state; for several leaks, I understand, have been discovered lately, by our intelligent carpenter, and have been stopped, and I am assured that the ship takes in less water than she did. I named thirteen inches, but it was twenty-three. I had been deceived for kind motives. I believe I do not yet know the extent of our danger, but I forbear to ask questions now, for often, what is intended to encourage me, sets my imagination at work.

Last Sunday we received the sacrament, in this cabin; it was a very interesting, and, as you may believe, a very affecting ceremony. None could kneel, but we received it as we could best contrive to do, and we have an excellent and pious chaplain on board. Today has been delicious repose; I have passed it in a comparatively happy manner (for the doors could be kept closed by holding). I could read, write, sit on deck; and after dinner, Lord Aylmer and Captain Doyle came into my little boudoir cabin, which is now comfortable again: and we sat looking out of the cabin window, and had a nice chat about Canada, those we had left behind, the present politics there, &c. All this was enjoyable; it breathed of peace, and calmed the mind: how valuable this, to us poor, forlorn mariners! Our spirits rise again, for our dear rudder works well, and they have ventured the topgallant sail up again. If this wind lasts, she may make Portsmouth after all, and be under a month on our passage. Three weeks, this day, since we parted, and what an awful three weeks!"

As I have undertaken to try and remember all that was interesting in our passage across the Atlantic, during our month spent on board the *Pique*, I ought not to omit mentioning that on one occasion, I think it was on the morning of the 21st when the topgallant yards were to be taken down, and the orders for so doing were issued, but no one particularly named to execute this very hazardous duty, in the then state of the masts: two young aspirants for glory were zealous in volunteering for this service, and disputed who should go up first. I heard this mentioned on the day it happened, but I am sorry to say I do not know the names of those young boys; but time will not make me forget the action, any more than the danger which called forth qualities so worthy of British seamen.

From that day of tranquility to the 12th of October, I could never take my pen in my hand; and I must make out my narrative of events from what I wrote afterwards and from memory.

On the 8th the wind came from the northwest, and gradually increased to a hurricane, and now I may be said to be describing the most awful part of our extraordinary passage across the Atlantic; and here I must fail. The little day of peaceful calm, which I have described from my journal, was followed by tremendous weather; and I recur again to those notes made when at anchor off the Casket rocks, where we anchored on the 12th.

"Monday 12th, at anchor off the isle of Guernsey. Very formidable position! Here, as a resource against worse, we anchored last night. To recount the variety of misfortunes which have happened to us, on the one hand, and the providential escapes on the other, would be an endless task. Such tremendous nights since I last noted down anything in this curious kind of journal; among our misfortunes, one of the principal chain pumps broke: this was dreadful, at the time, I well remember. The carpenters tried to repair the mischief, but in vain: it was then undertaken by the sailors, who with various contrivances of oakum, and other materials, succeeded in making the precious pump do its duty again: another testimony this, to the useful kind of practical knowledge to which a sailor's life leads him. During one of the most awful nights, in point of gale, the newly made Pakenham rudder, our only hope, gave way, and broke short off. This wretched event was, I confess, expected by me, for I had sat below, and watched the rising of the tiller, and irregularity of the rope's motions, which as they were brought through the cabin where we sat, I had full leisure to observe; but I was ridiculed for my fears, and I well remember, when Captain Doyle warned me not to support my feet on the ropes, as I was sitting on the ground, which I often did, when the ship rolled so unmerciful, I answered in a truly desponding voice, 'They will not long be useful to us.' The carpenter came in often, to examine the tiller, and I thought each time his countenance looked more suspicious of all not working well. At last, on his making some observations on the subject of the working of the rudder to Captain Rous, he answered, 'Never mind, don't talk any more about the rudder.' O how unwillingly I went to my swing cot on that night I well remember: I had taken to this as a last resource for getting repose, but in vain; and I may here remark, that such constant sleepless nights added many hours of suffering, when compared with those who, wonderful to say, slept profoundly during most of the long nights which I passed in loneliness. To omit bearing testimony to the consolations which I derived from frequently hearing the most appropriate and beautiful Psalms read to me, would be ingratitude to such divine resource. The happy choice of those so suited to our position was my constant comfort. I never knew half their poetical beauty before, and I hope I shall not forget them under happier circumstances. How truly I then estimated everything human! What was the world itself to us out of that ship? And if we did not then make our peace with God, could we ever dare hope to make it? How do we know what suffering on a deathbed may permit us to do? Surely we ought to value the being capable to the last hour, of reflection and prayer; to a pious and good person, with a self-approving conscience, this in itself is comfort; and had the distracting noises and motion of the ship been less, I could have imagined death in many a worse form than that in which it was threatening us. And I can look on many hours of my past life, at which I shudder more, as I look back at them, than I do on those which I passed on board the *Pique*.

It was on the night of the 9th, that the anxiety about the working of the rudder prevailed: these fears were justified; and during that awful night, as the officer on watch passed my cabin, I lay listening anxiously for his approach. Having counted the bells most regularly, I did not fail to hear when the awful event occurred. *Our rudder gone!* and there we were again in a heavy gale, and the ship's head come to the westward, and within a hundred miles of the Lizard Point. Fearful this! Again the deception was attempted of being better off without a rudder; but this will not answer twice. However, thank God, the wind was still favourable, and Captain Rous, prompt and energetic as usual, had again recourse to the sails, and the Almighty arm directing us, we actually sailed up mid-channel. How often, on that, and every night, were all the anxious heads poring over the chart, as it lay extended on the only table, and under the only lamp in the cabin. It seems that no reliance could be placed on the chronometers after the ship had struck on the rocks, but I believe I have not remarked, among our other mercies, that, however foul the weather, each day at twelve, there had been a gleam, so as to admit of an observation being taken, and I am glad I have thought of this circumstance among the other merciful assistance which was given us.

The night of the 10th was most anxiously passed by all who knew the danger. Captain Rous had a fall about this time, I think, of which, however, he made very light: he remained up on that night.* We had made one hundred and sixty miles in the twenty-four hours, without a rudder; and passing, between the Lizard Point on the coast of Cornwall, and Ushant on the French coast, without nearing either, found ourselves last night bearing for the only dangerous rocks in this part of the channel. Wind north, and driving us too much on shore, blowing fresh, when Captain Rous, with his usual promptitude, decided on anchoring off the coast of Guernsey. I shall not easily for-

---

* On our landing it was discovered that Captain Rous had broken in this fall two of his ribs.

get his finger placed on that evening, at the point on the chart where he proposed to anchor, and saying to me, "I will anchor you tonight about there." He made all the necessary arrangements: sounded unceasingly, till he found what he considered good anchorage, and then letting out one hundred and forty fathoms of cable, anchored in forty-two fathoms, I believe. So we remained all night, but I cannot say I slept, or felt easy in our position. The rolling of the ship continued, and she was very uneasy. Having out so much cable was considered safer, in order that in her present disabled state she might not strain. And now that I am writing this at two o'clock, p.m., the tide turning in our favour, the men having dined and pumped, which has been done every hour during the day and night since our misfortune, and their well-known chorus, to keep time as the poor fellows pump, sounding in my ears pleasingly, and yet producing tears, having done all this business, we are now heaving anchor, and about to try our fortunes once again. We are about eighty miles from St. Helen's: I pray God we may be there tomorrow. The barometer is rising, the sea calming and all looks better for us. Another rudder is preparing. All were too sanguine as to the success of our Pakenham rudder, but such seas would have destroyed anything. I have been on deck for the first time for many days, during which the dead lights were all in: the air, though cold, refreshed me; as I am, I confess, beginning to fail. I am very unwell in body and mind, hardly able to stand, and sometimes making more alarm for myself than perhaps there is cause for, as I did this morning, before I rose, when I fancied, being alone in my cot, that some strange noise, which I suddenly heard near the pumps, was caused by the leaks having burst and become unmanageable, and the ship sinking. Such fears of instant destruction are awful at the moment, but my nerves are weakened."

At anchor at St. Helen's. October 17, 1835. Since four o'clock this morning, and after a most anxious night, the last ever spent by us on board the *Pique*, God be praised, we anchored! After a sort of living death of three weeks' duration, the gratitude attending personal safety, is in itself delicious. I have found a corner of the cabin in the midst of confusion, and noises of all kinds; here I have sat quietly down to write, my thoughts fully occupied.

Once again, before I quit this eventful habitation, I write:

"The brave Captain Rous took advantage of a favourable wind yesterday, and brought us up through a misty and rainy night to St. Helen's; few went to bed during this most anxious night. It rained hard, but the gentlemen of our party remained round Captain Rous the whole night: it was too exciting for any one to remain below, who could be on deck. I had been particularly uneasy, dreading the darkness, and the chance of our being driven on the many dangerous places on the coast of the Isle of Wight. Captain Rous having at one time an idea of anchoring in St. Catherine's Bay: he however did better for us, for he steered by the sails as he had done before, and anchored, at four o'clock in the morning, at St. Helen's!"

How can I ever forget the tearful joy of their all coming down to congratulate me, who was lying on the sofa in my small cabin which I succeeded in lighting up in every possible way, in order to banish the terror and nervous excitement I was in, and taking a volume of *Sir Charles Grandison*, my maid read aloud, to try and draw our attention from the lengthened suspense. The sea was calm, and I had contrived to compose my mind by the reasoning powers of the medical gentleman on board, who had been very kind and attentive to me during our passage. He was an old sailor and I had some confidence in his reasoning, so I detained him an hour in conversation, which did me much good.

Oh! the joy of hearing them all in the adjoining cabin, taking some coffee, which Captain Doyle had been very busy making; and over this truly delicious repast, as they thought it, they were all talking together, and as happy and joyous as people just saved from destruction could be. Our minor miseries were, however, not quite over, but all appeared trifling, after what we had undergone.

I shall give a brief detail of our landing. Captain Rous went early on shore, to report himself. Having at daybreak telegraphed the sinking state of the *Pique*, some of the dockyard people were soon round the ship, and one of them, who came on board to examine her state, on going round one side turned to the head carpenter, and asked if the other side was in the same condition as the part he was then examining, where he found the bolts had sprung, and the whole in lamentable condition. The carpenter answered "*It is worse, sir, on the other.*" The shipwright said, raising his hands in astonishment: "It is enough, do not show me any more; I never saw any ship enter port in such a state."

It was expected that a steamer would be sent to tow us into Portsmouth harbour; but in this we were disappointed: but our good friend Captain Rous did not forget us, and the Port Admiral very kindly again sent the yacht (she had been once and dismissed; in the expectation that the steamer would arrive, and secure the *Pique* being safe in harbour early in the day). I began to look anxiously about me, fearing, after all, that our long discussed, delightful dinner on shore would not take place on that day. Of what this feast should consist had been often the subject of our efforts to raise each other's spirits during our awful voyage, and now that this seemed within our reach, it was not patiently to be borne, and we were quite determined to get on shore, somehow or other. The ship was all confusion, our goods separating from those belonging to Captain Rous, and everything would have appeared truly miserable could we have been ungrateful enough to think anything miserable after what we had escaped from.

At length, to my no small joy, preparations were made for getting on board the yacht; it blew very fresh, and Lord Aylmer requested that the cutter might be lowered, for our getting from the *Pique* on board the yacht: our minor misfortunes pursued us, for on lowering the cutter the accommodation ladder was nearly carried away; a few steps only remained, but as I declined having a chair to whip me down, which I always think a nervous operation, I preferred the other mode of descending, and notwithstanding my extreme weakness, we were, with some care, all safely deposited in the boat, and from thence put on board the yacht, and glided from the poor *Pique*, too thankful that she had not been our grave. We had been, while on board, towed by boats from St. Helen's to Spithead, where they soon anchored for the night, and we landed at the Custom House, but were not permitted any kind of privilege, but were obliged to send even our writing boxes to be inspected. This made us a little angry, but resistance would have been troublesome, and we were too happy to allow anything to annoy us long, and the keys were given to Captain Doyle; while the rest of our party proceeded in a carriage, sent for us from the George Hotel, where apartments had been taken when Captain Rous landed in the morning. And it would be utterly impossible to describe the joy with which we took possession of them in the comfortable hotel, and the excitement of that and the follow-ing days. Dinner was ordered, and the promised dinner proved as good as we had anticipated. I also found that I could sleep eight or

Rocket Apparatus for Saving Life from Shipwreck. A feature of late-nineteenth century rescue procedures. From *Canadian Illustrated News*, 9, Feb. 28, 1874. C61110, Courtesy of National Library of Canada/ Bibliothèque nationale du Canada

ten hours, and from that moment I ate, drank, and slept, while each in turn seemed to give me additional strength and happiness.

Everyone was kindly anxious and interested in our escape. The following morning we walked down to see the *Pique* towed past the look out: she was received with hurrahs! Did I not shed tears again at that sound! Many and grateful tears they were; and the same tune came to my ear, as the poor sailors were pumping, as the *Pique* was towed past us; that was the last time I heard those sounds; but shall I ever forget them? Never, I believe!

And now how did the scene change! We remained at Portsmouth till Saturday, in the hopes of seeing the state of the *Pique*, after she should be in dock: I was not sorry for those days of repose, or rather amusement; we were kindly entertained everywhere; Sir Thomas MacMahan's family were particularly friendly and attentive to us, though we had no previous acquaintance with them. We went also in company with Captain Rous, to dine at Mr. Thistlewaite's, at Southall Park; had the honour of meeting the Duke of Sussex on a visit there: as I sat opposite to his Royal Highness, and saw all sparkling and brilliant in the jewels and plate around me, and looked at the handsomely arranged and well-lighted rooms, I could not help feeling how delightful a contrast to our position on board the *Pique*! After all, there is nothing to be compared for comfort or luxury to an establishment at an English country-house. We may have a national pride in these things, as they are not, I really believe, to be found in the same perfection in any other country. Money is the only thing wanted: the taste for living well is certainly understood here. These remarks were suggested by my having been many years absent from England before I went to Canada. We were kindly and hospitably received at Admiral Sir Thomas Williams's, who has an excellent house in the dockyard, which was formerly the commissioner's; we were delighted with seeing the biscuit-baking, and there I had the pleasure of making an acquaintance with one, whom I have continued to like more and more, on every subsequent meeting. I found in this person, what I do sometimes find, a most intelligent, and really interested listener; she made me detail to her the particulars of our passage, encouraged and entreated me to write down and publish these, just in the simple way in which I had narrated them to her; but fatigued in mind, and indolent, for the time, as I really felt, I wanted courage for the exertion. On our arrival in London, I found my time so entirely occupied with answering letters of congratulations on our miraculous escape, some, indeed, written by persons whom I had not met for twenty years, that my pen had sufficient employment, touching, as of course I was so often obliged to do, on the eventful history of our passage across the Atlantic, in a leaky ship, without a rudder!

Added in the Isle of Wight, August 22, 1837. Looking over the foregoing sheets, now that I have had the opportunity of paying a visit to the *Pique*, and recalling to my eye, as well as my mind, past scenes, I again regret the idleness or the shyness which has prevented my having these sheets copied and circulated among those whom interest or curiosity might lead to their perusal. In their present form, they are almost useless; the scrawl I have indulged in allowing myself, will make the perusal troublesome to many; and I cannot bear to explain to a copyist my illegible writing, now that one of our party on board has just perused this statement, and pronounced it to be very correct as to facts, and most interesting to him as to recollections: while another who has read it, being a young connexion in the Navy, seems to think that it can be very well understood; I really do regret that I have kept it so long in my own desk, and I think I will have it fairly copied out, and let it be read by others.

When on board the *Pique*, I had the pleasure of meeting two of the officers who were on board with us during our voyage; and I was told the following circumstances. One of these gentlemen said, "*I believe there never were so many persons before saved by a sack of biscuit.*" On my requesting an explanation, he told me, that on the ship's stores being removed after she came into dock, it was discovered, that the water had penetrated the sack of biscuits, and by being saturated with the wet they had swollen, and positively proved a sufficient security against the leak which was discovered to be under this store of bread. I make no comments on this additional proof of mercy, but I record it here. How many other circumstances, trifling in themselves, but full of importance to us, have I not probably omitted, but my tale is already sufficiently long, and I have done!

As there is, or always ought to be, a moral to be deduced from every tale, may we not find one in mine? First, it proves that we never should despair of the Divine assistance under any circumstances, for we cannot know what fate God has prepared for us; next, as a woman, I may observe, though we seem privileged to be cowards, by the very weakness of our nature, and that our lives may, in fact, be often of less value to the community at large than those of the other sex, yet we have to admire, and should be grateful for, that attention and care, which is usually bestowed on us, in order to spare our feelings on all occasions where danger is to be apprehended; and we should therefore look up to those, who are not only our superiors in natural courage, as indeed nature herself points out the other sex should be, but who, while they are themselves aware of the extent of the peril, and meet every difficulty with prompt and proper exertion, guard their language and their countenance from betraying the alarming truth to those whom they would protect and preserve, at the hazard of their own lives. Such moral courage should meet with a suitable return, and to the younger part of my readers I venture to point out these things, for I have seen some of my sex inclined to take for granted, and as a matter of course, that they are always to be considered and saved in any danger, at the risk of life itself to the braver sex; this may be true, but then it should not be forgotten, that such privilege, while it proves to woman her natural dependence on man, and marks the distinctive relations between the sexes of protector and protected, this should also suggest that gratitude should be one of our virtues, and that, next to the Almighty, we are often called upon to be thankful to the brave and noble men for our safety and consolation in difficulty or danger.

Lady Aylmer added the following notations at the bottom of this page:

Ps. iii. iv. xviii. xix. xxii. xxiii. xxix. xxxix.xiii. xliii. li. lv. lvi.lxix. in our deep distress, lxxvii.; both appropriate.
xc. xcii. xcviii.; rejoicing and praise; xciii. particularly suited: xcviii. rejoicing: ciii. ditto.
civ. the most beautiful of all.
cvii. particularly suited.
cxxiii. cxxx. cxxxvi. and cxxxviii. quite beautiful.

NOTES

1. Lady Louisa Anne Whitworth-Aylmer, *Narrative of the Passage of the* Pique *Across the Atlantic* (London: J. Hatchard and Son, 1837), CIHM 21583.
2. Philip Buckner, "Whitworth-Aylmer, Matthew, 5th Baron Aylmer," *Dictionary of Canadian Biography*, vol. 4 (Toronto: University of Toronto Press, 1980), 904-08.
3. J. Russell Harper, "James Bowman," *Dictionary of Canadian Biography*, vol. 4 (Toronto: University of Toronto Press, 1980), 100-01.
4. Dror Wahrman, "'Middle-Class' Domesticity Goes Public: Gender, Class, and Politics from Queen Caroline to Queen Victoria," *Journal of British Studies* 32 (October 1993): 396-432.
5. Bonnie G. Smith, *Changing Lives: Women in European History Since 1700* (Lexington and Toronto: D.C. Heath, 1989), 182.
6. See Gertrude Himmelfarb, *Marriage and Morals Among the Victorians* (New York: Alfred A. Knopf, 1986), 4-5.
7. Cited in E. Holly Pike, *Family and Society in the Works of Elizabeth Gaskell* (New York: Peter Lang, 1995), 2.
8. Great Britain, House of Commons, *Report From The Select Committee Appointed To Inquire Into The Causes of Shipwrecks*, 15 August 1836, 39-41.

14

AWFUL SHIPWRECK: THE *FRANCIS SPAIGHT* (1836)[1]

JOHN PALMER

On 25 April 1839 Thomas Edwards, Secretary to the Royal Society for the Preservation of Life from Shipwreck, appeared before a British parliamentary Select Committee On Shipwrecks of Timber Ships. The committee's mandate was to inquire into the nature of timber shipwrecks and the accompanying disproportionate loss of life. The statistics were grim (see Appendix A). Edwards was asked by Sir Charles Vere if any particular instance stood out and he was informed that, yes, one did: that of the *Francis Spaight*.[2]

On 22 December 1836, the *Francis Spaight*, a 345-ton vessel, T. Gorman master, while en route to Ireland with a load of timber, was discovered dismasted and water-logged in lat. 47° long., 37° 24' lat., by the Newfoundland brig *Angeronia*. Captain John Gillard (Jellard) organized the rescue of the eleven survivors in a strong gale, with "a tremendous sea ... running, which frequently struck over the vessel and rendered it extremely dangerous to board her." Gillard and three men (William Hill, mate, John Towell, seaman, and Samuel Hicks, passenger) made their way in the *Angeronia*'s only boat, and "after much exertion and difficulty" rescued "six human beings from a state of suffering too horrible for description," then returned to pick up the remaining five crew members. The "gallant rescue" and the demonstrated "bravery" prompted the county magistrates of Teignmouth and the officiating minister of West Teignmouth to lobby for a public reward; in an application to the Shipwreck Institution, they noted that "no remuneration was sought at the time, and ... the rescued are wholly unable to provide a recompense."

The condition of the *Francis Spaight* paled when compared to the suffering of its surviving crew, who had been forced to resort to cannibalism. Their horrific attempt to survive was unfortunately not a rare occurrence, rivalled as it is by the fate of the *Earl Moira* and others.[3] The committee viewed the events of the *Francis Spaight* as perhaps typical of the 949 seamen aboard 73 ships lost or wrecked in 1836, whose fate remained unknown. It could "only be considered as an index of the suffering to *a like extent* in all those other vessels, the crews of which have never been heard of."[4] George C. Smith, Minister of the Mariners' Church and Honorary Secretary of the British and Foreign Seamen and Soldiers' Friend Society, and Superintendent of the Naval and Military Orphans Society, writing from the Naval and Military Office, Welclose-square, summed up for the committee the physical and psychological sufferings of crews in water-logged timber ships, saying that they were "more distressing and horrible" than those in any other form of maritime disaster, including those experienced in the worst hurricanes (see Appendix).[5]

The following first-hand account by John Palmer, a former deckhand and survivor of the *Francis Spaight*, provides insight into this dreadful event. He reminds us in citing the full poem that "there is no place like home," and for good reason in his case. His escape from a mundane and ordinary existence brought him, a young man from a family of means and "respectable parentage" who went seeking adventure, much misery. The editor adds closing remarks that comment on 1836 as a year of many marine disasters, and he includes a discussion of the fatal fire aboard the steamboat *Royal Tar* and the loss of the *Bristol*, both transatlantic passenger vessels. A final anecdote in this section comes from an unidentified captain's recollections of a collision in fog between his "fine, stout ship" and "a small schooner at anchor," which likely left no survivors and no other record of the event.

IT IS ALWAYS AT THE EXTREME HAZARD of their lives, that navigators, as well as others, adventure upon the boisterous ocean; and the past year (1836) will be long remembered as a remarkable one, for the many melancholy shipwrecks and fatal disasters at sea, that have attended it. Yet, seldom is it that it falls to our lot to record an instance attended with so great a portion of human misery, as the one narrated in the succeeding pages. The melancholy narrative cannot fail of exciting the sympathy of those who can feel for suffering humanity, wherever it may be read, and whatever the fate of the unfortunate sufferers may be disclosed to the heart and eye of sensibility.

The narrator, JOHN PALMER, who was a hand on board, (and to whom we are indebted for the melancholy particulars,) is a young man of unquestionable veracity, of respectable parentage, and of more than ordinary education; and who, it appears by his own confession, entered by a fictitious name, and without the knowledge of his friends, on board the British ship *Francis Spaight*, at St. John's (Saint John) N.B., bound from thence to Limerick; and which he was induced to do for no other reason (it being his first voyage,) than to gratify a strong propensity to "see the world," and which, he observes, he saw no great cause to regret until the 3rd day of the month proceeding that on which he entered,

[...] "when [to use his own words,] it was our misfortune to experience a gale, which for severity, (in the opinion of the oldest sailors on board,) was seldom surpassed, if ever equalled; and during which, while lying to under a close reefed mizzen topsail, the ship capsized, when three of her crew found a watery grave! Orders were immediately thereupon given by the officers to the survivors, to do all in their power for the preservation of the ship, as well as their lives, and who, after much hard labour, succeeded in cutting away her masts, when she righted; but, to inexpressible surprise and horror of all on board, it was discovered that not a particle of either water or provisions could be obtained to sustain the lives of those who had not shared the fate of their unfortunate companions! But this (as it afterwards proved) was only the beginning of our calamities. As there was nothing now that presented to our view but the horrible prospects of starving, without any appearance of relief, we were reduced to the most deplorable state imaginable! Peculiarly so as regarded myself, who had ever been a stranger to hardship, much less to hunger and want.

The wind continued to blow with unabated fury the two succeeding days and nights, and it was only by lashing ourselves to the wreck, that we were prevented from being washed overboard by the tremendous sea occasioned thereby; and when partially relieved in

Prospectus woodcut of Palmer's *Another Awful Shipwreck*. Note one survivor eating human flesh. BR 910.4 P12, Courtesy of the Harriet Irving Library, University of New Brunswick

this respect, our minds were agitated by the dreadful apprehensions that we had only escaped from a watery grave to experience tortures still more to be dreaded! Five days were passed in this state of painful anxiety, when our sufferings, produced by craving hunger and burning thirst, were too great to be longer endured; and to alleviate which, we were finally driven to the dreadful alternative of casting lots, thereby to determine who of our number should be put to death, that his body might serve as sustenance for the remainder! The lot fell on the youngest on board, a poor friendless youth, who had been apprenticed to the Captain, and who by the great hardships that he had endured, as well as long fasting, was reduced almost to a skeleton. Whether there was a previous understanding among some of the ship's crew, that he should be the one selected as a victim, without allowing him an equal chance with the others for his life, is well known to Him, from whom no human act can be concealed; but, whether such was the fact or not, such was the distracted state of my feelings at that moment, that it was impossible for me to determine. It is enough for me to remember, nay, at the present moment, my blood chills at the bare recollection of the heart-rending scene that ensued, when the fate of this poor unfortunate lad was made known to him! He first burst into tears, and entreated that his life might be spared for a few days, which not being allowed him, he reduced the time to a single day; and when he found that there was even an objection to this, he became frantic, declaring it his determination to defend himself to the last, although he retained hardly sufficient strength to support himself erect; but, being in this respect but little inferior to that of his other shipmates, although attacked by three or four of the most able-bodied, he succeeded, with his jackknife, in keeping them off for some minutes, when nature becoming exhausted, he fell prostrate on the deck, and in which condition he was instantly despatched, and his limbs detached from his emaciated body, and distributed among his still more wretched shipmates! Frequently had I heard and read that famine had led men to the commission of such horrible excesses, that insensible on such occasions to the appeals of nature and reason, they assumed that character of beasts of prey, and deaf to every representation, coolly meditated the death of a fellow-creature! But, foreign was it from my mind, that I should myself be brought, not only to be an eye witness to a scene like this, but to become, in reality, one of its melancholy subjects! Two days had, however, elapsed after the tragical death of the unfortunate youth, before I could be brought to follow the awful example of my starving companions! To what woeful extremities can poor human nature be driven by extreme hunger! Surely, none can be truly sensible of it, except those who have experienced it. It is not necessary for me to add, that to this state, I (who had been used to luxurious living, and who had unnecessarily left a home affording 'enough and to spare,') was brought!

However loathsome this food may be viewed by my readers, (some of whom may perhaps think, as I once thought, that even a lingering death by starvation, would be preferable to that of attempting to appease it by the use of human flesh,) it was found insufficient to support life but a few days, when a similar plan was adopted in the selection of another victim! And in a few days after, another! The first of the two appeared perfectly reconciled to his fate, and requested only a few moments to prepare himself for death, which he employed in fervent prayer for himself, and for our speedy deliverance, and then delivered up his life without a struggle! But, the piteous moans and lamentations of the latter, in consequence (as he represented,) of leaving behind him a beloved wife and several small children, dependent on him for support, were truly appalling, and could not have been withstood by any but such wretched beings as we were, whose sufferings and privation had driven to a state of desperation! This was, in reality, the situation of some of the unhappy survivors, who, deprived of their reason, and driven to a state of raving madness, and their strength admitted of it, it is not improbable that they would, like ravenous beasts, have fallen upon and destroyed one another, without any regard to the plan pursued in the selection of victims.

A few days previous to that on which we were relieved, four of our wretched companions expired, (by the names of O'Brien, Gorham, Beham, and Burns,) and all, apparently, in a perfect state of insensibility, as regarded their real situations. It was astonishing to witness how different were the effects produced by their sufferings. The ravings of O'Brien and Beham, in their last moments, were like those of madmen, and whose greatest efforts (with fists clenched, and with gnashing teeth,) appeared to be to commit violence on those of their shipmates by whom they were approached; and some of whom would, no doubt, have received serious injury, had they not retained sufficient strength to enable them to creep away beyond their reach. Burns, although he talked incessantly and incoherently, manifested a more harmless disposition. At one moment he would be engaged in singing some favourite sea song, and at the next would appear to imagine himself the commander of the wreck, calling on his shipmates (by wrong names) to attend to their duty, assuring them that there was every prospect of a short, pleasant, and prosperous voyage! The behaviour of Gorham was different from that of either of the three mentioned; at intervals he appeared more rational, and not insensible of his situation, and while speaking of his unfortunate family as bereaved of one on whom they depended for support, would weep like a child; but soon would appear to lose himself, and call on and talk to his children as if present, calling them by name, and entreating them to take pity on and indulge their father with even a few drops of water.

As regarded myself, although in body exhibiting the appearance of a living skeleton, yet I bore my sufferings and privation with a great degree of fortitude, until three days previous to that of our deliverance, when it was my fate (as I was informed by my shipmates,) to become delirious. When restored to my reason, I recollect that while I remained unconscious of my situation, all appeared like a dream. I imagined myself at home, in the presence of my affectionate parents, brothers, sister, &c., but confined to a sick bed, a prey to a burning fever, and tormented with most intolerable thirst. I plainly, as I imagined, recognized my friends, standing by my bedside, but who not only appeared to disregard my entreaties for water, but to view me with much apparent indifference; and it was, when endeavouring by gestures, (as I either was, or imagined myself deprived of the power of speech,) to acquaint them of the true state of my feelings and the tortures with which they were afflicting me, by refusing to indulge me with a little water with which to cool my parched throat, that my reason returned, and I became more sensible of my wretched condition.

By the return of my reason my mind was once more distracted by the most awful forebodings; being sensible that by the selecting of one victim after another, we were fast reducing our number, I could not but expect that my turn would by and by come; or, what was, if possible, still more to be dreaded, that it might be my lot to survive all my wretched companions, and be the last to perish on the wreck and thereby my afflicted parents ever left in suspense as regarded my wretched fate.

To determine whom it should be, the same plan of deciding by lot was adopted, which fell on the mate. The poor fellow appeared but very little affected thereat, having been frequently heard to declare that so great were his sufferings, that he envied those of his shipmates their fate, who had been doomed in this manner to yield up their lives; and could not but hope that if it should be found necessary to sacrifice another, that it might fall on his lot, as he had neither wife nor children to leave behind. His only desire was that he might die by strangulation, the deaths of the others having been caused by opening a vein. With the captain, the fate of his mate had quite a different effect; his attachment for him had been great, and he therefore used much persuasive argument to prevail on his unfortunate crew to postpone the sacrifice for a single day. He had, by soaking in salt water, preserved the liver and brains of the unfortunate youth (the first victim), and was the next morning about to share this, with the remaining food, among his companions, when to the inexpressible joy of all a vessel was descried bearing down for the wreck, which proved to be the brig *Angeronia*, Captain Gillard, bound from Newfoundland to Teignmouth.

When the Captain and crew succeeded in reaching our ship's deck, and beheld the awful spectacle which we presented, and the melancholy remains of the last victim on which we had subsisted for the three days previous, they appeared for a moment as if doubting the reality of what they saw; but convinced, they united in one general exclamation of horror and surprise! Our appearance at that moment, must indeed have been shocking in the extreme; but two of our number possessing sufficient strength to stand erect, the remainder were only able to creep about on their hands and knees. Our face, arms, hands, and other parts of our bodies, that had been exposed to the powerful rays of the sun, burnt nearly black; and our clothes having been continually wet, our emaciated bodies were chafed and nearly covered with painful sores.

We were by our kind deliverers conveyed on board the brig, where every thing was done that could be done to alleviate our miseries. Broths were made for us, but of which, as of water, we were permitted only to partake sparingly and to which we may impute the salvation of our lives, for had we been permitted to eat as much as our appetites craved, it must have proved fatal to us. By the kind assistance of my benefactors (for which may Heaven reward them), by the time the brig reached her destined port, I had by kind treatment gained sufficient strength to enable me, like another prodigal son, to reach that long wished for home, which had been the scene of many happy moments, but of which I had been unconscious, until I had unwisely deserted it, to experience trials and hardships of which none but those who have experienced similar, can have a true conception. By my great sufferings, my health still remains impaired, and my constitution (which was previously good,) so much broken, as to render it very probable, that until the day of my death I shall remain a living monument of my past folly.

True it is, as I have frequently heard it remarked, that dear-bought experience often proves a most valuable instructor, and that we are sometimes indebted to adversity for our wisdom. I had heard much of foreign countries and had long felt a strong inclination to visit them; and although I had not unfrequently read of, and listened with no inconsiderable interest, to the narratives of the surprising adventures of sailors, as they recounted their many hair breadth escapes, and the great perils and privations to which they were daily exposed while navigating the deep; yet it had but little effect to deter me from an attempt to accomplish my views, to gratify a too common propensity to adventure abroad, even at the risk of my life, 'to see the world!' Others, I argued, had been and returned in safety, and why not I? With this encouragement alone, I adventured. But, alas, too soon did I experience the difference between that peaceful and comfortable home, the habitation of endeared friends, the scene of every enjoyment that I most earnestly desire, to that of being tossed to and fro upon a boisterous ocean, and occasionally confined to a damp and dreary forecastle, subsisting on the coarsest food, and with none but perfect strangers, of almost every country, for my companions. But, what was all this to what I was afterwards doomed to suffer? The sad tale has been told; the melancholy particulars have been truly and faithfully recorded in the preceding pages.

Although while I remained on the wreck, my sufferings were so great as in one instance to deprive me of reason, yet, in my most rational moments, I could but contrast my own miserable situation with that of some of my young acquaintance on shore. That while they were, in all probability, reposing in security by the firesides of their friends, and blest with and enjoying every necessary of life that their hearts could wish, I was enduring all the tortures which extreme hunger and parching thirst could be productive of; and to relieve which, was finally driven to the awful extremity of eating the flesh and drinking the blood of those who had been my ship companions! My dear young friends, it is my sincere prayer that you may not follow my examples, and unwisely attempt to gratify a similar propensity 'to see the world,' but rather learn wisdom by my folly; take the advice of one who knows, who by his imprudence and too hasty conclusions, has been doomed to drink deep, very deep, of the cup of adversity! Never be so unwise as to exchange a certainty for uncertainty; if you have comfortable homes, and possess the means of procuring even a humble living, be satisfied therewith, for should you be otherwise inclined, you may have cause ever after to regret it. As regards myself, I can truly say with the poet, that

> Mid pleasures and palaces though we may roam,
> Be it ever so humble, there's no place like home;
> A charm from the sky seems to hallow us there,
> Which, seek through the world, is ne'er met with elsewhere.
>   Home, home, sweet, sweet home,

There's no place like home.

An exile from home, splendor dazzles in vain,
Oh! give me my lonely thatched cottage again;
The birds singing gaily, that come at my call,
Give me them with peace of mind, dearer than all.
 Home, home, sweet, sweet home, &c.

If I return home overburdened with care,
The heart's dearest solace I'm sure to meet there;
The bliss I experience whenever I come,
Makes no other place seem like that of sweet home.
 Home, home, sweet, sweet home, &c.

I have more than once heard it remarked, and by those who were
probably more wise than myself, that 'he who would know how to
prize health, should for a period be deprived of it.' A very correct
remark, in my estimation, and one that will with equal propriety
apply to some few in the humbler walks of life, who, although blessed
with health, and with the means of earning by their daily avocations a
comfortable subsistence, yet manifest much uneasiness and discontent, because there are others who appear to have been the greater
favourites of kind fortune, and to enjoy more profusely her gifts,
wrongfully imagining that the splendour of *wealth* and possession of
riches, are alone essential to their *happiness*; but, such an opinion I
know by sad experience, to be an erroneous one, for although it has
been with me from early age, (as with thousands,) the great object of
my pursuit, yet I can truly say, that I never did experience *true happiness* until that joyful moment, when, after having been driven to the
most awful extremities by hunger and thirst, I was presented by my
deliverers with a cup of *pure water* and a *bowl of broth*; and which I at
that moment, would have been found unwilling to have exchanged
for all the wealth of Peru. And such, I am confident, would be the
conclusions of those, who, although strangers to real want, yet too
frequently murmur against Providence; for debarring them from the
enjoyment of the luxuries and superfluities which has been placed
within the reach of others, would they condescend for a moment to
look down upon the thousands who are so far more miserable than
themselves, as to find it difficult to procure from day to day, food

sufficient to satisfy the cravings of nature? They would not, while enjoying the necessaries of life, conceive themselves so extremely unhappy, although deprived of the enjoyment of some of its luxuries. But such is the aspiring disposition of man, generally speaking, and such his natural thirst for wealth, that he is seldom found willing to *look down* and to contrast his situation with those who move in the lower ranks of life, (altho' it is not improbable that some were born to greater fortunes,) but is continually *looking up*, and envying the rich for their great wealth, although the possession thereof, it is possible, would render him ten times more unhappy than he would otherwise be. Pity it is, that such could not be made sensible that the real source of all human happiness is not *riches*, but CONTENTMENT.

It is a lamentable truth that a thirst for, or a pursuit after *imaginary* happiness, too much engrosses the attention of mankind generally, and too much do they expect to find it in the possession of great wealth. This is a great mistake, for no one can be pronounced happy, who depends upon fortune for his happiness. That man alone is most happy who is contented with the situation in which Providence has placed him. We live in a world naturally subject to lamentable events; and every day's instruction teems with lessons teaching us the vicissitudes, as well as the vanity and emptiness of all transitory things. Although we may at times see cause to rejoice, yet very soon we may see equal cause to mourn, by being unexpectedly humbled by adversity; and as these are vicissitudes to which the wealth and honours of this world can form no barrier, we ought not to indulge ourselves in repining, in uneasiness, or despondency, because we do not possess them to profusion.

How little disposed should we be to find fault with and to murmur at our condition in life, however humble it might be, were we to reflect for a moment how much more miserable they *might* be! I have seen the time when I would have been unwilling to have exchanged conditions with any one within the circle of my acquaintance; and I have seen the time, and that very recently, when I would have gladly exchanged conditions with the poorest beggar in existence; nay, would have given thousands, had I possessed them, for the privilege of sharing with him the humble fare bestowed on him in charity. Mysterious, indeed, are the ways of Providence; the same wheel which raises us today, on the smooth, unruffled ocean of prosperity, may, before the morrow, roll us in the stormy sea of adversity. The scenes of life are continually shifting, and mankind are ever subject to ills, perplexities, and disappointments; and we are too apt to find fault, and conclude that we are possessed of a greater share of worldly afflictions than our fellow men, or more than our proportion in the scale of justice; but on reflection, I am persuaded mankind are not so unequally provided for in this world as many imagine. 'God is no respecter of persons'; he favours one man no more than another, and his blessings are equally showered upon all his offspring.

In all the changing scenes of life, we behold man ever in a pursuit of happiness. It is his aim and object; nay, the very desire of his heart to be happy; and in hopes of being so, ere his days of this transitory life shall end, he toils and labours, with an unceasing and unwearied hand. No obstacles that meet him in his path are too great to be overcome; but, alas! before it is attained, how often does life itself, with all its anxieties and cares, vanish forever. It is a great mistake to account those things necessary and essential to our happiness, that are superfluous. Let the man of a firm health not account himself happy only on the enjoyment of this good, but may the thought of suffering nothing among so many calamitous events to which he is subject, make him yet more content. Let him enjoy himself, not only from the good circumstances that are his lot, but from the evils too, which do not befall him. The restlessness and inquietude peculiar to a great portion of mankind, through all the several stages of their existence, are the sole immolators of time. They are continually looking forward to a time, when they shall be rich in the possessions of the world; and even in him, who has the abundance of riches, 'a full basket and full store,' the same anxieties, the same uneasy spirit and restless mind, embitter the sweets of his life, and waste his time and years.

Let us remember that we are but sojourners here on earth, that we are fast hastening to our long homes, and let the benign anticipation of happiness hereafter, make us triumph over adversity, and instruct us in the proper improvement of afflictions, that they may efficaciously work out for us a 'far more exceeding and eternal weight of glory.' Thus suitably impressed with the hopes of consummated happiness and fruition in the realms of peace, and with minds dilated above the annoying influence of worldly troubles and adverse events, we can tranquilly withstand all the buffeting billows of time, and welcome the auspicious hour which transports us from these tenements of clay, to an 'inheritance incorruptible, undefiled, and that fadeth not away.'

Success and disappointment, mirth and despondency, alternately accompany us through the journey of time. One day we set forth on our road with vigour and animation, favoured by an auspicious atmosphere and serene sky, full of anticipation and elated with hope; but ere night arrives, to lay our weary limbs to rest, some incident has blasted all our expectations. The morn which beamed forth its radiance and dispensed to us pleasure, is supplanted by a sable night, which brings to us a sad reverse, of many pains, anxieties and sorrows. Hence, it is not an abundance of riches that can secure to us that degree of happiness and tranquillity of mind that all are anxious to experience. A good share of prudence is far more preferable; as for the want of it, the young and inexperienced frequently and rashly launch their frail barks before they are able to stem the adverse current of life, and are wrecked among the shoals and quicksands of adversity."

CLOSING REMARKS

The foregoing concludes the interesting narrative and address of PALMER, to which a friend begs liberty to subjoin some few remarks. As has been remarked at the commencement of the narrative, the year 1836 will be long remembered as a peculiar one for the many unfortunate occurrences at sea that have attended it. Scarcely a week has passed, that some awful shipwreck, great loss of lives in consequence of vessels taking fire, &c. has not been announced to us. Since the commencement of the year, it is probable that not a less number than one thousand persons, (men, women and children,) have become the victims of one or the other of these devouring elements, on, or in the vicinity of the American coast, attended with all the horrors, and in some instances, by the most aggravating circumstances that the human mind can conceive of.

To maintain a commercial intercourse with foreign nations, it is necessary, notwithstanding the perils to which they subject themselves, that there should be found some willing to adventure their lives; and it is not surprising that there should be many of that useful class, who, accustomed from their youth to a seafaring life, are found willing to face the most incredible hardships, for that support which they would find it difficult to obtain for themselves and families on shore. But, that there should be so many of quite a different class, a class composed of some of our most active and promising young men, of educations that would fit them for the most respectable stations, and produce them ample support, found willing, merely to gratify a silly propensity to see the world, to subject themselves to the dangers and perils of the sea, is indeed, astonishing. The fate of the unfortunate Palmer should afford such a lesson, which ought never to be forgotten. He (Palmer) was, it appears, of respectable parentage, a stranger to hardships, blessed with a competency, and with an education sufficient to qualify him for the performance of the duties of the profession in which he was about to engage; but, alas, what a reverse of fortune was produced by a single act of imprudence. He has, indeed painted his deplorable situation, while confined to the wreck, in deep colours, but we do not believe the picture too highly coloured; for what situation on earth is there in which man can be placed, so awful as that of being driven by hunger and thirst to drink the blood and eat the dead body of a fellow being! Such appears to have been the fate of this unfortunate young man — and which, we would again say, should serve as a beacon to deter others from an attempt to gratify similar propensities, which may, for aught they know, prove equally fatal.

Whoever has perused the melancholy account of the late awful conflagration which occurred on board the steamboat *Royal Tar*, when forty-nine of her unfortunate passengers perished; and the still more recent account of the loss of the ship *Bristol*, bound from Liverpool to New York, (when no less number than sixty-seven of her crew and passengers found a watery grave,) must be satisfied of the imminent danger to which mariners, and others who adventure upon the deep waters, are exposed. "Shipwreck [as a late writer observes] is always, even in its mildest form, a calamity which fills the mind with horror. But what is instant death, compared to the situation of those who are doomed to contend with hunger and thirst? Behold the ship safely gliding along upon the smooth sea, every heart bounding with joy, at the prospect of their soon reaching the destined port, and once more embracing those friends from whom they have long been separated, when, all at once, a cloud arises, the sun withdraws its light, the tempest rolls on, accompanied with all the horrors of midnight darkness; she drives headlong upon the rocks. Ah! fatal moment. Where now shall they seek for refuge? No kind friend is present to lend the aid sufficient to protect these unhappy sufferers; but a small solitary boat, or fragment of the wreck, must float them, they know not where; destined often, to satisfy the cravings of hunger and to prolong a lingering life, by casting lots for a victim to be sacrificed to serve for food for the rest." That the picture of horror and despair here presented to view, is not one of the imagination alone, the affecting narrative of the unfortunate Palmer affords a melancholy proof. Similar instances too frequently occur; nor do the two, of which we have made mention, and of very recent occurrence, in some respects, fall but little short of it. The awful scene of distress that attended the loss of the steamboat *Royal Tar*, as related by the few who were miraculously preserved from the dreadful conflagration, must still be fresh in the minds of my readers: the unfortunate passengers, comprising men, women, and children, to escape from the devouring element, hanging on to ropes and various parts of the burning vessel, until compelled by the approaching flames to loose their holds and to drop into the ocean, to rise no more; and to enhance still more the scene of horror, several unfortunate mothers, to put an immediate period to the sufferings of their tender infants, threw them overboard, and leaped after them to perish with them! Nor were the scenes which attended the more recent loss of the ship *Bristol* (almost within view of the harbour of New York), less distressing. The description given of the lamentable catastrophe by the few that escaped from the wreck, were in terms almost too shocking to describe! Mothers calling to their children, and husbands for their wives, and on the next wave they were buried in the deep! So sudden and unexpected was the disaster, that several of the passengers (principally women and children), perished before they could leave their berths. The ill-fated ship, on striking the shore, instantly bilged, filled, and all below were drowned. Not a groan was heard to denote the catastrophe, so awfully sudden was it. The ship, in a few hours went to pieces, and the ensuing morning presented a scene truly melancholy to behold. Sixty of the lifeless bodies of those who perished, were driven on shore. Such are some of the dangers, and such frequently the awful consequences of adventuring upon and exposing our lives to the boisterous ocean. On this melancholy subject, we think that we cannot present our readers with anything more appropriate than a description of a wreck at sea, by an eminent writer. He remarks:

"We one day descried some shapeless object, drifting at a distance — it proved to be the mast of a ship that must have been completely wrecked; for there were the remains of handkerchiefs, by which some of the crew had fastened themselves to this spar to prevent their being washed off by the waves. There was no trace by which the name of the ship could be ascertained. The wreck had evidently drifted about many months; clusters of shell-fish had fastened about it, and long seaweeds floated at its sides. But, where, thought I, is the crew? Their struggle has long been over; they have gone down amidst the roar of the tempest; their bones lie whitening in the caverns of the deep. Silence, oblivion, like the waves, have closed over them, and no one can tell the story of their end! What sighs have been wafted after that ship! What prayers offered up at the deserted fireside of home! How often has the beloved wife and affectionate mother pored over the daily news, to catch some casual intelligence of this rover of the deep! How has expectation darkened into anxiety, anxiety into dread, and dread into despair! Alas! not one memento shall ever return for love to cherish. All that shall ever be known is that she sailed from her port, 'and was never heard of more.'

The sight of the wreck as usual, gave rise to many dismal anecdotes. This was particularly the case in the evening, when the weather, which had hitherto been fair, began to look wild and threatening, and gave indications of one of those sudden storms that will sometimes break in upon the serenity of a summer voyage. As we sat around the dull light of a lamp, in the cabin, that made the gloom more ghastly, every one had his tale of shipwreck and disaster. I was particularly struck with a short one related by the captain.

'As I was sailing,' said he, 'in a fine stout ship, across the banks of Newfoundland, one of the heavy fogs that prevail in those parts, rendered it impossible for me to see far ahead even in the day time; but at night the weather was so thick that we could not distinguish any object at twice the length of our ship. I kept lights at the mast head and a constant watch forward to look out for fishing-smacks, which are accustomed to lie at anchor on the banks. The wind was blowing a smacking breeze, and we were going at a great rate through the water. Suddenly the watch gave the alarm of 'a sail ahead!' but it was scarcely uttered till we were upon her. She was a small schooner at anchor with her broad side towards us. The crew were all asleep, and had neglected to hoist a light. We struck her just amid-ship. The force, the size, and weight of our vessel, bore her down below the waves; we passed over her, and were hurried on our course.

As the crashing wreck was sinking beneath us, I had a glimpse of two or three half-naked wretches, rushing from the cabin; they had just started from their cabins to be swallowed shrieking by the waves. I heard their drowning cry mingled with the wind. The blast that bore it to our ears swept us out of all further hearing. I shall never forget that cry! It was some time before we could put the ship about, she was under such headway. We returned as nearly as we could guess to the place where the ship was anchored. We cruised about for several hours in the dense fog. We fired several guns, and listened if we might hear the halloo of any survivors; but all was silent. We never heard nor saw anything of them more!'"

NOTES

1. John Palmer, *Awful Shipwreck: An Affecting Narrative of the Unparalleled Sufferings of the Crew of the Ship,* Francis Spaight, *which foundered on her passage from St. John's, N.B. to Limerick in November last. The survivors after remaining aboard the wreck 19 days, during which they were driven to the most awful extremities, were relieved by the Brig.* Angeronia, *Capt. Gillard, on her Passage from Newfoundland to Teignmouth* (Boston, 1837), CIHM 50787.

2. Great Britain, House of Commons, Report From Select Committee On Shipwrecks Of Timber Ships, Minutes of Evidence, 18 June 1839, 2.

3. Another famous story of cannibalism in Newfoundland waters is described in Moses Harvey, "The Castaways of Gull Island," *Maritime Monthly* 1, 5 (May 1873): 435-47 [1867], and Ernest M. Howse, "The Horror on Gull Island: They Cast Lots and Then It Was Man Eat Man," *MacLean's* 82, 10 (October 1969): 48f, 48h.

4. Report From Select Committee On Shipwrecks Of Timber Ships, iv.

5. A revealing perspective on this topic is John R. Audette, "Historical Perspectives on Near-Death Episodes and Experiences," in Craig R. Lundahl, ed., *A Collection of Near-Death Research Readings* (Chicago: Nelson-Hall, 1982), 21-43.

15

DESTRUCTION OF THE OCEAN STEAMER *ARCTIC*,
BY COLLISION WITH THE *VESTA* (1854)[1]

HENRY HOWE

The shipwreck of emigrant and passenger ships have played a prominent role in the history of Newfoundland waters. The most famous was
the *Titanic*, of course, but there were numerous others that, in their
day, garnered similar international attention. In the era prior to the
nineteenth century, most immigrants or travellers crossed the North
Atlantic in a largely unregulated fashion aboard military and trading
vessels. Compared with what was to come, their numbers were modest.
This changed with the conclusion of the Napoleonic wars, when the era
of "the great migration" from Great Britain to British North America
began and some ships were built specifically and primarily for passenger travel. As some of our narratives have described, many, mostly less
affluent immigrants, travelled in steerage aboard timber ships and other
merchant vessels. This growing trend, coupled with the egregious and
ongoing shortcomings of a largely unregulated or poorly managed carrying trade, gave rise to a series of Passenger Acts between 1803 and
1872 that eventually helped to protect transoceanic human cargo.[2]
Such legislation and the steady transition from wood and sail to iron
and steam after mid-century played a major role in making transatlantic travel much safer and more comfortable than ever before; yet
these changes did not obviate marine disaster.

   A case in point was the collision of the American luxury vessel
Arctic, of the Collins Line, with the French *Vesta*, sailing from St.

Pierre, off Cape Race on 27 September 1854, which claimed 322 lives. Victims included the wife, one-year-old son, and other family members of E.K. Collins, the owner of the New York and Liverpool United Mail Steamship Company, better known as the Collins line. Although similar vessels of the Collins line in previous years had had various problems, the sinking of this vessel was still quite unexpected. The *Arctic*, with space for roughly 200 first-class passengers and improved safety features, belonged to a new generation of steam-propelled vessels, soon joined by vessels with screw propellers and iron hulls, which began to appear more regularly in the 1850s, constituting the first modern ships.[3] It was transitional type, a four-year-old, wooden-hulled, side-wheel paddle steamer, meant for comfort, dependability, and speed.

What was entirely unexpected and scandalous was the apparent treatment of the passengers; the circumstances surrounding the *Arctic*'s sinking raised a widespread public outcry, with not a single female passenger surviving. En route from England to New York, it encountered fog on the Grand Banks and collided with the propeller steamer *Vesta* under full sail. First impressions were that the *Arctic* was uninjured while the bows of the *Vesta* had been cut off. The *Arctic* responded initially by sending a lifeboat to the other ship; but then the captain discovered that the *Arctic*'s hull had been punctured and that it was rapidly taking water. Ironically, the *Vesta* had watertight bulkheads and survived the mishap; the *Arctic* did not. More significantly, chaos appeared to break out aboard the *Arctic*. When the water rose in the furnace rooms, the engine room crew abandoned its positions with the result that the ship was without power. From that moment the *Arctic* was doomed. Captain Luce desperately attempted to place what passengers he could aboard the five remaining lifeboats, enough for less than half the number on board. Four lifeboats were filled with passengers, including many women and children, but according to some observers, the fifth boat was taken by force by the chief engineer, several of his assistants, and other select survivors. The only senior officer left on board was Luce himself. In desperation and with the help of the third mate, he had a raft constructed for all the remaining children and women passengers. Finally the end came. The captain did not board the raft and remained with the ship as it went down, but he, while losing his own child, managed to survive.

Numerous and sometimes differing first-hand accounts of these events were published in newspapers and elsewhere. The sinking itself was tragic enough in the public eye, but the apparent "cowardice and greed" of too many of the crew resulted in an official report to the Secretary of the Treasury in the United States. This report cited neglect of the pilot rules as the main cause of the accident, and recommended that watertight bulkheads and additional lifeboats be required aboard steamships, as well as better crews and discipline.[4] This collision also occasioned the widespread introduction of steam whistles and the creation of separate east-bound and west-bound steamer lanes in the Atlantic. Lastly, it generated more debate on the relative merits of iron and wood hulls.[5]

This disaster attracted wide attention for many reasons. The narrative, following on the heels of the disaster, includes the initial public reaction in New York City, a lengthy and detailed statement by Captain Luce given at Quebec City on October 14, 1854, and another by passenger James Smith, followed by a memorial sermon delivered by Reverend Henry Ward Beecher of Brooklyn. One is again reminded that every shipwreck, large and small, had both its public and its personal dimensions.

⚓

THE OCEAN STEAMER *ARCTIC* formed one of the Collins line of American steamers, plying between New York and Liverpool, so called in contradistinction to those of the Cunard or British line, the latter having been built in England, and owned and controlled by an English company. The *Arctic* was built in New York, in 1850, at an expense of nearly one million dollars, and was one of the largest and noblest steamships in the world. Of beautiful proportions and great speed, she was the pride of her countrymen, as a specimen of their attainments in marine architecture.

On her homeward-bound passage, at noon, on the 27th of September, 1854, she came in collision with the French propeller *Vesta*, on the banks of Newfoundland; and a few hours thereafter the last vestige of her noble form, together with more than three hundred of her passengers and crew, disappeared beneath the waters. The fate of the smaller vessel was more fortunate. Provided by her more cautious builders with bulkheads, or water-tight partitions, between her different sections, she succeeded in gaining port in safety.

When tidings of this awful event reached our country, a profound sensation was created. The people of the city of New York, the most mercurial and impulsive of any in America, the earliest to be aroused by, and the earliest to forget, any startling event, were most intensely excited. The *Arctic* was a New York vessel; the pride of the great commercial metropolis; and numbers of her prominent citizens were known to have been on board of her. To give an idea of the effect there, we make brief extracts from a city paper of the day.

"The sorrow and excitement in New York, on the reception of the sad tidings, were beyond expression. Thousands of our citizens are bereaved of relatives, and tens of thousands have lost friends and acquaintances. Early in the morning the newspaper offices, and the office of the steamship company, were thronged with anxious inquirers for further news, and all day long the crowds were kept up by fresh arrivals. The flags on the City Hall, on the hotels, and the shipping in the harbor, were at half-mast through the day. Business was neglected, and the whole town bore on its outward features evidences of the sorrow within. There were hundreds of persons crowding Adams & Co.'s office, waiting their several turns to see Mr. Burns, one of the saved; and each concerned to ascertain whether there was not some possible chance that a beloved brother, or sister, or friend, in the Arctic, had escaped. Old men, as well as young, were sobbing like children, and telling their grief to the passers-by, with that absence of all reserve which so overpowering a misfortune is apt to produce.

In the office of E.K. Collins & Co., the proprietors of the line, a similar scene was being enacted. A large crowd had collected to hear the report of Mr. Brennan, an attaché of the engineering department, whose careworn looks, and marks of excessive fatigue, showed that he was one of the survivors of the sad catastrophe. A deep feeling of anxiety seemed to pervade the minds of all present, and eager questions were propounded to Mr. Brennan in rapid succession. Some described the personal appearance of absent ones, bound to them by affinities and deep friendship, some by ties of consanguinity, and others bound by nearer and dearer ties, and inquired if he had seen them enter any of the boats which left the vessel previous to the last one, on which he was saved. His words were anxiously waited for, and in some instances they were sufficient to buoy up an expiring hope, but in others to lead them to despair of ever meeting the loved ones again on earth.

At brief intervals, the announcement of the arrival of an installment of the telegraphic dispatch from Halifax would draw all to another part of the room, and, with feelings of mingled hope and fear, they listened in breathless silence to the words of the dispatch read by a gentleman connected with the office. When the reading of the installments was finished, many were the impatient exclamations because the names of the saved, in the boats which had arrived, were not forwarded first, instead of Mr. Baalham's account of the catastrophe; and when, at last, the concluding portion of the dispatch contained the list of names of those who were safe in Halifax, near a hundred hearts beat heavily and rapidly as they stood in expectation of the announcement of a name which was to make them rejoice, or drive them into a despairing gloom. The reading of the list was commenced. The announcement of several names was received with exclamations of deep joy, accompanied with words of thankfulness to heaven for the mercy extended to them. As the end of the list was approached, deeper sighs were drawn, and when it was announced that the names had been all read, '*Oh God! Oh God!*' were the words that many uttered in the deep anguish that wrung their hearts. The list was again read, but it only confirmed their worst fears; and after the announcement that no more dispatches would be received, those present left the apartment which had been the scene of such exciting interest, and its doors were closed for the balance of the day."

After the announcement by telegraph that Captain Luce, and several of his companions in suffering, had arrived safely in Quebec, the entire city was on the *qui vive*, waiting for the least word in confirmation of the intelligence, and fearing the next announcement would be that the statement was premature, and was not justified by the facts. But as another and another dispatch arrived, each one stating explicitly the safety of the noble captain, who chose to stand by the wreck and make himself his last thought in his efforts to save, a feeling of joy amounting to enthusiasm seemed to animate all; and when it was announced that Captain Luce's statement was being forwarded by telegraph, the most intense anxiety was manifested to know his words. The following is Captain Luce's statement to E.K. Collins, Esq., and dated at Quebec, Saturday, October 14, 1854:

"It becomes my painful duty to inform you of the total loss of the *Arctic*, under my command, with many lives; and I fear among them must be included your own wife, daughter and son, of whom I took a last leave the moment the ship was going down, without ever expecting to see the light of another day, to give you an account of the heart-rending scene.

The *Arctic* sailed from Liverpool on Wednesday, September 20th, at eleven a.m., with two hundred and thirty-three passengers, and a crew of about one hundred and fifty. Nothing of special note occurred during the passage until Wednesday, September 27th, when, at noon, we were on the Banks, in latitude 46°45' north, and longitude 52° west, steering west by compass.

The weather had been foggy during the day; generally a distance of half to three quarters of a mile could be seen, but at intervals of a few minutes a very dense fog, followed by being sufficiently clear to see one or two miles. At noon I left the deck for the purpose of working out the position of the ship. In about fifteen minutes I heard the cry of 'Hard starboard' from the officer on the deck. I rushed on deck, and had just got out, when I felt a crash forward, and at the same moment saw a steamer under the starboard-bow; at the next moment she struck against our guards, and passed astern of us. The bows of the strange vessel seemed to be literally cut or crushed off for full ten feet, and seeing that she must, probably, sink in a few minutes, and taking a hasty glance at our own ship, and believing that we were comparatively uninjured, my first impulse was to endeavor to save the lives of those on board the sinking vessel. The boats were cleared, and the first officer and six men left with one boat, when it was found our own ship was leaking fearfully.

The engineers were set to work, being instructed to put on the steam pumps, and the four deck pumps were worked by the passengers and crew, and the ship headed for the land, which I judged to be about fifty miles distant. I was compelled to leave my boat with the first officer and crew to take care of themselves.

Several ineffectual attempts were made to stop the leak by getting sails over the bows; but finding the leak gaining on us very fast, notwithstanding all our very painful efforts to keep her free, I resolved to get the boats ready, and as many ladies and children placed in them as possible; but no sooner had the attempt been made than the firemen and others rushed into them in spite of opposition.

Seeing this state of things, I ordered the boats astern to be kept in readiness until order could be restored, when, to my dismay, I saw them cut the ropes in the bow, and soon disappear astern in the fog. Another boat was broken down by persons rushing at the davits, and many were precipitated into the sea and drowned. This occurred while I had been engaged in getting the starboard guard-boat ready, and placed the second officer in charge, when the same fearful scene as with the first boat was being enacted, men leaping from the top of the rail, twenty feet, crushing and maiming those who were in the boat. I then gave orders to the second officer to let go, and row after the ship, keeping under or near the stern, to be ready to take on board women and children, as soon as the fires were put out, and the engines stopped. My attention was then drawn to the other quarter-boat, which I found broken down, but hanging by one tackle. A rush was made for her also, and some fifteen got in, and cut the tackle, and were soon out of sight. I found that not a seaman was left on board, nor a carpenter, and we were without any tools to assist us in building a raft, as our only hope. The only officer left was Mr. Dorian, the third mate, who aided me, with the assistance of many of the passengers, who deserve great praise for their coolness and energy in doing all in their power up to the very latest moment before the ship sunk.

The chief engineer, with a part of his assistance, had taken our smallest deck-boat, and before the ship went down, pulled away with about fifteen persons.

We had succeeded in getting the fore and main-yard and two topgallant-yards overboard, and such other small-spars and material as we could collect, when I was fully convinced that the ship must go down in a very short time, and not a moment was to be lost in getting the spars lashed together to form a raft, to do which it became necessary to get the life-boat (our only remaining boat), into the water.

This being accomplished, I saw Mr. Dorian, the third officer, in charge of the boat, taking care to keep the oars on board to prevent them from leaving the ship, hoping still to get most of the women and children in this boat. At last they had made considerable progress in collecting the spars, when an alarm was given that the ship was sinking, and the boat was shoved off without oars or anything to help themselves with; and when the ship sunk, the boat had got clear, probably an eighth of a mile, to leeward.

In an instant, about four and three quarters p.m., the ship went down, carrying every soul on board with her.

I soon found myself on the surface, after a brief struggle, with my own helpless child in my arms, when again I felt impelled downward to a great depth, and before I reached the surface a second time, had nearly perished, and lost the hold of my child. As I again struggled to the surface of the water, a most awful and heart-rending scene presented itself to my view: over two hundred men, women and children struggling together amidst pieces of wreck of every kind, calling on each other for help, and imploring God to assist them. Such an appalling scene may God preserve me from ever witnessing again.

I was in the act of trying to save my child, when a portion of the paddle-box came rushing up edgewise, just grazing my head, falling with its whole weight upon the head of my darling child. Another moment, I beheld him lifeless in the water. I succeeded in getting on to the top of the paddle-box, in company with eleven others; one, however, soon left for another piece, finding that it could not support so many. Others remained until they were one by one relieved by death. We stood in water at a temperature of 45°, up to our knees, and frequently the sea broke directly over us. We soon separated from our friends on other parts of the wreck, and passed the night, each one of us expecting every hour would be our last.

At last the wished for morning came, surrounding us with a dense fog, not a living soul to be seen but our own party, seven men being left. In the course of the morning, we saw some water-casks and other things belonging to our ship, but nothing that we could get to afford us any relief. Our raft was rapidly settling, as it absorbed water.

About noon, Mr. S.M. Woodruff, of New York, was relieved by death. All the others now began to suffer very severely for want of water, except Mr. George F. Allen and myself. In that respect we were very much favored, although we had not a drop on the raft. The day continued foggy, except just at noon, as near as we could judge, we had a clear horizon for about half an hour, and nothing could be seen but water and sky. Night came on, thick and dreary, with our minds made up that neither of us would again see the light of another day. Very soon three more of our suffering party fell down from exhaustion, and were washed off by the sea, leaving Mr. Allen, a boy, and myself. Feeling myself getting exhausted, I now sat down, for the first time, about eight o'clock in the evening, on a trunk, which providentially had been found on the wreck. In this way I slept a little throughout the night, and became somewhat refreshed.

Young Keyn, the German boy who was with us, suffered intensely. He happened to have some biscuit with him which had become soaked with the salt-water, and eating these only increased his thirst, and to make matters still worse, he drank some of the sea-water. His sufferings were beyond all description. Twice he jumped overboard, saying he would rather die than suffer as he was doing; and each time we pulled him back on the wreck. At one time he cut open a vein in his arm and sucked his blood.

About an hour before daylight, now Friday, the 29th, we saw a vessel's light near to us. We all three of us exerted ourselves to the utmost of our strength in hailing her, until we became quite exhausted. In about a quarter of an hour the light disappeared to the east of us. Soon after daylight a bark hove in sight to the north-west, the fog having lightened a little, steering apparently for us; but in a short time she seemed to have changed her course, and again we were doomed to disappointment; yet I felt hope that some of our fellow-sufferers might have been seen and rescued by them.

Shortly after we had given up all hopes of being rescued by the bark, a ship was discovered to the east of us, steering directly for us. We now watched her with the most intense anxiety as she approached. The wind changing, caused her to alter her course several points. About noon they fortunately discovered a man on a raft near them, and succeeded in saving him by the second mate jumping over the side, and making a rope fast around him, when he was got on board safely. This man who was saved proved to be a Frenchman, who was a passenger on board the steamer which we came in collision with.

He informed the captain that others were near, on pieces of the wreck; and, going aloft, he saw us and three others. We were the first to whom the boat was sent, and safely taken on board about three p.m. The next was Mr. James Smith, of Mississippi, second-class passenger. The others saved were five of our firemen. The ship proved to be the *Cambria*, of this port, from Glasgow, bound to Montreal, Captain John Russell.

From the Frenchman who was picked up, we learned that the steamer with which we came in collision was the screw steamer *Vesta*, from St. Pierre, bound for and belonging to Granville, France, and having on board one hundred and forty passengers and twenty seamen. As near as we could learn, the *Vesta* was steering east-south-east, and was crossing our course two points, with all sails set, wind west by south. Her anchor stock, about seven by four inches square, was driven through the bows of the *Arctic*, about eighteen inches above the water line, and an immense hole had been made, at the same instant, by the fluke of the anchor, about two feet below the water line, raking fore and aft the plank, and finally breaking the chains, leaving the stock remaining in and through the side of the *Arctic*; or it is not unlikely, as so much of her bows had been crushed in, that some of the heavy longitudinal pieces of iron running through the ship may have been driven through our side, causing the loss of our ship, and, I fear, hundreds of most valuable lives."

To this account of Captain Luce, we annex that of a passenger, Mr. James Smith, a native of Scotland, now a citizen of Mississippi. It contains some facts not given in any other narrative, and is enhanced by the pious emotions disclosed by the narrator:

"During the day, up to the time of the accident, the weather had been quite foggy, and I was somewhat astonished and alarmed several times when on deck, seeing the weather so thick, that I fancied not more than three or four of the ship's lengths ahead could be seen, and she going at full speed, without any alarm bell, steam whistle, or other signal being sounded at intervals, in some such manner as I had been accustomed to in a fog on other vessels. At about fifteen minutes after the meridian, eight bells had been struck, and while sitting in my state-room in the forward cabin, the earnest cry of a voice on deck (who I at the moment took to be the man on the lookout) to 'stop her, stop her; a steamer ahead,' was heard with alarm by myself and all others in the cabin; at the same time the man giving the alarm could be heard running off toward the engine-room.

I stepped out of my stateroom, and while endeavoring, with Mr. Cook, my room-mate, to calm the excitement among the ladies in the cabin, and before the man giving the alarm on deck had reached the engine-room, we were made aware of the concussion by a somewhat slight jar to our ship, accompanied by a crashing against the starboard bow. It was a moment of awe and suspense, but I think we all seemed to satisfy ourselves that the shock was slight, and that, as we were on so large and strong a vessel, no serious damage had happened or could well happen to such a ship, in an occurrence of such a nature. With such a reliance on my own mind, at any rate, I was very quickly on deck, and in detached accounts from other passengers, learned that a screw steamer, with all sail set, had struck us on the starboard bow, and glancing aft our starboard wheel and wheel-house, struck her again, and she passed off astern of us out of sight immediately in the thick fog. I saw on the first glance at our bulwarks that all was right with us, but instantly began to get alarmed from our careening over on the side we had been struck, as well as from the call for the passengers to keep on the port-side. I understood, also, at this time, that one of our boats had been cleared away and lowered with our first officer and six of the men, to render assistance to the other vessel, and that our ship was making round in search of her also.

I saw Captain Luce on the paddle-box, giving orders in one way and another, and most of the officers and men running here and there on the deck, getting into an evident state of alarm, without seeming to know what was to be done or applying their energies to any one thing in particular, except in getting the anchors and other heavy articles over to the port-side of the ship. I looked over the starboard bow and saw several large breaks in the side of our ship, from eight to twelve or fourteen feet abaft of the cut-water, and I was convinced that in the ten or fifteen minutes' time our wheels were further submerged in the water than usual. Our ship seemed to right herself somewhat after getting the deck weight upon the larboard, but it was too evident that Captain Luce himself, as well as all hands, was becoming aware of our danger; and, from the tremendous volume of water being thrown out from our steam pumps, I was convinced we were making water at a fearful rate.

Then came in full view before us the other vessel, presenting a most heart-rending spectacle; the whole of her bow, for at least ten feet abaft her cut-water, was literally crushed away, leaving, to all appearance, an open entrance to the sea; and how she had remained above water for so many minutes seemed a mystery. Her decks were covered with people, and all her sails on all three of her masts were set. We merely passed her again, and she was in less than a minute hid in the fog, but scarcely out of sight when we heard arise from her deck a loud and general wail of mourning and lamentation. It was just previous to, or at the same time that we thus came in sight of and passed her, that our wheels went over two or three separate individuals in the water, as well as a boat and crew, who had evidently left the other ship for safety on ours. One man, only, we picked up, an old weather-beaten French fisherman, who, having leaped from the small boat before she went under our wheel, caught a rope hanging from our ship and was finally pulled on board of us, and from whom we learned something of the other vessel. Captain Luce had, by the time of our coming in sight of the *Vesta*, become so convinced of our own critical situation, that our only or best chance was to keep under headway as fast as possible toward the land.

A deep-seated, thoughtful look of despair began to settle upon every countenance; no excitement, but ladies and children began to collect on deck with anxious and inquiring looks; receiving no hope or consolation, wife and husband, father and daughter, brother and sister, would weep in each other's embrace, or kneel together imploring Almighty God for help. Men would go about the decks in a sort of bewilderment as to what was best to be done; now laying hold of the hand pumps with redoubled energy, or with sickening effort applying their power to the hauling up of freight out of the forward hold, already floating in water before the lower hatches were opened. System of management or concentration of effort was never commenced or applied to any one object. Two separate ineffectual attempts to stop the leaking by dropping a sail down over the bow, were made, and the engines were kept working the ship ahead toward the land; but in the course of an hour, I should think, from the time of the collision, the lower furnaces were drowned out and the steam pumps stopped. Then it seemed to become only a question of how many hours or minutes we would be above water. The first officer with his boat's crew we had left behind from the first. The second officer, with a lot of sailors, had lowered another boat and left the ship, and a general scrambling seemed to be going on as to who should have places in the only two remaining boats that I saw on deck. The stern tackling of another had given way from the weight of persons in it while it was swinging over the side, and I think several must have been lost with that. I saw one lady hanging to the bow tackle of it after the stern had broken loose. One of those still remaining was a large one, on the quarter-deck, occupied by ladies and children and some few gentlemen. The other was on the upper deck forward, and in the possession of a lot of firemen. Things were in this condition at about two hours after the accident. Captain Luce was superintending the lowering of spars and yards, aided mostly by passengers, for the purpose of making a raft, and complaining that all his officers and men had left him. Most of the women and children were collected round the boat on the quarter-deck seemingly resigned to their fate.

Some few gentlemen exerted all their powers to prevail on others to work on the pumps, but all to no purpose; the ship kept on gaining in quantity as steadily as time progressed. The engines had stopped working, and I, seeing that the chief engineer, with some of his assistants and firemen, had got the forward boat in the water over by the bow, under the pretense I saw of working at the canvas, which was hanging over the bow, so as to sink it down over the leaking places, but seeing, as I thought, symptoms of their real intention to get off from the ship without too many in the boat, I dropped myself down near by them on a small raft of three planks about a foot wide each, and ten or twelve feet long and an inch in thickness, lashed together with some rope and four hand-spikes, and which I had just previously helped to lower into the water for the purpose of working from about the bow of the ship. Finding it bore me up, I shoved off, intending to get along side of the engineer's boat, but as I shoved off several firemen and one or two passengers dropped down into the boat, the engineer protesting against their doing so, and at the same time pushed off, and pulled well away from the ship, with about twelve or fifteen persons in his boat, declaring to those on board, at the same time, that he was not going off, but would stay by the ship to the last. At the same time, he, or those in the boat with him, continued to pull away in what I considered was the direction of the land, and were in a few minutes lost in the fog.

I now saw there was no probable chance for me but to remain where I was, on my frail little raft, until I could see some better chance after or before the ship went down. She had now settled down to the wheel-houses. The upper furnaces had for some time been drowned out. People on board were doing nothing but firing signal guns of distress, trying to get spars overboard and tearing doors off the hinges; nothing else seemed to present itself, as the means of saving the lives of some three hundred souls still on board.

I have crossed the Atlantic nine times now, and nearly every previous time have had in charge one or more of my family or near relatives, but now, I thanked my God that I had not even an

acquaintance with me in this my adversity. I tightened up my little
raft as well as I could, so as to make it withstand the buffetings and
strainings of the heavy rolling sea, and, with the aid of a long narrow
piece of plank, which I tore up with the others, using it as a paddle,
I kept hovering within two or three hundred yards of the sinking
ship, watching operations there, and keeping myself from being
drifted out of sight, so as to have what company there might be left
on the rafts like my own after our doomed vessel had sunk beneath
the surface. In this position, I saw three different small rafts like my
own leave the ship, one of them with three and another with two
of the firemen standing erect on them, the third with the old
Frenchman we had already picked up, and one of the mess boys of
the ship sitting on it. Those three rafts all drifted close by me, so near
that I was hailed by one and another of them with the request for us
all to keep near together, to which I assented, but told them that we
had all better try and keep by the ship till she went down. At this
time, I noticed that the large boat, which had been on the quarter-
deck, was in the water, and was being freighted pretty fully, to all
appearance, with several females and a good number of males, and
that the raft of spars was at the same time being lashed together, and
several getting on it. I noticed also a couple of large empty water-
casks, lashed together, with five men on them, apparently passengers,
leave the ship and drifting toward me, while within about fifty yards
they capsized with the force of a heavy swell, giving their living
freight an almost immediate watery grave. Three of them, I noticed,
regained the top side of the casks only to be immediately turned over
again, and the casks separating, I saw no more of them. My heart
sickened at so much of immediate death, and still I almost longed to
have been one of them, for at the same instant, and, as near as I can
judge, at about four and a half o'clock, the ship began to disappear;
stern foremost she entered under the surface, her bow rising a little as
she slowly went under; and I distinctly heard the gurgling and rushing sound of the water filling her cabins, from stem to stern, as she
went under; taking, I should think, from thirty seconds to a minute
in disappearing, with a large number of people still upon her deck.

Thus went down the noble steamer *Arctic,* leaving nothing
behind but a mixture of fragments of the wreck and struggling
human beings. I saw one large half-round fragment burst above the
surface, and several of the struggling fellow-mortals get on it; this,

and the raft of spars, with several on it, and the boat full of people, were all that I could distinctly make out as being left in the neighborhood of where the ship went down to windward; and the three small rails to leeward, along with my own, were left to pass the night now beginning to close in upon, and hide away from my sight (I wish I could say from my memory) this dreadful day; but such a night of extreme melancholy, despair, and utter loneliness, I hope I shall never again experience. I had, it is true, become familiarized with death, and felt as if it would be great relief to go immediately like the rest; and, for this end, I, with somewhat of satisfaction, thought of the vial of laudanum in my pocket; previously intended for a better use; but, oh! how unprepared was I to see my God, and for my family's sake how necessary I felt it was for me still to live a while longer, else would I have emptied that vial or rolled over the side of my plank most willingly.

The night was cold and chilly, the dense fog was saturating my already wet clothing. I was standing to the ankles in the water, with the waves every now and then washing me above the knees, no hope in my mind of being drifted to the land, and in a part of the ocean where it is expected a thick fog continually hangs over the surface, precluding the hope of any chance vessel, in passing near us, being aware of our situation. All circumstances seemed to say, it is but a question of how long the physical frame can endure this perishing state, or how long before a more boisterous sea turns over or separates the slightly fastened planks. Thus reflecting, I offered up to Him who ruleth the winds and waves, to Him unto whom we all flee in our deepest distress, a sincere petition for mercy, that, as I had now been called to account, I might notwithstanding my unworthiness, find an acceptance through the merits of Him who suffered for us, and who stands ready to aid, and who says, Knock and it shall be opened unto you, unto whom can we look, oh our God! but unto thee? Our whole life is, after all, at this hour, a mere question of a few short days, and what are all the mere vanities transpiring during an ambitious but short existence, compared to an assurance which maketh our latter end a fearless one. Relieved and consoled by this my last petition, I was somewhat calmly resigning myself to await my time, as long as my strength and power of endurance could hold out, when I discovered a large square basket, lined with tin, floating lightly by me. One of the steward's dish baskets it proved to be, and, paddling up to it, I got it aboard, and with the help of a small piece of rope I had round my shoulders, I lashed it pretty firmly on the top of the plank; thus, not only tending to make my raft more secure, but affording me a comparatively dry place to sit on the edge of it, and, with my feet inside, forming a shelter for my legs up as high as my knees. After getting this all arranged, and while sitting watching the water every now and then dashing over the top of it, and becoming convinced that it would soon be partly filled and add to my discomfort, as well as to the weight of the raft, I was again surprised to hear a distinct rattle against the side of the raft, which, proving to be a small air-tight tin can, a part of a set of such used as life-preservers, I seized hold of it, as an additional token of the presence of a protecting Providence. I cut out one end of it with my pocket-knife, and found it to answer the purpose of what, above anything else, I then needed, a bailing-pot, and by which I was enabled to keep my little shelter clear of water; and so acceptable, as a protection from the cold, damp blast, did I find this little willow house, that I soon found myself cramped down into the inside, thus keeping not only my feet and legs, but the lower part of my body somewhat warm. In this sort of situation, I wore away the tedious night, and the breaking dawn revealed to my sight nothing but thick mist, the unceasing rolling waves, and my own little bark; not a single vestige of all else that the night closed upon was now to be seen.

About midday the sun cleared away the mist, and the heat of his rays was truly grateful; but, oh! how desolate in its very cheerfulness, seemed the prospect he thus unfolded. Over the whole broad expanse of waters, not a sail could be seen, not a thing save the figures of the two firemen, about half a mile distant, still standing erect, and show-ing themselves at intervals, as every heavy swell raised them on its crest. I had not yet felt either hunger or thirst, for which I was truly thankful, for I had but a handful of dry broken crackers in my hat, which I felt determined to save to the last, and of course no water. I dreaded the craving of either. The day wore on still clear until about an hour before nightfall, when the two firemen (within hailing dis-tance of whom I had worked my way again) discovered a ship under full sail, broadside toward us; but it was with faint hopes of success that I hoisted my handkerchief, tied to the end of the strip of wood I was using as a paddle, the firemen doing the same with a shorter piece of wood in their possession. The ship, at one time, we noticed, laid to or altered her course for a moment, giving us a hope that she had discovered something, but the night closed in again, and with it all our hopes of a rescue.

I passed through this night in a dozing, dreary, shivering, half sensible sort of state, with all sorts of fancies before my drowsy and somewhat disordered mind, and all sorts of pictures in my wakeful moments, both of a pleasing and of a revolting character, floating before me on the dark surface of the water. Now and then, during the night, I fancied myself hailed by various surrounding parties, convinced, as I was, at the same time, that none others were within hailing distance but the two firemen. My disordered fancy, however, kept me for more than half the night, in an agreeable state of excitement, under the firm belief that companies of boats' crews were on the search for us, and most lustily did I answer every fancied or real signal. The morning dawned again, and with it a horrid scene of despair at the gloomy prospect of the same dense, foggy atmosphere, now and then fully developing to view the same two erect figures dancing about on the rolling surf; and, in my selfish liberality, I bargained with myself that I would endure still during this day, seeing that my two companions, who were obliged to be on their feet, supporting each other in a very precarious looking back-to-back attitude, were able to still exist. I felt a little hungry this morning, and ate half a biscuit. While warming myself by about two hours' paddling up toward them, during which the fog partially cleared away, and while close to them, we all became excited at the sight of a sail far to the south, as I thought, but broadside toward us. Like the one on the previous day, I had little hope of her coming much nearer; but, being determined to leave no effort untried which might possibly attract their notice, I stripped myself, and taking off my shirt, tied it by the sleeves to the end of my paddle, and, with my handkerchief on a small strip of wood tied on above it, I thought I had a tolerably conspicuous signal, and waved it to and fro for more than an hour, until the ship was nearly out of sight; and just as I had lowered it, in utter hopelessness, we all descried, at the same instant, in the opposite direction, another sail, end on to us, just entering, as it were, into our grand amphitheater, through a cloud of mist that seemed to rise and clear away above the vessel, forming a grand triumphal archway around, our Eureka, like a tower of promise, in the center. Feeling sure, at first sight, that this one was starting toward us, I did not long remain undeceived, for she began to increase in size as time wore slowly on; and, although she was falling to leeward considerably, as she advanced, still I felt sure, if she kept on the same tack, she would undoubtedly see our signals before passing beyond. My large signal, too, continued to drift me nearer to her track, and took me almost out of sight of my two companions.

When within about two or three miles of us, and about an hour and a half after she first hove in sight, we were relieved by her backing her sails, altering her course, and lying-to for awhile; then, hoisting a signal on her spanker-gaff, she put about and bore away, on and on, far in the distance, on the opposite tack, until my heart began to fail again, doubting whether she was beating to windward for us, or had gone on her way, rejoicing in the discovery and rescue of only a portion of the unfortunate wretches within range of her. But, again, how light and buoyant was the joy, as she at last put about, and stood directly for us; and on and on she advanced, like a saving angel, until we could see her noble looking hull distinctly rise and fall; within little over a mile distant from us, when she backed her sails again, and waited for some time in the prosecution of her mission of mercy, no doubt, relieving some of our scattering companions from a like precarious state. Soon, she sailed away again; and, at last, lying-to close by the two firemen, I saw her boat lowered with five men in it, who, picking up the two firemen in their course, came dashing along direct for my raft, and soon bouncing along side, I allowed myself to tumble aboard of them, unable, physically, to adopt anything of a grateful action, and morally, overpowered with gratitude to God and to those his instruments.

I remained speechless until I got on board the ship. Before getting on board, however, the boat went away off some distance to windward, and picked up the three other firemen, whom I had seen leave the *Arctic*, but who had been ever since out of view. We all got huddled upon the deck, somehow, although rather awkwardly, and making my way down to her neat little cabin, as well as my stiff feet and legs would allow, I had the pleasure of paying my respects to Captain John Russell, and found myself on board the ship *Cambria*, of Greenock, bound from Glasgow to Quebec. Captain Russell, the Reverend Mr. Walker, of the Free Church of Scotland, and his very kind and attentive lady, Mr. Sutherland, of Caithnesshire in Scotland, Mr. John McNaught, and several of the passengers of the steerage, paid us every attention that I could have desired; Captain Russell giving me up the berth which he had been using himself, and putting everything on board in requisition that might tend in the least to relieve and make us comfortable. I was surprised to learn that the old Frenchman, whom we had picked up from the *Vesta*, was our good genius on this occasion; being directly in the track of the approaching *Cambria*, he was picked up by the second mate of the *Cambria*, Mr. Ross, jumping overboard with a line, and, seizing hold of the old man, they were both pulled on board; and the rescued Frenchman, in the best English he could muster made Captain Russell aware that others were near, who then went to the mast-head, and, with his glass, made out the other four pieces of wreck, which we were all on, and, making his long tack to windward, came back in the midst of us, picking up first, from that half-round piece of wreck that I saw burst above the surface at the time of the ship going under, Captain Luce, Mr. George Allen, of the Novelty Works, and a young German, a passenger on the *Arctic*, by the name of Ferdinand Keyn.

They along with eight others of those who went down with the ship, had gained this piece of wreck, which turned out to be a segment of one of the paddle-boxes and, singular as it seems, Captain Luce, who had stuck by his sinking ship to the last minute, was thus saved at last on the very boards, which, as commander, were his post of duty. The same thing, however, had caused the death of an interesting son [sic], by striking or falling on him as it burst above water. The eight others, who had gained it with them, had, from time to time, perished on it; and Mr. Keyn was on the point of making the ninth, when the *Cambria* hove in sight. Mr. Allen, too, although saved himself, lost his wife and several other relatives, who were on board with him, and whom he saw placed on the raft of spars before the ship went under. I found those three my companions in the cabin of the *Cambria*, and being attended to like myself. The old Frenchman and the five firemen were comfortably quartered in the forecastle, all suffering much; and the old man having lost his 'compagnon de voyage,' the mess boy, who held out as long as he could, but finally rolled overboard. In the course of a few days, we all began to get around and feel pretty well, with the exception of the severe pains in our feet, which continued with very little intermission; and, at the same time, it was most congenial to our feelings, that, through the leadership of Mr. Walker, we had the daily opportunity of rendering praises and thanksgiving to a gracious God for his mercy and goodness toward us. Captain Russell feels the circumstance of his instrumentality in the matter with great gratification, on account of Captain Nye, of the Collins steamer *Pacific*, having some years ago run great risk in saving him and his crew from off the sinking *Jessie Stevens*, in a severe gale on the Atlantic."

Of the five boats that left the *Arctic*, only two were ever heard from, the one commanded by Mr. Francis Dorian, the third mate, the other by Mr. William Baalham, the second mate. The remainder, doubtless, sank in the storm of the succeeding Saturday. The persons in these boats, with eight or ten more on the rafts or fragments of the wreck, comprised all of the survivors of the catastrophe. Not a single female on board was saved; all perished!

Mr. Dorian's conduct, during these trying scenes, was noble. He was the only one of all the principal officers that remained faithful to the orders of his superior to the last. The recital of Peter McCabe, a waiter in the cabin, the solitary survivor of the large raft, which Mr. Dorian worked to construct with much zeal, unfolds to us other terrible incidents of this calamity. In common with the rest of the crew and passengers, McCabe seemed at first to have had no idea that the ship had encountered serious damage by the collision, but when he came on deck, he was soon undeceived. He was busy at work on the raft, when there came a dull rushing sound, and a long wail, and the *Arctic* went down. He was himself engulfed in the vortex of the sinking ship, and gave himself up for lost. The waters had closed over him, but presently he perceived, as it were, a dim light over his head, and he rose to the surface. He caught hold of a door, then of a barrel, then he swam to the raft, to which the seventy poor creatures were clinging. The sea was rough, not strong; but, in the confusion, the raft had been so imperfectly constructed, that the waves dashed over it, and the miserable passengers were swept from their hold. What follows, we will not attempt to paraphrase. Has human eye ever witnessed a scene of more awful and protracted agony?

"Those who had life-preservers did not sink, but floated with their ghastly faces upward, reminding those who still remained alive of the fate that awaited them. In the midst of all this, thank heaven, I never lost hope, but retained my courage to the last. One by one, I saw my unfortunate companions drop off; some of them floated off, and were eaten and gnawed by fishes, while others were washed under the raft, and remained with me till I was rescued. I could see their faces in the openings, as they were swayed to and fro by the waves, which threatened every moment to wash me off. The raft, at one time, was so crowded that many had to hold on by one hand. Very few words were spoken by any, and the only sound that we heard was the splash of the waters, or the heavy breathing of the poor sufferers, as they tried to recover their breath after a wave had passed over them. Nearly all were submerged to their arm-pits, while a few could with great difficulty keep their heads above the surface. The women were the first to go; they were unable to stand the exposure more than three or four hours. They all fell off the raft without a word, except one poor girl, who cried out in intense agony, 'Oh, my poor mother and sisters!' When I had been a few hours on the raft, there were not more than three or four left."

One of these three or four gave to Peter McCabe a paper, which he describes as like a "small map," and which, as he thought, was a kind of title-deed. A few minutes after he had given it, as though all energy had been exhausted in the preservation of that precious document, which he had at length been compelled to consign to the custody of another, his grasp gave way, and the owner of the title-deed was washed away. It is strange enough that McCabe, despite all of his efforts, could not succeed in preserving that precious paper; he made ineffectual efforts to get it into his pocket; he swam with it some time between his teeth, but all was in vain; the deed, which had been so dearly prized, was carried away from his mouth, and added for a moment to the relics of the wreck, then seen no more. A little incident of this kind seems to bring the scene before one's eyes with a more vivid reality even than the recital of the greater and more sweeping destruction. Before eight and a half o'clock that evening, every soul on the raft with McCabe were either dead or washed off; and "I," says he, "*was left alone*! But a few minutes before the last man went, I asked him the time. He told me, and *died in five minutes afterward*!"

Nothing could have been more exemplary on this occasion, than the resignation of the women, or the ready obedience displayed by the passengers. If all had acted as they did upon that fatal day, we should now be commenting upon a far less distressing tale; but the flight of the seamen and officers in the boats, full two hours before the vessel sunk was the cause of all the multiplied horrors of the disaster.* Individuals, however, displayed undaunted courage. The good conduct of one young man, who fired the cannon, an engineer learning under instructions, named Stewart Holland, was more conspicuous than that of any other person on board. "A more brave, courageous and self-sacrificing being," says Captain Luce, "I never saw." He tried to save all, without seeming to think anything about his own safety, never attempting to get into a boat. His end was heroic. Unmoved by the base desertion of others, he continued firing the signal gun, that, like a death-knell, boomed over the waters; and when the wreck sunk to its gloomy grave, he, too became numbered with the dead. Was death ever more noble?

Holland was from Washington City. His father, on first learning of the event, still clung to the hope that his son had escaped the perils of the wreck, by some such miracle as saved Captain Luce. He exclaimed: "My son is *not* lost; I will not give him up; but," he continued, "better a thousand times that he should perish in the manly discharge of his duty, than have saved a craven life by such cowardice and selfishness as marked the conduct of many of the crew." Such sentiments show a father worthy of such a son. Soon after his arrival in New York, Mr. Dorian addressed the following letter to Mr. Isaac Holland:

---

* A larger part of the seamen were foreigners, the offscourings of the marine service of many countries. Had they been of that class of brave, hardy, right-principled men that years ago composed the crews of our merchant vessels, their conduct might have been more like that exhibited on board the British steamer *Birkenhead*, which was lost on the coast of Africa a few years since. That vessel struck on a hidden rock, stove a plank at the bow, and went down in half an hour's time. A regiment of troops was on board. As soon as the alarm was given, and it was apparent that the ship's doom was sealed, the roll of the drum called the soldiers to arms on the upper deck. That call was promptly obeyed, though every gallant heart knew that it was his death summons. The women and children were placed in the boats, and nearly all saved. There were no boats for the troops, but there was no panic, no blanched, quivering lips among them. Down went the ship, and down went the heroic band, shoulder to shoulder, firing a *feu de joie* as they sunk beneath the waves.

"I am a stranger and can offer no apology for addressing you, further than my desire of adding my humble testimony to the merits of your noble boy. He was in the habit of daily coming to my room, telling me funny stories, etc., and, in this way, I had the pleasure of forming an intimate acquaintanceship with him. Believing that anything connected with him in the last scene might possess a dear, though painful, interest to you, I send you all I know. I regret it is so exceedingly scanty.

About two hours after the *Arctic* was struck, the firing of the gun attracted my attention; and I recollect that, when I saw Mr. Holland it struck me as remarkably strange that he alone, of all belonging to the engineering department, should be there. He must have had a good chance to go in the chief engineer's boat and be saved, but he did not, it seems, make the slightest exertion to save himself. His whole conduct can be accounted for by the simple word duty, and nothing else.

I recollect that, about an hour before the ship sank, I was hurriedly searching for spikes, to help to form a raft. I had just passed through the saloon; on the sofas were men who had fainted, and there were many of them, too. The ladies were in little groups, clasped together; and they seemed to me to be strangely quiet and resigned. As I emerged from the saloon, the scene that presented itself was one I hope never to see again. The passengers had broken up the bar; the liquors were flowing down the scuppers. Here and there were strong, stout-looking men on their knees, in the attitude of prayer; others, when asked to do anything, were immovable, perfectly stupefied.

In the midst of this scene, Stewart came running up to me; his words were 'Dorian, my powder is out; I want more; give me the key.' 'Never mind the key,' I replied; 'take an ax and break open the door.' He snatched one close behind me, and down into the ship's hold he dived, and I went over the ship's side to my raft. Half an hour later, when busy at the raft, a voice hailed me, and, on looking up, I again saw Stewart, when he hurriedly asked: 'Dorian, have you a compass in your boat?' 'No,' I replied; and off he went. He knew that any chance I had would be shared with him; and I have often thought how strange it was that that young man should, for a moment, quit his gun to inquire after my safety, and never, for a moment, think of his own. But such was Stewart Holland. I recollect distinctly his appearance as he hailed me from the deck. The right side of his face was black with powder, and two large spots on the left side. When he spoke, his countenance seemed lighted up with something like a quiet smile."

The clergy of our large cities preached discourses upon the loss of the *Arctic*. We conclude this article by a pathetic extract from a sermon by the Rev. Henry Ward Beecher, delivered in his church of the Pilgrims, at Brooklyn, the power of which will strike every heart. The text was the forty-sixth Psalm, first three verses: "God is our refuge and strength, a very present help in time of trouble: therefore will not we fear, though the earth be removed and the mountains be carried into the midst of the sea; though the waters thereof roar and be troubled, though the mountains shake with the swelling thereof."

"It was autumn. Hundreds had wended their way from pilgrimages; from Rome and its treasures of dead art, and its glory of living nature, from the sides of Switzer's mountains, from the capitals of various nations; all of them saying in their hearts, we will wait for the September gales to have done with their equinoctial fury, and then we will embark; we will slide across the appeased ocean, and in the gorgeous month of October we will greet our longed-for native land, and our heart-loved homes. And, so, the throng streamed along from Berlin, from Paris, from the Orient, converging upon London, still hastening toward the welcome ship, and narrowing every day the circle of engagements and preparations. They crowded aboard. Never had the *Arctic* borne such a host of passengers, nor passengers so nearly related to so many among us. The hour was come. The signal ball fell at Greenwich. It was noon also at Liverpool. The anchors were weighed; the great hull swayed to the current; the national colors streamed abroad, as if themselves instinct with life and national sympathy. The bell strikes; the wheels revolve; the signal gun beats its echoes in upon every structure along the shore, and the *Arctic* glides joyfully forth from the Mersey, and turns her prow to the winding channel, and begins her homeward run.

The pilot stood at the wheel, and men saw him. Death sat upon the prow, and no eye beheld him. Whoever stood at the wheel in all the voyage, Death was the pilot that steered the craft, and none knew it. He neither revealed his presence nor whispered his errand. And so, hope was effulgent, and lithe gaiety disported itself, and joy was with every guest. Amid all the inconveniences of the voyage, there was still that which hushed every murmur, *home is not far away*. And every morning, it was still one night nearer home, and at evening, one day nearer home! Eight days passed. They beheld the vast shallows of Newfoundland. Boldly they made at it, and plunging in, its pliant wreaths wrapped them about. They shall never emerge. The last sunlight has flashed from that deck. The last voyage is done to ship and passengers. At noon, there came noiselessly stealing from the north that fated instrument of destruction. In that mysterious shroud, that vast atmosphere of mist, both steamers were holding their way with rushing prow and roaring wheels, but invisible. At a league's distance, unconscious, and at nearer approach, unwarned; within hail and bearing right toward each other, unseen, unfelt, until, in a moment more, emerging from the gray mists, the ill-omened *Vesta* dealt her deadly stroke to the *Arctic*. The death-blow was scarcely felt along the mighty hull. She neither reeled nor shivered. Neither commander nor officers deemed that they had suffered harm.

Prompt upon humanity, the brave Luce (let his name be ever spoken with admiration and respect) ordered away his boat, with the first officer to inquire if the stranger had suffered harm. As Gourlie went over the ship's side, oh, that some good angel had called to the brave commander, in the words of Paul, on a like occasion, 'except these abide in the ship ye cannot be saved!' They departed, and with them the hope of the ship, for now, the waters gaining upon the hold and rising up upon the fires, revealed the mortal blow. Oh! had now that stern, brave mate, Gourlie, been on deck, whom the sailors were wont to mind; had he stood to execute efficiently the commander's will, we may believe that we should not have to blush for the coward-ice and recreancy of the crew, nor weep for the untimely dead. But, apparently, each subordinate officer lost all presence of mind, then courage, and so honor.

In a wild scramble, that ignoble mob of firemen, engineers, waiters, and crew, rushed for the boats, and abandoned the helpless women, children, and men, to the mercy of the deep! Four hours there were from the catastrophe of the collision to the catastrophe of sinking. In that time, near two hundred able-bodied men, well directed, might have built an ample raft, stored it for present necessity, filled the boats with discretion, and put off from the sinking ship with a flotilla, that ere many hours would have been hailed by some of the many craft that pass and repass that ill-fated spot. It was not so to be. All command was lost. The men heeded but one impulse, and that the desperate selfishness of an aroused and concentrated *love of life*. They abandoned their posts. They deserted their duty. They betrayed their commander. They yielded up to death more than two hundred helpless souls committed to their trust. And yet, even for these, let there be some thought of charity. Let us not forget the weakness of the flesh; the absence of the first mate, whom they were wont to obey; the terrible force of panic, even upon brave men; the sense of the hopelessness of effort to save so many, and the instinctive desire of self-preservation. All this is but a little.

But so much extenuation as there may be, let them have its benefit who certainly need every cover of charity, to save them from the indignation of an aggrieved and outraged community. Let it be remembered, also, that *individuals* among them acted most nobly, and, because the multitude were base, let not the exceptional cases be forgotten. Let that single officer, who did cling to the last manfully to his duty, the third mate, Dorian, be remembered; and that man who was set to fire the signal gun of distress, young Holland, who stood by his post until the ship sunk, and was in the very act of firing as the last plunge was made; and that engineer, who had a boy under his care, but refused to leave in the first boat, where a place was offered him, because he could not find his ward, and would not go without him. Let us charitably hope that many more such individual acts occurred, unnoticed and unreported, to redeem the crew and engineers from such disgrace as weighs heavily upon them. Many a poor fellow lies beneath the waves, unable to defend himself, who may have lost his life because he was faithful to the last; and his heroism may be without a witness, his name without a defender.

How nobly, in the midst of weakness and terror, stood that worthy man, Luce, in this terrible scene, calm, self-sacrificing, and firm to the end. Of all the witnesses, but *one* has disparaged his exertions. *He* says, that this noble commander *'seemed like a man whose judgment was paralyzed.'* Yet this man says, that when *he* was rushing desperately for the boat, Captain Luce withstood him, and tore the very raiment from his back, exclaiming: *'Let the passengers go in the boat,'* and with disgraceful naiveté he says, *'No more attention was paid to the captain than to any other man on board. Life was as sweet to us as to others'* (Patrick Tobin). Without doubt such a man would think his judgment was paralyzed who would not run; whose life was

not so sweet as his duty; who could die, but could not abandon a
trust as sacred as was ever committed to human hands. Nor do
I remember, in all my reading, any Roman heroism that can compare
with one incident recorded by one witness. When Captain Luce was
urged to enter one of the boats, he declined utterly. He was urged to
let his son go in — that son whom, afterward, sinking, he carried in
his arms, that son that, rising from the wave, was slain in his bosom
by the stroke of a piece of wreck. But should a man give precedence
to anything that belonged to him, over the hundred helpless creatures
that clung to him? His thrice heroic reply was: 'My son shall share his
father's fate!' Now, all over the deck, was there displayed every frantic
form of fear, of anguish, of bitter imploration, of transfixed despair.
Some, with insane industry, strove at the pumps; others rushed
headlong over the sides of the ship; the raft was overburdened; the
sea was covered with men struggling for a little time against their fate.
But let us remember that there were other scenes than these. There
were scores there who had long known that, by death, heaven was to
be entered. There were those who had rested the burden of their sin
upon Him who came to take away the sin of the world. Not in vain
had they prayed every day, for years, that they might be ready
whenever the Son of Man should come. There were mothers there,
that, when the first shock was over, settled their face to die, as if it
were to dream in peaceful sleep. Maidens were there, who looked up
in that tremendous hour as the bride for her bridegroom. Oh! in the
dread of crisis, upon that mournful sea, which mists covered, that the
tragedy of the water might not be seen of the sun, how many were
there that could say, '*God is our refuge and strength, a very present
help in trouble!*' There, friends exchanged their last embraces; they
determined to die, holding in their arms those best beloved, and to
yield up together their lives to the hands of God. Oh, noble loves!
that in such an hour, triumph over all fear, and crown the life with
true grandeur! Oh, noble trust! that, in the shock of such a sudden
death, could mount up above the waves, and behold the Redeemer,
and *rest* in him, to the taking away of all fear! In such an hour, every
one was tried by infallible tests. *Then*, the timid became heroic, and
the heroic became timed. Then it was neither wealth, nor honors, nor
station, nor pretense, that could give help. Strength, and skill, and
foresight, were all useless. Nothing was of worth, except a clear-eyed
piety that could behold the Invisible, a faith that could rest the very

soul in the hands of its Creator, and a hope that could behold so
much in heaven, that it willingly let go its hold upon the earth.
I will not doubt that, in those staterooms, many a prayer was uttered,
which attending angels wafted to heaven; in that cabin, there were
men and women who waited calmly for the event, as one waits
for the morning. At length the time was ended. That great ship,
treacherously stabbed, and drinking in the ocean at its wounds, gave
her last plunge. With one last outcry, the devoted company were
whelmed; and, high above all other sounds, there came a roaring
from the black, uplifted chimney, as if the collected groans of all
were mingled with the last groan of the ship itself.

Oh, what a burial was here! Not as when one is borne from his
home, among weeping throngs, and gently carried to the green fields
and laid peacefully beneath the turf and the flowers. No priest stood
to pronounce a burial service. It was an ocean grave. The mists alone
shrouded the burial-place. No spade prepared the grave, nor sexton
filled up the hollowed earth. Down, down they sank, and the quick
returning waters, smoothed out every ripple, and left the sea as if it
had not been."

NOTES

1. Henry Howe, "Destruction of the Ocean Steamer *Arctic*, by
   Collision with the *Vesta*, a French Propeller, on the Banks of
   Newfoundland, on Wednesday, the 27th of September 1854, by
   which Disaster More Than Three Hundred Persons Perished,"
   in *Life and Death on the Ocean: A Collection of Extraordinary
   Adventures, in the form of Personal Narratives* (Cincinnati: Henry
   Howe, 1855), 323-40, CIHM 36682.
2. Macdonagh, *A Pattern of Government Growth*, 22-53.
3. Robert Gardiner, ed., *The Advent of Steam: The Merchant
   Steamship Before 1900* (London: Conway Maritime Press,
   1993), 75-105.
4. Alexander Crosby Brown, "Women and Children Last: The
   Tragic Loss of the Steamship *Arctic*," *American Neptune* 14
   (1954): 261-62.
5. Maldwyn A. Jones, "Aspects of North Atlantic Migration:
   Steerage Conditions and American Law, 1819-1909," in Klaus
   Friedland, ed., *Maritime Aspects of Migration* (Cologne and
   Vienna: Bohlau, 1989), 321-32.

16

THAT TERRIBLE DAY (1892): THE *REASON*[1]

JESSIE HALE

Centuries-old Placentia, that former French fishing base of Plaissance until the eighteenth century, must have witnessed many "ships gone missing." The following brief oral narrative, the recollections of 96-year-old Jessie Hale, recorded in 1978, poignantly describes a family's private reaction to the wreck at sea of the schooner *Reason*, Captain Crann, on August 22, 1892.[2] In a severe gale, it carried away her brother Albert Joyce and other members of her community. There exists in this memory, which was never effaced, a matter-of-factness that is coupled with grief and religious devotion, and that ends with a telling silence.

Music was essential to the maritime world; not only did it serve as a record of past events, but it was integral to the vessel as workplace. Hale recalls this vessel with evident fondness and pride, for it was manned by a "singing crew" boasting "rich and vibrant" voices, who sang songs like "The Ocean Voyage" and "The Sailor's Farewell." There are of course numerous sea ballads, songs, and shanties associated with Newfoundland and Labrador fishery and sealing.[3] In his study of nineteenth-century sea songs, James Moreira explains, "Many places in the seafarer's world are steeped in cultural and occupational meaning, and in song they become symbols of group affiliations, experiences, and concerns."[4] According to Moreira, these songs helped to define the fishers' and sailors' identity and validated "the acceptance of risk as an occupational necessity, which in turn fosters pride and personal self-esteem."[5] Obviously, this sense of pride and esteem encompassed Hale's family and the community.

Such nautical songs also represent cultural artifacts that provide insight into the personal and collective experiences of seafaring.[6] Their sad themes of family and community reaction to wreck remain present even in more modern Newfoundland songs of the sea, many reworked or adapted from older versions. To illustrate, the last verse of "The Loss of the *Sailor's Home*" goes as follows: "When we arrived at Fortune/The people all came down/To hear how we lost the *Sailor's Home*/And how the rest were drowned."[7] One verse of the 1930s ballad "The Loss of the *Danny Goodwin*" describes the reaction in Rose Blanche on the southwest coast: "There are five poor widows, left behind who will bitterly cry,/All thinking of their loved ones who in the deep do lie,/But we must all remember they fought hard for their lives,/To sea they had to go and leave their children and their wives."[8] Another example is "The Loss of the *Barbara Ann Romney*," a fishing vessel lost in the 1950s. The lyricist writes, "'Oh mother dear,' the children cried, 'where is our father's boat?/He said that he was coming home the last time that he wrote.'/Grief-stricken was the mother's heart, the father and his crew, /For they're crashed in their ocean beds beneath the ocean blue."[9] Incidentally, not until the 1890s did a widow receive compensation of $80 from a government-sponsored and regulated Bank Fisherman's Insurance Fund, paid for with annual spring contributions of 50 cents by individually registered fishers.[10] Finally, like Hale's narrative, these secular songs sometimes contain religious imagery. For example, "The Loss of the *Jubal Cain*" reads, "We sympathized with those at home/And our loved ones that are gone, /We prayed that in the future/They'll have no right to mourn."[11]

I SHALL NEVER FORGET THAT DAY. The house shook, and its shaking woke me. Things were cracking outside. We were having a terrible storm. I felt it was all wrong. When I was thoroughly awake, I realized why.

This was the day my brother (Albert Joyce) was expected home.

He was with Captain Crann in the ship *Reason* and they had gone to the fishing banks five weeks.

I thought of the morning they had left home. It had been a bright, clear day. The wind was north, offshore, the sailors said.

In the early morning the boys had gone by with their bags. Quite a number of young girls had gone by, too, in freshly laundered dresses and sun-bonnets. I had seen my brother stop for a few minutes and talk with Celia Blythe. They had met at the garden gate on his way down to the ship.

Captain Crann loved to sing. He had a singing crew. The boys always sang as they weighed anchor. This morning they had sung "The Ocean Voyage" and "The Sailor's Farewell." Their voices had been rich and vibrant.

Now I looked out the window. Roofs were blown from some of the buildings. Fences were down. Pails, barrels, and numerous other things were blowing about.

From the front window I could see the harbour. Several boats had drifted from their moorings and the storm was increasing.

Downstairs the table was set as usual, but the place was deserted.

I saw my stepfather going up the road and I followed him. He was a serious man. That day he had cause to be serious. He had two brothers, three nephews, and a stepson on board that vessel. I followed him up the short road by the garden, and when we came to the road under Schoolhouse Hill I walked in the trench by the roadside and held onto the fence rail.

When I reached the road that led to the hill, or lookout, I think he saw me for the first time and held out his hand to help me.

I assured him I was all right. The wind was strong, and it was hard to walk on the high land. Once I felt my feet leave the ground, but I was holding onto the bushes near the path.

The path had been worn up the hillside. The brushwood and roots had been worn away down to the soft soil. The bushes on both sides were quite high, so the path was sheltered from the storm.

I went up so that I could see over the top and yet hold onto the brushwood. It was breathtaking. Out to sea everything was white as far as the eye could reach. Once in a great while you could see two black ledges known as the Western Rocks.

The ocean was mad. It surged, boiled, foamed. Even in the little creeks that were usually so placid, it had gone rampant.

Looking over the island, we could see that a number of buildings had blown down. Boats in the harbour were darting about as if they were creatures that had suddenly gone mad. Some had their crews on board; others were unmanned. Boatloads of men in oilskins were going out from the piers.

There were men on the hill standing near the great boulder called the Pulpit, where they leaned while they looked through their spyglasses. My stepfather spoke for the first time.

Addressing one of the men, he said, "What do you think, Captain Drake?"

"No boat could bide afloat today," the captain answered.

During the day people came, mostly those with relatives on the *Reason*. They spoke in low tones of the Sunken Keys, treacherous rocks that had to be passed on the way home.

In the late afternoon I went up to the lookout again. The storm had abated somewhat, but the ocean was white and angry looking, and where the waves struck against the cliffs, the crest of the waves seemed to break and for a second to be left suspended in the air.

The family gathered together when night came. It was the custom to have family prayer. We sat in our usual places.

My stepfather opened the Bible, waited a minute, then closed it and knelt down. We all did the same. Not a word was spoken. We rose when he did.

"O For The Touch of a Vision's Hand." The loss of a loved one at sea was often expressed in spiritual or religious terms. From *The Shipwrecked Mariner*, vol. 36, Shipwrecked Fishermen and Mariners' Royal Benevolent Society of London, 1889

NOTES

1. Jessie Hale, "That Terrible Day," *Decks Awash* 7, 2 (April 1978): 50, © The Centre for Newfoundland Studies, Memorial University of Newfoundland.
2. On the *Reason,* see David C. Barron, *Northern Maritime Shipwreck Database* (Bedford, NS: Northern Maritime Research, 1997), CD-ROM.
3. Two excellent collections are Kenneth Peacock, ed., *Songs of the Newfoundland Outports,* vol. 3, Bulletin No. 197, Anthropological Series No. 65 (Ottawa: National Museum of Canada, 1965); and Shannon Ryan and Larry Small, *Haulin' Rope & Gaff* (St. John's: Breakwater Books, 1978).
4. James Moreira, "Place and Transformal Meaning in Nineteenth Century Sea Songs," *Canadian Folklore Canadien* 12, 2 (1990): 69.
5. Moreira, "Place and Transformal Meaning," 83-84.
6. David A. Taylor, "Songs About Fishing: Examples of Contemporary Maritime Songs," *Canadian Folklore Canadien* 12, 2 (1990): 85.
7. "The Loss of the 'Sailor's Home,'" in Peacock, *Songs of the Newfoundland Outports,* 961-62.
8. "The Loss of the 'Danny Goodwin,'" Peacock, *Songs of the Newfoundland Outports,* 942-43.
9. "The Loss of the 'Barbara Ann Romney,'" in Peacock, *Songs of the Newfoundland Outports,* 937-38.
10. Raoul Anderson, "Nineteenth Century American Banks Fishing Under Sail: Its Health and Injury Costs," *Canadian Folklore Canadien* 12, 2 (1990): 115-16.
11. "The Loss of the 'Jubal Cain,'" Peacock, *Songs of the Newfoundland Outports,* 952-53.

17

MY FIRST SHIPWRECK: THE *CORISANDE* (1893)[1]

CAPTAIN BOB BARTLETT

Captain Robert Abram Bartlett, the narrator and victim of this shipwreck story and recently the subject of a CBC documentary, is the only writer in this collection who has been designated a person of National Historical Importance by the Historical Sites and Monuments Board.[2] Born in Brigus, Newfoundland, Bartlett descended from a long line of fishing and sealing captains, whose career path he followed. When only 18 years old, Barlett had been given his first command over a family schooner near his father's fishing station at Turnavik, Labrador. His first shipwreck, described in his autobiography and excerpted below, occurred at Cape Race while he was returning from Cape Cod.

Bartlett's chief claim to fame is rooted in arctic exploration. His biographer Harold Horwood calls him "the greatest Canadian ice captain who ever lived — the greatest, by general consent, of any nationality in this century."[3] After receiving his master's papers and well familiar with the Labrador ice-pack, he worked in 1898 as first mate aboard the *Windward*, part of Robert E. Peary's first and unsuccessful polar expedition, and then he went on to command several Newfoundland sealing vessels. When in July 1905 Peary again prepared to reach the North Pole, Bartlett was made captain of the *Roosevelt*. He also prepared supply caches for Peary, and in early 1906 he reached 87°6', which is roughly 150 miles from the North Pole. Three years later Bartlett again accompanied Peary, and he would have joined the famous arctic explorer and his African-American servant Matt Henson

at the pole, had he not been ordered back to the *Roosevelt*.⁴ This was
the first of two controversies about early twentieth-century arctic
exploration that involved Bartlett. The other involved Vilhjalmur
Stefansson and the unsuccessful Canadian Arctic Expedition of 1913-
14, when he commanded the *Karluk*. In later years, during which time
he became an American citizen, Bartlett was chosen as captain for
several arctic expeditions sponsored among others by the Royal Geographical Society, the National Geographic, the Museum of the
American Indian, the American Museum of Natural History, the
Smithsonian Institute, the New York Botanical Gardens, the American
Museum of Natural History, the Chicago Zoological Society, and the
Philadelphia Academy of Natural Sciences.

Bob Barlett was no stranger to shipwrecks. Apart from the episode
of the *Corisande*, he was present when the *Roosevelt* grounded in
1906, when the sealing schooner *Leopard* was wrecked in 1907 at
Cappahayden on the south shore of the Avalon peninsula, and when
the *Karluk* was crushed by ice in 1914 off Wrangel Island. However, his
memory of the demise of the "splendid ship" *Corisande* remained stark
and unforgettable although, at the time of writing his autobiography, it
had happened 30 years before. The narrative's significance is universal,
based as it is on the mature reflections of an experienced and eminent
sea captain and explorer. In Barlett's words, the shipwreck "brought me
up with a round turn in life. It sickened and depressed me." This
"catastrophe," happening around Christmas, "oppressed like death itself."⁵

⚓

I DIDN'T SIGN UP on that first deep sea voyage in the fall of 1893
without a good deal of thinking. For though I was eighteen and had
discovered that I was good enough to handle my father's schooner I
well knew that putting off in a big ship was to be an entirely different
kettle of fish. In the eyes of my friends and family I was a seafaring
man; in the eyes of the law I was nothing.

The law says that you have to do your apprenticeship first and
according to figure. Four years must be spent to get a second mate's
papers; another year for first mate and a sixth year for master mariner.
And these years have to be real years. They don't count in between
times. You have actually got to be on a ship every one of the 365 days
of them and see service on each day. There is no getting around the
law on such matters.

One thing that made me think hard was the sight of my father busying himself about our little schooner, the *Osprey,* which lay at the dock unloading her fish and skins which we turned in for credit at St. John's; with this credit he would buy up supplies for our small store at Brigus. Father's hair was just beginning to turn white; and though he was still the hale and hearty Skipper I had always known, I saw he no longer put his back into the heavy lifts and straps the way he had done a few years before. It was with a pang I thought of adding to his burden by going off and leaving him. But if I was to succeed him later on I must get my "papers." And to get them I must do more than seal and fish.

While our little vessel was lying alongside the dock and after I had my invoices and other papers pretty well checked up, I took a walk out around the hills behind the town. I was thinking things over very seriously. I could see ahead a few years. What chance would I have along with the rest of the fellows if they had papers and I didn't? I mean the legal papers that made them master mariners according to law. What good would it be if I could handle a vessel better than they, or as well as they, if the law didn't have me down in its books?

After a few hours I came back to the dock. My mind was made up. For awhile I was going to leave my friends and my family and all the Labrador fishing and sealing that I loved and go into the merchant service. It was not a happy thought. We of the sealing fleet looked down on the merchant service. The big ships that took cargoes were to us what a baggage car, I suppose, is to a cowboy. They were just big carriers of freight. There was no particular excitement about them except that they went to interesting parts of the world.

But my mind was made up; I had to get ahead. So I set forth at once rummaging around the docks for a berth. There was one big freighter, the *Corisande,* a square rigged ship of large tonnage and fine record. As luck would have it I fell in with her skipper that very afternoon.

I can see him now. He was a little fellow, more like a vice president of a bank than a commander of a big square rigged vessel. He was small, dapper and had a well-groomed look that goes more with the commercial landsman than with the care-free sailor. I don't say that sailors are not clean. They are the cleanest people in the world. But Captain Hughes had that clean look which comes from getting scrubbed up every morning in a bathtub at home and not

from being scrubbed down by the wind and brine over the side. He
wore gloves and he carried a stick with a shining ivory knob on the
end of it. Below the ivory the stick had his initials in gold letters. The
Captain wore a stiff shirt with studs in it and a navy blue suit that
was perfectly pressed. He certainly was the picture of a man who not
only took great pride in himself but wanted to show the world that
the sea was the finest profession going. There was just one thing
about him that worried me. That was the nervous way he had of
looking about him every now and then as if he were afraid something
was going to happen, he didn't know what.

"Good morning, lad," said he, waving his stick as a naval officer
might salute with his sword.

"Good morning, sir."

My feet felt nailed to the dock planking. I wanted to ask him
for a job on his ship. I didn't know how to begin. I had a desperate
feeling that he was going to walk away if I didn't say something.
Finally I came right out with it.

"I'd like to go to sea with you, sir."

He looked me up and down just as if he had suddenly discovered
my presence. I felt my face get red. I didn't look like a sailor
especially, though I was a good hearty lad with a fine coat of sunburn
from a summer down among the islands. I didn't even have any
seagoing clothes on; just a cap and an old suit and an open-necked
shirt that I guess was faded from scrubbing the fish oil out of it.

"What do you know about a ship?" said Captain Hughes.

"I just brought mine in," I told him. "Just a schooner, sir; but
she's all right. I can steer and reef and I have been in the *Hope* and
the *Panther*."

"Very well," said Captain Hughes briskly. "Be at the shipping
office at three."

That's all there was to it.

Remember this was October, the time of the year when the
summer hurricanes are over and the winter gales haven't started yet.
It was the ideal season for a trip down the Atlantic. I was to be an
ordinary seaman before the mast and I had shipped for the round
trip. As this was to be my first long voyage my mouth watered for
the experience. Little did I dream that it would end in tragedy.

I went aboard the afternoon before we sailed. My personal gear
I carried in a canvas sea bag and a big handkerchief tied together at

its corners. Besides what I had on I took an extra suit of woollen cloth for the cold trip back, a change of underwear, two towels, a big razor my father had given me and a spare pair of heavy fishing boots. When I opened my bag in the forecastle I found also a fine knitted muffler my mother had put in. Wrapped inside the muffler was a jar of her best blueberry jam which she knew was my favourite sweet.

We were towed out of the harbour at dawn next morning. While I was busy about the pin-rails faking down the various ropes in neat coils I had a heavy depressed sort of feeling. Part of it was pure home-sickness; but there was also a premonition that trouble lay ahead. I am not especially superstitious but now I have learned to trust my hunches about the future.

That time on the *Corisande* I surely was right. Scarcely had we left the dock when a fight started on deck. One man knocked another unconscious with a blow of his fist. Of course many of the men had been drinking as they always do just before leaving port on a long cruise. I guess even the skipper had it a bit up his nose too.

It took us sixty-nine days to make Pernambuco. The usual run was about thirty days. And all the while it seemed as if the *Corisande* knew she was doomed. I suppose I am stretching my imagination to say such a thing; but the others felt it as well as I. There were times when she suddenly trembled from stem to stern for no reason at all. There was more minor sickness aboard than there should have been. The ship's company were quarrelsome and ill at ease. At times a strange silence descended on all hands and we looked curiously into one another's faces to see if anyone knew the answer. A ship's cat we had aboard disappeared for no reason at all one calm night.

Captain Hughes must also have felt the shadow over us. He was no longer the same smart sailor-man I had signed on with. He stayed much in his cabin and when he came out he was irritable and captious.

About half way down my watch mate got laid out with a bad cut over his eye. As a result I did double wheel tricks, which in turn led to a boil on my neck getting chafed by dirty oilskins I hardly ever took off in the long hard watches. Soon the boil turned into a carbuncle that tormented me day and night with pain. The skipper wanted to lance the carbuncle. He declared that was the only way to cure it. Nearly every day he came at me with a long, thin knife he'd got out of the ship's medicine chest. But in his peevishness at my timidity his hand shook so that I was afraid to let him try it. This made him madder than ever. It got so that I was afraid to turn in. I felt sure he'd operate on me while I slept. Anyway, the pain was too dreadful to let me sleep. What finally saved my life was a series of hot barley poultices the cook put on when the old man wasn't looking.

Incidentally, this cook, like many cooks on such a voyage, was a great friend of all us sailors. I never forgot how, on the first day out, the cook caught me washing my teeth with fresh water. He said I'd have to go without that much water for my coffee because fresh water was scarce.

One day the captain had a regular forepeak row with this same cook. We had all been complaining about the beef being too salty and were tired of eating salt horse every meal. The cook usually took it out of the kegs and boiled it the same day. We had a big Swede who threatened to throw the fellow overboard if he didn't improve the grub. So the cook made a sort of crate that would hold about fifty pounds of salt horse. He spliced a rope to this crate and hung it from the jib boom so it would trail in the water. He figured this would iron out some of the brine.

The captain saw this gadget one day and threw a fit. "What sort of river barge do you think I'm running?" he yelled at the cook.

Cookie shook in his shoes.

"Haul that truck aboard!" screamed the old man.

"Don't you know that if we get our horse too fresh that gang of heathen down forward will eat too much of it?"

Finally we hit Pernambuco and beached the cargo. As we'd lost so much time, we took only ballast for the return. The weather was very bright with fresh wind night and day.

The *Corisande* now suddenly changed her ways. She began to make speed, as though, now that her death was getting close, she got sort of panicky and terrified. When the wind stiffened to half a gale she stood up straight and took it without a reef.

We raced another ship north. She had longer spars and carried more, but we left her hull down astern on the fourth day. Even this triumph didn't cheer us any.

The crew began to feel surer than ever something was coming. How did we know? We didn't. A man often feels that way on a ship that is making her last voyage.

"All dead below there?" sings out the mate one afternoon down the forecastle hatch. He'd never heard so much silence, he said. Nobody answered.

Off Cape Cod real cold hit us. The wind backed around into southeast by south. The sun faded out. Snow flurries came with every squall. The days were dark and overcast. The steady whine of the wind through the rigging never stopped.

The skipper had her laid dead for Cape Race. I guess the wind must have stiffened as we were logging over ten knots right along. This was too much for the old *Corisande*. The mate came and stood by me at the wheel one day. His face was dark as the sky. He shook his head and grumbled: "She can't stand this, she can't stand this"; twice over, like that.

By this time the mate wasn't on speaking terms with Captain Hughes. So he didn't say anything about what was on his mind to the old man.

Things began to get bad in the afternoon watch of the day before the final tragedy. A heavy sea was running. Twice the *Corisande* struck her nose, bowsprit and all, clean under. Two hands were busy chopping ice off her standing rigging. A big water cask lashed abaft the mizzen got adrift and nearly killed the cook. Soundings fore and aft showed she was making water. The heavy rolling and pitching and strain of the big spread we carried were pulling her seams right open.

We were due to round Cape Race the following morning. I had the middle watch, midnight to 4 a.m. Along about two I said to the mate, "We're near land, sir."

"You're landstruck, young 'un!" he bawled back at me to make me hear above the racket of the wind.

It was as black as your hat. But I'd heard sea birds off the port bow. I knew that meant land.

At four a.m. I turned in "all standing"; that is, with boots and slicker on. I even kept the strap of my sou'wester around my neck. There's no use denying it now, I was scared. What I was scared of, I couldn't have said. But I knew that sure as sunrise something terrible was going to happen. And something did.

An awful crash that threw me out of my bunk waked me. I didn't need to be told what it was. The ship had struck.

I rushed to the topside. To my surprise, the storm had disappeared. But the faint light of dawn showed me where it had

gone. Ahead was a vertical black wall that jumped right out of
the sea.

The cliff towered three times as high as our masts. I recognized it
at once as the Devil's Chimney, the most dangerous spot on the south
shore of Newfoundland. Over its top the storm still roared. Long
streamers of snow licked out toward our topmasts.

"We've got to work fast!" I heard the mate yell. His voice
sounded high and sharp with excitement.

I knew what he meant; we all did. The will of God had put us
into a lee that might last an hour or it might last ten minutes. With
the storm centre so near and the wind shifting northward it would be
in the west the minute the centre passed. Then our lee would be gone.

There was no confusion. We got our boats over the side. I ran
below and put on all my best clothes under my oilskins. Just as we
shoved off we got the first puff of wind from the northwest. It was
like a knife. Minutes counted.

In the half light and drifting snow we felt our way in. The wind
was coming in heavy blasts now. Surf was picking up. We could hear
it booming against the cliffs to the westward. As I rowed I kept looking at the poor old *Corisande* standing there alone and helpless like a
fat sheep surrounded by wolves with white teeth. If I hadn't been so
scared, I'd have cried.

Just before the gale's fury came full in we found a narrow opening
at the foot of which was a small sand spit. But before we could reach
it the wind struck full force. The boat I was in was swamped. We
floundered around in the icy water and somehow dragged ourselves
ashore. God, it was cold!

By a miracle we came through, all of us. We dragged our gear as
far as we could above the sea that rolled higher every minute. As soon
as we finished I crawled around on the rocks to get a last look at the
poor old *Corisande*. You see, I loved her. She was my first big ship.
She had weathered the storm and brought us in safely. Now I knew
there was no hope for her.

The most terrible thrill a seafaring man can ever feel comes when
his ship goes down before his eyes. I shall never forget that thrill
thirty years ago when the *Corisande* was being flung against the black
south cliffs of Newfoundland.

I strained my eyes to get a last glimpse of the ship's top-gallant
sails and royals as the huge combers sprang upon her with a smother of

Captain Bob Bartlett. Frontispiece from *The Log of Bob Bartlett: The True Story of Forty Years of Seafaring and Exploration.* New York and London: G.P. Putnam's Sons, 1928

foam. Then a flurry of snow shut her all out. Big waves forty feet high were rolling in. They made a regular thunder when they struck. I climbed higher and higher, but couldn't seem to get clear of their spray.

Then, of a sudden, the snow stopped. I stood looking down into a dreadful, foaming mess of sea, boiling like a gigantic pot. In the centre of it was the *Corisande*. Her masts were gone, just a tangle of spars and rigging hung over her port bow. Her hull had broken clean across the middle. While I looked, her after deckhouse went over the side. Then her whole stern slewed and lifted bodily over the fore wreckage.

I felt sick all over at the sight. I shut my eyes. When I opened them again the *Corisande* was gone.

That was my first shipwreck.

Cold and miserable I rejoined the others who were huddled in a cleft in the rocks. For a while it looked as if we should all be drowned by the surf that roared at our heels, or frozen to death by the zero wind that slashed down upon us from the cliffs. When I saw the sufferings of some of the men less hardy than I, I realized what it meant to have had my years of training down the Labrador with my father who had always insisted on us boys doing our full share of the work.

Finally one of the men said he knew where a fishing hut was on the plateau above us. He worked his way slowly up the dizzy cliff against which we crouched and finally reached the top. Here he was nearly blown into the sea by the blast which struck him. But he groped his way through the drifting snow and a few hours later staggered into the house he was looking for, where some fishermen had gathered to wait out the storm. When he told his story of the wreck they all hurried back with ropes and warm clothing and handed us up more dead than alive.

I reached home several days later. My mother was frankly overjoyed to see me again. What she wanted was to have me back safe and sound. But my father wanted to hear more about the wreck. To my surprise I found I couldn't talk much about it. Since then I have learned that the loss of a ship affects a seafaring man much like the loss of a dear relative; and it pains him greatly to discuss the circumstances of the sorrow.

The voyage was not without its benefits. I had made a deep sea voyage, and had taken the first step towards my master's papers which I knew I must have if I were to succeed in my chosen profession.

NOTES

1. Captain Robert A. Bartlett, *The Log of Bob Bartlett: The True Story of Forty Years of Seafaring and Exploration* (New York and London: G.P. Putnam's Sons, 1928), 61-74.
2. Much of the following biographical information is taken from "Captain Robert Abram Bartlett," *Encyclopedia of Newfoundland and Labrador* (St. John's: Newfoundland Book Publishers, 1981), 136-39.
3. Harold Horwood, *Bartlett: The Great Canadian Explorer* (Garden City, NY and Toronto: Doubleday, 1977), vii.
4. S. Allen Counter, *North Pole Legacy: Black, White and Eskimo* (Amherst: The University of Massachusetts Press, 1991), 189-209.
5. Bartlett, *The Log of Bob Bartlett,* 75.

APPENDIX A

TABLE 1. NUMBER OF TIMBER SHIPS WRECKED OR LOST AT SEA

Year	Wrecked	Lost	Total
1834	4	17	21
1835	15	34	49
1836	27	44	71
1837	7	25	32
1838	18	48	66
TOTAL	71	168	239

Source: Great Britain, House of Commons, Report From Select Committee On Shipwrecks of Timber Ships, 18 June 1839 (based on *Lloyd's Lists* and Custom House Returns).

TABLE 2. NUMBER OF SHIPS WRECKED OR LOST AT SEA COMPARED TO THOSE CLEARED FROM BRITISH NORTH AMERICAN PORTS, 1836-38

Year	Wrecked or Lost	Cleared	Percentage
1836	74	1,942	3.8
1837	51	1,815	2.8
1838	101	1,670	6.0
TOTAL	226	5,427	4.1

Source: *Ibid.* (Based on *Lloyd's Register Book of Shipping*.)

TABLE 3. NUMBER OF DISTRESSED SEAMEN AT ST. JOHN'S, NEWFOUNDLAND SUPPORTED BY LORDS ADMIRALTY

Year	Number
1838-39	20
1839-40	44
1840-41	71
1841-42	63
1843-44	29
1844-46	133
TOTAL	360

Source: Disbursements to Distressed Seamen by the Accountant-General of the Navy in Account with the Lords Commissioners of the Admiralty, 1838-1844 (Shipwrecked Seamen), GN2/19 No. 4, PANF.

APPENDIX B

THE CAUSES, SUFFERINGS AND REMEDIES
OF WATER-LOGGED SHIPPING

STATEMENTS respecting Timber Ships Water-logged, read to the Select
Committee of the House of Commons on Thursday, April 26, 1839;
George Palmer, Esq. in the Chair.

I consider the case of water-logged timber ships to be more distressing and horrible, from the extreme and protracted sufferings of the
crews, than any or all the maritime disasters reported during the
whole year in the severest hurricanes that endanger and destroy
our shipping.

Having been now more than forty years engaged in a practical
and most extensive acquaintance with sea calamities, I have long since
come to this conclusion, and I do, therefore, tender my very grateful
acknowledgements to the honourable gentlemen of the House of
Commons Committee, who are appointed to examine the circumstances connected with the frightful and alarming wrecks of our
North American timber ships in particular. Although property is
concerned in this inquiry, I do not consider that is of so much
consequence, because an increase of sea-wrecks, like an increase of
land-fires, terrify proprietors, and make them hasten to insure; and
thus assurance offices are improved in their revenue, and shipowners
being insured, the loss of a timber ship in their case is not felt
seriously, as it is natural to suppose that both ship and cargo are
insured at least to the full amount of their value, and especially in
an autumn return voyage from British North America.

I consider the case one that should interest the Government and
the nation more on the ground of humanity, philanthropy and
national interests, that sailors may observe a benevolent and kind
regard is manifested to the preservation of their lives, and that sailors'
families, by whom sailors are and can be influenced to almost any
thing, may see that some humane provision is made for the
preservation of their sons, and brothers, and husbands, and fathers,
"who go down to the sea in ships, and do business in great waters."
A popular writer, encouraged by a former Government many years
since, taught the nation a celebrated stanza to this effect: —

"Then, oh protect the hardy tar,
Be mindful of his merit."

Sailors are, under God, the right arm of the country, and it becomes Her Majesty's Government, and the honourable Representatives of the kingdom especially, to adopt every possible method for their preservation, particularly as the constituents of honourable Members are all more or less connected with the maritime profession in a great commercial country like the United Kingdom.

My first more direct consideration of water-logged timber ships arose from a most affecting circumstance in 1818, of what we term one of our Bethel or religious ships, when, after the crew had suffered most dreadfully in the main-top, they were compelled to abandon the ship, and endured the most fearful privations in an open boat at sea. Since then, my knowledge of water-logged timber ships has been constant and most agonizing, as Minister of the Mariners' Church, and Honorary Secretary of the British and Foreign Seamen and Soldiers' Friend Society, and Superintendent Manager of the Naval and Military Orphan Society.

The CAUSES of timber ships being water-logged I apprehend may be classed and comprehended chiefly as follows:—

First. Neglect in responsible authorities surveying the ships appointed for the North American timber trade in particular.

Second. Unseaworthiness, from age, or previous defects from storms or sea casualties.

Third. Deck-loading, so as to leave the crew sometimes without berths below, without bulwarks above, and exposed to the worst weather and the heaviest seas, and nothing but a ridge rope round the ship to secure doing duty over the deck timber.

The consequences or sufferings that follow, both personal and relative, are indescribable, and ought to awaken compassion and sympathy in every person pretending to the least humanity, patriotism or christianity. The very least of these may be considered as:—

First. Entire exposure to all the horrors of the tempest, unsheltered, undefended during the severest nights, and the most gloomy and appalling days of hail, rain and frost, in the chilling months and tremendous hurricanes of November and December;

no leeward place, but all to windward in a fore or main-top, or rigging, or catharpings, far off at sea.

Second. The internal agony and expectation of seeing a ship bear down, and then the terrible emotions of hope deferred for nights and days, or the horror of disappointment when a ship is sighted, approaches, but cannot rescue the trembling sailors, and then sails away, or is lost in the fog or tempests of midnight.

Third. The mental terrors of the prospects of lingering deaths under increasing sufferings during the succeeding nights after such a ship desertion, frequently producing the wildest insanity, the most shocking madness, and fearful suicide. I have experienced something of this in a ship of war likely to be deserted in the Western Ocean at midnight, after striking upon rocks on the French coast during the war.

Fourth. The agonizing tortures, mixed up with all these things, that sailors endure during the many winter nights and days, from intimate and endearing relationships on shore, as those of mother, wife or children, all of which are most painfully illustrated and confirmed in the extraordinarily afflictive case of the "Earl Moira" timber ship, from Miramichi, last winter.

Fifth. The corporeal sufferings from the most painful sensations, from the keenest hunger, and the most inflammatory burning thirst. Drinking salt water has produced a kind of awful delirium, and drinking blood a kind of stupified horror that is not even to be imagined.

Sixth. The horrible and only resources of murdering shipmates, and cutting up and hanging up and eating their raw and mortifying flesh for daily sustenance, with the prospect of even this failure, from the rapid process of putrefaction, of entire consumption. All these sufferings are to be considered as protracted for a fortnight or three weeks, or it may be, in a few cases, to one whole month. I say nothing of the horrors of a guilty retrospective conscience for mispent time and property, and health and strength, in short, in the vilest haunts of drunkenness and debauchery at a seaport town. I say nothing of the agonies of a prospective anticipation concerning a future and eternal state of being. I say nothing of the indignant reflections of a sailor's mind, and just reproaches he casts in his ravings against an ungrateful country that has neglected her sailors so much in body, in mind, in soul and in family; but I know what such feelings are, for I have experienced them myself, and heard them from thousands, and told them in public meetings all over the country, when a dying sailor exclaims, "Attend unto my cry, for I am brought very low," and mournfully utters this most affecting complaint of former days on shore, "I looked on my right hand and beheld, but there was no man that would know me; refuge failed me, no man cared for my soul." — Ps. *cxlii.* I say nothing of the domestic sufferings of mothers and widows, and orphans on shore, because these may be imagined, but cannot be fully comprehended, but by a personal examination, such as we have had at Rotherhithe and Wapping, and in the Mansion House with the Lord Mayor, concerning a destitute, afflicted, starving mother, and a distressed family of the widow and orphans of the "Earl Moira." There is not efficient provision made for such cases, as the wages cease when the ship is lost, and all ship's books and ship's papers are lost with her, so that bereaved families have no claim.

The affecting case of the "Earl Moira," which we are now publishing, will illustrate and confirm all these things, as we have been chiefly concerned in all the particulars of this case, and have now an orphan child of the chief mate in our asylum, and the infant as a pensioner on our Shipwrecked Sailors' Infant Society.

The REMEDIES are simple, and perfectly consistent with legislative interference. I should class them in the following arrangement:

First. All timber ships designed and fitting out for this trade should be specially reported to competent authorities for the most correct examination.

Second. A printed or painted testimony of sea-worthiness should be displayed on the shrouds of the ship, by order of the surveyors, for public and general observation.

Third. Persons should be appointed, especially in British and North American ports, to superintend the lading of all timber ships, and to exercise very particular inspection of *stowage*, especially in the autumn voyages, when timber ships have to cross the Atlantic in the months of November and December, as the "Earl Moira" had.

Fourth. Timber ships should have small casks of water, and portable potted or preserved provisions lashed in the tops and catharpings, or to the lower rigging, or about the lower masts, so that the sailors may not be starved to death in case of being water-logged. Such regulations would be of immense value in the estimation of our mercantile marine and their families, as it would show a kindly, humane and generous feeling, and provision for sailors, that would tend to endear the Government to them, and prevent, in a measure, those common desertions to foreign service that may endanger the very existence of the country in future naval wars.

Fifth. The very utmost vigilance should be commanded by law as to the character for habitual *sobriety* in captains and mates, as so many ships of all descriptions are lost through *intemperance* every year.

Sixth. A Trinity Board of veteran sea-commanders should be established, in particular for timber ships, to examine the nautical competency of all sea-officers who have charge of them; as many a young sea-captain is sent out with a *sea-nurse*, and ships are sacrificed from ignorance and incompetency.

It would be well for property, passengers, emigrants, troops, convicts, sailors, and the families, and the country at large, if a Committee of the House of Commons were appointed to investigate the whole of the state of our maritime population, with a view to the prevention of mutinies, and the efficiency of the Royal Navy, in the prospects of future naval conflict for the preservation of the throne, the government, the colonies, the commerce, the sea-boats, and the nation in general.

George Charles Smith

Naval and Military Office,
Welclose-square

Source: Appendix No. 2, Report From Select Committee On Shipwrecks Of Timber Ships, 95-97.

SIR HUMPHREY GILBERT
— Henry Wadsworth Longfellow

SOUTHWARD with fleet of ice
    Sailed the corsair Death;
Wild and fast blew the blast,
    And the east-wind was his breath.

His lordly ships of ice
    Glistened in the sun;
On each side, like pennons wide,
    Flashing crystal streamlets run.

His sails of white sea-mist
    Dripped with silver rain;
But where he passed there were cast
    Leaden shadows o'er the main.

Eastward from Campobello
    Sir Humphrey Gilbert sailed;
Three days or more seaward he bore,
    Then, alas! the land-wind failed.

Alas! the land-wind failed,
    And ice-cold grew the night;
And never more, on sea or shore,
    Should Sir Humphrey see the light.

He sat upon the deck,
    The Book was in his hand;
"Do not fear! Heaven is as near,"
    He said, "by water as by land!"

In the first watch of the night,
    Without a signal's sound,
Out of the sea, mysteriously,
    The fleet of Death rose all around.

The moon and the evening star
 Were hanging in the shrouds;
Every mast, as it passed,
 Seemed to rake the passing clouds.

They grappled with their prize,
 At midnight black and cold!
As of a rock was the shock;
 Heavily the ground-swell rolled.

Southward through day and dark,
 They drift in close embrace,
With mist and rain, to the Spanish Main,
 Yet there seems no change of place.

Southward, forever southward,
 They drift through dark and day;
And like a dream, in the Gulf Stream
 Sinking, vanish all away.

THE SHIPWRECK; or
THE STRANDING OF THE *WARRENS*, OF LONDON

On the Coast of Labrador, on the morning of the 25th October, 1813;
with part of the 70th Regiment on board, bound from Cork to Quebec.

— Robert Sands, School-master of the Regiment

Ye favour'd nine who on Parnassus hill
Doth rule your vot'ries by your sacred will,
I prostrate fall upon my bended knee,
And crave one favour you'd bestow on me;
One claim I have, if I am not mistaken,
Because, by Fortune, I have been forsaken —
The jade Misfortune ever follows me,
And from her fangs I never can get free;
But still my spirit, in unbroken tone,
Disdains her frowns and spurns her to begone.

When but a boy I on the sea was cast,
Grip'd by Misfortune most severe and fast,*
Till my companions sunk beneath the wave,
And found a premature, — a watery grave;
Thus leaving me upon an oar to ride,
Contending with the storm, the wind and tide,

---

* It is something remarkable that the author, though seldom at sea, has had
the misfortune to be twice compelled to bear the denomination of a "cast
away." — The first time was when he was a boy, of only 15 years of age.
He was solicited by a gentleman to go on board a boat to take a pleasure
sail and was easily induced to do so. There were five persons on board,
and one of them pretended to understand the management of small craft
of this kind. When we had rowed out to sea about two miles, we bent a
sail, and were to come into the harbour with a fine wind; but alas! the sail
had not been up more than five minutes, when the wind suddenly shifted
and laid our small vessel on her broad side. The evening immediately
preceding the accident, I had been reading an essay of Dr. Franklin's on
swimming, and his ideas were fresh in my memory. I therefore, agreeable
to his directions jumped into the water, and consequently saved myself
from the pain which one naturally feels on being thrown into that cold
element. I swam from the board towards the sea (for I could not attempt
the shore, as it was bold and rocky,) I knew I was too weak to be of any

Reliev'd at last I reach'd my native shore,
Thanks to humanity and to the oar.
Short way alas! we mortals see in fate,
Nor know ourselves until it is too late.
I then resolv'd that I no more should be
The sport of fortune on the raging sea,
I little know what was reserved in store,
For me to suffer upon Labrador.
But know, kind reader, in October last,
Along with hundreds bound for Quebec town,
A place of strength and one of some renown,
In August last two hundred men and more,
Embark'd with spirit from the Irish shore,
On board the *Warrens*, a most stately ship,
As e'er was launch'd from either dock or slip.

---

use to my miserable fellow sufferers, and I thought I should, by this means avoid the horrid sight of seeing them perish. I returned towards the boat about 15 minutes afterward, and the first thing I saw was a boy, younger than myself, lying on the surface in the last agonies of death; a sight shocking to me in the extreme, and one I never shall forget. I then swam towards the boat, and contrary to my expectation found the other three, who were all heavy men, clinging to her and by their weight turning her round on the gun-wale. I swam to the opposite end and succeeded in stopping the boat from her turning, and directed the men how to lay themselves on the gun-wale. There they lay till cold and fatigue forced one after another to drop into the deep to rise no more! The last one who survived, was the person who invited me on board. After falling into the water, he seized me by the skirt of the coat and tore me from the boat. I imagined he had done my business; but I struggled hard and brought him again to the surface, and placed him in his former situation. There he lay for nearly an hour, when his strength failed and he dropt, leaving me alone, and there I was 'till a boat coming that way by accident relieved me from my perilous situation, and landed me safely at the harbour. By the time I came there, however, I was nearly in a state of insensibility. I was carried to the first house on the shore, where every thing was done which could be done by humanity for my restoration and comfort, and these endeavours were so successful that, though it was about 6 o'clock in the afternoon that I was carried into this house, apparently lifeless, I walked to my father's house, a distance of more than half a mile, the next morning by ten o'clock. — This accident happened at Arbroath, on the east coast of Scotland, and the county of Forfar, being the place of my nativity. Happy, indeed, am I that the Labrador business was not so fatal in its consequences.

Of the Seventieth Regiment they form'd a part;
Many were active, healthy, young and smart,
All stout and ready orders to obey,
Or face their country's foes by night or day,
Commanded too by one who never fled,
Or slunk from dangers on a downy bed,
But ready ever in his country's cause,
To risk his life for her dear native laws;
The other Chiefs were men of proven merit,
Distinguish'd by a noble manly spirit.
Thus one should think we were from dangers free,
But dangers come which none can e'er foresee;
This was the case with us that dismal night,
For all were happy, none were in a fright.
For fifty days and something more we cross'd,
Along the ocean by the tempest tost,
Till we arriv'd upon Columbia's shore,
A place which few of us had seen before.
It would be dull, be tedious to relate
Each little story of our dismal fate,
Suffice it now my countrymen to tell
No serious accident to us befel,
Till in the gulph which leads to Quebec shore
A pilot came — we thought our dangers o'er:
He gave directions to three-finger'd Jack*
To keep the ship on such and such a tack,
But Jack more wise, bore to the starboard side,
Regardless of reason or of wind or tide,
And on the twenty-fifth at one o'clock

---

* Three-finger'd Jack, the chief mate of the ship, — a very assuming gentleman; one who considered himself to be always in the right. I happened to
be on the watch with him the night the accident happened; and, as he
had before worshipped heartily at the shrine of Bacchus, I found it almost
impossible to avoid a serious rupture with him. I, however, did avoid it,
after hearing a very great deal of insolence, and got down to bed, about
twenty minutes before the ship run aground. Morpheus had not then
visited me, and I felt the first stroke like electricity, and naturally
exclaimed, there is America now with a vengeance! The reason he was
called Three-fingered Jack, was on account that he wanted part of three
fingers. Seamen and soldiers both gave him this appellation.

Laid ship and us beside a sunken rock,*
The sudden noise below the vessel's keel
Made all on board a sad sensation feel,
Yet I shall ne'er forget how prudence wrought
And Calm'd the mind and social order brought.
All rose with freedom and their cloathes put on,
But none seem'd anxious that they should begone;
Then Samson ** came between the decks and said
"You know the ship upon the shore is laid,
"But don't despair, I hope the truth I tell,
"When I predict that all will yet be well;
"The ship is sound and whole in ev'ry part,
"And you may rest assur'd that ev'ry art
"Will still be us'd by those who have command
"To bring you safely to the nearest land;
"And for my part I pledge my honest word
"I shall all help within my pow'r afford —
"I pledge myself that I shall ne'er seek free
"'Till on the shore the last man landed be —
"But still be cool, obey those in command
"And be assur'd you'll safely get to land."
This lecture wrought like magic on the ear,
And banish'd ev'ry thought of dangerous fear;
Then all seem'd anxious to display their skill
And all were emulous to shew good will
In helping others from their dreary state
Ere the returning tide made it too late.
During the time that Phoebus had his light

---

*   It was the most providential thing I ever witnessed, to see the ship laid in
the place where she was; had she run only 8 feet further, she would have
been on a sunk rock, which most certainly would have beat in her bottom and in all probability would have been the cause of the death of
every person on board. Indeed, the place was completely spotted with
rocks of this kind, and it was next to a miracle we escaped running foul
of one or other of them.

** Mr. Samson, Lieut. and Adjutant of the regiment; a gentleman of a most
estimable character, and a man of humanity and judgment. It is singular
that this gentleman had a near relation immortalized by Burns, the Scottish poet. Would to God my weak pen could confer the same honour as
Mr. Samson; I am confident he deserves it.

And darken'd all the hemisphere with night;
The mind was anxious for our future fate;
But all with patience for the dawn did wait
'Till Phoebus darted o'er the eastern wave
And shew'd the spot where we our lives might save.
Two thousand yards and even something more
Our ship was stranded from Labrador's shore;
This space was cover'd by the briny sea
And almost frighten'd hundreds more than me.
Now was the time to try our utmost skill;
Now *hope or horror* ev'ry mind did fill,
Some brave exertion shew thy utmost parts,
Give life and hope and ease these troubl'd hearts;
Then Esculapius' son,* as good as brave,
With great McKay did dart upon the wave;
Fearless of dangers both went to explore
A place of safety on this barren shore;
Brave Richards too tho' in a humble sphere
Did like a man at this sad time appear;
He from the side into the boat did dart
And consolation gave to ev'ry heart;
They strove in vain to stem the ebbing tide
And lay the boat upon the water's side;
But sunken rocks and insulated sand
Would not allow them in the boat to land.
Then from the boat they wandered to the shore
And safely landed upon Labrador;
This once accomplish'd they return'd again

---

* Esculapius' Son, the Surgeon, who not only upon this, but upon several
other occasions, shewed a dauntless spirit, though at same time guided
by wisdom and humanity. Captain McKay and him were into the boat,
as soon as she was down the ship's side, and they along with serjeant
Richards, made good their landing on the shore. It would be vain to
praise one officer at the expence of another, for no one could say, who
was most active. All were actively employed in one department or
another, and it was to these joint and unwearied labours, that the
preservation of the people and the ship are, under Providence, to be
ascribed. The commanding officer was at this time confined by severe
indisposition; his orders were however given with promptitude and
executed with judgment.

To give true spirit and to banish pain,
The booms sure laid upon the vessels' side
And young and old did dart into the tide,
Ev'n I, tho' old, did dart into the wave
And wander'd thro' the deep my life to save.

Stop reader now and contemplate with me
This scene of mis'ry on the raging sea,
See hundreds wand'ring, waddling to the shore,
A place but seldom visited before,
A place indeed, which sov'reign pow'r ne'er claim'd,
A place but seldom, almost never nam'd,
Yea held in horror in historic page
Abhor'd by savage and despis'd by sage.

See young and old attempt to gain the land;
All leave the vessel in St. Lawrence strand,
Rank and distinction now are laid aside,
All travel loaded thro' the briny tide;
E'en female weakness now must strength acquire
And age assume the form of youthful fire.
Suppose all landed on the desert coast
Sore hurt indeed but not one creature lost.
Reflection then must take the place of fear;
Now does our state to ev'ry mind appear,
All drench'd and cold, scarce any thing to eat,
No house or home our misery complete;
What shall we do in this sad desperate state
To find a home and something too to eat,
The wood our refuge and our cov'ring too;
The scene tho' wretched still 'twas something new.
See trees in millions tow'ring tow'ring rise
And almost reaching to the azure skies.
See millions laid upon their sides by age
Or by the horrid tempest's stormy rage.
True emblem here of human life and too
This forest doth to human nature shew —
Here trees do grow, and here they fade away
Like us, poor mortals, creatures of a day.

The moral draw, kind reader, if you can,
And know that thou thyself art but a man.
Come now invention, O inspire the brain
Infuse some comfort and ah! banish pain,
Direct our conduct, shew thy utmost skill,
O guide our minds and regulate our will;
For now, indeed, 'tis thee that should inspire
Our ev'ry thought, and be our full desire.
Here unprovided we must fade away,
Unless inventive pow'rs should now display.
See what our wants and happiness doth crave,
Give us but these, no other will we have.
The chilling cold reminds us of a fire,
And thus to gratify the first desire,
Some trees we fell and lay them in a pile,
Which kindled once, made young and old to smile,
Reviv'd the spirits and made nature glow,
And all reliev'd from misery and woe;
Thus life and health to all at once were giv'n,
And all did think this forest almost heav'n.
Now night approaching something else demands,
A cov'ring here in these wild desert lands.
What shall we do, a house or home to have
To give us comfort and our lives to save?
Lord, how my spirit glow'd, when on this shore
I heard my native tunes play'd o'er and o'er,
When Charlie Fleming, on his oaten reed,
Play'd o'er the hills and thro' the woods with speed,
When Tannahill he did revive to me,
And Robin Rattres play'd with mirth and glee.
The rain now fell in torrents on the trees,
The wind did fawn us with a gentle breeze,
While at the fires we snugly all sat round,
Compos'd and happy on the mossy ground;
The time moved on without the smallest fear,
Until the sun did in the east appear,
The ship ere then had shifted from the bed,
Where most unhappily she had been laid,
And in deep water did in safety ride,

Unmov'd by storm, by tempest, or by tide.
Then all prepare to move down to the strand,
And leave this white inhospitable land;
The boats are seen approaching to the shore:
Now all exult and think their dangers o'er.
Long did we wander o'er the level beach,
And fondly hop'd the boats and ship to reach;
The seamen then their utmost skill did try
To find a place whereon their boats might lye;
McKay, Drawwater and good Mr. Scott,
All struggled hard each to secure a boat,
To save the people from the swelling sea,
And from this second peril set them free;
I well remember how the waves did roll,
And each supported by a wooden pole,
Did bear the weary trav'lers thro' the tide,
And laid them softly on the gun-wales side;
The men, who did the King's commission bear,
Did one and all like heroes appear;
The reader knows at least he ought to know,
True courage from humanity does flow,
And that the man who swims the troubled sea,
To save his fellow must a hero be.
(This I have witness'd on the ocean wide,
Where two at once jump'd in the briny tide,
And sav'd a youth from sinking in the wave,
When strong exertion only then could save)
Three boats now loaded forward did proceed,
And to the ship now sail'd with rapid speed,
But what did grieve and fill us all with pain,
The boats could not that day return again.
Thus were our friends still left upon the shore,
To spend another night in Labrador;
They from the waters to the wood retire,
Again they build, again they kindle fire;
Some travel forward thro' the barren wood,
Some walk for pleasure, some in search of food.
At last a hut a party did descry,
Whose inmates run or rather off did fly;

Unus'd they were to see a human face,
Except the ancient, the true Indian race,
Yea probable it is, and something more,
No stranger had they ever seen before;
But men like these who know no human crime,
Are easy pleas'd almost at any time:
No guilty horrors hang about the heart,
Nor do they know the least deceitful art;
A look or motions seeming to be kind,
At once attracts, at once doth ease the mind.
This was the case with these good happy men,
Our tender look caus'd them return again,
They kindly offer meal and drink to those
Whom but before they did account their foes;
Civilization look at this and cry,
Let fears now drop from ev'ry Christian eye;
To our disgrace some men to virtue lost,
Have robb'd, have plunder'd on the British coast;
Have murder'd those who swam across the wave,
And stolen all that which swelling seas did save;
Oh! cursed avarice! the wounds are deep,
And causes thousands more than me to weep;
But here on shore our friends we cannot leave,
Nor suffer them one moment there to grieve;
Our grand exertion to bring them on board,
To save their lives and keep our honest word,
Must now be us'd; to-morrow this we'll try,
Humane's the call and dangers we'll defy.
To-morrow come, the boats again are man'd,
Again they stretch towards the point of land.
Now all our friends come down the woody hill,
Broke up by time and many a turning rill,
And long they wander'd thro' the briny tide,
Until they reached where the boats did ride:
Then male and female both the young and old,
Got safe on board, tho' drench'd with wet and cold,
We now exulting in our future stays;
We'll forward be by such and such a day;
But winds did baffle and the tides ran so,

That for some time we could not forward go;
At last a fav'rite wind, as I remember,
Sent us to port on the fourth of November.
How thankful then should ev'ry one now be,
That he is sav'd from dangers of the sea.
'Tis he that made us can alone preserve,
And he's more kind to us than we deserve.
Else for our sins we'd been from mercy driven,
Sweep'd from the earth and also banish'd heav'n,
Let us improve the time which God has lent,
And seek his love and seriously repent.

Source: Robert Sands, *The Shipwreck; or The Stranding of The* Warrens, *of London, On the Coast of Labrador, on the morning of the 25th October, 1813; with part of the 70th Regiment on board, bound from Cork to Quebec.* Quebec: New Printing Office, 1814, CIHM 52394.

VERSES ON THE LOSS OF THE *HARPOONER TRANSPORT*,
RESPECTFULLY INSCRIBED TO MISS ARMSTRONG,
THE ONLY PERSON OF THAT FAMILY SAVED
FROM THE UNFORTUNATE WRECK

The war was hush'd, its sanguine toil was o'er,
And warriors hop'd to view their native shore;
Each breast elated, warm'd by patriot zeal,
Glow'd for his home, and for his country's weal!
For Albion Bound — sweet liberty's abode!
High o'er the deep, the floating transport rode;
With songs of joy, her anchors left their bed,
And wide aloft her swelling sails were spread
To court the breeze: — the breeze auspicious blew,
Adieu Quebec! exclaim'd the joyous crew,
And o'er the river's waves the stately vessel flew,
Wolfe's field of glory soon was left behind,
The dreaded Gulph was clear'd, and fair the wind;
But thick and cold, November's blast grew strong,
And swift the bark roll'd gloomily along;
For rimy clouds had veil'd the sun of noon,
The night was dark, and sunk the waning moon!
When unexpected, with terrific shock,
The plunging vessel struck the fatal rock!
Then rushing billows enter'd ev'ry pore,
With sweepy havoc, and tremendous roar!
While deafening cries, in dire confusion peal'd,
And while the ship, by pressing waters reel'd,
Each *husband* panted to protect his *wife*!
Each *mother* struggled for her *infant's* life!
But, ah! too soon, her pond'rous planks divide,
She sinks, engulph'd, in ocean's whelming tide.

'Tis done! 'tis past! that hyperborean shore,
Once hoar with brine, now foams with human gore!
Gore of my friends, high prais'd for all that's just;
Friends, gone for ever to their kindred dust!
Scarce had they pray'd, scarce slept, awoke, and sigh'd,
Scarce threw a look to Heav'n, but sunk and died!

The deed is done! that Cape, emboss'd with green,
Where death so late displayed his tragic scene,
Waves his tall plume to ev'ry wanton breeze,
And while his rocks shoot treacherous in the seas
Stands reckless of the grief, his shelves have spread,
That mourn the living, dying, and the dead!

Come, Muse of Woe! with ev'ry calming word
Inspire my mind, and tune each plaintive cord —
Assist my theme, to comfort Harriet's breast,
To lull her cares — restore her wonted rest:
Resume that smile, which ne'er was seen but lov'd,
That look of bliss, which ev'ry heart approv'd!
Oh, think not I have lightly mourn'd the tale,
Where thou, sweet maid, outliv'd the ruthless gale —
On FANCY'S WINGS OF GRIEF, I saw thine eyes
Distill each boiling tear, and heard thy cries:
Saw thy drench'd tresses, and angelic form,
Wave, shrink, and droop, amid the bitter storm!
I heard thy pray'r, and mark'd thine anxious look,
While fears of death thy panting bosom shook!
I heard thy voice around the rocky shore,
Exclaim aloud, amid the billow's roar,
"Where my Father? where my *tender* Mother?
Where my Sisters? where, alas, my Brother?
And are they gone? Oh God! accept my breath,
And let me join them in this SEA OF DEATH!
For I am here, a wandering orphan tost,
Houseless and bare, upon a frozen coast!"
But thou, sweet maid, wilt never friendless rove,
For those that know but *half* thy truth and love,
Now prize thy worth, and ev'ry look approve.

How bless'd my friend, amid the howling blast,
Whose manly arms enclos'd thy virtuous waist,
And proudly daring, spoil'd each yawning grave,
That roar'd for prey in every surging wave!
His worth made tenfold, by his care to thee,
Imparts, a balm that soothes thy misery!

For oh! his heart can sympathize with thine,
As I to both can sympathize with mine.
Then cease to mourn, sweet Harriet, dry thine eyes,
For thou art sav'd to prove a richer prize:
Thou'lt live on earth, a charm to ev'ry friend,
And smile an *angel* when *that charm shall end*!

H.

Source: *Montreal Herald,* January 7, 1817. Reprinted in *Mercantile Journal*
[St. John's], May 30, 1817.

A FULL-RIGGED SHIP

1. Flying jib
2. Outer jib
3. Inner jib
4. Fore topmast staysail
5. Fore-course or foresail
6. Lower fore topsail
7. Upper fore topsail
8. Lower fore topgallant sail
9. Upper fore topgallant sail
10. Fore royal
11. Main course or mainsail
12. Lower main topsail
13. Upper main topsail
14. Lower main top-
  gallant sail
15. Upper main top-
  gallant sail
16. Main royal
17. Cross-jack (pr. cro'jack)
18. Lower mizzen topsail
19. Upper mizzen topsail
20. Lower mizzen top-
  gallant sail
21. Upper mizzen top-
  gallant sail
22. Mizzen royal
23. Driver or spanker

From E. Keble Chatterton, *Sailing Ships*. London: Sidgwick and Jackson, 1909

APPENDIX D

GLOSSARY

Note: These are some of the terms which appear in the preceding narratives. They are taken and adapted from the *Oxford Companion Nautical Dictionary* and the *Oxford English Dictionary*.

Aft hold	A large compartment below decks and toward the stern of a ship mainly for the stowage of cargo but also, in earlier days, for stowing provisions for a voyage and often ships' gear.
Baldder	Also "Bald-headed." A sailing term used to indicate a square-rigged ship without her royals set or a fore-and-aft rigged ship with her topmast struck down.
Bowsprit	Also "Boltsprit." A large spar projecting over the stem of large sailing vessels to provide the means of staying a fore-topmast and from which the jibs are set.
Breakers ahead	Waves breaking over rocks or shoals, an often useful warning to ships off their course that they are standing in danger.
Bul works	Likely "Bulwarks." The planking or woodwork, or steel plating in the case of steel ships, along the sides of a ship above her upper deck to prevent seas from washing over the gunwales and also to prevent persons on board from falling or being washed overboard in rough weather.
Capstan	A cylindrical barrel fitted in larger ships on the forecastle deck and used for heavy lifting work, particularly when working with anchors and cables. It is normally placed on the centreline of the ship and driven mechanically either by steam or electricity.

Chest-tree Also "Chesstrees." Two pieces of oak secured to the topsides of a square-rigged sailing ship at the point where the curve of the bow begins to straighten out for the run aft, one on each side of the ship. Normally, a chest-tree would have a hole through its centre, but occasionally they were fitted with a sheave. The bowlines with which the main tacks were hauled down were led through the hole or the sheave in the chest-trees to give the crew a clear haul.

Counter The arch forming the overhanging stern of a vessel above the waterline, its top, or crown, being formed by the aftermost deck beams and its lower ends terminating in the wing transom and buttocks.

Cutter A term that embraces a variety of small vessels. In its older meaning, it referred to a small, decked ship with one mast and bowsprit, a gaff mainsail on a boom, a square yard and topsail, and two jibs or a jib and a staysail.

Davits Small cast-iron cranes, fitted with hoisting and lowering gear in the form of blocks and tackles and placed along both sides of the upper deck of passenger liners and ferries, from which a ship's lifeboats are slung.

Forecastle Pronounced "fo'c's'le." The space beneath the short-raised deck forward, known in sailing ships as the topgallant forecastle, to be seen in smaller ships.

Foresail The principal sail set on the foremast. In square-rigged vessels, the lowest square sail on the foremast. In fore-and-aft rigged vessels, the triangular sail before the mast.

Frigate Also "Frigot." A class of ship in the navies of all countries. During the sailing era frigates were three-masted ships fully rigged on each mast, and armed with 24 to 38 guns on a single gundeck.

Furl	"Furl to the sails." The operation of taking in the sails of a vessel and securing them with gaskets, or, in the case of square-rigged ships, hauling them in on the clew lines and buntlines and rolling them up to the yards.
Gib-boom	Also "Jib-boom." A continuation of the bowsprit in large ships by means of a spar run out forward to extend the foot of the outer jib and the stay of the fore topgallant mast.
Graphel	Also "Grapnel" or "Grapple." A small four-pronged anchor often used in dinghies and similar small boats.
Gunwale	A piece of timber going round the upper sheer strake of a boat to bind in the top work. Also the plank that covers the heads of the timbers in a wood ship.
Hawse-hole	The hole in the forecastle deck, or upper deck in the case of vessels without a forecastle, right forward in the bows of a ship, through which the anchor cable passes.
Heel	The after end of a ship's keel and the lower end of the sternpost to which it is connected. Also the lower end of a mast, boom, or bowsprit in a sailing vessel.
Helm	Another name for the tiller, by which the rudder of small vessels, such as yachts and dinghies, is swung. Also the general term associated with orders connected with the steering of the ship.

Jolly-boat	A small boat used for a variety of purposes, such as going around the ship to see that the yards are square, taking the steward ashore to purchase fresh provisions, and so on. Propelled by oars, hoisted on a davit at the stern of the ship.
Keel	The lowest and principal timber of a wooden ship, or the lowest continuous link of plates of a steel or iron ship extending the whole length of the vessel. To which the stem, sternpost and ribs or timbers of the vessel are attached. The backbone of the ship and its strongest single member.
Larboard	The old term for the left-hand side of a ship when facing forward, now known as the port.
League	A measurement of distance, long out of use. A league at sea measured 3 1/8 nautical miles, the equivalent of four Roman miles, but those on land had different values according to the country. These ranged from a minimum of 2.4 to a maximum of 4.6 statute miles. Usually at sea, for practical purposes, the league was taken to be three nautical miles, the odd fraction being omitted.
Leeside	The side of a ship, promonotory, or other object away from the wind.
Mainmast	The principal mast of a sailing vessel; it holds the mainsail. On a square-rigged vessel, the mainsail, usually the termed maincourse, is the lowermost (and largest) sail carried on the mainmast.
Masthead	The top of the mast, to which the shrouds and stays attach to secure the mast.
Mizzen	Also "mizen." The name of the third, aftermost mast of a square-rigged sailing ship or of a three-masted schooner, or a small after-mast of a ketch or a yawl.

Moorings	A permanent position in harbours and estuaries to which ships can be secured without using their own anchors.
Poop	The name given to the short aftermost deck raised above the quarterdeck of a ship. Only larger sailing ships had poops.
Quarterdeck	The part of the upper deck of a ship that is abaft the mainmast, or approximately where the mainmast would be in the case of those ships without one.
Rudder	The most efficient means of imparting direction to a ship or vessel under way. The rudder was the logical development of the older steering oar, and began to replace it in ships in the mid-13th century.
Scud	In a sailing ship, to run before a gale with reduced canvas, or under bare sail in the case of gales so strong that no sails could be left spread. It was apt to be a dangerous practice, with the risk of the vessel being pooped.
Shrouds	The standing rigging of a sailing vessel, which gives the mast its lateral support, in the same way as the stays give it fore and aft support.
Spanker-gaff	Also "spanker." A spar to which the head of a spanker (an additional sail hoisted on the mizzen-mast of sailing ships to take advantage of a following wind) was attached. It was the name used for the final form of the driver.
Spars	A general term for any wooden support used in the rigging of a ship. It embraces all masts, yards, booms, gaffs, and so on.

Stern	Also "sterne." The after end of a vessel, generally accepted as that part of the vessel built around the sternpost, from the counter up to the taffrail.
Sternport	The left hand side and rear of the ship.
Tiller	A wood or metal bar that fits into or round the head of the rudder, by which the rudder is moved as required.
Topgallant	The top at the head of the topmast, and thus in a loftier position than the original top-castle or top.
Trysail	A small sail, normally triangular, which is set in a sailing vessel when heaving-to in a gale. Also the fore and aft sails set with a boom and gaff on the fore and mainmast of a three-masted square-rigging ship.
Twain	A distance of two fathoms.
Yardarm	The outer quarters of a yard, that part which lies outboard of the lifts, on either side of the ship either port or starboard. They were the positions in a square-rigged ship where most of the flag signals were hoisted and, in the older days of sail, where the disciplinary code on board was posted and where punishments of death by hanging took place.

BIBLIOGRAPHY

A. PRIMARY SOURCES
GOVERNMENT PUBLICATIONS

DOMINION OF CANADA. STATUTES

An Act respecting Inquiries and Investigations into shipwrecks and other matters, c. 38 (1869).

GREAT BRITAIN. HOUSE OF COMMONS. REPORTS

Select Committee on Shipwrecks (1836).
Select Committee on Shipwrecks of Timber Ships (1839).
First Report from the Select Committee on Shipwrecks (1843).
Second Report from the Select Committee on Shipwrecks (1843).
Report from the Select Committee on Lighthouses (1845).
Unseaworthy Ships. Preliminary Report from the Royal Commission, I (1873).
Unseaworthy Ships. Minutes of Evidence before the Royal Commission with Digest of Evidence and Appendix, II (1873).

GREAT BRITAIN. HOUSE OF COMMONS. STATUTES

43 Geo. III, c. 56 (1803)
44 Geo. III, c. 744 (1804)
53 Geo. III, c. 36 (1813)
56 Geo. III, c. 83 (1816)
56 Geo. III, c. 114 (1816)
57 Geo. III, c. 10 (1817)
58 Geo. III, c. 89 (1818)
59 Geo. III, c. 124 (1819)
1 Geo. IV, c. 7 (1830)
4 Geo. IV, c. 84 (1823)
5 Geo. IV, c. 97 (1824)
6 Geo. IV, c. 116 (1825)
7 & 8 Geo. IV, c. 19 (1827)
9 Geo. IV, c. 21 (1828)
4 & 5 Wm. IV, c. 62 & 63 (1834)

5 & 6 Wm. IV, c. 53 (1835)
1 & 2 Vic., c. 56, LI (1838)
1 & 2 Vic., c. 113, XXVI (1838)
3 & 4 Vic., c. 21 (1840)
5 & 6 Vic., c. 107 (1842)
13 & 14 Vic., c. 93 (1850)
17 & 18 Vic., c. 104 (1854)
18 & 19 Vic., c. 91 (1855)
25 & 26 Vic., c. 63 (1862)
32 Vic., c. 11 (1869)
34 & 35 Vic., c. 110 (1871)
36 & 37 Vic., c. 85 (1873)
39 & 40 Vic., c. 80 (1876)
42 & 43 Vic., c. 72 (1879)
43 & 44 Vic., c. 43 (1881)
45 & 46 Vic., c. 76 (1882)
46 & 47 Vic., c. 41 (1883)

NEWFOUNDLAND. STATUTES

*An Act to make Provision for the Constitution of a Marine Court of
Inquiry in this Colony,* c. xiii (1866).
*An Act to amend an Act passed in the twenty-ninth year of the reign of
Her present Majesty, entitled "An Act to make Provision for the con-
stitution of a Marine Court of Inquiry in this Colony,"* c. 8 (1867).

CONTEMPORARY LEGAL PUBLICATIONS

ANSPACH, LEWIS AMADEUS. *Summary of the Laws of Commerce and
Navigation, Adapted to the present State, Government, and Trade of
the Island of Newfoundland.* London: Printed for the author, by
Heney and Haddon, 1809.
MURTON, WALTER. *Wreck Inquiries. The Law and Practice relating to
Formal Investigations in the United Kingdom, British Possessions and
before Naval Courts Into Shipping Casualties and the Incompetency
and Misconduct of Ships' Officers.* London: Stevens and Sons,
1884.

OTHER PRIMARY SOURCES

ANGER, DOROTHY, ed. *Noywaʹmkisk (Where the Sand Blows ...): Vignettes of Bay St. George Micmacs.* St. John's: St. George Regional Indian Council, 1988.

BARRON, DAVID. *Northern Maritime Shipwreck Database.* Bedford, NS: Northern Maritime Research, 1997. CD-ROM.

BLACHFORD, WILLIAM. *Sailing directions for the island of Newfoundland and coast of Labrador: including the straits of Belle Isle and banks.* R. & W. Blachford, 183?. Canadian Institute of Historical Micro-reproductions [hereafter, CIHM] 49076.

BRAY, THOMAS. *A Memorial Representing the Present State of Religion on the Continent of North America.* London: William Downing, 1700.

Disbursements to Distressed Seamen by the Accountant-General of the Navy in Account with the Lords Commissioners of the Admiralty, 1838-1844. GN2/19 No. 4, Provincial Archives of Newfoundland and Labrador [hereafter, PANF].

DOUGLAS HOWARD. "Account of the Wreck of H.M. Transport *Phyllis* 1795. Copy of Narrative of my father's shipwreck in 1795 — written by himself." Douglas Papers. M.G. 24, A3, vol. 5, National Archives of Canada (NAC). Copy held at Arts and Culture Library, St. John's.

Ex-voto du capitaine Edouin. [1709]. Collection of Sainte-Anne-de-Beaupré, Québec. [Photocopy]

"His Majesty's Commission For The Well-Governing of His Subjects Inhabiting In Newfoundland." [1630] Centre for Newfoundland Studies, Memorial University of Newfoundland.

PURDY, JOHN. *The new sailing directory for the Island and banks of Newfoundland, the gulf and river of St. Lawrence.* London: Printed for R.H. Laurie by J. Rider, 1827. CIHM 40624.

Seamen lodged by Sundry persons. Account Book. GN2/19 No. 4, PANF.

WILLIAMSON, JAMES A., ed. *The Voyages of the Cabots and the English Discovery of North America Under Henry VII and Henry VIII.* London: The Argonaut Press, 1929.

SHIPWRECK NARRATIVES AND OTHER PUBLISHED PRIMARY SOURCES

"Account Of A Wonderful Escape From The Effects of A Storm In A Journey Over The Frozen Sea In North America," in *Wonderful Escapes!* Dublin: Brett Smith, 1818, 148-62.

An Authentic Narrative of the Loss of the Barque Marshal M'Donald, *Off Newfoundland, On her passage from Quebec to Limerick, On the 7th of Dec. 1835; Including Interesting Particulars of The Sufferings of the Crew, as related by Thomas Goodwin and Joseph Shearer, two of the Survivors, who were landed at Portsmouth, by the* Arab Transport, *August 22nd 1836.* Bath: W. Browning, 1836.

AYLMER, LADY LOUISA ANNE. *Narrative of the passage of the* Pique *across the Atlantic.* London: J. Hatchard and Son, 1837. CIHM 21583.

BARTLETT, CAPTAIN ROBERT A. *The Log of Bob Bartlett: The True Story of Forty Years of Seafaring and Exploration.* New York and London: G.P. Putnam's Sons, 1928.

Brief account of the missionary ships employed in the service of the mission on the coast of Labrador from the year 1770 to 1877. London: Printed by G. Norman for the Brethren's Society, 1877.

Captain Cartwright and His Labrador Journal. Ed. Charles W. Townsend. Boston: Dana Estes, 1911.

Carrie Clancy, the heroine of the Atlantic. Philadelphia: Old Franklin Publishing House, 1873. CIHM 55081.

CRESPEL, EMMANUEL. *Voyages of Rev. Father Emmanuel Crespel in Canada and his shipwreck while returning to France.* Frankfort-on-the-Meyn: Louis Crespel, 1742. CIHM 35453.

DARTNELL, GEORGE R. *A brief narrative of a shipwreck of the transport "Premier" near the mouth of the River St. Lawrence.* London: J. How, 1845.

DEWAR, NEIL. *Narrative of the Shipwreck and Sufferings of Neil Dewar (Who has lost both his Legs and Arms,) Seaman of the* Rebecca of Quebec *Wrecked On the Coast of Labradore, 20th November, 1816.* Greenock: Neil Dewar, 1816. Arts and Culture Library, St. John's.

————. *Affecting Narrative of the Extreme Personal Sufferings of Neil Dewar, (Who has lost both his legs and arms,) Sometime Seaman out of Greenock, but late of the Schooner* Rebecca *of Quebec, Wrecked on the Coast of Labradore, 20th November, 1816, and of the Painful Enterprises and Death of Captain Maxwell and Crew, Belonging to the said schooner* Rebecca. 2nd ed., with additions. Glasgow: William Lang, 1822. CIHM 50246.

————. *Narrative of the Shipwreck and Sufferings of Neil Dewar Seaman of the* Rebecca *of Quebec Wrecked On the Coast of Labradore, Who Had Both His Legs and Arms Amputated For the*

Third Time, by Drs. Corkindale and Cumin, of Glasgow. Ed. James Smith. 3rd ed. Greenock: Neil Dewar, 1843.

"Extract from Cambden's *Annals.*" *The Voyages and Colonising Enterprises of Sir Humphrey Gilbert.* Vol. 2. Ed. David B. Quinn. London: Hakluyt Society, 1940; rpt. 1967, 428.

FELLOWES, WILLIAM DORSET. *A Narrative of the Loss of His Majesty's Packet, the* Lady Hobart, *on an island of ice in the Atlantic Ocean, 28th of June 1803.* London: J. Stockdale, 1803.

FERRAR, W.A. *Narrative of a shipwreck off the coast of North America in the winter of 1814.* [S.l.: s.n.], 1858. CIHM 44458.

GEARE, ALLAN. *Ebenezer, or a monument of thankfulness, being a true account of a late miraculous preservation of nine men being inclosed in islands of ice.* London: A. Bettesworth, 1708.

GILLY, W.O.S. *Narratives of Shipwrecks of The Royal Navy, Between 1793 and 1849.* 2nd. rev. ed. London: John W. Parker, 1861.

GOODWIN, THOMAS. *An authentic narrative of the loss of the barqe [sic]* Marshal M'Donald *off Newfoundland.* Bath: W. Browning, 1836. CIHM 21520.

The Greenlanders' Saga. Trans. George Johnston. Ottawa: Oberon Press, 1976.

H. "VERSES on the loss of the *HARPOONER* Transport, respectfully inscribed to Miss Armstrong, the only person of that family saved from the unfortunate wreck." *Montreal Herald,* Jan. 7, 1817. Reprinted in *Mercantile Journal* [St. John's], 30 May 1817.

HALE, JESSIE. "That terrible day." *Decks Awash* 7, 2 (April 1978): 50.

HOUISTE, M. GAUD. *Naufrage du navire morutier* La Nathalie. Coutances: J.V. Voisin, 1827. In Barbier, Ant.-Alex. *Dul. des anv. anonymous.* Tome III. Paris: Daffis, 1875.

HOWE, HENRY. "Destruction of the Ocean Steamer *Arctic,* by Collision with the *Vesta,* a French Propeller, on the Banks of Newfoundland, on Wednesday, the 27th of September 1854, by which Disaster More Than Three Hundred Persons Perished." *In Life and Death on the Ocean: A Collection of Extraordinary Adventures, in the form of Personal Narratives.* Cincinnati, OH: Henry Howe, 1855.

The Jesuit Relations and Allied Documents: Travels and Explorations of The Jesuit Missionaries in New France 1610-1791. Vol. 3. Ed. Reuben Thwaites. New York: Pageant Book, 1959, 235-45.

The Journal of James Yonge, 1647-1721, Plymouth Surgeon. Ed. F.L. Poynter. New York: Longman's, 1963.

Jukes' Excursions. Eds. Robert Cuff and Derek Wilton. St. John's: Harry Cuff Publications, 1993. Revised edition of Joseph Bette Jukes, *Excursions In and About Newfoundland During the Years 1839 and 1840.*

LONGFELLOW, HENRY WADSWORTH. "Sir Humphrey Gilbert." In *The Poems of Henry Wadsworth Longfellow.* New York: Thomas Crowell, 1901.

"Loss of the *Aeneas* Transport." In R. Thomas, *Interesting and Authentic Narratives of the Most Remarkable Shipwrecks, Fires, Famines, Calamities, Providential Deliverances, and Lamentable Disasters on the Seas in Most Parts of the World.* London, 1835; rpt. Freeport, NY: Books for Libraries Press, 1970, 265-68.

"Loss of the British Brig *Jesse.*" [1835] In R. Thomas, ed., *Remarkable Shipwrecks.* Freeport, NY: Books for Libraries Press, 1970, 358-59.

"Loss of the *Cumberland* Packet." In *Shipwrecks and Disasters at Sea or Historical Narratives of the Most Noted Calamities, and Providential Deliverances from Fire and Famine on the Ocean.* Manchester and Liverpool: Samuel Johnson and T. Johnson, 1838, 360-66.

A Narrative of the Loss of His Majesty's Packet The Lady Hobart *on an Island of Ice in the Atlantic Ocean, 28th of June 1803: Spectacular Account of the Providential Escape of the Crew in Two Open Boats By William Dorset Fellowes, Esq. Commander. Dedicated, By Permission, to the Right Hon. The Post Master General.* London: John Stockdale, 1803. CIHM 35106.

A Narrative of the Shipwreck and Distress Suffer'd By Mr. Thomas Manson, of Lympson in Devon, and his Ship's Crew, near the Coast of Newfoundland, in the Year 1704. London: Andrew Brice, 1724.

Narrative of the sufferings of the crew of the Eliza, *Capt. Boswell, of this port, as affectingly detailed in a letter.* North Shields, Quebec: J. Pollock, 1824. CIHM 62907.

PALMER, JOHN. *Awful shipwreck, an affecting narrative of the unparalleled sufferings of the crew of the ship* Francis Spaight, *which foundered on her passage from St. John's, N.B. to Limerick in November last. The survivors after remaining aboard the wreck 19 days, during which they were driven to the most awful extremities, were relieved by the Brig* Angeronia, *Capt. Gillard, on her Passage from Newfoundland to Teignmouth.* Boston: G.C. Perry, 1837. CIHM 50787.

Particulars of the fatal effects of the late dreadful high wind. London:
Smeeton, [1828?]. CIHM 53187.

PEACOCK, KENNETH, ed. *Songs of the Newfoundland Outports.* Vols.
1-3. Bulletin No. 197, Anthropological Series. Ottawa: National
Museum of Canada, 1965.

*Perils of the ocean and wilderness, or, Narratives of shipwreck and
Indian captivity, gleaned from early missionary annals.* Boston:
P. Donahoe, [1856?]. CIHM 53412.

"Richard Clarke's Account of the Casting Away of the *Delight.*" [1584]
In David B. Quinn, ed. *The Voyages and Colonising Enterprises of
Sir Humphrey Gilbert.* Vol. 1. London: Hakluyt Society, 1940,
423-26.

RYAN, SHANNON, AND LARRY SMALL, eds. *Haulin' Rope & Gaff: Songs
and Poetry in the History of the Newfoundland Seal Fishery.* St.
John's: Breakwater Books, 1978.

SANDS, ROBERT. *The Shipwreck; or The Stranding of The* Warrens, *of
London, On the Coast of Labrador, on the morning of the 25th
October, 1813; with part of the 70th Regiment on board, bound
from Cork to Quebec.* Quebec: New Printing Office, 1814. CIHM
52394.

SAUNDERS, ANN. *Narrative of the shipwreck and sufferings of Miss Ann
Saunders.* Providence, RI: Z.S. Crossmon, 1827. CIHM 40276.

Sea Sketches about Ships and Sailors. London: Leisure Hour Office,
The Religious Tract Society, 1853.

SHEA, JOHN GILMARY. *Perils of the Ocean and Wilderness: Narratives of
Shipwreck and Indian Captivity, Gleaned from Early Missionary
Annals.* Boston: Patrick Donahoe, 1856.

"Shipwreck off Newfoundland." In *Sea Sketches about Ships and
Sailors.* London: Leisure Hour Office, Religious Tract Society,
1853.

Shipwrecked Mariner. Vol. 36. London: London Shipwrecked
Fishermen and Mariners' Royal Benevolent Society, 1889.

*Shipwrecks and Disasters at Sea or Historical Narratives of the Most
Noted Calamities, and Providential Deliverances from Fire and
Famine on the Ocean.* Manchester and Liverpool: Samuel Johnson
and T. Johnson, 1838.

SMITH, JOHN. *Narrative of the Shipwreck and Sufferings of the Crew and
Passengers of the English brig* Neptune *Which was wrecked in a vio-
lent snow Storm on the 12th of January, 1830, on her passage from
Bristol to Quebec.* New York: J. Smith, 1830. CIHM 48082.

The Terrors of the sea: as portrayed in accounts of fire and wreck. New York, ca. 1890. CIHM 17909.

THOMAS, R. *Interesting and Authentic Narratives of the Most Remarkable Shipwrecks, Fires, Famines, Calamities, Providential Deliverances, and Lamentable Disasters on the Seas in Most Parts of the World.* London, 1835; rpt. Freeport, NY: Books for Libraries Press, 1970.

WIX, EDWARD. *Six Months of a Newfoundland Missionary's Journal, From February To August, 1835.* 2nd ed. London: Smith, Elder, 1836.

Wonderful escapes! containing the interesting narrative of the shipwreck of the Antelope *packet, upon the coast of an unknown island; with an account of the dangers and sufferings of the crew.* Dublin: printed by B. Smith, 1818.

B. SECONDARY SOURCES

MODERN POPULAR ACCOUNTS

"A.G. flashback: Loss of the Anglo Saxon." *Atlantic Guardian* 9 (1952): 19-20.

"A.G. flashback: The *Queen of Swansea* tragedy." *Atlantic Guardian* 9 (1952): 52-54.

BREEDE, CLAUS. "Shipwrecks and Cannon Balls in the North Atlantic." *Rotunda* 6 (1973): 17-23.

BROWN, CASSIE. *The Caribou Disaster and Other Short Stories.* St. John's, NF: Fianker Press, 1996.

———. "Heroes of St. Lawrence." *Atlantic Insight* 1 (1979): 92-95.

———. *Standing into Danger: A Dramatic Story of Shipwreck and Rescue.* Garden City, NY: Doubleday, 1979.

———. *A Winter's Tale: The Wreck of the* Florizel. Toronto: Doubleday, 1988.

———, AND HAROLD HORWOOD. *Death on the Ice: The Great Newfoundland Sealing Disaster of 1914.* Toronto: Doubleday, 1988.

CAREY, JOHN. "The rescue of a race: a brief account of the salving of the Eskimo." *Moravian Missions* 3 (1905): 58-60.

CAVE, GLADYS M. "Northward: The *Proteus.*" *Atlantic Advocate* 53 (1963): 37-40.

"Christmas Day Wreck." *Decks Awash* 14 (1985): 51-52.

COTTER, H.M.S. "The Great Labrador Gale, 1885." *The Beaver* 263 (1932): 81-84.

DEVINE, JOHN M. "Mostly about myself and others." *Cadet* 2 (1915): 14-16.

DOWNEY, F.J. "The passing of a ship." *Cadet* 3 (1916): 14-15.

"Extract from the 'Newfoundlander' 30 July 1872." *Newfoundland Ancestor* 4 (1987): 14.

FELLOWES, W.D. "The Loss of 'Lady Hobart.'" *Atlantic Advocate* 56 (1966): 61-68.

FITZGERALD, J. "Sealers Wrecked Off Fogo, April 1870." *Newfoundland Ancestor* 4 (1988): 34-35.

FITZHENRY, JOHN J. "An 'Anglo-Saxon' romance!" *Newfoundland Quarterly* 40 (1941): 25-30.

FOWLES, JOHN. *Neil Dewar of Greenock*. London: Cape, 1974.

GALGAY, FRANK, AND MICHAEL MCCARTHY. *Shipwrecks of Newfoundland and Labrador*, Vol 1. St. John's: Harry Cuff Publications, 1987.

———. *Shipwrecks of Newfoundland and Labrador*, Vol. 2. St. John's: Creative Publishers, 1990.

———. *Shipwrecks of Newfoundland and Labrador*, Vol. 3. St. John's: Creative Publishers, 1995 .

"Ghostly tales." *Them Days* 3 (September 1977): 32-43.

GRENFELL, WILFRED T. "The Wreck of the Mail Steamer." *Them Days* 13 (December 1987): 8-13.

GUY, R.W. "One Hundred Years of Shipwrecks Along the Straight Shore." *Newfoundland Quarterly* 74 (Summer 1978): 3-5, 7-8, 10-11.

HARDING, GEORGE. "The Menace of Cape Race." *Harper's Monthly Magazine* (April 1912): 674-84. This article was summarized in the *The Literary Digest* 44 (January-June 1912): 960-63.

HARRINGTON, MICHAEL F. "Atlanticdote." *Atlantic Advocate* 47 (December 1956): 21.

———. *Sea Stories from Newfoundland*. St. John's: Harry Cuff, 1986.

———. "The Wreck of the *Harpooner*." *Newfoundland Quarterly* 45 (September 1945): 26-28.

HARVEY, MOSES. "The Castaways of Gull Island." [1867] *Maritime Monthly* 1, 5 (May 1873): 435-47.

———. "Two thousand miles on an ice-floe; or the voyage of the Polaris party." *Maritime Monthly* 2 (August 1873): 135-47.

"Heroism." *Youth's Companion* 41 (January 16, 1868): 11.

HOWSE, ERNEST M. "The Horror on Gull Island: They Cast Lots and Then It Was Man Eat Man." *MacLean's* 82 (October 1969): 48f, 48h.

JOHNSTON, ARTHUR. "Tragic Wreck of the 'Anglo-Saxon.'" *Newfoundland Quarterly* 66 (Summer 1968): 24-26.

————, AND PAUL JOHNSTON. "Labrador Gale." *Them Days* 4 (1979): 54-57.

"Loss of H.M. Brig *Drake*." *Decks Awash* 14 (July-August 1985): 76.

MCCARTHY, MIKE. "Letters from Gull Island: The *Queen of Swansea* Tragedy, December 12, 1867." In Galgay and McCarthy, *Shipwrecks of Newfoundland and Labrador*, 27-32.

MORRIS, DON. "The Castaways of Gull Island." *Atlantic Advocate* 66 (May 1976): 40-43.

MORRIS, EDWARD P. "The wreck of 'The Queen': A Christmas memory of forty years ago." *The Newfoundland Quarterly* 6, 3 (December 1906): 7-9.

MOWAT, FARLEY. *The Farfarers*. Toronto: Key Porter, 1998.

————. *The New Founde Land*. Toronto: McClelland and Stewart, 1989.

————. *Wake of the Great Sealers*. Toronto: Little, Brown, 1973.

————. *Westviking: The Ancient Norse in Greenland and North America*. Toronto: McClelland and Stewart, 1973.

————. *This Rock Within the Sea: A Heritage Lost*. Boston: Little, Brown, 1969.

MURPHY, JAMES. *Newfoundland Heroes of the Sea*. St. John's: [the Author], 1923.

"On the Rocks." *Decks Awash* 13 (March-April 1984): 67-68.

NEATBY, LESLIE H. "Wrecked on the Coast of Labrador." *The Beaver* 297 (Autumn 1966): 21-25.

PRIM, CAPTAIN JOSEPH, AND MIKE MCCARTHY. *The Angry Seas: Shipwrecks on the Coast of Labrador*. St. John's: Jesperson Publishing, 1999.

PROWSE, D.W. "An old colonial judge's stories: Wrecks and riots." *Newfoundland Quarterly* 10 (July 1910): 17-19.

————. "Old-time Newfoundland." *Cornhill Magazine* 89 (April 1904): 539-47.

————. "Old-time Newfoundland." *Cornhill Magazine* 91 (February 1905): 208-15.

PROWSE, D.W. "Reminiscences of a Colonial Judge." *Canadian Magazine* 39 (September 1912): 438-41.

"The *Queen of Swansea* Tragedy." *Atlantic Guardian* (March 1952): 52-54.

"Shipwrecks." *Them Days* 15 (July 1990): 16-21.

SMALL, JOSEPH H. "Burgeo statistics." Ed. H.W. Cunningham. *Newfoundland Quarterly* 40 (April 1941): 31-36.

SNOW, EDWARD ROWE. *Great Gales and Dire Disasters Off Our Shores.* New York: Dodd, Mead, 1952.

"Trapped in the northern sea." *Literary Digest* 44 (May 4, 1912): 960-63.

WAKEHAM, P.J. "Island of Death." *New-Land Magazine* 39 (Spring-Summer 1981): 21-29.

———. "Loss of Three Immigrant Ships." *New-Land Magazine* 5 (Spring 1964): 3-10.

———. "The Tragedy of the Sailing Ship 'Queen of Swansea.'" *New-Land Magazine* 2 (Winter-Spring 1962-63): 3-5, 26.

WHITELEY, GEORGE C. "Wreck of the Brigantine *Queen.*" *Newfoundland Stories and Ballads* 10 (Summer-Autumn 1963): 12, 15, 17, 19.

WHYMPER, FREDERICK. *The sea: its stirring story of adventure, peril and heroism.* London and New York: Cassel, Petter and Galpin, 1878. CIHM 17843.

BOOKS

ANDREWS, K.R. *Trade, Plunder and Settlement: Maritime Enterprises and the Genesis of the British Empire, 1480-1630.* Cambridge: Cambridge University Press, 1984.

ARIÈS, PHILIPPE. *The Hour of Our Death.* New York: Random House, 1982.

ARMOUR, CHARLES A., AND THOMAS LACKEY. *Sailing Ships of the Maritimes: An Illustrated History of Shipping and Shipbuilding in the Maritime Provinces of Canada, 1750-1925.* Toronto: McGraw-Hill, 1975.

AUDEN, W.H. *The Enchafèd Flood or The Romantic Iconography of the Sea.* New York: Vintage, 1967.

AUGER, RÉGINALD. *Labrador Inuit and Europeans in the Strait of Belle Isle: From the Written Sources to the Archaeological Evidence.* No. 55. Québec: Université Laval, Centre d'études nordiques, 1991.

BAILYN, BERNARD. *Voyagers to the West: A Passage in the Peopling of America on the Eve of the Revolution.* New York: Vintage, 1988.

BARKHAM, SELMA. *The Basque Coast of Newfoundland.* Nfld.: Great Northern Peninsula Development Corporation, 1989.

BARNABY, K.C. *Some Ship Disasters and Their Causes.* London: Hutchison, 1968.

BARRON, DAVID. *Atlantic Diver Guide.* St. John's: Atlantic Diver, 1988.

BASS, GEORGE, ed. *Ships and Shipwrecks of the Americas: A History Based on Underwater Archaealogy.* New York and London: Thames and Hudson, 1988.

BECK, ULRICH. *Risk Society: Towards a New Modernity.* London: Sage, 1992. Originally published as *Risikogesellschaft: Auf dem Weg in eine andere Moderne.* Frankfurt: Suhrkamp Verlag, 1986.

BRIÈRE, JEAN-FRANÇOIS. *La Pêche française en Amerique du Nord au XVIII siècle.* Saint Laurent, Quebec: Fides, 1990.

BROEZE, FRANK, ed. *Maritime History at the Crossroads: A Critical Review of Recent Historiography.* St. John's: International Maritime Economic History Association, 1995.

BROWNE, P.W. *Where the Fishers Go: The Story of Labrador.* Toronto: The Musson Book Company, 1909.

CAMRY, NICHOLAS, AND ANTHONY PAGDEN, eds. *Colonial Identity in the Atlantic World, 1500-1800.* Princeton, NJ: Princeton University Press, 1987.

CELL, GILLIAN T., ed. *Newfoundland Discovered: English Attempts at Colonisation, 1610-1630.* London: Hakluyt Society, 1982.

CHARBONNEAU, ANDRÉ, AND ANDRÉ SEVIGNY. *1847 Grosse Ile: A Record of Daily Events.* Ottawa: Canadian Heritage, 1997.

CHATTERTON, E. KEBLE. *Sailing Ships.* London: Sidgwick and Jackson, 1909.

COATES, KEN, AND BILL MORRISON. *The Sinking of the* Princess Sophia: *Taking the North Down with Her.* Toronto: Oxford University Press, 1990.

CODIGNOLA, LUCA. *The Coldest Harbour of the Land: Simon Stock and Lord Baltimore's Colony in Newfoundland, 1621-1649.* Kingston and Montreal: McGill-Queen's University Press, 1989.

COUNTER, S. ALLEN. *North Pole Legacy: Black, White and Eskimo.* Amherst: The University of Massachusetts Press, 1991.

COWAN, HELEN I. *British Emigration to British North America: The First Hundred Years.* Toronto: University of Toronto Press, 1961.

CUFF, ROBERT H. *New-Founde-Land at the Very Centre of the European Discovery and Exploration of North America.* St. John's: Harry Cuff, 1997.

DAVIS, RALPH. *The Rise of the English Shipping Industry in the Seventeenth and Eighteenth Centuries.* London: David & Charles, 1962, 1972.

DE JONG, NICHOLAS A., AND MARVEN E. MOORE. *Shipbuilding on Prince Edward Island: Enterprise in a Maritime Setting, 1787-1920.* Ottawa: Canadian Museum of Civilization, 1994.

DICKASON, OLIVE P. *Canada's First Nations: A History of Founding Peoples from Earliest Times.* Toronto: McClelland and Stewart, 1992.

DRUETT, JOAN. "She was a Sister Sailor": *The Whaling Journals of Mary Brewster, 1845-1851.* Mystic, CT: Mystic Seaport Museum, 1992.

EBER, DOROTHY HARLEY. *When the Whalers Were Up North: Inuit Memories from the Eastern Arctic.* Kingston and Montreal: McGill-Queen's University Press, 1989.

FINGARD, JUDITH. *Jack in Port: Sailortowns of Eastern Canada.* Toronto: University of Toronto Press, 1982.

FISCHER, LEWIS R., AND GERALD E. PANTING, eds. *Change and Adaptation in Maritime History: The North Atlantic Fleets in the Nineteenth Century.* St. John's: Maritime History Group, Memorial University of Newfoundland, 1985.

FISCHER, LEWIS R., AND STUART PIERSON, comps. *Atlantic Canada and Confederation: Essays in Canadian Political Economy.* Toronto: University of Toronto Press (in association with Memorial University of Newfoundland), 1983.

FISCHER, LEWIS R., AND ERIC SAGER, eds. *The Enterprising Canadians: Entrepreneurs and Economic Development in Eastern Canada, 1820-1914.* St. John's: Memorial University of Newfoundland, 1979.

FRIEDLAND, KLAUS, ed. *Maritime Aspects of Migration.* Cologne and Vienna: Bohlau, 1989.

GARDINER, ROBERT, ed. *The Advent of Steam: The Merchant Steamship Before 1900.* London: Conway Maritime Press, 1993.

GEERTZ, CLIFFORD. *The Interpretation of Culture: Selected Essays.* New York: Basic Books, 1973.

GIDDENS, ANTHONY. *Modernity and Self-Identity: Self and Society in the Late Modern Age.* Cambridge: Polity Press, 1991.

GOLLIN, GILLIAN LINDT. *Moravians in Two Worlds.* New York and London: Columbia University Press, 1967.

GOSLING, W.G. *Labrador: Its Discovery, Exploration and Development.* London: A. Rivers, 1910.

GOSSETT, W.P. *The Lost Ships of the Royal Navy, 1793-1900.* London: Mansell, 1986.

GOUGH, B.M. *British Mercantile Interests in the Making of the Peace of Paris, 1763: Trade, War, and Empire.* Lewiston, NY: Edwin Mellen Press, 1992.

GUILLET, EDWIN. *The Great Migration: The Atlantic Crossing by Sailing-Ship, 1770-1860.* 2nd ed. Toronto: University of Toronto Press, 1963.

HARPER, JOHN RUSSELL. *Painting in Canada: A History.* Toronto: University of Toronto Press, 1966.

HEAD, C. GRANT. *Eighteenth Century Newfoundland.* Toronto: McClelland and Stewart, 1976.

HENDERSON, GRAEME. *Unfinished Voyages: Western Australian Shipwrecks, 1851-1880.* Nedlands, Australia: University of Western Australia Press, 1980.

HIMMELFARB, GERTRUDE. *Marriage and Morals Among the Victorians.* New York: Alfred A. Knopf, 1986.

HOCKING, CHARLES. *Dictionary of Disasters at Sea During the Age of Steam Including Sailing Ships and Ships of War Lost in Action, 1824-1962.* London: Lloyd's Register of Shipping, 1989.

HORWOOD, HAROLD. *Bartlett: The Great Canadian Explorer.* Garden City, NY and Toronto: Doubleday, 1977.

HOUSTON, CECIL C., AND WILLIAM J. SMYTH. *Irish Emigration and Canadian Settlement: Patterns, Links, and Letters.* Toronto and Buffalo: University of Toronto Press and Ulster Historical Foundation, 1990.

HOWELL, COLIN, AND RICHARD J. TWOMEY, eds. *Jack Tar in History: Essays in the History of Maritime Life and Labour.* Fredericton: Acadiensis Press, 1991.

HUDSON, KENNETH, AND ANN NICHOLLS. *The Book of Shipwrecks.* London and Basingstoke: Macmillan, 1979.

HUMPHREYS, JOHN. *Plaisance: Problems of Settlement at This Newfoundland Outpost of New France, 1660-1690.* Publications in History, No. 3. Ottawa: National Museum of Canada, 1970.

HUNT, LYNN, ed. *The New Cultural History: Essays by Aletta Biersack.* Berkeley: University of California Press, 1989.

HUNTRESS, KEITH, ed. *Narratives of Shipwrecks and Disasters, 1586-1860.* Ames, IA: Iowa State University Press, 1974.

JOHNSON, ARTHUR, AND PAUL JOHNSON. *The Tragic Wreck of the Anglo-Saxon, April 27th., 1863.* St. John's: Harry Cuff, 1995.

LANDOW, GEORGE P. *Images of Crisis: Literary Iconology, 1750 to the Present.* Boston, London and Henley: Routledge and Kegan Paul, 1982.

LEHUENEN, JOSEPH, AND JEAN-PIERRE ANDRIEUX. *Naufrage!: Histoire illustrée des désastres maritimes aux Iles Saint-Pierre et Miquelon.* Beamsville, Ont.: W.F. Rannie, 1977.

LUNDAHL, CRAIG R., ed. *A Collection of Near-Death Research Readings.* Chicago: Nelson-Hall, 1982.

LYON, DAVID. *The Sailing Navy List: All the Ships of the Royal Navy, Built, Purchased and Captured, 1688-1860.* London: Conway Maritime Press, 1992.

MACDONAGH, OLIVER. *A Pattern of Government Growth, 1800-60: The Passenger Acts and Their Enforcement.* London: MacGibbon and Kee, 1961.

MALLOY, DAVID J. *The First Landfall: Historic Lighthouses of Newfoundland and Labrador.* St. John's: Breakwater Books, 1994.

MARBLE, ALLEN. *Surgeons, Smallpox, and the Poor: A History of Medicine and Social Conditions in Nova Scotia, 1749-1799.* Montreal and Kingston: McGill-Queen's University Press, 1993.

MARCEL, EILEEN REID. *The Charley-Man: A History of Wooden Shipbuilding at Quebec, 1763-1893.* Kingston: Quarry Press, 1995.

MARSDEN, PETER. *The Wreck of the Amsterdam.* New York: Stein and Day, 1975.

MARSHALL, INGEBORG. *A History and Ethnography of the Beothuk.* Montreal and Kingston: McGill-Queen's University Press, 1996.

MATTHEWS, KEITH. *Lectures on the History of Newfoundland, 1500-1840.* St. John's: Memorial University, Maritime History Group, 1973.

―――, AND GERRY PANTING, eds. *Ships and Shipbuilding in the North Atlantic Region.* St. John's: Memorial University of Newfoundland, 1978.

McCANN, LARRY, CARRIE MACMILLAN, eds. *The Sea and Culture of Atlantic Canada.* Sackville, NB: Mount Allison University, 1992.

McCUSKER, JOHN J., AND R.R. RUSSELL. *The Economy of British America, 1607-1789.* Chapel Hill, NC: University of North Carolina Press, 1985.

McGREGOR, GAILE. *The Wacousta Syndrome: Explorations in the Canadian Langscape.* Toronto: University of Toronto Press, 1985 .

MILLER, KIRBY A. *Emigrants and Exiles: Ireland and the Irish Exodus to North America.* New York and Oxford: Oxford University Press, 1985.

MOORE, ARTHUR R. *"A Careless Word ... A Needless Sinking": A History of the Staggering Losses Suffered by the U.S. Merchant Marine, Both in Ships and Personnel During World War II.* King's Point, NY: American Merchant Marine Museum, 1983.

MORGAN, KENNETH. *Bristol and the Atlantic Trade in the Eighteenth Century.* New York: Cambridge University Press, 1993.

MORRIS, ROGER. *Atlantic Seafaring: Ten Centuries of Exploration and Trade in the North Atlantic.* Camden, ME: International Marine, 1992.

NEARY, PETER, AND PATRICK O'FLAHERTY, eds. *By Great Waters: Newfoundland and Labrador Anthology.* Toronto: University of Toronto Press, 1974.

NYLAND, NICK. *Skørbug, beskøjter og skibskirurger: Traek af søfartsmedicines historie.* Esbjerg: Fiskeri-og Søfartsmuseet, Saltvandsakvariet, 1994.

O'BRIEN, BRENDAN. *Speedy Justice: The Tragic Last Voyage of His Majesty's Vessel Speedy.* Toronto, Buffalo and London: University of Toronto Press (with the Osgoode Society), 1992.

O'FLAHERTY, PATRICK. *The Rock Observed: Studies in the Literature of Newfoundland.* Toronto, Buffalo and London: University of Toronto Press, 1979.

OMMER, ROSEMARY E. *From Outpost to Outport: A Structural Analysis of the Jersey-Gaspé Cod Fishery, 1767-1886.* Montreal: McGill-Queen's University Press, 1992.

———, ed. *Merchant Credit and Labour Strategies in Historical Perspective.* Fredericton: Acadiensis Press, 1990).

———, AND GERRY PANTING, eds. *Working Men Who Got Wet.* St. John's: Memorial University of Newfoundland, 1980.

PIKE, E. HOLLY. *Family and Society in the Works of Elizabeth Gaskell.* New York: Peter Lang, 1995.

PLUMMER, KEN. *Telling Sexual Stories: Power, Change and Social Worlds.* London and New York: Routledge, 1995.

POPE, DUDLEY. *Life in Nelson's Navy.* London: Unwin Hyman, 1987.

PRITCHARD, JAMES. *Anatomy of a Naval Disaster: The 1746 French Naval Expedition to North America.* Montreal and Kingston: McGill-Queen's University Press, 1995.

PROULX, GILLES. *Between France and New France: Life Aboard the Tall Sailing Ships.* Toronto and Charlottetown: Dundurn Press, 1984.

PROULX, JEAN-PIERRE. *Histoire et naufrage des navires le* Saphire, *la* Marguerite, *le* Murinet, *et l'*Auguste. Ottawa: Parks Canada, 1979.

PROWSE, D.W. *A History of Newfoundland from the English, Colonial and Foreign Records.* London and New York: Macmillan, 1895.

QUINN, D.B. *Explorers and Colonies: America, 1500-1625.* London and Ronceverte: The Hambeldon Press, 1990.

REDIKER, MARCUS. *Between the Devil and the Deep Blue Sea: Merchant Seamen, Pirates, and the Anglo-American Maritime World, 1770-1850.* Cambridge: Cambridge University Press, 1987.

RENO, JANET. *Ishmael Alone Survived.* Lewisburg, PA: Bucknell University Press, 1990.

RODGER, N.A.M. *The Wooden World: An Anatomy of the Georgian Navy.* London: Collins, 1986.

ROMPKEY, RONALD. *Grenfell of Labrador: A Biography.* Toronto: University of Toronto Press, 1991.

RYAN, SHANNON. *Fish Out of Water: The Newfoundland Saltfish Trade, 1814-1914.* St. John's: Breakwater, 1986.

———. *The Ice Hunters: A History of Newfoundland Sealing to 1914.* St. John's: Breakwater, 1994.

SAGER, ERIC W. *Seafaring Labour: The Merchant Marine of Atlantic Canada, 1820-1914.* Montreal, Kingston and London: McGill-Queen's University Press, 1989.

———, AND GERALD E. PANTING. *Maritime Capital: The Shipping Industry in Atlantic Canada, 1820-1914.* Montreal: McGill-Queen's University Press, 1990.

SHARP, J.J. *Discovery in the North Atlantic from the 6th to 17th Century.* Halifax: Nimbus Publishing, 1991.

SMITH, BONNIE G. *Changing Lives: Women in European History since 1700.* Lexington and Toronto: D.C. Heath, 1989.

STARKEY, DAVID J. *Security and Defence in South-West England before 1800.* Exeter: Exeter University Press, 1987.

STORY, G.M., ed. *Early European Settlement and Exploitation in Atlantic Canada.* St. John's: Memorial University of Newfoundland, 1982.

TANNER, TONY, ed. *The Oxford Book of Sea Stories.* Oxford and New York: Oxford University Press, 1994.

THOMPSON, FREDERIC F. *The French Shore Problem in Newfoundland: An Imperial Study.* Toronto: University of Toronto Press, 1961.

TUCK, JAMES, AND ROBERT GRENIER. *Red Bay, Labrador: World Whaling Capital, A.D. 1550-1600.* St. John's: Atlantic Archaeology, 1989.

WILSON, GARTH S. *A History of Shipbuilding and Naval Architecture in Canada.* Ottawa: National Museum of Science and Technology, 1994.

ZIMMERLEY, DAVID WILLIAM. *Cain's Land Revisited: Culture Change in Central Labrador, 1775-1972.* Social and Economic Studies, No. 16. St. John's: Institute of Social and Economic Research, Memorial University, 1975.

ARTICLES

ANDERSON RAOUL. "Nineteenth Century American Banks Fishing Under Sail: Its Health and Injury Costs." *Canadian Folklore Canadien* 12, 2 (1990): 102-21.

AUDETTE, JOHN R. "Historical Perspectives on Near-Death Episodes and Experiences." In Craig R. Lundahl, ed., *A Collection of Near-Death Research Readings.* Chicago: Nelson-Hall, 1982, 21-43.

BAEHRE, RAINER. "New Directions in European-American Migration." *The Northern Mariner/Le marin du nord* 4, 3 (1994): 51-62.

BARBER, JANETTE M. "A Historic Shipwreck at Trinity, Trinity Bay," *Newfoundland Quarterly* 77, 2-3 (1981): 17-20.

BARKHAM SELMA. "Documentary Evidence for 16th Century Basque Whaling Ships in the Strait of Belle Isle." In G.M. Story, ed., *Early European Settlement and Exploitation in Atlantic Canada.* St. John's: Memorial University of Newfoundland, 1982.

———. "A Note on the Strait of Belle-Isle During the Period of Basque Contact with Indians and Inuit." *Études/Inuit/Studies* 4, 1-2 (1980): 51-58.

BIERSACK, ALETTA. "Local Knowledge, Local History: Geertz and Beyond." In Lynn Hunt, ed., *The New Cultural History*. Berkeley: University of California Press, 1989, 75-78.

BOSHER, J.F. "The Imperial Environment of French Trade with Canada, 1660-1685." *English Historical Review*, 108, 1 (January 1993): 50-81.

BRIÈRE, JEAN-FRANÇOIS. "Pêche et politique à Terre-Neuve au XVIIIᵉ siècle: la France véritable gagnante du traité d'Utrecht?" *Canadian Historical Review* 64, 2 (June 1983): 168-87.

————. "The Ports of Saint-Malo and Granville and the North American Fisheries in the 18th Century." In *Global Crossroads and the American Seas*. Missoula, MT: Pictorial Histories, 1988, 9-18.

————. "The Safety of Navigation in the 18th Century French Cod Fisheries." *Acadiensis* 16, 2 (Fall 1987): 85-94.

BROEZE, FRANK. "'Our home is girt by sea': The Passenger Trade of Australia and New Zealand." In Klaus Friedland, ed., *Maritime Aspects of Migration*. Cologne and Vienna: Bohlau, 1989, 441-65.

BROWN, ALEXANDER CROSBY. "The '*Arctic*' Disaster: Maury's Motivation." *U.S. Naval Institute: Proceedings* 94 (1968): 78-83.

————. "Women and Children Last: The Tragic Loss of the Steamship *Arctic*." *American Neptune* 14 (1954): 237-62.

BUCKNER, PHILIP. "Whitworth-Aylmer, Matthew, 5th Baron Aylmer." In *Dictionary of Canadian Biography*. Vol. 4. Toronto: University of Toronto Press, 1980, 904-08.

BURTON, VALERIE. "The Myth of Bachelor Jack: Masculinity, Patriarchy and Seafaring Labour." In Colin Howell and Richard J. Twomey, eds., *Jack Tar in History: Essays in the History of Maritime Life and Labour*. Fredericton: Acadiensis Press, 1991. 179-98.

CADIGAN, SEAN. "Seamen, Fishermen and the Law: The Role of the Wages and Lien System in the Decline of Wage Labour in the Newfoundland Fishery." In Colin Howell and Richard J. Twomey, eds. *Jack Tar in History: Essays in the History of Maritime Life and Labour*. Fredericton: Acadiensis Press, 1991, 105-31.

CAMERON, LAURA. "Old /New/Maps/Territories." *Histoire sociale/Social History* 28, 55 (May 1995): 241.

CELL, GILLIAN T. "The Cupids Cove Settlement: A Case Study of the Problems of Early Colonisation." In G.M. Story, ed., *Early European Settlement and Exploitation in Atlantic Canada*. St. John's: Memorial University of Newfoundland, 1982, 97-114.

CHRISTENSON, RUTH M. "The Establishment of S.P.G. Missions in Newfoundland, 1703-1783." *Historical Magazine of the Protestant Episcopal Church* 20 (1951): 207-29.

CLARKE, JOHN, AND JOHN BURRONE. "Social Regions in Mid-Nineteenth Century Ontario." *Histoire sociale/Social History* 28, 55 (May 1995): 194-96.

CRANE, SUSAN A. "Writing the Individual Back into Collective Memory." *American Historical Review* 102 (December 1997): 1372-85.

CRONON, WILLIAM J. "A Place for Stories, Nature, History and Narrative." *Journal of American History* 78 (March 1992): 1347-76.

ENGLISH, CHRIS. "The Development of the Newfoundland Legal System to 1815." *Acadiensis* 20, 1 (Autumn 1990): 89-119.

————. "From Fishing Schooner to Colony: The Legal Development of Newfoundland, 1791-1832." In Louis A. Knafla and Susan W.S. Binnie, eds., *Law, Society, and The State: Essays in Modern Legal History*. Toronto, Buffalo and London: University of Toronto Press, 1995, 73-98.

FISCHER, LEWIS R. "A Bridge Across the Water: Liverpool Shipbrokers and the Transfer of Eastern Canadian Sailing Vessels, 1855-1880." *The Northern Mariner/Le Marin du nord*, 3, 3 (July 1993): 49-59.

————. "The Sea as Highway: Maritime Service as a Means of International Migration, 1863-1913." In Klaus Friedland, ed., *Maritime Aspects of Migration*. Cologne and Vienna: Bohlau, 1989, 293-308.

————, AND HELGE W. NORDVIK. "Maritime Transport and the Integration of the North Atlantic Economy, 1850-1914." In Wolfram Fischer, R. Marvin McInnis, and Jurgen Schneider, eds., *The Emergence of a World Economy, 1500-1914*. Wiesbaden: Steiner, 1986, 519-44.

FISCHER, LEWIS R., AND GERALD E. PANTING. "Maritime History in Canada: The Social and Economic Dimensions." In John B. Hattendorf, ed., *Ubi Sumus? The State of Naval and Maritime History*. Newport, RI: Naval War College Press, 1994.

FITZHUGH, WILLIAM W., ed. *Cultures in Contact: The Impact of European Contacts on Native American Cultural Institutions, A.D. 1000-1800*. Washington and London: Smithsonian Institution Press, 1985.

GAFFIELD, CHAD. "The New Regional History: Rethinking the History of the Outaouais." *Revue d'études canadiennes* 26, 1 (1991): 64.

GRAHAM, GERALD S. "Britain's Defence of Newfoundland." *Canadian Historical Review* 23, 3 (September 1942): 260-79.

HANDCOCK, W. GORDON. "The West Country Migrations to Newfoundland." *Bulletin of Canadian Studies* 5, 1 (April 1981): 5-24.

HARPER, J. RUSSELL. "James Bowman." In *Dictionary of Canadian Biography*, Vol. 4. Toronto: University of Toronto Press, 1980, 100-01.

HILLER, JAMES. "The Moravians in Labrador, 1771-1805." *The Polar Record* 15, 99 (1971): 839-54.

JACKSON, GORDON. "New Horizons in Trade." In T.M. Devine and Gordon Jackson, eds., *Glasgow Volume I: Beginnings to 1830.* Manchester and New York: Manchester University Press, 1995, 214-38.

JANZEN, OLAF. "The French Raid upon the Newfoundland Fishery in 1762: A Study in the Nature and Limits of Eighteenth-Century Sea Power." In *Naval History: The Seventh Symposium of the U.S. Naval Academy.* Wilmington, DE: Scholarly Resources, 1988, 35-54.

————. "'Une Grande Liaison': French Fishermen from Ile Royale on the Coast of Southwestern Newfoundland, 1714-1766 — A Preliminary Survey." *Newfoundland Studies* 3, 2 (Fall 1987): 183-200.

————. "'Une Petite République' in Southwestern Newfoundland: The Limits of Imperial Authority in a Remote Maritime Environment." In Lewis R. Fischer and Walter Minchinton, eds., *People of the Northern Seas.* St. John's: International Maritime Economic History Association, 1992, 1-33.

————. "The Royal Navy and the Defence of Newfoundland During the American Revolution." *Acadiensis* 14, 1 (Autumn 1984): 28.

————. "Showing the Flag: Hugh Palliser in Western Newfoundland, 1764." *The Northern Mariner/Le Marin du nord* 3, 3 (July 1993): 3-14.

JONES, MALDWYN A. "Aspects of North Atlantic Migration: Steerage Conditions and American Law, 1819-1909." In Klaus Friedland, ed., *Maritime Aspects of Migration.* Cologne and Vienna: Bohlau, 1989, 321-32.

KAPLAN, SUSAN A. "European Goods and Socio-Economic Change in Early Labrador Inuit Society." In William W. Fitzhugh, ed., *Cultures in Contact: The Impact of European Contacts on Native American Cultural Institutions, A.D. 1000-1800.* Washington and London: Smithsonian Institution Press, 1985, 45-69.

KEMP, PETER, ed. *The Oxford Companion to Ships and the Sea.* London and New York: Oxford University Press, 1976.

KOLLTVEIT, BARD. "Scandinavian and Baltic Transatlantic Passenger Lines." In Klaus Friedland, ed., *Maritime Aspects of Migration.* Cologne and Vienna: Bohlau, 1989, 133-44.

KORTE, BARBARA. "English-Canadian Perspectives of Landscape." *International Journal of Canadian Studies/Revue international d'études canadiennes* 6 (Fall/Automne 1992): 9.

LAHEY, RAYMOND J. "Avalon: Lord Baltimore's Colony in Newfoundland." In G.M. Story, ed., *Early European Settlement and Exploitation in Atlantic Canada.* St. John's: Memorial University of Newfoundland, 1982.

LANDRY, NICOLAS. "Les pêches canadiennes au XIXᵉ siècle." *The Northern Mariner/Le Marin du nord* 2, 4 (October 1992): 23-30.

LAQUEUR, THOMAS. "Bodies, Details, and Humanitarian Narrative." In Lynn Hunt, ed., *The New Cultural History.* Berkeley: University of California Press, 1989, 176-204.

LOCKERBY, EARLE. "The Deportation of the Acadians from Ile St.-Jean, 1758." *Acadiensis* 27, 2 (1998): 45-94.

MACDONALD, JOHN, AND RALPH SHLOMOWITZ. "Mortality on Immigrant Voyages to Australia in the 19th Century." *Explorations in Economic History* 27 (1990): 84-113.

MACKENZIE, KENNETH S. "A Ready-Made Flotilla: Canada and the Galway Line Contract, 1859-1863." *Mariner's Mirror* 74, 3 (August 1988): 255-65.

MACPHERSON, KENNETH, FRANK BROEZE, JOAN WARDROP, AND PETER REEVES. "The Social Expansion of the Maritime World of the Indian Ocean: Passenger Traffic and Community Building, 1815-1939." In Klaus Friedland, ed., *Maritime Aspects of Migration.* Cologne and Vienna: Bohlau, 1989, 427-40.

MARSDEN, PETER. *The Wreck of the Amsterdam.* New York: Stein and Day, 1975.

MARTIJN, CHARLES A. "An Eastern Micmac Domain of Islands." *Actes du vingtième res des Algonquinistes* (Ottawa: Carleton University, 1989), 208-31.

MARTIJN, CHARLES A. "Innu (Montagnais) in Newfoundland." In William Cowan, ed., *Papers of the Twenty-First Algonquian Conference*. Ottawa: Carleton University, 1990, 227-46.

――――. "The Inuit of Southern Quebec-Labrador: A Rejoinder to Garth Taylor." *Études/Inuit /Studies* 4 (1980): 194-98.

MAZA, SARAH. "Stories in History: Cultural Narratives in Recent Works in European History." *American Historical Review* 101 (December 1996): 1494-95.

MCGHEE, ROBERT. "Possible Norse-Eskimo Contacts in the Eastern Arctic." In G.M. Story, ed., *Early European Settlement and Exploitation in Atlantic Canada*. St. John's: Memorial University of Newfoundland, 1982, 31-40.

MOLTMANN, GÜNTER. "Steamship Transport of Emigrants from Europe to the United States, 1850-1914: Social, Commercial and Legislative Aspects." In Klaus Friedland, ed., *Maritime Aspects of Migration*. Cologne and Vienna: Bohlau, 1989, 279-92.

MOREIRA, JAMES. "Place and Transformal Meaning in Nineteenth Century Sea Songs." *Canadian Folklore Canadien* 12, 2 (1990): 69-84.

NEARY, PETER. "Frederic Edwin Church and Louis Legrand Noble in Newfoundland and Labrador, 1859." In Larry McCann, with Carrie MacMillan, eds., *The Sea and Culture of Atlantic Canada*. Sackville, NB: Mount Allison University, 1992, 15-46.

NORDVIK, HELGE W. "Norwegian Emigrants and Canadian Timber." In Klaus Friedland, ed., *Maritime Aspects of Migration*. Cologne and Vienna: Bohlau, 1989, 279-92.

PASTORE, RALPH T. "The Collapse of the Beothuk World." *Acadiensis* 19, 1 (1989): 52-71.

――――. "Fishermen, Furriers, and Beothuks: The Economy of Extinction." *Man in the Northeast* 33 (Spring 1987): 47-62.

PERLIN, ALBERT B. "History and Health in Newfoundland." *Canadian Journal of Public Health* 61 (1970): 314.

PETTERSON, LAURITZ. "From Sail to Steam in Norwegian Emigration, 1870-1910." In Klaus Friedland, ed., *Maritime Aspects of Migration*. Cologne and Vienna: Bohlau, 1989, 125-32.

POULIOT, LEON. "Charles Lalement." *Dictionary of Canadian Biography*. Vol. 1. Toronto: University of Toronto Press, 1966, 411-12.

PRATT, T.K. "Sea, Land and Language: Shaping the Linguistic Character of Atlantic Canada." In Larry McCann, with Carrie

MacMillan, eds. *The Sea and Culture of Atlantic Canada.* Sackville, NB: Mount Allison University, 1992, 27-41.

PRYOR, JOHN H. "Winds, Waves, and Rocks: The Routes and the Perils Along Them." In Klaus Friedland, ed., *Maritime Aspects of Migration.* Cologne and Vienna: Bohlau, 1989, 71-86.

QUINN, D.B. "Newfoundland in the Consciousness of Europe in the Sixteenth and Early Seventeenth Centuries." In G.M. Story, ed., *Early European Settlement and Exploitation in Atlantic Canada.* St. John's: Memorial University of Newfoundland, 1982, 9-29.

REDINGTON, MICHAEL. "An Island's Story." *Galway Archaelogical and Historical Society Journal* 10 (1917-18): 154-57.

RICE, RICHARD. "Sailortown: Theory and Method in Ordinary People's History." *Acadiensis* 13, 1 (Autumn 1983): 154-68.

RINGER, JAMES. "A Summary of Marine Archaeological Research Conducted at Red Bay, Labrador." *Research Bulletin* (Parks Canada) 248 (March 1986): 1-19.

RUFFMAN, ALAN. "The Multidisciplinary Rediscovery and Tracking of 'The Great Newfoundland and Saint-Pierre et Miquelon Hurricane' of September 1775." *The Northern Mariner/Le Marin du nord* 6, 3 (July 1996): 11-23.

RULE, JOHN. "Wrecking and Coastal Plunder." In Douglas Hay et al., *Albion's Fatal Tree: Crime and Sociaty in Eighteenth-Century England.* New York: Pantheon Books, 1975, 167-88.

RYAN, SHANNON. "Fishery to Colony: A Newfoundland Watershed, 1793-1815." *Acandiensis* 12, 2 (Spring 1983): 34-52.

———. "Newfoundland Sealing Disasters to 1914." *The Northern Mariner/Le Marin du nord* 4, 3 (July 1994): 19-37.

SAGER, ERIC W., AND LEWIS R. FISCHER. "Atlantic Canada and the Age of Sail Revisited." *Canadian Historical Review* 63, 2 (June 1982): 125-50.

———. "Patterns of Investment in the Shipping Industries of Atlantic Canada, 1820-1900." *Acadiensis* 9, 1 (Autumn 1979): 19-43.

SANGER, C.W. " 'On Good Fishing Ground but Too Early for Whales I Think': The Impact of Greenland Right Whale Migration Patterns on Hunting Strategies in the Northern Whale Fishery, 1600-1900." *American Neptune* 51, 4 (Fall 1991): 221-40.

———. " 'Saw Several Finners But No Whales': The Greenland Right Whale (Bowhead) — An Assessment of the Biological Basis of the Northern Whale Fishery During the Seventeenth, Eighteenth and Nineteenth Centuries." *International Journal of Maritime History* 3, 1 (June 1991): 127-54.

SCHWARTZWALD, ROBERT. "Introduction." *International Journal of Canadian Studies/Revue international d'études canadiennes* 10 (Fall/automne 1994): 5-13. Special issue on "Identities and Marginalities."

SINCLAIR, PETER R. "Fishermen of Northwest Newfoundland: Domestic Commodity Production in Advanced Capitalism." *Journal of Canadian Studies/Revue international d'études canadiennes* 19 (1984): 34-48.

SKELTON, R.A. "Cabot (Caboto), John (Giovanni)." *Dictionary of Canadian Biography*. Vol. 1. Toronto: University of Toronto Press, 1966, 146-52.

———. "Cabot, Sebastian." In *Dictionary of Canadian Biography*. Vol. 1. Toronto: University of Toronto Press, 1966, 152-58.

STEPHENS, W.B. "The West-Country Ports and the Struggle for the Newfoundland Fisheries in the Seventeenth Century." *Report and Transactions of the Devonshire Association for the Advancement of Science, Literature and Art* (1950): 90-101.

STEVENS, ANNE E., AND MICHAEL STAVELEY. "The Great Newfoundland Storm of 12 September 1775." *Bulletin of the Seismological Society of America* 71, 4 (August 1991): 1398-1402.

STEVENS, WILLIS. "Progress Report on the Marine Excavation at Red Bay, Labrador: A Summary of the 1983 Field Season." *Research Bulletin* (Parks Canada) 240 (March 1986): 1-15.

STONE, LAWRENCE. "The Revival of Narrative: Reflections on a New Old History." *Past and Present* 85 (1979): 3-24.

TAYLOR, J. GARTH. "Moravian Mission Influence on Labrador Inuit Subsistence: 1776-1830." In D.A. Muise, ed., *Approaches to Native History in Canada*. Ottawa: National Museum of Man, 1977, 16-29.

THORNTON, PATRICIA A. "The Demographic and Mercantile Bases of Initial Permanent Settlement in the Strait of Belle Isle." In John J. Mannion, ed., *The Peopling of Newfoundland: Essays in Historical Geography*. St. John's: ISER, 1977, 152-83.

———. "The Transition from the Migratory to the Resident Fishery in the Strait of Belle Isle." In Rosemary Ommer, ed., *Merchant Credit and Labour Strategies in Historical Perspective*. Fredericton:

Acadiensis Press, 1990, 138-66.

TRUDEL, FRANÇOIS. "The Inuit of Southern Labrador and the Development of French Sedentary Fisheries (1700-1760)." In Richard A. Preston, ed., *Papers from the Fourth Annual Congress, 1977, Canadian Ethnology Society.* Canadian Ethnology Service Paper No. 40. Ottawa: National Museums of Canada, 1978, 99-121.

TRUDEL, MARCEL. "Cartier, Jacques." *Dictionary of Canadian Biography.* Vol. 1. Toronto: University of Toronto Press, 1967, 165-72.

TUCK, JAMES A. "1984 Excavations at Red Bay, Labrador." In Jane Sproull Thomson and Callum Thomson, eds., *Archaelogy in Newfoundland and Labrador, 1984.* St. John's: Newfoundland Museum, 1985, 230-31.

TURGEON, LAURIER. "Colbert et la pêche française à Terre-Neuve." In Roland Mousnier, ed., *Un Nouveau Colbert.* Paris: Sedes, 1985, 255-68.

————. "Naufrages des Terreneuviers Bayonnais et Luziens, 1689-1759." *Bulletin de la Société des Sciences, Lettres et Arts de Bayonne,* nouvelle série 134 (1978): 115-123.

————. "Towards a History of the Fishery: Marketing Cod at Marseilles During the Eighteenth Century." *Histoire Sociale/Social History* 14 (November 1981): 295-322.

————, AND DENIS DICKNER. "Contraintes et choix alimentaires d'un groupe d'appartenance: Les Marines pêcheurs français à Terre-Neuve au XVIe siècle." *Canadian Folklore Canadien* 12, 2 (1990): 53-68.

TURNER, VICTOR. "Social Dramas and Stories About Them." In W.J.T. Mitchell, ed., *On Narrative.* Chicago: University of Chicago Press, 1981, 137-64.

VIGNERAS, L.-A. "Corte-Réal, Gaspar." *Dictionary of Canadian Biography.* Vol. 1. Toronto: University of Toronto Press, 1967, 234-35.

————. "Corte-Réal, Miguel." *Dictionary of Canadian Biography.* Vol. 1. Toronto: University of Toronto Press, 1967, 236.

WAHRMAN, DROR. " 'Middle-Class' Domesticity Goes Public: Gender, Class, and Politics from Queen Caroline to Queen Victoria." *Journal of British Studies* 32 (October 1993): 396-432.

WESTFALL, WILLIAM. "On the Concept of Region in Canadian History and Literature." *Journal of Canadian Studies* 15, 2 (1980): 3-14.

WHITELY, W.H. "The Establishment of the Moravian Mission in Labrador and British Policy." *Canadian Historical Review* 45, 1 (1964): 29-50.

ZUCKERMAN, MICHAEL. "Identity in British America: Unease in Eden." In Nicholas Camry and Anthony Pagden, eds., *Colonial Identity in the Atlantic World, 1500-1800.* Princeton: Princeton University Press, 1987, 119-57.

UNPUBLISHED THESES AND PAPERS

BARBER, JANETTE M., AND VERNON C. BARBER "The Newfoundland Marine Archaeology Society Survey Expedition in 1981." Unpublished report, St. John's, 1981.

———. "The Trinity Site: A Shipwreck of a Mid-1700's Merchant Vessel." Unpublished paper, Newfoundland Historical Society, 1979.

BARBER, VERNON C. "Newfoundland Marine Archaeology Society, Project Proposal." Unpublished paper, St. John's, 1975.

———. "Shipwrecks of Newfoundland with Particular Comment on H.M.S. *Sapphire,* Sunk in 1696." Unpublished paper, Newfoundland Historical Society, 23 April 1975.

DAVIS, DAVID. "Sealers Wrecked off Fogo." Unpublished notes, 34-35. PANF.

FITZPATRICK, CAPTAIN THOMAS. "Wrecks and their Causes." Unpublished paper, H.F. Shortis Papers, Vol. 2. 391, 74. [PANF]

HILLER, JAMES. *The Foundation and the Early Years of the Moravian Mission in Labrador, 1752-1805.* Unpublished M.A. thesis, Memorial University of Newfoundland, 1967.

———. "Jens Haven and the Moravian Mission in Labrador." Unpublished paper, Newfoundland Historical Society, 23 October 1968.

KEYES, JOHN. *The Dunn Family Business, 1850-1914: The Trade in Square Timber at Quebec.* Unpublished Ph.D. thesis, Laval University, 1987.

SMITH, SHELI. "The 1983 Isle Aux Morts Survey." Unpublished paper, Newfoundland Marine Archaeology Society, 1983.

THORPE, F.J. "The Cod Fishery in French American Strategy, 1660-1783." Unpublished paper presented at the Annual Meeting of the Canadian Historical Association, June 1989.

WALPOLE, KATHLEEN A. *Emigration to British North America Under the Early Passengers Acts, 1803-1842.* Unpublished M.A. thesis, University of London, 1929.

WETZEL, MICHAEL G. *Decolonizing Ktaqmkuk Mi'kmaw History.* Unpublished LL.M. degree, Dalhousie University, Halifax, 1995.

INDEX